PRAISE FOR *THE DARK WOR*

"S.C. Parris weaves a beautiful story within a world that will leave you breathless. *The Dark World* is a refreshingly new take on the Vampire and Lycan war that has slathered the dark fantasy realm since *Underworld*, and will take the entire community by storm. Xavier Delacroix could very well be the new Lestat."
– Kindra Sowder, author of *The Executioner Trilogy*

"S.C. Parris may be a young writer, but in *The Dark World* series, she reaches for something remarkable: a vision of horror firmly rooted in the great gothic tradition of vampire literature, but completely original. *The Dark World*, populated by mixed monstrosities, magically gifted humans and the descendants of Count Dracula himself, will be instantly recognizable to lovers of vampire tales but accessible to those new to the genre. Some great story-telling here, with something for everybody. S.C. Parris is a talent to watch."
– Jamie Mason, author of *The Book of Ashes*

"With intricate characters just as delicious as those from Game of Thrones, you truly can't help but become invested in the sequel and thirst for more!"
– A.Giacomi, author of *The Zombie Girl Saga*

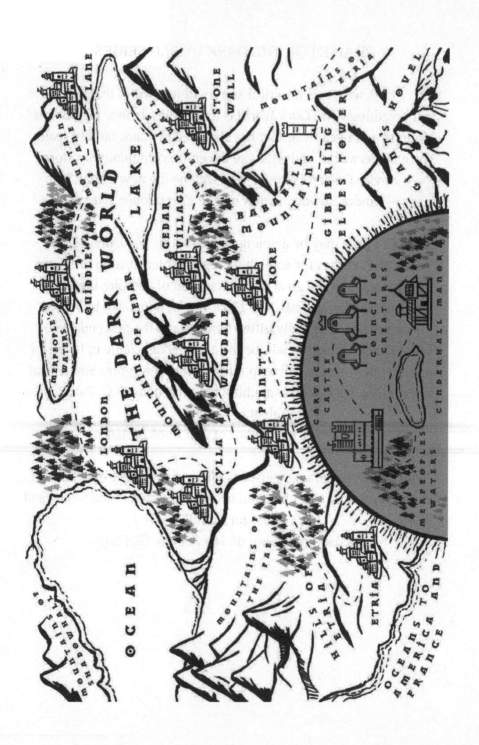

THE IMMORTAL'S GUIDE

THE DARK WORLD BOOK II

S.C. PARRIS

A PERMUTED PRESS BOOK

ISBN: 978-1-68261-081-7
ISBN (eBook): 978-1-68261-082-4

The Immortal's Guide:
The Dark World Book Two
© 2016 by S.C. Parris
All Rights Reserved

Cover art by Christian Bentulan
Map provided by: The Noble Artist, Jamie Noble Frier

Permuted Press, LLC
permutedpress.com

Published in the United States of America

*To my father, for being an endless well of
sometimes-maddening support.*

Other Works by S.C. Parris:

"A Night of Frivolity" short story
The Dark World Book One

Chapter One

THE GUEST

With a cold sweeping breeze, the calm night air was disturbed by the appearance of three cloaked figures. The tallest of them readjusted the collar of his gold traveling cloak and nodded to his companions.

Neither of them said a word as they nodded in return, before staring down the hill, the dark path before them illuminated by the moonlight above. They stepped together, their destination clear.

The tall white house jutted through the rolling hills as though it had been dropped there overnight, and the tallest Vampire smiled, for this was precisely the case.

"Isn't this most troublesome?" he asked, hearing their footsteps behind him.

"How exactly do you mean?" the one to the left of him asked.

"Dracula's death, of course. I have heard Xavier has been named the new King."

The man on his right spoke up, "Well, what does this mean for us?"

"Honestly?" The man in the middle stopped walking, tearing

his gaze from the high house to stare incredulously at the man on his right. "Our family name is in danger!"

"I do not follow," the one on his left said.

He stared at the two of them through the shadow of his hood. "Honestly?!" he cried again. "Well, we are almost there...I am sure he will explain..."

And with a small snort at their less-than-average minds, he walked ahead, his stride never breaking as he came to the black gate.

With a pale hand, he pushed it open and stepped through, his robes sliding against the dirt ground. He did not turn as the other two cloaked figures followed.

He reached for the knob of the door and turned, stepping into the house. The strong smell of stale blood reached his nose, and with a quick hand, he removed the hood from his head, letting his long blond hair settle behind his back.

The other two cloaked figures entered the house after him.

A small blonde woman entered the room. "Ewer," she said, "you are back."

"Yes, Minerva," Ewer Caddenhall said, smile warm. "Where is he?"

"Darien or the other?" she asked, brow furrowing.

Ewer stepped to her, staring down at her small frame. "Darien, of course. I have no business with the other. He is Lucien's guest, is he not?"

Lucien Caddenhall, who had removed his own hood some time before, walked around the wooden table and left the dining room, his black cloak swishing silently around his boots.

Minerva looked up at Ewer with deep blue eyes. "My Lord is upstairs. He has been pacing."

"Has he now? Well, it would be in horrible taste to keep him waiting any longer." His old face grew concerned. He ran a pale hand over the front of his cloak. It unfastened itself and slid from his back, landing gently upon the wooden table. The golden robes he wore shimmered in the light of the candles that surrounded them. He moved to the stairs to his right, leaving the siblings staring fearfully up at him as he climbed.

It was not long before he reached the landing, the voice dancing to his ears with remarkable impatience: "Ewer. *Come to me.*"

He left the top step and glided over the creaking floorboards, moving past the old doors along the hallway before reaching the only one that was closed, its ancient wood peeling. With one slow breath, he allowed his thoughts to leave him. He did not want the Vampire to know what he was thinking before he'd had a chance to mouth the words. It would be most undesirable.

The door flew open as he hesitated, and when he stepped across the threshold, it closed sharply behind him.

He did not spare breath, unable to see a thing before him, and he felt he was alone until the black figure on the other side of the room stirred.

The sound of snapping fingers brought to light a ball of fire a man held in his dark palm. He sat in a chair facing the door, his face sharp with interest. The ball of fire lit up the room—which Ewer saw was bare of decorations, save a small table in the corner—but did nothing to still the cold that flew all around them.

"Ewer," the man said, his black eyes cold in the light of the fire. "What news have you for me?"

He bowed low. "I have learned of Dracula's death."

"The Great Vampire is dead?"

"Yes."

"This is not some lie? You are sure your sources are trustworthy?"

"I am sure."

The man in the chair glared at the Vampire across from him, although the corners of his mouth twitched ever so slightly upwards. "Go on."

"It happened," Ewer began, "at the Council of Creatures...during the meeting...It seems Eleanor Black ambushed the castle with her Creatures...cornered Dracula and Xavier—"

"*Eleanor Black*?" the man whispered, interrupting the Vampire's words, his eyes appearing thoughtful against the brilliant glow of the fire in his hand. "Xavier? What of the Vampire?"

"He has been made King, my Lord." Ewer eyed the dark man in the chair carefully for any sign of surprise, or even anger.

Neither showed itself. The dark Vampire remained seated, part of his face hidden in the shadows the fire could not reach. He snarled after another moment, causing Ewer to take a cautionary step away.

"His dying wish was to make Xavier King?"

"It...appears so," Ewer said.

A short, breathless silence filled the room before Darien said, "Is this all you have learned?"

"Yes." Ewer's old face broke into relief...the relief, perhaps, that he was no longer needed.

But then Darien said, "Call for Yaddley, I must hear what he has uncovered."

"Right away, my Lord." He turned to leave.

Darien raised a hand. "Stay here, Ewer. Call for him...I do not want any of you out of my sight."

"Of course, my Lord," he whispered, for he knew the news of Dracula's death would cause a tighter rope to be pulled around the Caddenhall family. After all, their one source of innumerable protection was now permanently dead.

Ewer closed his eyes and passed along the message, and soon footsteps could be heard against the creaking floorboards of the hallway.

Darien flicked a hand and the door swung open, allowing both Vampires to eye the tall, muscular arrival: Yaddley's broad shoulders could barely squeeze through the doorway of the room.

Darien said nothing, but studied Yaddley's strong features before speaking. "What have you uncovered?"

"There are Enchanters who are worried about their place in the Dark World. It has become known that Dracula gained his immortality by convincing an Enchanter to cast the spell on him."

"And what spell is this?" Darien asked, eyes wide.

"A potion, really," he replied. "A concoction the Enchanter created within several days."

"Who else has it?"

"No one. The Enchanter in question is unknown, but there have been rumors in various Enchanter Guilds. They believe a man by the name of Peroenous Doe was the one who created it. If this is true, the Enchanter faces backlash from other Enchanters—even Vampires. It has long been known many Creatures dislike the former King's title as King of *All* Creatures."

A loud, painful scream issued from below them and Yaddley cast a nervous glance to Ewer, who did not return the gaze.

Darien smiled. "Is that all, Yaddley?"

"Yes, my Lord."

"It may prove useful in the future, thank you," he said before turning his gaze to Ewer. "Call for Lucien."

Ewer's jaw clenched at this harrowing demand, but he closed his eyes all the same, and moments later footsteps could be heard nearing the door. Darien did not bother to flick his hand to open it this time—it opened on its own.

Lucien Caddenhall stood there, his black robes stained with blood, his naturally brown eyes now a deep, fierce red. His blond hair fell wildly around his head and he made no attempts to smooth it out as he addressed the dark Vampire staring at him coldly from his chair. "Yes, Darien?"

Ewer's eyes widened with his insolence. "You will call him 'Lord!'"

But Darien, smiling, raised a hand to silence the old Vampire, and gazed upon the bloodstained robes of Lucien. "You were busy with your...guest?"

"Yes."

"I can only continue to wonder what you can gain from that Vampire...what grudge my dear brother holds against him."

Lucien did not appear troubled by these words. "Why have you called me up here?"

Darien's smile disappeared. He leaned forward in his seat, bringing the palm that held the ball of fire closer to his face, a face brimming with seething interest, if not anger. "I have called you up here because you have just returned from gathering information, I do hope."

His expression remained blank. "Creatures from all over the Dark World are searching for a book."

Darien's face fell. He leaned back against his chair. "A book? What good is a book to *me*, Lucien? What is this great book's name?"

"The Immortal's Guide."

Darien gasped, and his free hand clutched the arm of his chair. "How has it become known to all Creatures of the Dark World?"

"News has spread of Xavier's search for the book. Other Creatures cannot wait to look for it themselves."

"They *cannot!*" Darien whispered harshly. "That book is a night-mare!"

Ewer's brow furrowed. "A nightmare? You have read this book, my Lord?"

"Read it? You do not *read* a book like *The Immortal's Guide!* You survive it!" Darien yelled. "No one else can possess it. I have tried, but ultimately failed. Only Dracula...no, now it is Xavier who can have the book in his possession—and even that I do not wish on him!"

Yaddley and Ewer exchanged concerned glances, then said simultaneously, "What *is* this book exactly?"

He looked up at them, something like horror in his eyes, his mouth trembling. "It holds knowledge. Horrible...terrible truths."

Ewer narrowed his eyes at Darien's sudden, flustered demeanor. "You said you 'survive' this book? What do you mean by that exactly?"

But Darien had taken to muttering under his breath, long gone from the cold room where three Vampires remained, staring after him with bewildered faces.

Lucien snarled coldly. "If I'm no longer needed," he whispered, before turning to open the door, his black robes swaying against the creaking floorboards as he disappeared down the long hall.

Once the door shut, Yaddley and Ewer hesitated. Darien sat in the chair, his black eyes misty with remembrance, the ball of fire gone, the room doused in darkness.

When Yaddley reached for the door's handle, Darien sat up, alert. Through the darkness, he whispered, "He is here. How could he have found us?"

"Who is here, my Lord?" Ewer asked.

The dark Vampire stood. The chair crashed to the floor just before the sound of a door opening below jarred them where they stood.

Darien pushed past Yaddley and ran down the hall, Ewer at his heels. There was a fear Ewer could feel in his dead heart, his entire being. It was most encumbering, but that was to be expected for a Caddenhall Vampire bound to their Master.

Darien began to descend the stairs, a dark hand sliding down the railing. And when he reached the last step, the gasp escaped his lips. Ewer followed the gaze towards the Vampire that stood in the open doorway, and Darien said the name with a snarl:

"Damion."

※

Damion Nicodemeus stared at his brother, the two tall Vampires behind him atop the stairs. He smiled, aware it did not reach his eyes.

The cold wind blew into the room behind him, sending the many candles around the modest room to die. He removed his hood, the smile still on his lips, for he had found the house at last.

"Are you not...overjoyed to see me?" he asked Darien, who still lingered on the last step.

When Darien did not respond, Damion continued, "You look surprised...did you think I would not know where the house was? I have my ways, brother." He stepped further into the dining room, ignoring Minerva, who moved forward as though to greet him, although hesitant.

The door closed behind him, and the candles resumed their dances, flickering as if a small wind had only temporarily blown them away. He eyed the numerous flames before turning from them and moving into the other room, its brown walls reminding him of comfort, the fireplace within a far wall unlit, the furniture cozy. Gray and dark brown armchairs rested against corners in between numerous bookcases stuffed with old, peeling books.

He stepped with purpose, ignoring the glares of the others, to a small door pressed to the back of the room, and with a strong hand he pushed it open. He descended the dark steps down into the small basement, eyeing the blond Vampire that stood next to large bloody rags.

Lucien turned and bowed low. "My Lord."

Damion waved a hand, bidding him to stand, keeping his gaze on the pile of bloody rags just before them, a twinge of anticipation filling his dead heart. *How much had the Vampire told?* A slow smile found its way to his dark face and he tilted his head, trying to make sense of where the Vampire ended and began.

8

Dragor's once brown and gray hair was covered in blood, as was the Vampire's face, now bruised beyond recognition. A deep gash in his forehead spilled blood down his nose and onto the stone floor. The clothes he wore were smeared in blood as well, from previous bouts with Lucien.

Damion said, *"Excellent job,* Lucien. Did he talk?"

"He sang like a Phoenix," Lucien remarked, staring down at Dragor.

He tore his gaze from the bloodied Vampire to eye Lucien. "Where is it being kept?"

"Dracula had it last."

"What do you mean, 'had it last?'"

"Dracula is dead, my Lord," Lucien said.

Damion stared at him blankly, as though he had not heard a word of it. Then, slowly but surely, the words found their places in his mind. With a harsh laugh, he exclaimed, *"Dead?* When I left the Vampire City, Dracula had taken off to some Council meeting."

"Yes, my Lord, that is where he was murdered," Lucien said. "The sword was in his possession last—"

"Surely, you lie," he said, the shadow of doubt lingering just upon his tongue.

"I cannot lie to you, my Lord."

"Indeed, you cannot." And as he thought these words over, his eyes darkening the more it reached him, he tried again: "What happened? Who killed him? Who is King?"

"I know not who killed him, but it is known far and wide that Xavier Delacroix is King."

"Xavier?! King?!" he bellowed. Surely *this* was a most cruel lie, for what on Earth was Dracula playing at?

Damion felt a pang of disgust for Xavier: the information he must now have access to—things Damion did not. "How...what... wh-who has the sword now?" he asked desperately.

"I do not know," Lucien said.

"You must find out who has it. And do so quickly."

The Vampire nodded before disappearing from the basement in a quick wind, the smell of dried blood filling the air as he did.

Damion felt his mind spin. How could someone have *killed* Dracula? Who has the sword now? And Xavier. King?! Indeed, what *happened* in the few days he was bed-ridden at the infirmary inside the City?

Damion glared at the bloodied Dragor at his feet. Indeed. Did the Vampire tell Lucien everything he knew? Would his song change if he knew who it was Lucien worked for?

With an odd twitch of dark fingers, Dragor was lifted into the air, his head rolling lazily over a shoulder.

Damion shouted, "Up! Up! Wake up, Dragor!"

The bloodied mass made a weak utterance. His swollen eyes fluttered open as though roused from a deep sleep, the blood leaving his forehead to race down his slightly-aged face in droves. "D-Damion?"

His hand still outstretched, Damion demanded, "The sword. What can you tell me of the sword?"

Dragor blinked, his swollen face falling into contempt with the words; he attempted a snarl, yet his mouth could not open wide enough. Blood poured down to the stone floor beneath his hovering feet.

Damion sent the Vampire flying against the hard floor. Dragor cried out in pain when he hit the wall with a terrible thud and fell silent, his swollen eyes not opening against the light of the torch just above him.

Damion moved to him, bending low over a bleeding ear. *"Tell me more about Dracula's sword. The more you do, the more I shall think about letting you out of here alive."*

Dragor responded, "You...are wasting...your time. I know nothing."

"You know more than you are willing to tell!" he yelled, grabbing the Vampire's blood-soaked shoulder. Rising to stand, he lifted the Vampire with him, holding him high against the wall. "Do you mean to tell me that you, Dragor Descant, know *nothing* of Dracula's sword?"

"Yes, Damion, yes. That...is what I mean to tell you... I know nothing of the great sword—Dracula...would never speak, never speak freely of it," Dragor whispered, spurts of blood leaving his lips with the words.

Damion let out a cry of frustration. To come all this way...he had been expecting mountains of information with the number of things he'd instructed Lucien to do to the Vampire once he'd obtained him. But this? This was not worth the days of wondering whether he would finally possess the power to rule. This was not worth the damned Vampire's exile from his post! Perhaps he had chosen the wrong Vampire... Perhaps Dragor was not as close to Dracula as he had once thought him to be...

Releasing the Vampire from his grip, he watched him hit the stone floor a harsh grunt leaving his throat. He stared down at Dragor, the swollen eyes fluttered closed, and then the wounded Vampire dipped into unconsciousness.

Damion eyed an axe, a mallet, and several other sharp, bloodied objects that rested around the room, and knew that Lucien had stolen them from various Creatures—no respectable Vampire carried around such blunt objects.

Taking a deep, cold breath, he decided he would have to keep Dragor Descant alive. Although he claimed he knew nothing, perhaps it was a lie; it was known far and wide that Dragor's will was unnaturally strong. With one last glance to the bloodied mass upon the hard floor, he swept from the basement.

He climbed the stairs and was met with the tall back of Ewer Caddenhall. The Vampire faced the windows opposite the basement door, his golden robes flowing around him, giving him the air of a divine being.

For a reason unknown to him, he hesitated, and then Ewer's brittle voice said, "The sword you seek is in a place you won't want to venture, Lord Damion."

His eyes narrowed. "What?"

Ewer turned, his blond hair shaking as he moved, sharp eyes piercing with his stare. "I know what you want and I know who has what you want. And I know," he took a small step forward, "that you won't obtain it."

"What is this?" he snarled. *I do not have time for games, strange words...*

"I am helping you, Lord Damion, although you are not my Master. I am warning you: Release the Vampire below. There is no need to keep him here. Very soon, others shall come to obtain him. They will know something is wrong—even in this time of turmoil."

"What are you talking about, Ewer?!" Damion yelled, very much wishing to obtain the blood from his home.

A smile flickered across Ewer's face and he turned to look out the window once more. "Nothing, Lord Damion. I speak of nothing if you will not care to listen."

Damion glared at the back of the blond head, and then, with a final snarl, he moved, stepping past the old Vampire towards the dining room. A name caused him to still in his tracks:

"Eleanor Black has the sword, Lord Damion," Ewer's wheezing whisper sounded. "If, of course, you care to know."

He turned at once, marching up to Ewer, turning the Vampire to face him completely. "*What,*" he bared fangs, "*did you just say?*"

"*Eleanor Black,*" he said, Damion felt his face fall. *No, she could not have the sword...* Unable to think of anything more, he stepped from Ewer, keeping the blue eyes within his sight. *This was a lie,* Damion thought, *it had to be. She wouldn't have the sword—*

"Leaving so soon, brother?"

Damion turned to see the Vampire leaving the stairs, his eyes curious, yet he could not find the words to respond, not when the words of Ewer filled his mind without end.

"What is wrong here, Ewer?" Darien asked.

The Vampire bowed slightly. "Nothing, Master. Lord Damion was preparing to leave."

Darien turned back to his brother. "What is wrong?"

Damion blinked at the voice and eyed the younger Vampire. "Nothing," he whispered hoarsely, turning away from both Vampires' intent gazes. "Nothing. I must... I have to... *Out of the way!*" And he stalked past Darien, swirled around the corners of the table heading to the door. Before he could cross through the doorway, before he could rid himself of the spell that plagued Caddenhall Manor, Damion turned and gave one last bewildered glance towards the deep blue eyes of Ewer Caddenhall and saw in them what he had feared most: deep understanding. Fear filling his dead heart, Damion Nicodemeus pushed open the door, and disappeared from their eyes in a second's blink.

Chapter Two

THE DRAGON'S CAVERN

"**Y**ou can have this one," one man said with a quick grin to the other.

Xavier Delacroix walked deeper into the old room and eyed the small, uncomfortable bed that rested up against the wall. Strands of hay peeked through the small pieces of cloth, red and draped across the small, stiff mattress. "I'll sleep on the floor, thanks," he told his companion.

Nathanial Vivery removed his hood, and in the faint glow of the candle, his golden eyes glowed. He swept a pale hand through the short, red hair that flew every which way upon his head and turned his eyes to the sheath against his companion's waist. "If you are not comfortable here, we can move on. There is a city not far from here. Scylla."

He removed his own hood and turned to stare at Nathanial, his dark green eyes shining in the low candlelight that did nothing to brighten the growing darkness that swelled inside them. His black hair lay unbound against his back and trailed behind him as freely as the cloak he still wore. It was not long before he moved a strong hand to the hilt of the sword upon his waist. "We can't risk it. Eleanor's put out a search party for me. If we did not appear here when we did, I am sure we would have run into them."

Nathanial's golden eyes danced to the only window in the room. The fog beyond the glass rolled on and hid the bottom of green hills in the distance. "If we stay here any longer they may think to look here... And what will we do for sustenance? Sneak downstairs and take one of the humans while they're too drunk to function?"

"If it comes to that, yes," Xavier said.

He seemed keen on objecting, but said, "Cedar Village is not far from here, Xavier."

Xavier snarled, sending the candle's flame to flicker with the small breeze. "I am not scared of Eleanor's men. If it comes to facing them, we will."

"This isn't about pride or fear, my Lord. This is about your safety. The Creatures present at the Council of Creatures meeting—those who survived—are pursuing the book. What good would it be if they knew your location? Followed us until we found it and claimed it for themselves?" he said.

"But they cannot possess the book, can they? Eleanor said so herself."

"They may not be able to have the book in their possession, but they can travel through it once opened. There is no spell upon it—no enchantment, no curse, it's anyone's claim—but they will not be able to hold it in their hands for much longer then it would take for the book to suck them in."

Xavier looked away from him and gazed towards the small candle upon the old dresser, vaguely realizing that its knobs were missing. His thoughts were, instead, on the words Nathanial spoke. "And that would be most unwanted, correct? With the rate the humans are dying, thanks to Eleanor's Creatures and scared Enchanters, more Creatures' deaths are the last thing we need since—"

"Dracula's death sent the Dark World into disarray. The Enchanters are scared because the news broke of Peroeneus Doe giving Dracula the elixir for immortality. They are scared of any confrontation from other Creatures regarding the potion, that's why they're blasting away any being that looks like they might wish to question them about it. Regardless of if they're human or not."

"But these other deaths, the ones more...gruesome..." Xavier said, never removing his gaze from the small flame, even as Dracula's name was spoken.

"Done by Eleanor's Creatures, yes. Although several of them may have been caused by some stray Lycans—yes, there *are* still Lycans out there, regardless of what you heard Victor say, Xavier— it's been reported in various newspapers that several murders have taken place all over the world, many caused by the most unthinkable magic out there. Things not even Enchanters would dream of doing."

He looked away from the candle and towards Nathanial at last. "It's reached newspapers, has it?"

"Of course. With the reign of terror and crushing power that is this new Creature, it was only a matter of time before the humans' newspapers picked it up—even if they don't know the true cause of them."

Xavier said nothing, thoughts still claiming his mind. They soon fell into silence, and without realizing much of what he was doing, he moved across the small room and sat down upon the uncomfortably small bed, his brow furrowed.

Nathanial leaned against an old wall, his eyes hard with concentration.

After several minutes, Xavier emerged from his thoughts: "Eleanor has the Ares."

"Yeah, what about it?"

Xavier looked up and noticed the other Vampire appeared troubled. "Well, if she has the sword, could she not be planning to use it on me? Once her men find me, of course."

"She wouldn't be able to hold it for long. Like I said, any Creature that touches it that isn't a pure-blood Vampire gets repulsed by it."

"So it's a sword that was forged to kill Vampires, but only those of pure descent can use it?"

Nathanial stared at him. "Dracula didn't tell the truth in the hall, Xavier. He wasn't about to let Eleanor know the reality behind the sword. When he visited Tremor, Tremor took note of the sword and realized the pain it gave Dracula. He made it so only Dracula could touch it. Hold it. It still had the same effect—that it could kill Vampires—but only a pure-blood Vampire would be able to use it: he transferred some of his own energy into the sword."

Xavier took in this information with darkened eyes. "But Dracula killed that Creature, Michael, when he was in Lycan form. How was that possible?"

Nathanial pushed himself away from the wall. "I believe he confronted an Enchanter in the Modifying Magical Weapons Sect and made it so he could kill any Creature with the sword."

He blinked, thinking he had misheard a few words. "Modifying what?"

"Dracula really kept the Order locked tight, didn't he? What, you couldn't go out into the Dark World and see more than just the Vampire City?" Nathanial let out a small growl of disbelief at the look on the Vampire's face. "He really didn't wish to tell you anything, then. The Modifying Magical Weapons Sect is one of the many Enchanting Sects in the Dark World. There are about five-hundred or so Sects to date. Each dealing with different matters. There are the Modifying Magical Weapons Sect, the Mess-Cleaned Sect, the Enhanced Power Sect, the Renewing Reports and Regulations Sect... I could go on. My point, Xavier, is that there are several Sections of Powers, each given to distinct Creatures able to perform the tasks—"

"Like the Erasers and Cleaners," Xavier interjected.

"Precisely," Nathanial said.

"A friend of mine had trouble that had to be sorted. The Erasers and Cleaners were called to handle the mess." Xavier remembered the night two Erasers landed right in front of him, telling him of a message Victor left dealing with the Caddenhalls and Lillith... It all seemed so miserably far away.

Nathanial's voice snapped him out of his thoughts: "The Erasers and Cleaners are members of the Mess-Cleaned Sects. Whatever mess that has occurred will be settled. It is all a matter of contacting them, although I am sure you were not happy to have those two bumbling idiots about, were you?"

"Not exactly." Xavier remembered the two Erasers who had a disturbing affinity for finishing each other's sentences. And then he remembered the Cleaners, three Etrian Elves who seemed displeased with their job.

"Well yes, there are several Sections of Powers about in our world, hopefully we will not have to call on any of them in our search for the book," Nathanial said, studying Xavier's face.

"Right."

Nathanial studied him for a moment more before faking a yawn. "It's getting late; I should head in." The sky outside the window had blackened. When Xavier turned his head back to the Vampire, he wasn't surprised to see that he was now alone.

With his departure, Nathanial had put out the candle and Xavier made no attempts to bring it to life. He abandoned the uncomfortable bed and removed the sword from his waist, placing it against the wall. He then sat, back to the wall, an arm across a knee as he allowed a sigh to escape his chest. His thoughts drifted to how he was to acquire this book, especially since many more Creatures seemed to be searching for it, although they didn't know the horrors that awaited them—nor did he—but he felt it was his duty to protect them now that the odd energy of Dracula's blood flowed through his veins.

He opened his eyes and stared at the dark sky outside, wondering just what it was that he was supposed to gain from traveling through the book. Yes, others mentioned the vast knowledge contained within its pages, but knowledge of what exactly? Ever since Dracula was turned to ash, he'd felt as if he was thrust unwillingly into this new Dark World. The veil of protection and secrets had been lifted and he was forced to come to terms with a world he barely knew, a destiny so unceremoniously given, while being expected to accept it with open arms.

He knew he couldn't pretend that nothing had happened at the Council Meeting. Everywhere he turned, others eyed him with awe-filled, sometimes apprehensive, eyes. He knew they knew about his blood. He could sense it easily. It was the same look Dracula received when he was alive.

Xavier brought his hand to his face and curled it into a fist. The pulse resonated through his hand and arm, and he knew this was the difference he held. His hand never pulsed in such a way before Dracula's death. What was so different now? *Why* was something different now?

That was the question Xavier found himself asking most of the time. *Why? Why not Victor? Why me?* Surely, Victor was a much better candidate for this, having lived by Dracula's side for all those years. But apparently he had only witnessed the Dracula that they had all seen right up to his death. They knew nothing of the Vampire's past and his mountain of secrets that stemmed through years of murder, stealing, and blood.

And was that okay? Was it all right that Lillith and Victor knew nothing of Dracula's true nature? How much did Darien know? He was still alive, with the Caddenhalls, going by the name of Demetrius Bane, the Head Officer of the Alliance for All Dark Creatures in the Vampire County of Lane.

The Caddenhalls. The thought of the Vampire family brought

his attention to the Vampire that he'd left with Lucien Caddenhall. Dragor Descant. How was the Vampire fairing? Would it be worth a trip to Lane to see?

But of course, he wouldn't be able to travel to Lane just yet. They still had to go to Cedar Village and search for the book. If it was not there, then they had to move onto Quiddle, a famous Vampire city Xavier repeatedly read about in his studies of *Quiddle: A Usurper's Paradise*. If they did not find the book in Quiddle, then they would travel to Lane, their "last resort," to put it in the words of Nathanial Vivery.

It had been three weeks since he'd left Victor's manor with Nathanial. In that amount of time, could the news of the book have exploded so rapidly? But who broke the news? It had to have been someone that was present at the Council Meeting...but no one came to mind.

Xavier closed his eyes, letting his head rest against the wall behind him. He'd prided himself on being able to think silently for several hours a day, but he found he'd exhausted himself this night. It seemed even *thinking* was another journey he was sent on, a silent one to recover clues and secrets within his mind.

And as the unpleasant memory of several Elite Creatures ambushing him and Nathanial two nights before surfaced, he willed it away, and drifted off to sleep, the Ascalon pulsing beside him.

✳

The small breeze blew past him, and he laid eyes upon her. He saw her hair tangle together behind her head, the silkiness reminding him of a cloak.

He watched as she crossed the street to greet him, her dread spreading through his veins with ease. "I sent Amentias and Aciel to various places throughout the Dark World and they have both returned to me with interesting news," he told her once in quiet speaking distance.

She stared at him, her eyes narrowing. "What news?"

"Dracula's death is the story on Creatures' tongues. It appears they are aware of what happened, although the story is always different as to *how* it happened," he said.

"And?"

He heard the slight edge to her voice and hurried on: "And they know of the book."

"*What?*"

He bowed his head lower, deliberately hiding his face underneath his hood. "Yes, my Queen. They...wish to...acquire it—"

Her movement was sudden and he had had no time to react: The café building he just departed from was sent up in flames, the screams heard plainly inside. He leapt back in shock and stared at the humans who'd lingered behind, now burning in the high flames. He turned to eye her in bewilderment. "Eleanor—"

She lifted a slender hand to silence him and began to walk away from the burning building, which was now drawing eyes and screams of fright from others in their nearby homes. He followed after her, allowing himself to be swept up in the darkness she had placed around them with a quick swish of a pale hand. It kept them hidden from the eyes of humans and a few nicely disguised Creatures that swept urgently past, eager to see up close the building that was now almost completely gone—

"They cannot lay eyes upon that book!"

He had to rush to keep up with her. He was surprised to find she had not left the ground and taken flight, given the speed she now traveled.

He panted after her, feeling his blood begin to boil with anxiousness. "My Queen, what...are we going...to do?!" he gasped.

She did not break stride. "*You* must secure the book! Do whatever it takes but make sure no Creature finds it—*especially Xavier!* He will not be able to truly rule if he does not have it. And—" She turned to him so abruptly, he almost barreled into her. "The sword, you still have it?"

"Yes, yes I have it, but what does that have to do with the—" he began, but she walked further away from him, the darkness engulfing them now growing warmer with her escalating rage.

He walked after her yet again, refusing to speak lest she decide to set him on fire instead of any of the dim, curtain-drawn buildings they were passing now. He turned his head to look behind them, trying to see whether any of the commotion had died down.

Thick smoke climbed into the night sky and on the ground, the gathering of humans and Creatures had thickened. Several horse-drawn carriages were stationed outside the burned café and he assumed the Watch had arrived. Wondering how many of the people in their dark cloaks decorated with badges were actually Vampires, he allowed himself to face the long, dark hair of Eleanor Black in front of him.

They continued walking along the sidewalk and rounded a sharp corner into an alley. A tall, dark figure appeared at the end, blocking the light from a nearby streetlamp.

Eleanor took a step forward, hands loosely intertwined in front of her as she addressed the dark figure. "Are you the one with the information I seek?"

The voice that came back was deep and smooth, and for the first time, Thomas caught the scent of cold blood. Vampire.

The figure said, "I am, if you are the one who is looking for the information I have. Miss Eleanor Black?"

"I am," Eleanor said.

The figure took several steps forward. As, he drew closer, Thomas was able to see his face. He had an air of great charm that was not uncommon to the colder Creatures of the Night, this Thomas

22

could see in the man's deep blue eyes. His dark hair reached his neck in a sweep of something resembling elegance, and his voice was smooth, still, as he spoke yet again. "Well, Miss Black, what do you wish to know?"

"I have heard you know of a human woman who holds the blood of Dracula," she said.

Thomas's eyes widened and he stepped forward, standing between both Creatures, yet he could only glare at Eleanor in sheer incredulity. "What?!"

She turned to him, her eyes a fierce red, yet she did not speak.

He knew at once that she was forbidding him to take part in the conversation that would ensue.

He stepped into the shadows behind her and remained deathly silent, his dark eyes watching with deep interest.

The Vampire continued on then, as if Thomas had not interrupted the conversation at all. "I do. I laid eyes upon her at Victor Vonderheide's ball a month ago. There were a number of humans there, as it is Victor's custom to mingle humans and Vampires fearlessly, but she was indeed like no other I've seen."

"How so?" Eleanor smiled.

His deep eyes glazed over ever so slightly as he answered her, his words no longer one of bestowing information, but of sweet, sublime obedience. "This woman was an absolute entrancement, my Lady. She was every bit a human, but I could not smell her blood—I had no desire to drink from her, but then again, I did adorn my ring that night, like so many others alongside me." He blinked. "I caught no name, but Victor was upon her before I could get a good look. He took her upstairs and that was that. As for her harboring the blood of Dracula, it is only a guess of mine, and what I've heard from rumors here and there about the Vampire World." He then looked at her as if attempting to apologize for his lack of certain information. "Is this what you wished to know, my Lady?"

"That is exactly what I wished to know, dear constable. Thank you."

The constable seemed to lapse into a state of supreme contentment, for he looked =oblivious as to where he was and with whom; he blinked several times and a thick drop of drool dribbled out the side of his open mouth, now curled up into a wide, handsome smile. When Eleanor turned from him and stepped away, his blue eyes returned to a state of utmost seriousness. Thomas eyed the Vampire as Eleanor swept past him and continued to walk briskly through the small alleyway back the way they had come.

The Vampire looked angry, perhaps even hurt. His blue eyes turned dark red, and he took a quick step towards the retreating Eleanor.

Thomas exhaled, preparing to let the cold of the early morning engulf him, as he had no hope of facing a Vampire in his current human form, yet he had not gotten very far at all before the constable called after her, not with a voice of outrage and disbelief at who he had just spoken to, but with anxiousness: "Wait! What about our deal?"

Thomas stared at the constable, dumbfounded. *What on Earth was happening here?*

Eleanor's voice danced in the night air. "What deal, Vampire? The deal was that you would give me information on a human woman with direct relational ties to Dracula. You have given me no such thing. There is no deal."

Confused, Thomas turned to stare at Eleanor. "What—" he started to say before the huge gust of air blew past him, a large shadow sweeping over the alleyway.

Eleanor rose a few feet off the ground. The constable crashed to the cold stone where she had been just seconds before and was now getting to his feet, although he looked disoriented. It was as if he could not see anything at all. He took a step and staggered before crashing to his knees.

She floated above the Vampire, her frame ethereal, her face surrounded by her long, flowing hair, her many necklaces clinking together, causing the Vampire to jump to his feet, staring blindly up at the air above, clearly not seeing her.

Eleanor's eyes turned red, her skin paled so that she was a ghost against the darkness. She looked down at the Vampire, contempt alive in her eyes.

Thomas allowed the darkness that she'd placed to enter him, allowing himself to take the form of a Vampire as he would not be able to stomach the blood of the constable otherwise.

With a harsh laugh and wave of her hand, several deep gashes appeared along the Vampire's body, continuing to appear until, at last, his limbs were fully severed. His torso was cut in half. His head disconnected from his neck and rolled to where Thomas stood, the black eyes wide and distant, staring up at him, dull.

With a disgusted snarl, Thomas kicked the head away from him and stared at Eleanor, who had landed lightly upon her feet. She stepped towards him, her eyes their murderous red.

"Come Thomas," she said. "We must retrieve the sword."

He pulled his hood over his head, his own eyes red as he recognized the blood that splattered the walls as sustenance.

The darkness about the alleyway was removed and the light surprised him. The sun made the blood shine even as it began to darken, and moving to follow Eleanor's lead out of the alleyway,= he stepped over the bottommost part of the constable's torso, as well as a thumb and several fingers, but it was one ringed finger he stepped upon that made him halt.

Stooping to examine the ring, he saw that it gleamed brilliantly. He pried the ring off the cold finger, slipping it in the pocket of his cloak as Eleanor disappeared, sending a gust of wind to blow past him.

Mind gone on how the Vampire had done all he could to please

Eleanor, he grimaced, aware that she had caused him to do the same by holding his dear Mara against him...

The sound of footsteps on the sidewalk behind him caused him to realize where he stood, and he closed his eyes, following Eleanor's lead, disappearing from the bloody alleyway and the murder that just occurred.

※

He awoke the next morning with a start and the sword moved with his hand: The silver blade gleamed in the sunlight pouring through the small window. His eyes wide, he shifted his gaze from one cob-webbed corner to the other, the feeling of vulnerability flooding every sense. The sensation that he had not been alone upon waking would not release its hold upon his dead heart.

Nathanial appeared beside the old dresser in the next second, his face shifting from anxiousness to concern as he looked down at the tense Xavier upon the floor. "What's wrong?"

Slowly rising to his feet, Xavier let the Ascalon fall in his hand. "I'm not sure. I felt as though..." Then, for a reason unknown to him, he mouthed the name—the true reason for his discontentment.

"What was that?"

Xavier looked at him, yet his mouth could not move, the words would not form, for how foolish would they sound? Instead he turned, and placed the Ascalon in its sheath at his waist. "Nothing," he said, grateful the Vampire had not realized the name.

"Are you certain?"

"I am," Xavier responded, his mind swimming with confusing question.

"Very well." Nathanial sighed. "There was a murder right across the street last night."

He whirled. "What?"

"It's why I came in to wake you. Apparently it happened in the alleyway right across from this inn. I managed to catch the scene before the Watch pounced upon it like a pack of beasts. There was a considerable amount of blood splattered all throughout the alleyway as well as torn body parts: fingers, arms—even the head was torn from the neck."

He was painfully silent as he took in this information, his thoughts clamoring together once more, although he was not sure, nay, did not want to be sure, that he knew in which direction they were traveling—

"And," Nathanial said, apparently not finished, "a small café was burned to the ground not far from here. There were still people inside."

"You're not serious?"

Nathanial leaned up against the dresser. "Unfortunately, I am. We must leave, Xavier. With all of this...death so close, I'm sure it is the doing of Eleanor's men—"

And all at once he realized what it was he felt deep inside, the presence all around him, within his heart...

"Eleanor," he said aloud so that Nathanial was ushered into silence. "It was her!"

Nathanial raised an eyebrow. "What?"

Xavier stared at him, unabashed as he said, "Can you not see it? It was *her*, Vivery! I-I felt her presence nearby—she is the cause of the murder, I'm sure of it."

Nathanial said nothing for a time, then moved from the dresser and strode toward Xavier, placing a hand upon his shoulder, staring him carefully in his emerald eyes. "Just to be clear...you are saying that you somehow knew Eleanor was...nearby? That she's the one who committed that murder, possibly burned down the café?"

He stared back into the golden eyes and it was as if he was able to think clearly at last: his breathing slowed, his thoughts dissipated, and the feeling of derision that so filled his mind with Eleanor's presence began to dissolve.

And Nathanial, satisfied that the confused, overwhelmed expression left Xavier's face and cleared from his eyes, released his grip upon the Vampire's shoulder and stepped away. "We're heading for Cedar Village next. We must keep moving."

Xavier stared at him. The thoughts of Eleanor returned against his will, and he recalled how upon waking he'd felt as though she was right in the room with him. Now, she felt much farther away.

But that couldn't be right, he forced himself to think, *I wouldn't be feeling her... I shouldn't be...*

She wouldn't be roaming the Dark World by herself after what happened at the Council Meeting, surely. She'd leave that job for her many loyal Creatures, currently searching for himself and the book.

As they left the small room, and the old door creaked closed behind them, Xavier was convinced that he was rattled with all of the things that had and were happening to him. Upon descending the old stairs and stepping through the vacant dining area towards the door, he was sure that Eleanor's presence was his overactive imagination at work.

Chapter Three

CHRISTIAN DELACROIX

The empty fireplace held his thoughtful gaze before his black eyes closed with deep concentration, his mind clouded with thoughts on the new...guest within his home and the depressing information he had heard only three days before.

He recalled his shock when Lillith rode to him that faithful night, her blue eyes larger than usual. She did not bother to gain entrance into Delacroix Manor by way of the front door, but decided to appear before him in his bedroom. She had knelt at his bedside, hands tightly clenching the sheets. There was no ring on any finger.

"Christian!" she half-screamed, half-whispered. "Dracula—he's *dead*."

"Dead?" He stared at her. "You're joking... You're *not* joking..." he'd said, rising to sit up.

She'd risen slowly with him, and moved to sit atop the bed, never turning her gaze away from his black eyes.

He could see there was something else much more prominent going on than the Great Vampire being dead. He did not speak, but waited until she could muster the strength to say it. At last, her

29

mouth moved and the words that left those lips seemed a chore to comprehend, for they couldn't have been true in the least. He blinked and ran a hand over his mouth, the shock of it all too much to take in so late in the night.

And then he would say: "My brother—Xavier Delacroix—is king of the *entire* Dark World?"

"Yes, Christian," she'd said, nodding.

"Why hasn't he come and told me this himself? Where is he?"

She stood from the bed then and turned to look down at him. "He visited Victor and I earlier this night..." She fell into a hesitant silence for a moment. "Victor...I know he felt the difference. Xavier had to leave us. Victor and I soon received numerous visits from various Vampires explaining Xavier's...quest to destroy Eleanor Black—that she is a threat to the Dark World..."

Christian stood, his chest illuminated in the dim moonlight cast through the open windows. "He's left to chase after Eleanor Black?"

"That is what I was told."

His eyes darkened as he stared at her. She had taken to his dresser, apparently engrossed in deeper thought. It wasn't until he'd moved to retrieve a shirt from the dresser that she'd blinked and said, "We are not sure what...what is going to happen from here on, Christian. The Vampire City has surely received the news by now. Victor's rode to the City for the night...he could not bear to remain in his home any longer and I expect things shall be...hectic on the surface for the next few weeks as word spreads. Because you are his brother, I'm sure others shall be knocking your door down for information— but be weary, Christian. Eleanor's men apparently have the ability to change breeds at will. You won't be able to smell their true nature. And...and the woman. Alexandria. Don't let anyone know you have her living with you here—it will raise suspicions. You do understand, don't you, Christian?"

He turned to her. During the time she had been talking, he had flung the shirt over his arms and had buttoned it, the prospect of sleep trivial now. She was staring at him with a look of bewilderment and he furrowed his brow; her features returned to normalcy: perfect, inquisitive beauty.

"No, Lillith, no, I don't understand, if I'm to be perfectly honest. When did this all happen?"

She took a breath and began to tell him of the Council of Creatures meeting that Xavier had traveled to upon Dracula's request that she'd heard by way of Victor.

He'd sat upon his bed, amazed. It wasn't until she had finished that he dared move from his stupor: he strode to the window, staring out at the crescent in the sky, wondering what on Earth it was that his beloved brother was doing now.

She said nothing more to him and it was only when he felt the slight breeze blow against his back did he know she had departed, leaving him with his thoughts. And now he looked down at his hands and was surprised to see them trembling. With effort, he closed them into fists, bashing them against his head. It was maddening that he'd had no bloody idea what in the world was happening around him—to his own brother! Dracula, dead. Xavier, King. It made no sense. Why was it that he was always the last to know?

The following hours after Lillith had left his room, Delacroix Manor was indeed met with visits from all kinds of Vampires disguised as humans, Enchanters claiming to be personal friends of Lord Xavier, and entrancing Faes who had come to pay their respects to Count Dracul.

Every time the door bell sounded, Christian would let out an aggrieved groan. He'd had nothing to tell these Creatures—many he was meeting for the first time—and he wished they would leave him alone.

He'd finally gotten his wish when no callers had come before breakfast the next day to ask him where it was that Lord Xavier had traveled to, leaving the Dark World in disarray. It wasn't until night fell around the Manor and he prepared to go feed did he stop in his tracks and realize not a single Dark Creature attempted to pay him a visit. It was then that he was able to go into town and choose his victim, feeding on her with additional flourish, for he had had no late-night stragglers wishing to know what happened to Xavier.

Thinking this freedom permanent at last as he moved about his home the next afternoon, feeling light as his ring was stowed safely in a drawer beneath piles of freshly laundered clothes, Christian was now free to focus his attentions on other things. Or, more specifically, other people.

Yes, the curious human was once again at the forefront of his mind. They still knew not her purpose, and now they would never know—the Great Vampire was permanently dead—so what was he to do with her? He could not have a human woman living with him. He and humans did not bode well. He found them pitiable, no matter their social standing, and the only time he was ever interested in them was when he was to drink their blood and keep his life. But with her, with Alexandria Stone, it was different.

He could not drink her blood, he could not even *smell* her blood, could not feel it pulsing in her veins. For this, he was extremely grateful. He could not bear the sight of her, how her eyes pierced his far too easily for a human's to ever do so. She was maddening, and just what role did she play in the Dark World? If Dracula needed her, surely, she held some power, some deeply hidden power that had to be unlocked through some unknown ancient rite...

He tried to recall anything special he knew from her. The fact that she destroyed his ring with her mere smile those two months ago was interesting enough. No human had ever left him so vulnerable; no human had forced him to feed upon another so quickly to sustain his urges.

Alexandria Stone.

What an insufferable vixen. He was reminded, inexplicably, of how hard she had cried into his chest, of how she shook with fear in Victor's room, yet still she remained in his arms...and then the memory of her blood the night he had stumbled upon her in the large paws of Lore returned to him, and his eyes closed with the sweetness of it.

That blood. How irresistible. How intoxicating. And yet... His eyes opened as it came to him. He could not smell her blood when she was awake and aware, but when she was sleeping, her scent would linger at his nose. It would find him anywhere. And how interesting that was. That her blood overpowered the smell of the drunken, unbearable women he ran into on a nightly basis. And he would return home, only to be drawn to her chambers, only to stand near her bedroom door for the smell of her would call him so...

But he would do nothing more, knew he could do nothing more. She was important to Dracula, needed to be kept alive. He would not fall into the bad graces of his dear brother by killing the very thing Dracula wished for. So he would leave her doorway, he would leave her gentle frame as she slept, unaware of her incredible blood.

The growl was involuntary as it left his chest and he realized the very thought of her made him feel incredibly misplaced. Just what was she? *Who* was she? Why did Dracula request her and why was he, Christian, the one to find her? *Why?*

He decided that if she was never found, he'd have finished his training with Damion and he'd be working alongside Xavier right now, fending off Eleanor Black. But he wasn't and the fact that he wasn't and that she'd chosen him to watch over her confused him. Why had she chosen him?

It was Xavier, he thought. He had scared her, and looking back on it, Christian knew she had found an inkling of comfort in his arms, if ever briefly. It was no wonder she would chose the one...person that had shown her kindness. Though he also knew Xavier's words that he could not watch over her, had propelled him to want to do it, to prove himself in this vast, dangerous world.

It was now that he was so miserably alone with the human that he realized just how irritable of a job it would turn out to be.

Ever since she left Victor's Manor in tears, she'd been distant, this he could not help but notice. She remained in her room for vast amounts of time and would reject the food given to her by the help. He would walk by her room and see a new dish sitting in front of her door, completely untouched. It would remain there for hours until a maid or cook would stoop and pick it up to replace it with a fresh plate of food.

It did not take him long to realize that she was unhappy, that she was alone and that she was very much being held here against her will, for surely she had a home, surely she had a family who cared for her, who was missing her something terrible. Christian was sure she thought about them every night...and with this thought came the reminder of his own parents' death.

Xavier had woken him to tell him that their parents were dead and that they had to leave before the monsters returned to kill them as well. It was early morning when they'd finally packed enough clothes and left their home forever. He would never forget when he saw the remains of his father, completely unrecognizable, just before the door. He'd almost lost his breakfast at the damned smell, but he held it in, for he would not show weakness in front of Xavier...the boy who had been like a rock through that most horrible time.

Christian remembered his brother, who did not look down at the corpses of his mother and father like he had done, eyes wide with tears at their states. No, Xavier had focused on a point in the distance, a point far away from where they were and seemed to place himself there, and his eyes darkened that day, the light never returning to them.

He was their pillar of strength ever since and they were forced to grow up fast. They were required to move mountains to live each day, sometimes finding shelter from the rain beneath the roofs of abandoned houses, sometimes cowering in alleyways where nothing but dead rats rested in their graves. All of it seemed a far cry away from where they were now, with their many-roomed mansion, their own live-in help, their own stable, the property that included a beach along the side, and Christian's thoughts were turned to the man who had given them this new life, who had seen them in their state of depreciation and who had promised them riches, the best life money could buy.

Of course, he was no man, Christian later discovered. The fact that the man was indeed a Vampire made Christian slightly scared, yes, but inexplicably intrigued. Creatures that could live forever on nothing but the life-force of humans were fascinating to him: He was twenty-four then, and nothing seemed more perfect for him, nothing seemed the better way to escape a world so filled with death and constant hunger. He craved the escape. He was willing, much more willing than Xavier, who had come later to find Christian on the floor of the Vampire's manor, blood spilling from a wound to his neck.

Christian could barely remember his brother's screams. They had filled his ears and heart and then he had lost consciousness, only to be awakened a few hours later by the taste of another's blood. His mind had gone blank as the pain when the blood crept down his throat and entered his system was incredible, one he never wished to revisit. Instead, he turned his thoughts to Xavier, how his brother had looked when he, Christian, had removed himself from the floor, his face paralyzed with an expression most unreadable as Christian stared at him in renewed wonder.

At first, he thought Xavier would shrink from him, fall into a state of denial and flee the manor, but instead, the brave man that has always been Xavier Delacroix turned to the Vampire who stood there, eyeing Christian softly, and demanded he change him as well.

The Vampire obliged and Christian watched as he touched Xavier's neck, yet Xavier did not wince as Christian had done. He stood, as still as stone, prepared to die for his brother. Prepared to be reborn for his brother.

The next moments of Xavier's transformation were moments Christian vowed he would never forget. What made them special was not the way Xavier's eyes pierced his once it was done, nor was it the length to which his hair had grown and darkened once it was done. No, it was the scream that left his lips when he was upon the floor, writhing in pain, his eyes open, placed upon Christian's. They never moved the whole time he was dying. Xavier was strong, even in death.

Christian watched Xavier fall silent after a time, and the Vampire moved to cut his finger. He then placed it over Xavier's lips, spilling his blood for the other Delacroix brother to claim.

Christian recalled the way Xavier's eyes flew open once the blood had touched the tip of his tongue. Xavier was on his feet before the wound in his neck had fully healed.

They had learned that they could not go long without blood, and the Vampire who had turned them showed them how to feed, who to pick, how exactly to do it, and, if necessary, how to kill the human if you did not want to drink all of their blood yet did not wish to have them turned either.

"Creating another is a vast responsibility," he had said to them, and ironically enough, within the next year, the Vampire that had given them new life, that had taught them and cared for them like a father, was gone, never to be seen again—they were left to fend for themselves.

It was after this that they started their excursions, making a name for themselves amongst the other wealthy elite. The pile of bodies leading to their door had certainly drawn the notice of other Vampires, yet it was Victor Vonderheide that appeared, wanting to meet with the Vampires so new, so unguarded in their nature. Xavier was the one to answer the door as Christian had left to feed the night

Victor came and when Victor mentioned the "King of Their Kind," Dracula, Xavier obliged to meet him.

Christian had returned home to an empty manor and waited months before Xavier appeared again to tell him of a city full of Vampires, of Vampire Armies, of a very interesting Vampire named Dracula.

Yes, Christian saw less and less of Xavier after that, but he would never forget when Xavier returned to his home on the surface with a note from Dracula telling them that they would receive humans as their servants and that they were to wear golden rings that would stifle their urges. It was with great reluctance that he'd placed his ring upon his finger, and once it was on, Christian felt as though he were nine all over again and his parents had just died by the claws of Lycan Creatures. The effect was indeed stifling, suffocating; he felt he could not breathe properly with it on and it took several years to get used to, but after the eightieth year or so, Christian forgot the damned thing was on at times.

The next surprise was when Xavier returned from the Vampire City to tell him that he'd been made Head of the Vampire Order, an outfit established by Dracula, where only the best Vampires of the Armies and around the World were chosen to work alongside him on matters regarding the entire Dark World. At this news, Christian was bewildered, and he was more disconcerted when Xavier Delacroix's name began to sprout up everywhere he dared turn. The Vampire was starting to get noticed by more than just Vampires atop the surface; every Vampire city and town across the Dark World was starting to recognize the name of Dracula's new favorite Vampire.

At first, it drove Christian insane: There were many times he had been mistaken for being Xavier, only to have to explain that he was his brother. The look on their faces would be enough to make Christian wish he'd never accepted the damned Vampire's offer to become what he was.

And then, slowly, but surely, he grew accustomed to the glances and glares he'd receive from other Vampires, and it didn't bother him as much. He remained on the surface, living his life as he was shown to: drink and kill. He started to see humans as prey, never the interesting, complex creatures they really were. He had not realized this until he met Alexandria Stone, who had awoken in him a reality he had not wished to ever face again: That humans were more than just prey, that humans had lives. They lived, not only to feed his urges, but to experience life. With her weeping, he was reminded of this wholeheartedly, and he did not like the distant feelings, or the thoughts this spurred on.

Wondering why on Earth he allowed her to consume his thoughts so much, he forcefully turned his attention back to the empty fireplace and examined the cobwebs across the mantle, the logs that sat cold and untouched for years, yet she was still there and would not leave...

With a final sigh, he stood from the white couch and turned his gaze to the white door, where he could hear faint footsteps moving away beyond it.

＊

It was well into the evening when the two uneasy Scotland Yard Officers arrived. Christian had been in his room when they had called. A maid had conjured up enough courage to knock upon his door.

Now he sat before them in the moderately-sized sitting room as a fire blazed in its grate, watching them both with cold, indifferent eyes. His thoughts, once he'd left the white living room for good this day, had only ventured to the human he was tasked with watching over. He had not seen her once since he'd left the room, but it was not like he was expecting to see her flittering about aimlessly after all.

"M-my Lord, Your Grace, L-Lord Christian," one officer stammered.

He regarded the man with a hint of disgust. He had known the moment he had seen him that this man was a mere human. He did not know that he sat before a full-fledged Vampire (for Christian had left his ring in the bowels of the dresser), nor would the man know that the officer he had arrived with was a Vampire as well. No, he would only feel a remarkable chill he could not explain, would only desire to bask in the glow of such a beautiful man, if only to wonder how it was he came to gain his apparent death-filled glow.

He turned his bored gaze to the Vampire officer sitting just beside the human. His deep blue eyes were calm as he stared back at Christian; it was as though he only regarded the Delacroix Brother as someone unworthy of the special attention so many others agreed to place upon him.

"What brings you to my home?" Christian said, sinking further into the red armchair, desiring nothing more than to be done with this and to resort to his hunt for the night.

"There has been a murder...a-a massacre," the human said, his hands shaking in his lap.

An eyebrow rose and then settled back down. "A murder or a massacre?"

"For all intents and purposes," the Vampire said now, "both. A constable was murdered in an alleyway just across from *The Dragon's Cavern* and a café has been burned to the ground—the matron and his family who resided in the small apartment upstairs are dead."

He sat forward in his seat. "The Constable...was murdered?" he asked, all former boredom leaving him, his thoughts running to the smooth-talking Vampire who had once talked Nicodemeus Manor out of alarm. Christian still remembered the taste of the maid's most welcoming blood. "Who would kill a man such as the constable?"

The Vampire across from him sat higher in his own red armchair. "We believe it to be a most...*heinous murder*, something only a...*new breed* of murderer can accomplish before dawn, presumably, of course."

Christian blinked, understanding that this Vampire spoke of the new breed of Creature that now freely terrorized the Dark World. "And why would you bring this depressing news to a man of my stature?"

"Is it not obvious?" the Vampire said, his blue eyes narrowing.

"Is it?" the human man said dimly from his seat.

"Yes, of course," the Vampire said as though explaining the alphabet to a child. He turned back to eye Christian. "Your brother, my Lord, was seen leaving *The Dragon's Cavern* yesterday morning."

"Yesterday?" Christian asked. "This happened *yesterday?* Why are you bringing this to my attention now?"

"Matters had to be attended to before we could consult you, my Lord," the human said.

The Vampire never removed his stare from Christian. "Yes, we could not move away from the precinct for long. We had to be there to speak on matters, see who would be sent to locate your brother, for he is a suspect in the murder of the constable, Christian."

"But you just said a-a most heinous murderer could have done it, would have done it!"

"And is Lord Xavier not a most heinous murderer, my Lord?"

The human sat upright in his seat, his shaking, sweaty hands now clutching tight a handkerchief he'd removed from his coat pocket to dab at his forehead. "Now see here, Arthur, you can't just go making accusations like that! Lord Xavier Delacroix is a most respected, most admired man throughout Europe—the idea that he would commit a m-murder...it's inconceivable!"

"Is it?" Arthur said.

"Yes!" Christian Delacroix said, clutching the arm rests on his own red chair. "My brother would never kill another Vam...man!"

"Can you say that standing trial in front of a judge, a jury?"

He sank back in his seat slowly. "A what?"

"The constable's death has called for retribution. The hu—" he began, realizing the human man sat beside him. It was a second before he shifted in his seat and continued on with a more careful tongue. "There are...people out there that desire to see things resolved. If you, the man's very brother, can stand before twelve men and state that Xavier Delacroix would never, as long as you have known him, kill another man, I'm sure it would help his case."

"But, I don't understand," Christian said, his black eyes wide with confusion. "Why would I have to stand trial? Aren't there... procedures that could be followed to...to make all of this...go away?" His eyes darted to the human to see if the man had caught the implication of his words. The man did not: he appeared engrossed in the handkerchief upon his lap.

Arthur swept some black hair off his shoulder as he rose to his feet. The man looked up, surprised to see movement, blinked, and then rose to his own feet as the Vampire said, "Procedures, Lord Christian? What on Earth are you talking about? No one is immune to the law, no matter if they bear the surname Delacroix or Vonderheide. Am I understood?"

Christian glared up at him. Because Xavier was not here, because Xavier could not be located, because Xavier left the Dark World when he was needed the most, he, Christian Delacroix was being punished for a crime an Elite Creature committed. Someone needed to be seen doing *something*, this Christian was aware of. Yet it did not still the boiling outrage in his chest that this Vampire would come here and demand he stand his own brother's trial.

"Are we understood, Lord Christian?" Arthur said again.

Christian's eyes were deep with rage. "We are understood, officer." He did not rise as both officers bowed low and walked, one with grace and poise, the other with trembling legs and a feeble disposition towards the wooden doors leading into the main hall.

Chapter Four

THE SWORD'S CALL

The deep forest held trees that hung heavily from their roots, partly obscuring his view of the modestly-sized cabin just several feet from where he stood. It was not morning here, it was miserably dark amongst the trees.

He stepped over branches and leaves and up to the door, never bothering to knock, but opening it softly, stepping over the threshold. The fireplace cracked and sparked with life, and against a far corner, something stirred.

The figure moved forward out of the darkness of the corner, dark eyes gleaming. "Thomas, she has just left, but you are free to stay here and wait for her to return."

"I have no intention of leaving if she is to return," Thomas responded, stepping further into the cabin, the door closing behind him.

He saw the gleam in the man's black eyes as he stepped forward into the light of the fireplace, and the man said, "So. She wants the sword secure, does she?"

"Yes," Thomas said. He did not release the sword from his grip, but took a seat in an armchair nearest the fireplace, allowing his gaze to travel to the dancing, jumping flames.

"Thomas," the voice reached his ears and the footsteps traveled to the back of his chair as the strong hand was placed upon it. "Do you know what she is planning to do with the sword?"

"I know she needs it secure, safe—anywhere the Vampire cannot reach it, Amentias."

The chair grew white, and he took a cold breath before moving away from Thomas, the sword, and the fire that burned. "I was just wondering, of course."

Thomas shifted in his seat, turning to stare upon the back of the Vampire. "Where did she go?"

Amentias sighed again and turned to stare at the man within the chair, his eyes crimson. Thomas could smell the cold blood of him even in his human form: Amentias was hungry. "She would not tell me, but Aciel went with her. I imagine if he was needed, it was to a place that required the...excellence of his *much desired skill*." The last three words drowning in sarcasm.

"Then she should be here soon, I imagine," Thomas said, settling back into the armchair, no longer turning his gaze to the fire. He stared into the red gem planted in the guard of the Ares.

As if on cue, the fire died, casting them into darkness. Thomas looked up and heard Amentias move to the windows facing the front of the cabin. Through the gloom, he could see the crimson eyes shifting in the night, looking for any sign of another presence.

And then: "There is no one there...at least, no one I can sense..."

"Then why did the fire go out?" he asked from his chair.

The crimson eyes turned to him and Thomas admired the surreal eminence of the Vampire's gaze. He wondered if that was how he looked when in his own Vampire form.

"I do not know," Amentias responded.

He rose from the armchair, keeping the Ares close, and moved to the other set of windows on the other side of the old door. He looked out into the clearing and, indeed, no one was there. It was a new moon, so there was no light shed upon the ground. But even so, Thomas swore he almost saw something move closer to one of the bending trunks of the many trees.

"What should we do?" came a desperate whisper from nearby.

"Get the fire started again," he responded, turning his gaze from the darkness of the night. Perhaps he had just imagined the movement.

From outside, several leaves crunched as if weight were being applied to both them and the soft ground beneath, causing him to turn to the window. "Well, we are not alone, that much is clear." He realized he smelled nothing but Eleanor's stretching lilac and blood. It was a smell that never left him, much to his dismay.

"But who could it be?"

"I am not sure," he said, never breaking his gaze from where he believed the person stood near the trees.

And in the next moment, it happened: The whole cabin groaned as if something heavy was standing right atop it.

"*What is that?*" he heard Amentias whisper from his place in the shadows.

Thomas did not answer: too engrossed was he by the figure that had just appeared in the clearing. It wore a long, dark cloak and seemed to be surrounded in a black mist. The face could not be seen—it was hidden under a sweeping hood.

A bead of sweat trickled down the side of Thomas's face as he stared at the figure. Wondering who was beneath the hood, he raised his free hand to wipe the bead of sweat from his face, and just then, the figure lifted a single arm straight toward the door of the cabin and it blew open, sending a large gust of air to breeze through the room. Thomas was pushed against the armchair, which fell forward just before the empty fire. To his left he heard the shuffling, muffled sounds of Amentias. It was as if the Elite Creature was struggling against something.

"Amentias!" Thomas called. There was no reply, just the continued shuffling sounds permeating the darkness. Edging closer to the darker reaches of the cabin, he felt the sword tremble slightly in his hand, but ignored it; perhaps he was overcome with fear, yet nowhere else in his body was shaking. He tore his gaze from the darkness ahead, where the muffled sounds continued to beckon him and turned to the sword.

His eyes widened as he stared at it. Its red gem was glowing, shedding an eerie light against his arm and clothes. Even the black, dried blood seemed to be glowing along with the gem in the guard of the sword. Thomas stared at it in silent awe as the red light traveled throughout the entire sword, growing even brighter as it extended to his hand. He watched as it traveled up his arm, extending to his chest, his other arm, each leg, then at last, his face. He felt as though he was surrounded in a warm breeze.

Rising slowly to his feet, he glanced up towards the end of the cabin and saw Amentias struggling to fend off the cloaked figure that had traveled into the cabin some minutes before, the red light making it possible to see.

The Ares trembled in his hand and lifted, bringing his arm to extend directly across from him. The sharp, bloodied blade was pointed toward the figure whose hood had been thrown off his head to show bright blonde hair shaking vigorously atop a pale, young face.

"Let him go!" Thomas yelled, eyes narrowing as to better see this young man.

His grip around Amentias's throat slackened and Amentias fell to the wooden floor, his body limp. The young man turned to eye Thomas and he gaped back. The young man's eyes shined toward him, not a color he could discern against the red glare, but a color that made him freeze where he stood all the same.

"Who are you?" he asked.

The man said nothing, but continued to glare toward Thomas, his eyes catching the sword in Thomas's hand. "His...sword," he breathed, transfixed.

He followed the man's glare to the sword before returning his eyes to him. He looked no more than eighteen. "Who are you?"

The young man seemed to realize he was being spoken to at last, for his eyes darted up to Thomas's face. "Javier. Javier Theron."

"Javier," Thomas repeated. He lowered the sword's blade. "Well, Mister Theron. Why have you come here?"

Javier appeared lost as he looked down at the motionless body of Amentias upon the floor, around toward the open door, and finally, upon the blood-stained sword tight in Thomas's grip. He did not respond.

Thomas's brown eyes shifted across the young man's face. He *did* look incredibly lost. With a small step forward, the sword still stretched out in front him, he stepped toward the Vampire, and the red light that surrounded him intensified until it was all he could see. The cabin, Amentias' motionless body, the empty fireplace, the knocked over armchair, the young man in front of him—it all disappeared as the red light consumed his eyesight. He could hear a distant scream somewhere far away from where he was, could smell an intense fragrance, one he could not recognize, tasted the sweat dripping into his open mouth...and then he saw her.

She was floating toward him, a red sweeping dress hanging about her body, her startling brown-green eyes piercing his. The red light cleared from around her, replaced by a pure white aura. He gaped at her, perusing his mind for words, for anything, something to whisper to this incredibly beautiful woman. She opened her mouth and the sweetest voice echoed through the air: "You are not the one I seek. Why do *you* harbor the sword forged from his blood?"

Thomas suddenly desired nothing more than to drift off into a deep, harmless sleep, but he had to keep her in his sights. There was something so familiar about this woman. "Who...who are you?"

"That is of no concern to you," she said, laughing faintly. "Dear Creature. Release the sword, it is not yours to cart. The longer you hold it, the more you shall lose."

He attempted to thwart off the heaviness that was falling over him, but even as he did this, something happened: The red light flashed black for the instant of time he stared at her and she was no longer glorious, nor beautiful; her eyes were black, no white could be found in them, her hair the deepest color that blended seamlessly with the darkness around her. Her dress was no longer a thriving red, but now dark and tattered, torn and ripped in certain places showing parts of her white skin, devoid of life.

"*Release the sword, Creature. It does not belong to you. And what does not belong to you will surely be the downfall of your soul—of everything you are trying to accomplish.* It will not work," she breathed. Her voice no longer sweet and delicate but twisted.

He wanted to ask her what she meant, but he had a feeling he already knew. He fell to his knees, staring up at her, and before his face hit the cold floor, he saw a flash of white, sharp fangs between her pale lips.

"Thomas," the sharp hiss reached his ears as soon as he had closed his eyes. "*Thomas*, get up! She will be here soon—you *must get up!*"

Rough hands grabbed hold of his arms, pulling him up to stand. The sword lay upon the floor, the dark cabin coming into blurry view, the shadow of Aciel's cloak swaying to where Amentias lay upon the floor. Slight movement to the right told Thomas that Javier was still there, and he shook his head, trying to straighten his thoughts, and wipe the image of the mysterious woman from the back of his eyes.

What just happened?

A sharp breeze burst through the open door and blew the cloaks of all who stood in the cabin. She walked in with purpose, looking a bit harried, but beautiful just the same. "Who is this?" she said, laying eyes upon Javier.

Aciel stood from Amentias as if he were nothing more than the overturned armchair near the fireplace, and turned to Eleanor. It appeared he had not even noticed the young man. "My Queen, this can be explained—"

She turned to him. "Can it, Aciel? Can you tell me why Amentias is unconscious, Thomas is disoriented, and this...boy is here doing whatever it is he is doing?"

"I—"

"Of course, you cannot," she sighed. "Aciel, I asked you to remain nearby until Thomas arrived. When he did, why did you not enter the cabin and let them know you were here?"

"Because—"

"Because you would enjoy seeing what would happen to my men. You are jealous that I entrusted Thomas with the Ares. You are envious that I asked Amentias to protect Thomas, besides yourself, in case anything was to happen in my absence. Is this correct?"

Aciel looked terrified. "I...my, my Queen—"

"Thomas, what happened here?" she said, turning to him. He leaned up against the open door, clutching his heart. "Thomas?"

He did not look at her but breathed heavily, such was the tightness that gripped his lungs. "We were waiting...waiting for you to return when the fire died." He coughed into his hand, confused to see blood in his palm. "Then *he*," he said with a glance toward Javier, "appeared...outside—Amentias was weak from lack of blood, the boy came in, blew open the door, strangled Amentias... The boy was, is, confused...he doesn't know why he is here."

Eleanor narrowed her eyes, moving closer to Thomas. "And you...what happened to you?"

He avoided her gaze. "I...blacked out, Eleanor."

"Blacked out? Why would you black out here? This cabin is secure, Thomas."

"I know," he sighed, the wildness of his heart slowing. "The sword," he muttered, regretting it as soon as he said it. Eleanor's face lit up mischievously and her eyes darted around, looking for any trace of the ruby gem.

With a satisfied gasp she bent down near the overturned armchair, staring at the Ares on the floor. She reached out for it, but soon recoiled as if an invisible barrier was around the sword and stood, reaching for Thomas. "Grab it," she commanded.

"No," he said, absolutely certain he was to go nowhere near the sword again if he could help it. The mysterious woman's beautiful face still swam before his eyes.

"But you must. You must grab it. You are the only one who can hold it—you, who killed Drac—"

"I am never going to touch it again!" he yelled, this time staring straight into her eyes. But she had turned from him and looked around at the three cloaked men, all of whom looked apprehensive.

"Amentias," she said. "Grab the sword."

He blinked several times, his eyes adjusting to the darkness, and he rose from the floor, obeying the distant voice that called to him. His black eyes were riddled with weakness as he eyed them all and then caught the silver gleam of the sword upon the floor. With a heave of effort, he extended his arm. The Ares shook violently and then rose five feet into the air before zooming into his outstretched hand, before letting out a feeble red light and then darkening.

Eleanor breathed a sigh of relief. "Well, that settles things. *Amentias* shall be the one to hold the sword...it seems *he* is not one to...overreact."

Thomas growled in disgust but said nothing. He could not deny that he was happy to be free from it, but he found himself longing to speak to the mysterious woman, to hear more of what it is she had to tell him.

Eleanor turned to Javier, "My dear boy. What are you doing here?"

He looked up at her, his eyes a vivid red. "I...am here because I felt a...sort of pull to this place."

Her eyebrows raised in interest. "You are a Dark Creature."

"Yes, a Vampire," he whispered.

Thomas glared at him. "Of course you are." Eleanor smiled. "And where do you come from?"

"The City."

"The...City?" She spared a glance to Thomas, who returned it with equal question.

"Yes," Javier answered. "The Vampire City...in London? Have you heard of it, Miss?"

Eleanor laughed. "Have I heard of it, my dear boy? Who hasn't heard of the Vampire City in London?" Catching herself, she breathed, "What have you been doing in, ahem, the Vampire City?"

"I was...training," he said.

"Training with whom?" Eleanor asked, running a loose finger across her many necklaces.

"Master Dracula," he said.

The gasp could not be hidden even as she tried to stifle it by faking a short laugh. Through the gloom, her dark eyes widened with surprise. "You've been *training* with Dracula?"

"Y–yes."

Amentias collapsed onto the floor, his back resting against the old wooden wall of the cabin, the sword clanking to the floorboards, free from his grip. When Thomas eyed him through the darkness, Amentias was gasping for air, his red eyes gleaming through the night, sweat glistening down his pale face.

"He needs blood," Thomas observed.

Eleanor waved a hand to Aciel. "Take care of it." It seemed she did not wish to travel too far from the newcomer.

Aciel gave her one glare before retreating into the darkness, kneeling in front of Amentias. Thomas could not see what Aciel was doing, but the smell of fresh blood filled his nose, then the sound of greedy gulping reached his ears. At that moment a quick movement to his right caused him to turn: Javier had started forward, the sight of Aciel's blood raising his senses.

Eleanor placed a slender hand upon Javier to keep him contained, and soon Aciel stood. Amentias regained his composure: With a sharp breath, his black eyes shined in the dark and his pale skin filled with color as he took human form.

Javier stared at him, not understanding. "What—"

Eleanor clasped a cold hand over his mouth. "In time, dear boy," she said. "But first tell me more about your training with *Master* Dracula."

"He...would not like for me to tell anyone else," Javier began.

"He has no place in the matter anymore, it would seem, young Vampire."

"What do you mean?"

"Don't you know?"

"Know what?"

She looked around at Aciel and then Thomas before turning back to Javier. "You really *don't* know what happened to Dracula?"

He looked around with uncertainty before returning to her. "I don't."

Eleanor clasped her hands together. "Well!" It was hard to not notice the absolute glee in her voice. "There is so much we must learn from each other, dear Vampire."

Thomas pushed himself off the old door. "*Don't* tell him about Dracula." The obvious joy upon her face most sickening. It propelled him forward.

She turned to him slowly, her smile fading. "Why, I had no desire to tell him anything about the dear Vampire, Thomas. I wished to leave that to you."

What? he thought in alarm, the memory of Mara billowing into ash returning to him. He fought a wave of sick. "I *won't*," he growled, his heart thundering within his chest.

Eleanor glared at him. "Yes, you will. Tell him what happened to Dracula."

The growl escaped his chest before he could call it back and the young Vampire stepped away, but he paid no heed to the pressing stare: his eyes remained trained on Eleanor's growing rage.

"I cannot!" Thomas spat, sweat streaming down his face. He felt it within him before he realized it: the heat, the enragement, the absolute anger. His eyes were black, devoid of any white, and he was aware his teeth had begun to sharpen and lengthen, so enraged was he at Eleanor's obvious glee at the death of the Vampire...but why should that matter now? The intensified in waves, one right after the other, bearing down upon his body. He lurched forward, clutching his sides, and he felt the beast begin to fully form—

"Don't be a fool, Thomas!" Aciel yelled.

He stared at them from his knees. Amentias had risen from his seat on the floor, the Ares clutched tightly in hand, waiting for Eleanor's word to strike. Eleanor breathed heavily, Javier, behind her, looked flustered, ready to strike Thomas as well, but no one moved.

The screams left Thomas's lips from the pain searing through his heart. He glared at Eleanor, the hatred stretching across his face when she and the others disappeared from view and he once again stared upon the mysterious woman in a haze of red light.

"Thomas... She will destroy you and take even more away from you than she already has... You do not have to suffer like this. Let me help you."

"You...you can't help me!" he screamed, yet he was still upon his knees glaring up at Eleanor—

"Yes, I can. If only you would return the sword to its rightful owner. Do this, and I shall give you life anew, one...with the woman you love."

"What is happening?" he heard the distant, cold voice ask to another, somewhere far away, indeed.

"I...I don't know, my Queen," the familiar voice responded, echoing through the image of the mysterious woman.

"Thomas," she breathed, and as he watched her, her image darkened once more, her eyes black, her dress dark and torn, her fangs shining through. A wave of cold swept through him, reaching his heart and the pain seemed to numb.

With a gasp, he clutched his heart, and Eleanor was there before him, looking confused. She breathed heavily, her Vampire form gone. "Thomas, what the hell was that?"

He did not speak—he did not think he could—but moved to his feet, sweat continuing to drip down his face, onto his shirt, damp with his profusion. He stumbled to the door and leaned up against it again, unable to look upon any of them. He stared straight ahead, his mind still numb with what he'd just seen.

"My Queen," Amentias said, moving forward, the Ares still erect in hand. "What is the next plan of action?"

She turned to him. "I will take our young friend with me for more words. He is misguided; I wish to...enlighten him on matters of importance."

Amentias's brow furrowed in the dark. "Matters of importance?"

"Matters of importance," she repeated. "I have just returned from several Enchanters and Giants who are looking forward to joining my cause. We are growing every day; we must not lose momentum. I need you and Aciel to travel to the Enchanter town of Cedar Village,

I hear Xavier is heading there in his search for the book. We must not forget the ones we are up against."

"No, my Queen," he said, but he did not move. "I...cannot carry this sword freely. I shall need a sheath."

"Of course," Eleanor said, digging into her cloak, removing a worn sheath from around her own waist. "You and Aciel are to leave immediately."

Amentias bowed low, sliding the sword into its place at his side. "Right away, my Queen."

Aciel bowed low as well, and both ventured towards the door.

Thomas felt their gazes, Amentias's concern, Aciel, mere indifference. Once their feet touched the leaf-ridden ground, they disappeared.

Eleanor's scent drifted to his nose as she drew closer. "Thomas, whatever is happening to you...make sure it does not affect your allegiance to me. You are to go to your home. I shall send someone when you are needed in the next phase. Do you understand?" The voice reached his ears cool and cold, he understood then that he was nothing more to her than another soldier in her ranks, another hand to carry around a sword she could not touch. A mere tool to her greater plan.

It was a plan Thomas was not so sure he desired to follow anymore.

He stared at her, his teeth sharpening again, the thoughts growing within his still-pounding mind. His jaw clenched and his teeth ground against each other, but he forced himself to look into those eyes. "I understand," he whispered.

Her face was expressionless, but he swore he saw a flicker of derision in those dark eyes.

His thoughts continued to collide within his mind, completely uncontrollable the more he focused upon them. She was using him, using them all for her meaningless end—and what *was* that? To acquire a most maddening Vampire that was once his, Thomas's one focus, that was once his very life...

But that was until he had lost Mara; all of this seemed so useless. What was the point of it all? He did not have the reason he had joined Eleanor Black in the first place, and now...now he had absolutely nothing. Nothing at all!

The growls increased, the anger burning deep in his heart, the thought of Mara placing them there. He stared without really seeing, Eleanor reaching Javier, clasping a hand upon his shoulder, but the young Vampire was staring towards him with blood-red eyes, his face the poster of swelling horror and fury.

"What is he?" Javier asked.

Eleanor turned to watch him at last.

With her gaze, it happened: his face stretched outward to accompany the many rows of large teeth that had begun to grow, his size could not fill the doorway and the wood began to tear away, leaving a large hole in front of the cabin. Saliva dripped onto the floor, and his beady black eyes found Eleanor and the Vampire. He growled and started forward, the wood upon the floor flying up as he ran for them—

"No, Thomas!" Eleanor said a snarl escaping her lips. Her red eyes widened, and in a large gust of wind that tore the walls from their roots, she and Javier had gone.

With a frustrated growl, Thomas skidded to a stop where she had been just moments before. He stared around at the destroyed cabin, his desire to reach her, to tear into her paramount...and yet, he truly wondered if he would actually harm her.

It was strange that he'd even desired to do so. What was wrong with him?

"If only," the voice returned, "you would return the sword to its rightful owner... Do this, and I shall give you life anew, one...with the woman you love."

Perhaps he would see her, he would hear her voice and learn more from her, learn how she knew of Mara, if what she'd said was truth.

But the more he remained there, the more he realized he would not hear her voice anymore. All that remained was a sweeping silence, the soft rustle of leaves. He heaved a great sigh, returning to human form, the cold of the night, the freshness of the wind ice against his sweat.

He was vulnerable, naked, his clothes ripped, yet the desire to tear Eleanor apart burned hot in his heart.

Mara. Eleanor was the reason she was dead.

He bent low, gathering what remained of his clothes, the glint of gold several feet in front of him, half-buried in the dirt next to a dark tree. He moved forward and bore down upon the object, kneeling to see it better. It was the ring he'd snagged from the Vampire Eleanor had killed. He picked it up. It seemed to pulse in his fingers. How odd. But he had no time to worry about unusual rings, he had to get home and get a fresh pair of clothes and wait for Eleanor's word on what to do next.

He wondered, now that he no longer had the love of his life at his side, just what it was that was holding him to Eleanor. He could surely leave her whenever he wished. His father was no more, gone somewhere Thomas could not know, the true Lycans becoming scarce; they were few and far between, indeed.

He thought on the sword and the woman who'd spoken to him. *Who was she?* There was something dreadfully important he had to be doing now. A search to find something...but no, no, he was to return to his home and await Eleanor's instruction. Yes, that was right.

And the brown-green eyes faded from view with this thought; he closed his eyes, allowing the breeze to carry him home.

Chapter Five

FIRST MOURNING

Victor Vonderheide entered the office and looked around, his expression unreadable against the torch's light. Two more Vampires walked in behind him, moving simultaneously to the front of the desk that Victor stood behind. He placed a finger on the surface and dragged it, his grimace apparent in the light of the torch: a fine coat of dust clung to his finger.

The Vampire closest to the door waved a hand and it closed behind him. "Victor, speaking as your friend, I know how hard this must be for you—"

"Has...no one entered this room since?" he interrupted, his eyes held to the dust on his finger, thoughts swarming with the burden he now held.

Westley's brow furrowed while Craven cleared his throat and continued speaking, "Ex-excuse me, my Lord?"

Victor raised his eyes from the dust and stared at the remaining Chairs. "This room, no one has entered since..."

Craven stared at him. "No, no, of course not, my Lord. No one would have dared enter—this floor was and still may be off limits if you desire it. No one has trespassed out of honor and respect for... for..."

"Dracula," he finished.

"Well, yes," Craven said.

Westley spoke up next, his deep voice drawing Victor's eyes to him. "My Grace, there is much that must be done. You have been briefed, but there are cities to protect, towns to govern—the Dark World is in disarray. Quick, necessary order must be established at once lest we fall to the hands of Eleanor Black."

Victor stared at him, trying to make sense of where Dracula's many secrets ended and began. "I admire your desire to...uphold the sense of direction and order you have been privy to these past years, but I am a different Vampire, and I will decide what is best for my people."

Westley stared at him. "Victor, I understand how you must feel, but the rules Dracula upheld—"

"Were the same very rules that allowed the Dark World to fall."

Craven glared at him. "What are you talking about?"

"Surely you won't feign ignorance to what this Vampire has done to the Dark World?" Victor asked, watching them closely for any slip, any sign as to what they did for the late Vampire.

Westley folded his arms across his chest. "This has to do with what happened at the Council of Creatures Meeting, doesn't it?"

Victor moved from behind the desk, striding to the empty fireplace, their gazes, he knew, trained on him. "What happened that day was unfair," he began, "Creatures who were present are not even wishing to speak."

"And for good reason!" Westley said. "If they speak, do you not imagine it would leave them open to the one Dark Creature that wishes to silence them?"

"If you speak of Eleanor Black, I do not imagine she would wish to silence any of those Creatures—what is known far and wide is that Dracula is dead, what else would she wish to hide?"

"What was passed back and forth that day," Westley said, pulling Victor from the empty fireplace. "*Words*, Victor. I was told by the few Enchanters that managed to survive that Peroeneus Doe was the only Enchanter present in the room when Eleanor told a great tale."

"A tale, Westley?" Victor said, all thoughts of the Chairs' importance fading. "What tale is this?"

"He said she spoke of Tremor the Great, how Dracula was born to a human father, an Ancient mother. He said that she mentioned how the sword Dracula carried with him for years was in actuality a sword Tremor created to fend off the first Vampires Dracula produced before you—before he consulted Peroeneus, himself, in order to have the Enchanter place the curse of immortality upon him."

He turned to face the Chairs fully. "Curse? A curse of immortality?"

The Goldchair nodded. "I do not know what he told you, or if he told you anything when he turned you, Victor, but that is the truth of the Vampires' existence that we have come to know."

"He, he did not-- *how did Eleanor get to know all of this?*"

"She paid Tremor the Great a visit, apparently."

"Tremor...*Tremor*," he said thoughtfully, trying his damndest to think of where he'd heard it before. "Who is this Tremor?"

Westley spared a glance to Craven, who returned it. They looked despondent. *What's that for?*

"Victor," Westley said softly after a while, "Tremor the Great is the Ancient Elder. Surely you have read of the Ancient Creatures— the first Creatures in existence alongside the Phoenixes of the Nest?"

The Phoenixes! The Chairs should know something about them. "I have read of them," he said, watching the dark eyes of Westley for any sign of secrecy. "But in the books, it never mentioned any of this—any of their...place in our World. Only that they were no longer living and that they paved a great way for our kind."

"Well, yes, that is true," Westley Rivers said. "But those books are wrong, this we know now thanks to Eleanor Black. Tremor is still living, if only weakened, slowly deteriorating."

"Did Peroeneus Doe tell the surviving Enchanter anything else?" Craven asked, joining the conversation. "I, for one, would like to know why Dracula sought him out in order to gain the curse of immortality."

They all stared at each other, and Victor waited, desiring to hear what more the Vampires said, if they were truly within Dracula's palm as intensely as Xavier.

After a few minutes of silence, Victor strode the length of the office and stood before the green curtains that hung across a wall. "This Peroeneus Doe," he said, "what has happened to him? I'm sure with his knowledge of that day Eleanor has not let him speak freely."

"As far as it is known, the Enchanter has gone into hiding, and the Enchanter that shared the news of what happened at the Council of Creatures Meeting has disappeared from the face of the Dark World," Westley said.

The truth, Goldchair? Or yet another lie?

For he knew the Chairs had been lying to him the moment he'd arrived at the City, to see what could be done. All they'd told him was that he was to take the Great Vampire's place and ignored all other questions with maddening skill.

More silence filled the room, and then Craven whispered, "What...is your first order as King, Victor?"

He turned at these words, the last few striking him the most. "I wish to be alone for the time being, Craven, Westley."

They both stared at him, not moving.

A smile found its way to his lips and he stepped towards them. "I need time—more than anything else I imagine—to settle my mind and come to terms with what has taken place so rapidly over the past few days. Becoming King is, as I'm sure you know, the step up from my previous role in the Vampire Order." *A role you both know was one of the dog, playing fetch for a Master that was never there.*

They said nothing, their silence one of bewilderment, and then Westley nodded, moving for the door. Craven, however, remained before the desk, staring at Victor with a forlorn expression.

"Silverchair?" Westley called.

Craven did not turn, and when three more minutes passed and Westley prepared to step towards him, he said: "What has become of the Vampire Order?"

Victor's smile faltered when Westley interrupted: "Surely, it's over with. All previous Members are insane or gone or no longer in the Vampire City."

Craven turned to face his comrade. "Yes, that is *your* assumption, but I must know from his own mouth," he said, turning back to face Victor who had replaced his smile. "What is your word on the Vampire Order, your Grace?"

"Westley is right," he said. "It cannot continue. And even if it were to, I don't see who we could get to fill the ranks of the Vampires that graced the Order before. They were chosen because...because Dracula was, more than likely, prepping them to take his place as King. *All but myself,*" he added silently. "It cannot continue."

He watched them with his wild stab in the dark, knowing it foolish if it were true and they were prepared to do all they could to keep it a secret, yet Craven blinked and said, "Ah."

They moved for the door without another word.

Once the door closed, the smile faded from his lips, and the torch's light went out, casting the room into complete darkness.

What did the Chairs know?

His mind ran to Dracula, how the Vampire could have left the Dark World in such a state: no law, Vampires terrified, all manner of communication between the towns and cities now gone.... He recalled Xavier's face when the Vampire had come to his home to tell them of

Dracula's death. There, in that time, in that moment, Victor realized there was more to Dracula than he had ever seen. A darker side, perhaps, a side of secrets and holes he'd never allowed to be revealed. It begged the thought: had Xavier seen that side of Dracula?

Of course, of course he did, he decided, *after all, the bloody Vampire had been chosen as the new King of All Dark Creatures, hadn't he?* Yet where did that put he, Victor? Was he destined to be pushed to the background forever, only doing Dracula's dirty work while other Vampires like Xavier received all the glory?

Anger pooled through him as he thought of all the things Xavier must know that he did not, he knew grief and clear hatred for Dracula as the Vampire was no longer here, no longer alive to keep him unaware. He knew very human feelings, incredibly sharp and vivid against his heart and he hated it. Was he so vulnerable now that the only being that he would ever know to show him compassion and kindness, unmatched by his life as a human, was now gone? Gone and dead, forever unable to answer the multitude of questions that arose within his mind?

He felt the ring upon his finger pulse and stared at it, his thoughts clamoring to their protective powers. Yet he had felt his ring was more of a hindrance than protecting. It seemed to be sucking his lust for blood from his body. It was as though it were a Vampire of its own, feeding on the emotions that spurred within him. They felt incredibly strange and secluded, as though he were not experiencing them at all, but another was—someone human.

The feeling of sadness, so ruthless and unmasking as it was, reached him with yet another pulse of the ring. Marveling at the complexity with which he felt so innately *alive*, he stared at it in shock, his hand shaking against the power it exuded. The feeling of sadness growing and expanding to cover the entire office, the turmoil of grief enveloping him in full. He felt the burning in his eyes, the burning which, he knew long ago, to give way to tears.

He raised a hand and wiped his cheek and stared at the wetness of his hand in silence. He could not find the voice to scream or even whisper. *A tear?*

His heart beat against his rib cage in urgency and he felt as though time, which had always been nothing to him, a faraway thing to never be bothered with, was closing in on him, and fast.

And it was with a glance to the empty, cold grate that he started, allowing the tears to fall hot and fast, allowing them to wash away the barrier held severely in place before.

He knew then that he was vulnerable, not because of his new position as Temporary King of All Creatures, nor was he vulnerable because he had no firm grip on leading an entire Dark World, but he was vulnerable because he had felt the one emotion a human, upon being turned into a Vampire, silently vows to never truly feel again:

Love.

✳

They'd left the streets of London once free from the pandemonium, the rubble that once was a notorious café, and now traversed the woods of some foreign terrain. It was, at least, foreign to Xavier, for he had never ventured this far south of London before.

The plain stretched out for miles all around them, and as they grew level with the last array of trees that once surrounded them at every turn, Xavier turned to stare upon Nathanial. "How much farther is it?"

Nathanial Vivery stepped up to the Vampire. "It is just beyond these plains."

"And what is its entrance?" he asked, knowing that every Vampire city and town had their own unique entrances, be it a well, the base of a mountain, or a simple run-down manor.

"Its entrance, my Lord, is a gate," he said stepping out of the woods, his worn brown boots squishing against the wet grass.

"A gate?" he asked, following. "How can a gate be the entrance into a Vampire city?"

Nathanial said nothing as they walked across the grass, neither having enough energy to fly.

Xavier did not press the question further, although his own mind swam with questions. He had never been to Cedar Village before but often heard Dracula speaking of it. The Great Vampire would never tell he, Xavier directly where the Vampire town was located. He'd read no piece of article or summary about this Vampire town in any books Dracula would have him read, nor was he aware if anyone in the Vampire Order knew where the town was. How strange it was that Dracula would keep such a town from Xavier's knowledge. *But perhaps*, Xavier thought as they walked, *it was not that strange at all.*

He eyed the red-haired Vampire ahead of him through the darkness. It was very possible, he decided then, that Dracula was protecting this Vampire. It did seem Nathanial Vivery had Vampires he knew in this town. Perhaps Dracula did not want knowledge to spread of Nathanial Vivery's whereabouts until the time of his death.

A cold sigh escaped his lips. Dracula's death. It was a topic of thought and discussion he would remove himself from. Ever since they left Victor's Manor weeks ago, their minds were glued, irrefutably, to finding *The Immortal's Guide*. He had had no time to think on or question Dracula's motives. Or, at least, that was the lie he told himself whenever the opportunity for free thought arose. The truth was, and this Xavier Delacroix could not ignore, he desperately desired answers to all the questions Dracula left him with. And he knew—hoped—all these answers would be in this book Dracula had left for him to journey through. It was one of the things that propelled him forward. The other, naturally, was Eleanor Black.

The memory of her undeniable presence found its way to the forefront of his thumping skull just then and he was once again forced to relive, with terrible vividness, how he had felt upon waking in that horribly small room in *The Dragon's Cavern*.

The presence of her so strong, so alive with hunger for him, he was surprised that Nathanial had not felt it. This begged the sudden thought: Did Nathanial not feel it, or did he not *want* to feel it? To entertain what he had to see as Xavier's most outlandish claims?

For even to Xavier, the idea seemed mad. That he could feel Eleanor Black's whereabouts throughout the Dark World. Know when she killed, if she were near... It was preposterous. He'd be mad to even entertain such a thought. Yet, the creeping dread was returning, this he knew. It was not as strong as it had been when she had first revealed herself to be alive, but, yes, there it was in the pit of his gut, swirling, waiting, desiring to grow with more power, desiring the one she wanted—

He smacked into the back of a still Nathanial and looked up. They had reached the end of the plains, the valley dipping downward into a sloping hill, but this was not the reason for Nathanial's abrupt stop, Xavier saw.

For where the grass stopped, cobblestoned road took its place. A massive city lay out all before them...completely on fire. Xavier stared as high flames danced through the night, burning tall buildings, the Vampires within, surely...and he vaguely wondered how they had not seen the flames as they approached.

Nathanial, who stared blankly upon the chaos said, "The spell upon it keeps it from the eyes of any Creature, any human, until they reach the gates." He lifted a finger to point towards the black gates that surrounded the city.

Out of the madness of flame and terrible screams, there came deep, harrowing laughter. And all at once Xavier felt it: the minor boiling dread within his gut expanding until it was all he could feel.

"Hold it, boys!" the rough voice sounded from within the sky, causing Xavier to turn his gaze upward.

As the city burned beneath him, the Elite Creature hovered above, staring down upon the madness he and the others created. "It's not here! Seems like the Vampire was telling the truth, eh? We're best trying our luck in Raffle—" But his eyes, alive with the orange of flame, spotted them amidst the madness and Xavier felt his blood run cold.

Damn.

Before he could do a thing, the Creature was upon him, hands pressed to his collar, pulling him up into the air.

Nathanial shouted something Xavier did not catch, the howl of the brazen wind screaming in his ears and the Creature released him with a cry of pain. He fell back against the air, landing roughly atop the grass, able to pull the Ascalon from its sheath just as Nathanial waved a hand and a solid blue wall appeared before them, keeping the remaining Elite Creatures at bay.

He rose to his feet with Nathanial's help: The Vampire pulled at the shoulder of his cloak, and whispered in his ear, "Follow my lead."

Before Xavier could ask just what that lead was, Nathanial inhaled the smoke-filled air, and blew it back out, except it left his lips as flame, burning the wall in turn.

"What on—?" he breathed, unable to say anything more: Nathanial had placed a hand on his shoulder, pulling him into a suffocating darkness before he knew it.

Chapter Six

A NIGHT OF SECRETS

Christian stared at the burned café as a streetlamp's light flickered nearby. True to the officer's word, the apartment upstairs had been burned through as well, but not completely. Part of it still remained, if blackened, the furniture within nothing but black ash upon a charred, withering wooden floor that was barely holding up.

"Terrible, isn't it?" a voice nearby said.

He turned, yet another Scotland Yard officer stood several feet away. This Vampire's badge gleamed in the flickering street lamps' light as he stepped closer, his deep red traveling cloak swaying about him as he moved.

There was silence, and then the officer said, "I see the trip two of my peers took to your home this evening went along with a most undesired outcome. You do not believe my words." The Vampire raised two pale hands, bringing them fluidly together before himself as though he were prepared to beg. Before Christian could ask what the Vampire was prepared to do, he'd closed his eyes and bowed his head, his next words a whisper on the chilling night wind, "Please,

Lord Christian, accept this apology on behalf of all of Scotland Yard—indeed, on behalf of all Vampires still residing in London."

Christian gazed at him with understanding: There was more going on at the precinct than the two officers from earlier would have him see. "Apology accepted," he said, "but I daresay this does not keep me from speaking on behalf of my brother at his trial?"

The officer's hands dropped to his sides as a couple of humans passed along the sidewalk, both staring up at the burned café in sadness as they passed. It had been a popular place. He then said, "I'm afraid not, no. Believe it or not, this is why I have come to seek you out, my Lord."

"Indeed?"

"Yes," the officer said, gesturing for them to walk along the sidewalk, to which Christian obliged. "It would appear there are Vampires throughout London—and regretfully within our own precinct—that would see your brother hang for a crime they believe he has committed."

Christian was silent. What could this Vampire have to tell him that the other officers from before could not? When they reached the end of the street, several coaches rumbling slowly past, he said, "Of this I am most painfully aware, as I was shown earlier today. This is of no interest to me—"

"My name is Devon Strumer, my Lord, and I do not come to you to speak on what is already known. I come to tell you of what you perhaps, are not aware: That there are Vampires here who believe your brother is innocent—some hold solid proof."

Christian stopped walking. "There is proof to my brother's innocence? Who holds it?"

"I do, of course, my Lord," Devon said after a nearby woman had resumed walking by, her poodle barking madly at them over a large shoulder. "I was with the constable the night he was murdered. I even saw who did it."

Christian's gaze widened. "If you hold such proof, Devon Strumer, why did you not tell the others?"

He did not look the least bit upset when he said, "I told them what I knew, but they did not believe me. To know that Eleanor Black had been right in London, right down the street from where they worked...they did not want this to be true. But, Lord Christian, I saw her, with my own eyes." He stopped and pointed towards a darkened alleyway. No streetlamps light could throw relief over the alleyway's contents due to the two high buildings on either side of it, yet Christian could still smell the thick scent of Vampire blood all throughout. "Here is where it happened, my Lord. On the other side of the street is *The Dragon's Cavern* where Xavier Delacroix was seen leaving with a red-haired Vampire. I pointed out to my peers that if Xavier Delacroix had committed the murder, he would not have acquired a room at *The Dragon's Cavern*—it's much too revealing, right across the street, you see.

"The fact that my superiors disregarded this clear evidence as nothing tells me there is more going on here, my Lord."

He then cleared his throat and looked uncomfortable all of a sudden. It seemed his next words were a chore to get out.

Christian raised an eyebrow, wondering just what more he would hear.

"Lord Christian," Devon said at last, "I wish to help you and Xavier wherever possible. But in order to do this I would need to know...just what it is Lord Xavier is doing with his time."

Ah, so this was what the showmanship was all about, Christian thought, a small sigh escaping his chest with the realization. It made perfect sense: lead Xavier's brother along with talks of apologies and evidence to the crime. He focused his attention on a beautiful woman that had exited a nearby shop ahead of them, and he said, "I know nothing of my brother's whereabouts Vampire, however, all of the Dark Creatures that were actually present at the Council of

Creature's meeting may be able to aid your search for the truth." And with that, he began to walk towards the woman, who had begun to step from them, having caught his hungry stare.

Devon held out a hand to still Christian before he could make it far at all, the woman's back getting swallowed by darkness.

Christian whirled to stare upon the Vampire. "What are you—?"

But the look in the officer's eyes stilled his tongue: they were a fierce red, his fangs bared, and a soft wind rose up around them both.

"You are a fool for not seeing what is happening here, Christian!" Devon said, his hand still held out. "The Vampires rally against you—against your brother! Your brother has made more enemies than anyone can count! Thanks to his lack of explanation after the Council of Creatures meeting, everyone is making up their own stories, coming to their own conclusions about how Dracula could have been killed, and many point to Xavier as the culprit!

"I *saw* Eleanor Black kill the constable, but she did not see me, and the constable did not know I was there—I was not supposed to be, this I will admit, but I followed him. My curiosity got the better of me. Do you know why the Constable was meeting Eleanor in that alleyway, Christian?"

He didn't dare answer.

"It is because he was going to give her information on a certain human who seems to hold interesting blood. Eleanor wants to know who this human is. The constable said he recalled a woman whom he'd seen at Victor Vonderheide's ball some months ago. He spoke of how he *could not smell blood* from her—"

"Why do you tell me this?" Christian whispered, his vision turning red. He recalled with horror the sight of Alexandria standing just before him...her blood unable to reach his nose...

"Because, my Lord, the constable spoke *your* name! He spoke the name of Christian Delacroix—how the human woman came with *you* to that party and was later taken up to Victor's room—a room you were seen running to the moment you entered the Vampire's home!"

His mind drew a blank, and it was as though he'd witnessed the Vampire's words leave the lips as someone far away from where he stood. Guilt filled his dead heart, and he fought to keep the damned emotion from reaching his face, but even as he tried to still this, the truth flickered in his eyes, and he stepped away.

A maniacal smile graced the Vampire's lips. "Then this is true, you know of such a woman who supposedly holds no blood?"

"I, I know nothing of what you speak, Vampire," Christian said at last, trying his best to collect himself, although his gaze would not leave their shade of apprehensive red. "Why would I know a human woman if not to drink her blood?"

"Why don't you tell me, Christian? Just what are you and your brother doing? Why have we not seen any trace of him since he left the meeting with that red-haired Vampire?" He took a step towards him, ignoring a horse-drawn carriage that splashed water near where they stood. "What are you and your brother hiding?"

"We hide nothing."

"Then why do you visit the sight of the burned café this night?"

"I was on my way to find my dinner, if you must know. The sight of the café caught my interest for a moment."

"Indeed?"

"Indeed!" *How could this have happened? Why would the constable tell Eleanor Black of Alexandria Stone? What the hell am I supposed to do now?* "This has been more than entertaining," he said with something of contempt. Shocked, more than anything, that it would come to this and so soon, "Mr. Strumer, but I must be on my way." He turned from the Vampire without another word and began to step down the sidewalk before the Vampire could stop him a second time.

As he walked, he became aware an enthralling scent filled his nose. Indeed, it was nothing compared to the smell of the many humans' blood that filled the dirty street, no, it was something more, something... enticing.

Alexandria finally slept.

And even as the thought crossed his mind, he turned in expectant apprehension to see if the Vampire had noticed this brilliant smell as well.

Devon Strumer was not there. He had disappeared in an alarming gust of wind, and Christian, terror rising in his dead heart, turned his thoughts to Delacroix Manor, hoping the damned Vampire had not singled out the place the blood drifted from.

✳

It was not long before her eyes opened and she found herself not upon the cold ground of a dark wood, but within a vast bed, several pillows tucked underneath her head and all around her. She had but a second to become aware of her awakening, the dream losing its vividness rapidly before she felt the presence in the room.

She froze, feeling the gaze upon her, and she turned her head, the figure within the doorway seeming to glow through the darkness. She blinked, lifting her hands from beneath the sheets, rubbing her eyes; the light died, his eyes black, as far as she could tell, in their piercing gaze.

A breath escaped her lungs, and how peculiar it was that he stared at her lips, now, as though the slight parting had drawn all his attention. A fresh awareness reached her: she was freezing cold.

The sheets she remained underneath did nothing to halt this chill, and indeed how much greater it seemed from meeting the strange... man. She desired to be lost once more within her dreams. At least there, he did not harm her...or threaten her with his piercing stare like he did now.

The absolute nothingness within his eyes, the complete loathing that existed whenever their paths crossed in the house... It was clear he hated her, and she couldn't say the feelings weren't returned. She felt like his prisoner, although he was said to be protecting her (from what, she had no idea), and it was in his contemptuous gaze that she saw her reality. Without that gaze bearing upon her, she found this whole situation much easier to stand.

It took her by surprise then, when he took a single, solitary step into the room, yet appeared to have taken a thousand. And still his black eyes would not leave hers.

Before she could muster enough resolve to stammer a word (what could she say to him?), he had opened his mouth and had spoken, his fangs showing themselves through glimpses of his words. Daggers flashing amidst a blood-stained night.

"You were talking," he said slowly, his voice deep, seeming to resound against the high walls, "in your sleep. I...wondered if anything was amiss."

Strange. She could have sworn his eyes darted around the room, as though he were anxious, worried. But the more she looked, the more his dead-on gaze appeared to have never left her frame atop the bed.

She remained against the pillow, not daring to lift her head. The fear that if she blinked too much, or took her eyes off him, he would disappear filled her. "I spoke in my sleep?" she asked, her voice barely able to leave her throat.

"You did." His eyes remained on her.

She would not ask what she said, no, it was embarrassing enough that he had been called to her because of mutterings within her sleep. She was painfully aware her hand shook; she moved some hair from her face, grateful that the contact made to her hair steadied her movement, if only slightly.

She had taken to thinking of Christian like a regular man, nothing more than a handsome, wealthy Lord, if only to calm her frantic nerves, but she found this difficult to continue when he stood before her, glaring at her like she did everything wrong. His skin white, his hair black, his face etched into perpetual boredom. Or was it hatred? Yes, he stared at her like he desired her dead, and she braced herself for the death that he was sure to inflict upon her.

Yet it never came.

She found her mouth forming the words, "What did I say?"

She could have slapped herself.

There was a flicker of something on that face, then, a flicker of surprise, shock even, but as she stared, she realized she must have imagined the change: Christian's face remained blank, and alarmingly so.

His hands came together in a fluid motion. She found it akin to further torture that he did not reach forward and grab her neck, choking her to death. They interlaced before him, and he inclined his head slightly, the smallest trace of a smile gracing his lips.

"You mentioned...Dracula's name," he said.

"'Dracula?'" she repeated in confusion.

"Yes, and you were whispering...a plea...to be saved."

Red canvassed her cheeks. *Don't tell me...*

"What called me here, more than anything," he admitted, much to her growing horror, "was the utterance of my name."

She froze, not knowing what to say or do, for he had confirmed her growing suspicions. She did not know what was worse: That she had spoken his name in her sleep, or that he didn't look the least bit fazed by it.

She blinked hard, forcing the thought to leave her mind. What would she care what he thought of her uttering his name in her sleep? *He should care*, a damning voice answered back.

Nonsense.

She opened her eyes and cleared her throat, realizing she must at least apologize for calling him to her chambers when he was not needed. (What was he needed for, then?)

Alexandria pushed herself off the pillow and tried to steady the rushing dizziness that accompanied her movement. Her body was attacking her for lack of proper exercise—for being cooped up in one room for so long. *It wasn't my fault,* she reasoned with the air as she gazed unsteadily upon him.

As her eyes adjusted to Christian's tall frame near the doorway, she pointed her next words in that general direction.

"I'm sorry, my Lord, for interrupting your sleep, if I did, but as you can see, I'm perfectly fine."

The devil himself wouldn't believe that lie, she knew, which was why she wasn't entirely surprised to see him smile widely. He showed no fangs, and she found it amazing that he could look so...human. But with his next words, she knew that could never be truthfully so.

"No, you are not," he said, his words very much in opposition with the smile now fading, becoming something less strangely pleasant, more deadly, serious.

"I...I beg your pardon?" she breathed, terror growing with the thin line his mouth formed.

"You are not fine," he responded, taking yet another simple step towards her bed. "You have been taken from your family...your past life gone, perhaps forever, I can hear your cries throughout the manor during the day, and you do not eat what is sent up to you. You are far from perfectly fine, Miss Stone."

She did not speak, but stared, not daring to admit to herself that he was correct.

"I only say this," he said, deciding he had crossed some line with his words, "because you are a guest here, for as long as it is desired of those above me. I...would implore you, Miss Stone, to use my home as you see fit. You needn't lock yourself away in this room. There is, after all, nothing that may harm you here."

She definitely couldn't imagine away the concentrated gaze he gave the room at large once more before his eyes fell upon her.

The sudden sigh that left his lips reached her in a cold breeze and she could not help but feel it was one of satisfaction...but whatever for? As the cold touched her skin, she clutched the sheets. She wore nothing but a thin chemise. It was then that she wished the lone candle placed atop her bedside table did more than emit a faint, useless glow throughout the room, though she'd remembered blowing it out before she slept.

"My Lord," she breathed, grateful that it was dark where she sat, "I must...thank you for your gracious hospitality. It has indeed been... hard remaining here when one does not even know why one must..."

She had hoped, somewhat, at least, that he would catch this suggestion to know more about her reasoning for being tied to Delacroix Manor. But what left his mouth next did nothing to answer any of her questions, much to her dismay.

"Naturally."

"Lord Delacroix—"

She found her words cut by the cold hand placed abruptly upon her mouth. He had moved at a terrible speed to stand behind her, and it was with a simple motion that he pulled her closer to him, keeping her ability to scream subdued.

At once, the slowly boiling fear that had gripped her heart in flutters and pangs now roared with the rising scream that bubbled in her throat.

"Shh!" he demanded and she found her ability to scream taken from her as well. He kept her in place, facing the now-empty doorway; he waved another hand through the dark air and the candle's light was obediently extinguished.

In complete darkness, Alexandria sat with her back to Christian, trying hard to remember what it was to breathe, the feel of his cold skin through his shirt stifling her ability to think properly: Rushing blood and terror marred her mind.

She sat in what seemed a painful silence. His hand was rough on her lips, and although she had forgone the notion of screaming some time ago, he had not removed it from its place. It wasn't until she heard faint footsteps in the hall that she realized the reason for his abrupt movement.

They watched in silence (Christian, the only one not breathing at all), as the man's silhouette entered the doorway. He stopped and turned towards the room, Alexandria not sure if the person could see them through the gloom. The newcomer said, in a smoothly deceptive voice, "Lord Christian...is that you?"

"Yes," Christian responded.

The man took a step into the room and Alexandria fidgeted just the slightest beneath Christian's tight grip. Another, perhaps even colder, wind entered the room with the man's movement.

"You've returned home from feeding so...soon, my Lord. What...caused you to return here so quickly?"

"I could, instead, ask you why you have entered my home without my consent."

Alexandria could not see the face of the man that stood before her, but was aware he was not amused.

"But you knew I was here for...ah...several minutes now, my Lord," came the smooth reply. "You were aware—"

"But I knew not where in my home you were, Mister Strumer," Christian said, his grip upon Alexandria's mouth never slacking in the dark. "It was not until you reached the stairs that I realized—"

"And you prepared this...little deterrence in the case that I would happen upon the smell of your secret," he interjected.

"I fail to see what you mean."

He took yet another step. "I know another—perhaps the woman—is here with you, in this room. Her smell has evaded me since I reached your home, but all the more you and your brother's secrets must be shared. Especially with those that desire only to aid you."

"We hold no secrets here, Devon, and if we did, we would not share them with others—especially those aiding the ones that would see my brother's name destroyed."

"I have already told you, I am not among those that would see you or your brother's name run through the streets, Christian! I only desire to know—so that I may *help* aid your pursuits—"

"My only pursuit this night was to acquire some blood."

"Yet I know you smelled that strange blood just as I!" he went on stubbornly. "And I know the source of that smell. That blood came from *this very manor!*"

"Mr. Strumer!" Christian snarled. "There is nothing here, wherever the source of that blood may be it, does not come from this home. Now please, take your goddamned leave from my manor!"

"Delacro—"

"I don't want your help, officer! Nor do I need it. Now, for the last time, before I must forcefully remove you myself—*take your leave!*"

There was a snarl of frustration and then Alexandria was pushed back against Christian further with a rush of brazen wind, and Christian released her from his hold.

"It would be best if you did not sleep just yet, Alexandria," he said, stepping away.

Almost losing her balance with his movement, she swayed backwards, ready to fall to the floor. But she steadied herself, her heart pounding viciously within her chest, she moved on all fours to the center of the bed. Taking a steadying breath, she turned to eye him.

She could see nothing through the dark, except for the strange glint of his black eyes. Under that gaze, under that simple stare, she felt like a small animal surveyed by its condescending predator. Nothing more than a bundle of veins carrying what this animal desired most. She stammered: "Wh-who was that?"

"An annoying Vampire with a penchant for knowledge that doesn't concern him," the dark answered back.

"Wh... How did he kn-know I was here?"

The black eyes turned deep red, a red she could see easily through the gloom. The gasp left her lips without thought.

"*He smelled your blood,*" Christian said.

He smelled my blood? she thought in confusion before the small breeze blew past her with his words. It was a breeze that never left. She had felt the cold when near him in Victor's home, and she had definitely felt the cold in great lengths just moments ago when he had pressed her to him, forbidding her to speak. She looked away from his gaze, aware he had not taken his eyes from her shaking frame atop the bed. "How...could he smell my blood? I...I was aware you and your brother—the other V-Vampires, c-couldn't..."

"That is true," the red eyes said, "yet when you are asleep it appears... It would be best, it seems, if you were to join me for a late night drink—" and she looked up at these words, hardly daring to believe he said them "—in the white living room. I am sure a cup of tea, would be sufficient enough to keep you from falling to sleep. I will wait for you there."

And before she could whisper her confusion, her resounding fear at the sudden intrusion into Delacroix Manor, his strange request, a new chilling wind drifted through the room, furthering the cold she continued to feel, and she knew she was once again alone.

She could barely think on her most bizarre situation for long when the candle within its holder sparked to life, casting a feeble glow upon her and the bed she remained in.

✳

Christian appeared in the white room in the next instant and snarled. He marched towards the white couch and took his seat forcefully.

He would not allow his thoughts to turn to her. No, he couldn't. *That* he definitely would not do. Not when the sight of her tossing and turning atop the bed was so fresh in his mind, the smell of her blood so damned *strong* in his nose. It took all his restraint to keep from moving to her and sinking his fangs into her sweet, tender neck...

Another snarl escaped him as he jumped to stand, no longer finding sitting an option. How could he sit when there was a Vampire—and perhaps more, many more—that had smelled her blood and had moved to its location with ease, only steps away, perhaps, from discovering the true source of the scent?

How could he possibly sit when there were others that desired to seek out the source? How long did he have until they arrived upon his doorstep requesting with hungry eyes and heavy snarls to acquire the source of their bloodlust?

He blinked and found himself before the unlit fireplace, staring maddeningly into the cobwebbed grate. He was overthinking things, surely. Surely Devon Strumer, being at odds with the other watchmen at Scotland Yard, would not speak on what he had smelled, would not speak on the woman, for did they not disbelieve his word anyway?

But it was always true that he could convince them, which was why it was vital to keep Alexandria Stone awake for as long as humanly possible. What would happen when she finally slept, he would deal with when it came. For now, he had to keep her awake, keep her blood withdrawn. He had deduced while he watched her that the only way this would be achieved was to keep her with him at all times—a maddening proposition. But there was nothing, at least not in his narrow queue of options, that he could do.

He sighed, marveling at how his little task was beginning to wear upon his senses. It seemed the secret that was Alexandria Stone would not remain behind Delacroix Manor walls. And it was his job to make sure that no other Creatures knew of her...that no other Creatures got suspicious...but here was a Vampire telling him that Eleanor Black was searching for her! Just what was he supposed to do about *that*?!

The pang of hunger blinded him, and all thought of Eleanor, of Alexandria, died as he realized he had not fed for the night. Placing a shaking hand on the cold marble of the fireplace, he exhaled another cold breath, the hunger pervading his being even more. God, blood. He needed it dearly. It had not helped seeing her there on the bed, her fear elevated, the smell of her blood so easy to call to his senses.

Letting out a quick cry of frustration, he turned his thoughts from her and tried to clear his head, tried to think only about what was happening right now. Right this moment, she was preparing, he hoped, to meet him here. She would expect tea and also food, would she not? She would expect these things and he had not bothered to prepare them in the many years he roamed the Earth as a Vampire. *Humans and their food*, he thought in disgust.

A thought came to him. Was he not in possession of a house full of maids who attended to these very matters almost daily? But he would have to rouse one...and he had very little power available to compel one to rise.

The door opened behind him just then and he froze, the smell of the woman's blood drifting through the air to reach his nose, moving all thought, all action to the notion of satiating his boundless urges.

"Oh!" the startled voice breathed, and he turned to eye the woman that stood within the large doorway, her brown eyes filled with fear. "My Lord!" she curtsied, never staring at him directly. "My deepest, I didn't, *I didn't*, I shouldn't—" And she inhaled sharply, turning to leave.

Ah, he thought dazedly, eyeing her shaking frame, her utter inability to speak before him. Yes, yes, this was what he needed...and how could he say no, how could he say no when she was just there... just waiting to be his...waiting to be taken?

Christian moved without knowing he had done it, he moved the length of the large white room, his ring long removed, thrown to the floor just before the fire, his gaze held, intent.

His hand reached out to grasp at her retreating back, oh how smooth the fabric that was her dressing gown, his fingers gracing her shoulder.

He barely heard the gasp escape her lips, but he did see her brilliant brown eyes, how they danced with alarm at his presence, how her lips trembled with what she had done. He knew she could see the hunger his eyes held, he knew she could see, in that moment, just who he truly was...*what* he was.

Which was why he was not surprised when she stepped towards him, her lips shaking, allowing the low sound of her voice, her sweet, drawing voice, to enter his haunted ears, ears that caught every breath, heard every pulse of her scared heart.

She said, "My Lord, your eyes..."

"*Yes*," he whispered. The hunger was all he could feel, her blood all he could smell, the pulse of lust just there beneath her skin, calling him, drawing him ever closer. And yes, he felt the skin of her neck, her blood—his food.

"M-my L-Lord," she whispered, the door closing behind her, eyes still held on his face. He thought how lovely it was that she did not jump at the sound of the door closing, her fate being sealed. She was a willing target, yes so very willing...and now he slid a hand around her waist, pressing her closer, the blood only surging thicker in her veins, sending his own dead heart to soar with absolute need.

He barely heard her pleading for her life, a life that belonged to him now, no, all he knew was her neck, how soft it was, how the vein there pulsed and rushed with her heightened apprehension.

The thought occurred to him then to keep her subdued, yes, it did, but he had no power for that, so much of it he had used keeping Miss Stone from screaming. There was nothing he could do now but place a hand over the woman's mouth. Her fear grew when he did this. Oh, how he felt it soar in her heart...the muscle thumping wildly, but what did that matter? All too soon it would stop.

And all too soon, the desire to taste this human, the desire to gather the blood she housed, the desire to strengthen his own dead body, was gone.

He lingered there, feeling her heart thunder in her chest. He lingered there, feeling her blood rush through her body. He lingered there for moments more, knowing, completely, that not a second ago he was prepared to feed from her—and now it was gone.

What? he thought in blind confusion, still weakened, knowing he *needed* this blood...so why could he not claim it?

"P-please," she breathed, her voice clear now that he was no longer warped with insatiable hunger...but it made no bloody sense!

And before he could think on just what it was he could do, should do, he realized the sound of muffled footsteps were just outside the white double doors.

He had no time at all to release her before the door opened and Alexandria Stone appeared, her gaze trained on the scene before her. Before she could say a word, he released the maid, unable to think, she stumbled away from him, barreling into the closed door right beside the only other human to ever hold his gaze.

"Have I...intruded on something?" he heard Alexandria say, never fully looking at her. He found it much easier to keep his stare trained on the frightened woman. She was gazing upon him as though she could not believe what just happened. He barely believed it himself. His urges...gone. Just like that!

"Intruded?" he forced himself to say, for he had seen the maid's mouth open in preparation to speak. He stifled the growl that arose. "I was just...telling this maid here that you were to join me," and he eyed the maid, "for a late night cup of tea."

The maid drew herself up to stand, though it seemed she could not do this without the door's help. She shook. She appeared to be aware she was given an order at last, and waving some hair that peeked out from underneath her sleeping cap away from her face, she hastily wiped away her tears, Alexandria reaching out to grasp at her shoulder.

She jumped at the touch, Christian smiling at her fear. *It was only right.*

"Are...are you all right?" Alexandria asked, stepping deeper into the room, allowing the door to close behind her, sealing the rush of terror the maid nursed, would feel for the rest of the night, indeed.

"I-I'm..." Her gaze drifted to Christian's face, though she appeared to be trying her hardest to remain staring at Alexandria. "I'm fine, Miss Stone. My L-Lord was just...just telling me wh-what h-he desired for you upon y-your arrival. I shall f-fetch your tea."

"But—"

She stepped around Alexandria with shaking legs, pulled open the door, and walked through it, not bothering to keep the door from slamming behind her as she went.

Alexandria blinked. "What...forgive me if I am being too bold, but what was that?" She turned to face Christian, and he had to blink to make sure he was seeing her properly, for it could not be true that she could have cleaned up so well.

She wore an incredibly well-tailored day dress, though how she had fastened the dress to fit so tightly about her body with not a maid's help, he would never know. The clear crystal gems embedded into the dress's red fabric just below her ample bosom were placed in the shape of a diamond, and as the dress flowed into its many skirts, a mixture of gold and red roses stitched into the hem.

Her beautiful brown-green eyes held great traces of sleep, but her beauty had not diminished.

She needed food, he realized with a small start. *But then again... so do I...*

"Lord Delacroix," she said.

Blinking away the thoughts of how strange it was he had lost all desire to taste the maid's blood, he turned his thoughts to her question. And how troublesome it was.

"There was a death in her family," he said, "she was so distraught she decided to take a walk throughout the manor...she found herself here and shared in her troubles with me."

"Oh," Alexandria said, her expression darkening.

Had she believed him so easily?

She remained near the door, her long brown hair disheveled as it flowed down her back and over her covered shoulders. He found his eyes to linger upon her neck for just a moment, before his gaze moved to her sharp eyes at last, eyes that bade him an equal match in intensity.

"Please," he said, deciding this would be much more bearable if she were seated; he moved aside to allow her to see the long white couch behind him. "Take a seat, Miss Stone."

For some reason unbeknownst to him, she jumped at his voice, her eyes tracing his movements with a searching gaze, as though she desired to know something more.

Yet it was not long before she stepped forward, her eyes on the couch; her lifeline, for all the attention she paid it.

Perhaps if she does not eye me, she thinks I will disappear, he amused himself. And then sudden question fell upon him: Was this what she truly desired?

She sat upon the couch, perched on the edge of it like any respectable woman of title, and this begged the question, *did* she hold some title? He recalled how he knew nothing of her. Her intensity, her fear, he was not even sure she feared him: she looked calm. He marveled at her calmness when he stood just before her, a Vampire, clearly able to rip into her flesh, break her small, delicate fingers before she clasped them before herself like she did now.

Was it, in fact, that she did not fear him? Was it that she was content to move about as she saw fit now that he had given her permission to do so? But how could that be? How could it be that she so easily went from a state of sheer terror in her bedroom but now, out of her self-made cage, she showed not the slightest of care that he was near?

And why did he think on these things as though they hurt his pride? As though they mattered?

The door opened, bringing both of their gazes towards it, and the maid from before appeared carrying a tray of two steaming cups of tea, a small bowl of sugar cubes placed upon it as well. She moved, shakily, across the room to place the tray atop the table just before the couch. She curtsied without a word, never gazing at Christian. Then she stepped away, prepared to disappear behind a white door, before he said, "Could you prepare an early breakfast for us? Miss Stone has not eaten in days...she could use the health do you not think?"

The woman did not turn at his voice but froze, and it was though he'd physically pinned her there, and then she nodded, opening the door and moving through it without a glance back.

When the door closed, Alexandria said from her seat, "An early breakfast, my Lord? Do you think it...fair to place such stress on the woman when she is clearly grieving?"

He turned to eye her.

She held a cup of tea and took a single sip as he stared, made a face of disgust, and then began to place nearby sugar cubes one by one, into the gray liquid.

He marveled at her unfazed countenance. Who was she?

As she stirred her tea, he said, "Do you doubt that you hunger, Miss Stone?"

The stirring stopped just as quickly as it had started and she stared straight towards the fireplace across from her with his words. "I do not," she said after a time, lifting the tea to her lips once more. Her hands shook.

Ah, he thought darkly, *she was still terrified*. How brilliant she was at hiding it. Watching her intently, he remained standing, figuring it would only frighten her further if he were to take his seat upon the white couch as well.

"Alexandria," he said, for what did one say to a human he was bidden not to kill? "The rest of this night promises to be...interesting, surely."

She seemed to be quivering, her response careful, "How long must I remain awake, my Lord?"

"Until morning," he said. "Listen, you needn't be scared—"

"How do you come to that conclusion?"

"You shake...clearly...your tears...your stare—"

"My stare?" she breathed, bringing her gaze back upon him. "What do you mean my stare? What do you know of any human's stare, my Lord?"

Nothing, in truth, he thought. Nothing I would like to remember.

Aloud, he said, "Alexandria...if we are to work together, if I am to protect you, you must not fear me—"

"You—you're joking!" she whispered. And although her voice would not rise, her eyes blazed with obvious fear and anger. "How is it that you expect me not to fear you when...when your stare is akin to an iceberg—your expression not showing the least bit difference when you speak on matters most delicate—"

"Matters most..." he began before her incredulous stare bade his tongue to still. He turned from her, sure to place his stare upon the unlit fireplace as well, the surprise of her words, her stare, drawn plainly upon his face. He could almost smile, she had spoken so fiercely, yet clearly her fear still riddled her. Yes, that was what Christian was most adept at seeing in a human—their fear, their vulnerability, and their blood...

Christian turned his attention to her words: the things that had been stinging his ears the longer he stared upon the derelict fireplace.

How was it that he expected her not to fear him? He knew the night would go on awkwardly if she were to sit far from him, avoiding his gaze, yet this was what most humans did when in his presence, this he was far from used to. Why then did her fear riddle his mind with question when other humans' fear drew out in him his truth?

He turned back to her at last, deciding no human, no matter who they were, would make Christian Delacroix attempt to bend his ways.

She bowed her head, wiping away tears.

Pretending he had not seen this show of fear, of desperation, he took a step away from the couch and said, slowly, "Fine. Fear me, if you will, Alexandria. It makes no difference. But we shall be accompanying the same room for the remainder of this night. And as I cannot...harm you, and as you are most safe because of this, you are free to relax and find comfort wherever you may—forgive me for my...foolish desire to make you at ease. It is clear my words cannot do this, given what I am."

When she finally did speak, she said, into her hands, "V-very well, my Lord." She sighed, closing her eyes, her eyelashes long and wet.

He stared at her, finding her adamant gaze impressive. She had gone from curious, to angry, shocked, outraged, and finally, stoic blankness. And all in a matter of minutes.

He could not suppress the small smile that found its way to his lips then, the white doors opening, the maid returning, pushing a cart laden with two loaves of bread, a plate filled with grapes, a jar of whipped butter, a knife, and several modest slices of ham.

The maid stepped into the room, the wheels of the cart sliding across the smooth floor before she came to a rest at the table before the couch. She stepped around the cart and moved towards the table where the tray of tea sat. She picked up the tray, and her hands shaking far too much to hold it properly. He stepped to her, placing a hand upon her own, able to smell her scent: one of dried sweat and various foods.

Her other hand slid off the handle of the tray at his words, slapping down hard onto the marble table with her alarm. Squeezing her hand once, he leaned over her and lifted the tray into the air, his untouched cup of tea steaming directly into her face causing the small tears that formed to mix with the sweat that had already been there.

Christian moved from her, allowing her to hold the tray herself. She looked as though she were on her death bed: her eyes were downcast and she said not a word, turning from them both and stepped to the doors as quickly as she could.

The maid balanced the tray with one hand, opening the door with the other, before sweeping through it and disappearing behind it as it closed, but Christian knew she had not moved from the door. He heard her silent sobs, heard her ragged breathing as she cried, tray still held in her hands.

He turned his gaze back towards Alexandria. She had never glanced at them. She stared at the cart, her eyes lingering mostly upon the plate of ham, although hesitancy kept her from rising, hunger shining in her brilliant eyes.

He raised an eyebrow in amusement.

Tonight was going to be interesting, indeed.

Chapter Seven

THE GIANT

"Where is he?!" the gruff voice pierced his ears through the darkness: the fire had died some time before.

"I don't know!" another voice sounded. "It's too bloody dark. Anyone find a torch?"

He had pulled Xavier to the safety of the closest building in the burning city, thoughts of his father's whereabouts never once leaving his mind. He had known the town was not Cedar Village, but he did not dare tell Xavier this: he needed his book, and the Vampire would only question what book it was.

He stifled a groan. Mountains of cracked marble and stone lay atop him, crushing him to the floor. He lifted a hand to wipe dust from his eyes, and then pushed against the debris to better figure out his next course of action. He shifted the large piece of marble halfway across his body and saw dust-covered black hair just feet from him, beneath a particularly large piece of ceiling. Stamping down the wave of panic that Xavier was trapped beneath stone as he was, he focused on the sudden sounds somewhere around him.

Various pieces of rubble were being shifted haphazardly as they searched for life throughout the wreckage. They had attacked the building shortly after they'd entered it, a thunderous boom sounding before the ceiling of the building had collapsed. He knew he had little time before they discovered him lying there or before they found a torch and lit it, destroying the cloak of darkness that was an aid as well as a hindrance.

He carefully continued to move the piece of ceiling off his midsection, but it slid to the floor, scraping loudly against it, and the Elite Creatures stopped their search.

Damn.

"Someone's alive," one of them said at last, this voice a third, a woman's.

"Careful how you search, don't want to accidentally step on the one she wants," one grunted.

Nathanial could hear them edging around the debris, felt his heart leap as one neared him: He could smell the wind on the Creature's boot. "We're here and we can't see a thing. Tell me again why we don't cast one of them light spells?"

"Because," the woman said, "we weren't taught those spells. She has enough on her plate to teach us the Enchanting Arts."

"Can't you two shut up," the deep voice growled. "Sniff around for the blood of anything, living or dead. If Xavier's here, we'll definitely smell him."

There were noises of agreement and the sound of sniffing reached Nathanial's ears. Knowing he had little more than a second before he was discovered, he sat up slowly, his every movement taut as he rose to stand without making a sound. He heard their footsteps and their sniffs as he felt around for Xavier. He had just managed to pull himself towards the Vampire's hair when one of the Creatures said, "I've got one."

And before he could push the debris off Xavier, the arm wrapped around his neck and dragged him away, towards the place the others were searching. Someone snapped their fingers and light filled Nathanial's eyes: The woman had found a torch and was staring at him with curiosity, her face long, her hair auburn and wavy, falling over small shoulders. "Who is this?" she asked.

"That is Nathanial Vivery, Catarina," the first Creature to speak announced. And as he neared and entered the light of the torch, Nathanial could see his features were wild: deep black eyes set inside a hard face stared at him, not in wonder, but in amusement. His face was lined with feral black hair that melded unseeingly with his wide black beard. "He is the son of the Vampire, Igorian Vivery."

His eyes widened. *How can they know of father?*

"Where is Xavier?" the Vampire that held Nathanial whispered harshly into his ear.

"Yes," the deep-voiced Creature asked, "where is the Vampire?" His black eyes roamed the darkness beyond the torch to where Xavier lay beneath rubble he could not see. "Catarina," he said to the woman, "search there."

She moved past Nathanial, his eyesight once again taken from him. He knew the spell to have light but he would have to utter it, something he could not do with the pressure the Creature placed upon his throat.

"Jackal, hold that Vampire, we may need him. He has damn good knowledge of magic," he said, moving past the Vampire that held Nathanial to where Catarina's torch danced as she bent low over the body of Xavier.

"It's him." She barely breathed, yet her voice carried to where Nathanial stood, restrained. *"Bloody hell, we've got Xavier Delacroix."*

✳

Nathanial felt a rough, jagged surface under him and opened his eyes to find that he was face down on a gigantic black boulder, water pounding against his back. The rain obscured his vision as the thick, murky night darkened the figures that strode several feet away him.

It was a few moments before he realized he was hearing voices in the thundering rain and he continued to lie there, listening to what was being said.

"Well, why won't 'e wake up?"

"I dunno! We had him," one countered.

"Bloody 'ell," the deep-voiced Creature whispered.

Nathanial saw the blonde-haired Creature move away from the larger one and idly walk over to another place he could not see. He wouldn't dare lift his head and give himself away—it seemed they did not know he was awake.

He eyed the Elite Creature called Catarina through the rain. She moved away from the others for the briefest of moments, allowing him to see the big lump of wet cloak upon the dark ground at their feet.

He narrowed his eyes, trying his best to see Xavier's face, his black hair, perhaps the flash of green of the Vampire's cold eyes. Yet he could see nothing but the large cloak. It obscured the Vampire's body. A flash of anxiousness passed through his dead heart as he lay there, wondering what had caused Xavier to remain unconscious. A ceiling had fallen on him after all, but he should be recovered by now.

A pair of hands descended from darkness and Nathanial felt himself being pulled up to stand. The Elite Creature snarled in his ear, the rain pressing against his hair, sending dark red patches to cover his eyes, but he could still see one of the Elite Creatures and Catarina. They pulled Xavier to his feet as well, though the Vampire was still not awake: his head lolled to a shoulder lazily and his eyes never opened behind his heavy lids.

Wondering just what was going to happen, where they were going to be taken, he felt himself being pushed towards the waiting Elite Creatures. Gritting his teeth as they drew closer to the grinning beard of the Creature and the sneer of Catarina, he could not see a way out, and he began to steel his heart for whatever it was that would come next, be it death or Eleanor Black.

"He's not waking up, Nathanial," the deep-voiced Creature said. "What's wrong with him?"

"I don't know," he said.

"How can't you know?" he asked, staring at Nathanial with narrowed eyes, smile gone. "He's your King, innit he? He's under like he's been spelled. Did you spell him Nathanial Vivery?"

"How do you know my name?"

"Name?" the Creature repeated, turning a grinning face to Catarina who returned it over Xavier's shoulder. "You're Nathanial Vivery. You're bloody well famous you are. Of course, we know your father well—"

He snarled. "What're you talking about?" He felt the hands release from his arms and heard the Creature behind him step away through the pounding rain, but he did not turn to face him, his eyes placed intently on the grinning face of the Creature in front of him. That grin unsettled him.

The Creature said, "Why, we've just seen him, Mister Vivery. Told us we wouldn't find the book we need there. Now tell us, what did you do—what spell did you place on Xavier to keep him asleep?"

"I placed no spell upon him!" Nathanial shouted just as the ground beneath their feet began to shake tremendously and he felt his heart drop even further into his stomach. He looked around at the dark sky, aware he could see the tops of trees. *It could not be.*

They were lifted even further into the night air and Nathanial almost lost his footing, swaying loosely against the rocking of the boulder beneath them. It was then that he realized what the gigantic black boulder was.

He looked wildly at the smiling, bearded Creature, disbelief pooling through him. "Giant?!" he screamed.

They laughed at him and the one that held Xavier shook him roughly in an attempt to rouse him further.

Terror washed over Nathanial in paralyzing waves as he recalled the time he'd witnessed a single Giant killing three hundred different species of Dragon, rendering them almost extinct. He had been powerless to do anything, for his spells and his Vampire strength were no match for a Giant's. The last of the Dragons now lived in the deepest of valleys, the highest of mountains, keeping to themselves to remain alive.

The Giant's head was rough, as rough as the earth, and it was cold, he realized, because its head was normally in the skies. He tore himself away from the Creature's cold glare and stumbled over to where the massive boulder curved downward. The rest of the Giant's head was just as black and rocky, and he could see the top of two large eyelashes, below them the large eyeballs that stared straight, ignoring the pattering of rain.

He followed the Giant's gaze and he could make out a vast array of trees he recognized as the gateway to the Mountains of Cedar, beyond which lay the very village they had to get to. Were they indeed heading towards Cedar Village? Was it possible these Creatures were searching for the book as well?

With every step the Giant took, Nathanial felt himself sway, felt the tremble of its working body, and he wondered if the Giant even knew it had visitors atop its head. Fear held its icy grip around his dead heart. Nathanial heard a surreal call somewhere miles from where they were, but also, deep within him: It sounded inhuman, ethereal, and it lasted only a second, but he was sure he'd heard it even through the thundering rain and the low voices of the Elite

Creatures. And it was in hearing that call, he knew himself to feel just the slightest bit better; somehow, someway, he would get out of this mess, he would get Xavier to safety—

"Hey, Vampire!" Catarina called to him. "Get away from the edge, the moment this big lug gets to those trees, we'll be swarmed by baby Dragons, their mothers don't live far off—in the mountains just there," she said, pointing to an invisible outline in the distance. It was impossible to see due to the murkiness of the night and the rain. "We need you to work your magic—keep 'em away. Got it?"

He turned to her, her expression unreadable, but Xavier lay at her feet and it was with reluctance that he agreed, nodding curtly to pass along the message without words. She strode to the others who had taken seats towards the rear of the giant's massive head, leaving Xavier wholly unattended.

They had neared the trees now, and as Catarina predicted, three large Dragons appeared, their red and yellow scales shimmering through the night and rain. Although they were "babies," they were still massive, their long sharp tails reaching several yards in length alone, not counting the rest of their immense bodies. Their red eyes glared at the Giant, who did not stop, but continued to walk directly into the thick of the trees, their leaves just brushing his shoulders.

Nathanial wondered why the Giant was stepping so blindly into the fray of waiting, protective Dragons as the roars escaped their throats and the jets of fire—barely dispersed by the rain—blew forth, attempting to halt the massive Creature from going any farther. Yet their attempts did nothing, for the Giant continued to walk through the trees, their trunks breaking away as it walked past them.

Nathanial turned to watch the Elite Creatures, who he saw had noticed the Dragons but did not seem to mark them as a major concern, for they remained seated, Catarina included, and stared out towards the rear of the Giant. They seemed to be arguing over what to do with Xavier, none of them turning to watch him, and it was then that

Nathanial moved, as steadily as he could, over to Xavier and kneeled at his side, eyes placed intently on the backs of the three Creatures.

In his movement, a Dragon realized the Giant had guests atop its head and began to circle the massive skull, letting out minor roars. The other Dragons had remained in the entrance to the thicket of trees as they realized the Giant could not be stilled by their impressive but measly attempts at thwarting it off course.

Nathanial heard the call again, this time, however, it was much louder, and lasted for a second longer than before. The ethereal voice drifted through his mind as though only he was meant to hear it, and once again he knew that he would be safe no matter what happened, although he could not see how that was so.

As the Dragon circled, his large wings beating slowly, Nathanial had a very wild idea. He grabbed Xavier and hoisted him over his shoulder, moving to the edge of the Giant's head, his eyes placed intently on the circling Dragon.

"Hey!" the deep voice of a Creature shouted through the downpour and the small earthquakes the Giant made far below them.

He did not turn to see what the Creatures were doing, but jumped into the air as the Dragon came round to his end once more. He landed roughly on the Dragon's back and the Dragon let out a cry of shock and anger and dove furiously, leaving the three Elite Creatures atop the Giant's head, their cries and shouts lost in the rain.

Nathanial held onto Xavier as the Dragon dove past the branches and leaves and headed down, down, down into the depths of the trees, far away from where the Giant cleared a path. Chancing a glance back, Nathanial saw that the Giant had covered a significant distance since he'd jumped and had almost reached the Mountains of Cedar, the three faint specks atop its head jumping furiously, though they would not leave the Giant's head. *Curious.* He was brought back to the Dragon he rode when it came to an abrupt stop, sending him flying across the top of its hard, scaly head, through the air, and smack into a tree, Xavier flying from his arms.

It was several minutes before he forced himself to open his eyes amidst the startling pain of his landing, to find the large red eyes of the Dragon a few inches from his face. Before he could speak, it said, in a low voice, "You're mad, you know that?"

"I take my chances," he replied, trying his best to ignore the pain that seared throughout his back.

"Hmph." It turned, its long tail swishing dangerously, and Nathanial rose from the ground. It turned back to eye him near a thin tree, and said, "I suspect you're not like those other ones...yes, something is different about you. I smell it in your blood."

He'd managed to sit up without screaming, but knew he could move no further: the pain that passed through his body was alarming, so piercing it remained within his veins.

"You are in pain and yet you move. Interesting, Vampire," the Dragon said, bristling. "Where were you and those Creatures headed?"

"I don't know," he said at last, turning his gaze to face the Dragon. The rain fell sparsely now that they were down on the ground, the barrage of leaves above stilled most of the rain from hitting the earth, but enough of it fell to create mud, which clung to the side of his face and ran all along his back and hair.

"You protected that Vampire," the Dragon said, turning its eyes to a place behind Nathanial. "Loyalty is honored amongst my kind. We have lived lives of misunderstanding, misery, we must be able to trust our own...but I see," it continued not bothering to give Nathanial a chance to speak, "that those other Creatures were against you. Yes, they were similar to you, but only in appearance. In blood, they were extraordinarily different. And what they did to that Giant... most impressive..."

Nathanial was not sure what the Dragon was talking about, nor did he care—he had to get Xavier to safety, had to get him to Cedar

Village. He decided to lift himself to stand at last, but barely made it off the ground before the Dragon let out a puff of black smoke from its nostrils and strode over to him, staring him down, red eyes forbidding him to stand.

"Loyalty is sometimes best in moderation. How can you save that Vampire when you yourself have been hurt?"

He stared up at it in disbelief. "You don't understand—"

"What don't I understand, Vampire?"

"I have to get Xavier to safety. We must get to Cedar Village—"

"No," it countered, "you must regenerate. Drink blood, as you do. You can barely move and yet you push yourself so hard. You remind me impossibly of Worca, Vampire."

"Worca?"

"My mother's friend. Incredibly determined yet she does not know when to still. She always finds something to defend, be it our clan, or the mountains."

"You defend the Mountains of Cedar?"

"We are the Guardians!" it answered, as if Nathanial should have known it all along. "A Dragon must defend *something*, must guard *something*. It is in our blood, our nature. Normally, I would kill you and your friend, but after seeing what you did for him, I can only admire, and if possible, aid you. You said you need to get to the village of Cedar, did you?"

"Yes, I do," he said, wondering if what he thought would happen would indeed.

The Dragon stepped away from Nathanial and, through the rain and mud, lifted its long neck and let out a stream of thick, hot fire that surged upwards, despite the rain, burning the tops of the trees.

It was not long before two pairs of red and yellow wings beat through the leaves, heading towards them, the Dragon who had spoken before saying, "Rise, Vampire. We can do nothing while you remain upon the ground," as they neared.

Chapter Eight

NEW BLOOD

She passed him for the tenth time, her brow furrowed deep in thought.

It was something the constable said. It was something he'd said about that woman...that he felt he could not bite her. Yes, that was it. *He could not bite her, felt most unnatural in her presence.* But why on Earth would that be? Why would he feel that way? Why would he not be able to smell her blood? To lust after her like any respectful Vampire should in the face of a human?

"My Queen, forgive me but it is urgent," he said. "He has been spotted."

She stopped pacing as though something physically placed itself in front of her. "What?" she asked the Creature.

He stood and stared around the room, his eyes briefly falling over Javier's figure on top of the stool and the shadows of humans that stood against the walls. The single bright light conjured from her hand shone above them, its energy made of pure will.

He turned his gaze back to Eleanor Black. "Xavier Delacroix has been spotted in London, my Queen."

"*What?*"

"Apparently, the death of a Vampire in a prominent position amongst the humans has risen alarm...there have been reports by several Vampires who have seen Xavier Delacroix leaving an inn right across from where the death occurred."

She froze. "Truly?" she whispered. *He had been right across the street. Right across the bloody street? Then why could I not sense him? Smell his most delicious blood, even?*

"Yes, my Queen."

She snapped out of her thoughts with his words. "Do you have reports of where it is Xavier could now be?"

He appeared confused, but said, "Cedar Village, of course."

Her eyes flashed in remembrance at these words and she nodded, signaling his leave.

Once the door closed behind him, she turned her attention back to Javier, noticing that he was most curious as to the conversation at hand. "Javier," she said, attempting to break his concentration. "I have decided that your training shall resume with me."

He said nothing, but stared at her hard, as though thinking of why it was she was so concerned with Xavier Delacroix.

Feeling his gaze press into her, she inhaled, and swept a hand. "Take your leave—rest. You shall need it, my child."

He stood from the stool, his face still set in heavy thought, and roamed to the door. He spared a quick glance back before opening it, and stepping through.

The door closed behind him, her gaze moving to the humans around the room. *Their confusion, their fear.* With a small smile, she took a slow breath, the coldness consuming her skin, her blood.

Many humans gasped and many more cowered, some clawed at the walls, and one even attempted to dart for the door, tripped over his own feet, and hit the stone floor hard. He did not resurface.

"Humans," she said loudly, and they froze, waiting with bated breath. "You have followed me here under your own desires. You have been allowed to see where it is I dwell. I have told you of a world you have not known until now... Tell me, why do you shake and squirm as though I shall bring harm to you? I will not hurt those who so willingly agreed to join my cause. So please, release yourself from this ignorance, this fear. Kneel before me, and we can begin your paths to immortality."

Slowly, a handful removed themselves from the walls, their eyes wide with fear, and they moved as one to place themselves upon their knees.

She allowed her gaze to move around the dungeon, and she guessed it would take a few months, but the moment the humans turned into her Creatures, she would be one step closer to stopping Xavier from acquiring *The Immortal's Guide* and the Goblet which she held in her possession.

And the sword.

It grazed her mind and she thought of Amentias and how he was holding up with Dracula's sword. There was the possibility he had started to act as strange as Thomas did, but if he did, she was sure Aciel would return to her with complaints, as the Creature was prone to do.

Turning her attention from these Artifacts, all in her possession, she smiled and eyed the humans coldly. After a short while, she waved a hand through the air and the light in the room went out, dropping her and the humans into complete darkness. There were cries and screams from the humans but her voice surpassed the din: "Rise humans, and prepare. Your training starts now, and I hope for your sakes that you all survive. I do not want to travel to the Dragons' mountains to deliver your corpses."

※

Christian entered the small room and stared at the small table in the center, the woman that sat around it.

He had only left Alexandria Stone to go feed, for she had agreed that she would be fine if he left to satiate his urges. And he'd left her with the promise to himself that he'd be quick in enjoying the maid, that his time was very limited, but time it was all the same. He had arrived in the help's quarters, had located her room with ease, for Alexandria was not there to stifle his urges...he had fed with relish, yes he had, but he had returned to the white living room to find Alexandria fast asleep atop the couch. He had returned to smell not only her overwhelming blood but the maddening blood of a Lycan as well...

He recalled all too vividly how he had stormed out of his home to eye James Addison upon the ground, skin torn from leg, barely alive, and he had been grateful Damion and Lillith were nearby. He had smelled the beast's blood, and stayed to help decide what would be done with Xavier's favored servant.

Ignoring her eyes, he nodded his curt greeting and stepped into the small room, taking a seat just opposite her, the light of the sun beginning to brighten the sky. He stared at the window behind her head, wondering what more could be done to keep all of this under wraps.

He stared at her and saw that she had been staring at him from across the table, her brown-green eyes still wet, and up close, he could see she looked tired: the dark circles underneath her blotched eyes were deep.

"Miss Stone," he said, wondering why she'd called him here, "please, if you were not well, you did not have to meet me now."

She wiped a tear from an eye. "I-I suppose I'm shaken still. That servant...he was your brother's, wasn't he?"

"Yes, he was," he said, staring at her uncertainly. Crying humans were one thing when they were not in his direct line of sight, or better, when he was to take their blood for his own, but to have one so close, just before him once again, and alone at that—he knew not what to do at all.

Clearing his throat, he tried his best to pull her from, he was sure, most troubling thoughts. "Alexandria," he said again, feeling incredibly misplaced.

She still cried, never ceasing. She didn't seem to hear his words at all.

He stared at her aghast, not knowing how one human could produce so much *water*. Blood, yes...but *this many tears?* He rubbed his temples, weary of her strange tears, his eyes closing as the warmth of the sun pressed against his sleeve and hand. What a change from where he would normally be on a morning—in his bed, or in the white living room, gathering and shifting through thoughts that would bother him most.

At last the frantic crying ended, and he opened his eyes with this sudden silence to find that she had dampened a nearby napkin, using it to dry her tears and wipe at her nose. He blinked, wondering just what it was she desired from him, for surely she could have cried this much in her room, where, thankfully, he was not privy to this most pathetic sight.

"I...I'm sorry...my Lord," she said then, her voice still breaking as she looked at her full plate. "But seeing James upon the ground like that...and for it to be my fault—"

"What do you mean it was your fault?" he asked, wondering just what she was talking about.

She sighed deeply, gulping the last threatening tears down, and she never looked upon him directly. "That...beast was drawn here... because of me."

He stared at her, his mind running fast with thoughts on whether this could possibly be true. "How," he said at last, "do you figure?"

He thought of her blood, the haze of red light that surrounded her as she lay upon dirt ground surrounded by curious eyes.

"My dream," she said. "Not only did I see James get attacked. I-I went out—out into the courtyard...I-I lifted a hand...and t-told the...creature to go—"

"You *what?*" he whispered, confusion pooling through him.

"And it, it obeyed...it *listened,*" she said with the air of wonder. "But I know that it was called here because of me...it was the same creature that came for me once before."

He stared at her and said nothing, mind working hard. If Alexandria were truly the one to drive the Lycan away, *if* she were... then what did that mean? Did she hold some special power that fended off Lycans?

His eyes widened with the thought. "You said that it was the same creature that came for you once before?"

"Yes," she said, setting down her cup of tea.

"You mean when I found you in the woods just outside Lord Nicodemeus's home?"

"Yes."

"Then that Lycan last night," he said, "that was Lore. It had to be."

She did not seem the faintest bit scared or shocked by that name. "Lore?"

He ran a hand over his mouth. "The Lycan King...he...I fought him when you were found," he said, thoughts incredibly fogged. How could it be possible...Lore...*again?*

She shifted slightly in her seat. "I'm sorry, did you say '*king?*' That beast is a king of those...those other beasts?"

"Yes," he answered, mind long gone with thoughts of Lycans, Alexandria's red light. "Every Creature has a leader they rally behind. And all Dark Creatures pay heed to the King of us all."

"And that is...?"

"Xavier, of course," he said, not bothering to eye her, his mind still burdened with thoughts of Lore and why he had been here... Why Alexandria was able to make him turn tail and run...

He opened his eyes with the memory: The dark of the night all around, the smell of dirt and Lycan stench thick in the air...and then a flash of red light...a Lycan left alone to stare upon a mysterious woman...

He stood, unable to remain seated as the thought of her red light returned to him, the smell of her blood.

"Was there a red light around you when you told Lore to leave?" he asked her carefully, ignoring her fearful stare at his anxiousness.

"I...I believe so," she whispered, and her brilliant eyes seemed to harden with concentration.

His mind raced even as he stood glaring down upon her. Who in the World was she? To have a power that fended off Lycans, a most brilliant blood that sent him mad with the desire to taste her...

"How did you feel, Miss Stone, when the red light surrounded you?" he asked her, having decided that if she felt different if this red light emanated from her, or her blood, it would naturally bring about some changes to her being.

"How did I feel, my Lord?" she repeated, a hand rubbing at her temples, and he realized she must not have slept at all after she had seen James upon the ground.

He slowly sank back into his chair. Her eyes followed his movement with something like fear. Ignoring this, he said, "Yes, how did you feel? I am sure you were not the same when this red light filled you in your dream."

Her eyes then blanketed with remembrance. "I don't believe I was any different, my Lord."

"Truthfully?" he asked, disappointed. If she was not any different in demeanor or appearance, he thought then, perhaps it had been just a dream. But why would Lore come for her? And how did he leave with no coercion at all?

"Perhaps I was mistaken," she said after a time, "perhaps I just...I was wrong and the Lycan had nothing to do with me—"

"Given your...track record with the beasts, Alexandria, I can't believe that. No, you were right to bring this to my attention. Whatever you possess within you, Lore seems unquestionably drawn to it."

She looked resigned to his words, as though she would not have him believe it, but things were too late for that, he knew.

She wiped away more stray tears and nodded slowly, her long dark brown hair waving along her back and shoulders as she did so. "Then I'm wanted by this...Lycan...King," she said in a low voice, her eyes appearing to fog with resounding fear.

He eyed the slender hand that rested atop the table, and he felt, miraculously so, that he desired to reach out and touch her fingers, graze the trace of her knuckles...crush her fingers in his own—

The door to the breakfast room opened then and he turned to see the intruder, surprised that it was James's aunt, her eyes still red with tears. In a shaking hand, however, she held a neatly folded piece of paper.

"Forgive me, my Lord, Miss Stone, but it would appear," and she gasped, apparently trying to hold back an avalanche of tears, "Officers of Scotland Yard request your presence at the precinct, Master Christian."

Christian stared at the woman. It was not until Alexandria said, "My Lord, may I accompany you?" that he realized what the woman had said. *What the devil do those Vampires want now?*

"Yes, yes," he whispered to the room as he stood, removing himself from the table. He eyed the woman before saying, "Can't keep them waiting. You are free to check on James at your leisure, of course."

"I...thank you, my Lord," she said, a large tear leaving a brown eye.

Christian turned back to watch Alexandria. "We leave after you've had your breakfast, Miss Stone."

She nodded. Satisfied, he turned back to James's aunt and stepped towards her. "He will be fine," he said, doing his best to ignore the doubt in his dead heart. He feigned his most reassuring smile as Alexandria sniffed behind him.

Chapter Nine

CEDAR VILLAGE

They pounded against the clear sky. The rain had let up when they had taken off in pursuit of the Giant and now that the morning sun brightened his vision, Nathanial could easily see the commotion that lay ahead: several fully-grown Dragons had awoken to the trembles of the ground the Giant had cast as he moved the earth beneath his feet and were stretching their wings and tails, moving their heads to eye what was happening. The Giant had stopped before the ice-capped mountains and the three Elite Creatures on its head had taken to the skies, flying towards the small village that lay just beyond a rushing river.

Cedar Village.

"Hurry, we mustn't let them get there!" Nathanial commanded into the Dragon's long ear.

It obeyed and let out a roar, beating its wings faster as it glided in earnest across the morning sky. The others glided along next to it, the slumped body of Xavier placed carefully in between the shoulder blades of a neighboring Dragon.

109

"Don't bother with the Giant!" the Dragon Nathanial rode yelled to its brother. It had swooped ahead and began to circle the massive Creature who stood as still as a mountain himself, large eyes closed. "There's no point—!"

His words were silenced as the massive Creature lifted into the sky, and for one moment, it seemed to Nathanial that the sky had caved around itself, for all became dark as the largest Dragon of them all spread its massive wings and blocked out the light of the sun.

It let out a thick stream of fire and the Elite Creatures stilled in their quest to pass it; they remained airborne, apparently too mesmerized by the Dragon before them to do anything more than stare. The Giant remained still, the spell placed upon it incredibly effective.

"You wish to pass into the village of Cedar?" the Dragon's deep voice boomed through the air and its large black eyes scanned the small valley before the mountains, eyeing the Elite Creatures.

The Dragon Nathanial rode neared the massive Dragon that continued to stare at the speechless Creatures before it and cried, "Worca!"

Upon hearing her name, Worca turned her long face to the approaching Dragon, her red and black scales gleaming in the morning sun as she hovered in the sky. "Rwnerog, you abandon your post at the gateway for—" Her thick voice dropped as she eyed Nathanial atop Rwnerog's back.

"Worca, these Vampires" —he motioned with his head to where his brother carried Xavier next to him— "were held prisoner to those Creatures. We must let them pass."

"Pass?" Worca bristled, allowing a thick stream of hot black smoke to issue from her nostrils. "What has that Vampire done that changes your opinion about the disgusting Creatures, Rwnerog?"

"He has defended another of his own—protected another of his own—such loyalty shall not be overlooked—"

"By you? Or by your mother, dear Rwnerog?" Worca said, the mentioning of his mother apparently meant to sting. "*Who* has that Vampire protected?"

Nathanial lifted himself to sit higher atop the Dragon (for he remained low against the Dragon's back as it flew and had remained as such while it hovered, the wind it created far too much to face), and addressed the massive Dragon before him, his voice loud over the howling winds created both by how high they were in the sky and by the Dragons' beating wings: "Xavier Delacroix is the Vampire I have protected."

Worca made a swishing motion with her long tail and turned to face the Vampire the other Dragon held. "That is Xavier?" she asked, eyeing the dark, damp cloak that draped loosely over the scale-ridden back. "You should have said so sooner, Vampire."

Nathanial was no closer to asking her why when she turned from them, moving to the Elite Creatures that had been trying to sneak past her. She let out a stream of fire and they let out screams of fright, flying over the mountains, still pressing for the tiny village beyond the bubbling stream. She followed them relentlessly, flying below them in order to forbid them to land, her large wings blowing the roofs off houses, and uprooting many smaller Creatures who were sent flying into the air. Rwnerog continued towards the small village with an indignant flap of his wings. As they neared it, Nathanial looked down to see the Creatures that were now leaving the small cottages, looking up in bewilderment. They landed roughly, stopping just before the river, Nathanial catching a Vampire in the window of a dark cottage whose black door was opening against the morning. His eyes shifted to the motion the swishing curtain made as this Vampire hid himself from the light of the sun.

"Nathanial." The deep voice of Rwnerog called him back to where he remained, and the large head jerked towards the other Dragon that had just landed a few feet from them, Xavier sliding off its back and hitting the grass in a rumpled heap, arm dangling oddly over his face.

He slid from Rwnerog and flew to Xavier, landing beside him. The Dragons had joined each other and were watching intently from a distance while the Creatures that had left their small cottages pointed and watched them all with obvious interest, their voices carrying in a collective wind.

Nathanial eyed Xavier's arm and attempted to move it, not surprised to find it was loose. "Broken," he whispered darkly.

"Can you not heal him?" the Dragon asked, staring down upon Xavier.

"What?"

"You bear the blood of the magical ones, Vampire," he said calmly, turning his strong gaze to match Nathanial's eyes. "It is thick in your veins."

"How do you—?"

"What's happened here?!" a deep voice said then, shunning Nathanial's words.

He looked up to see several Creatures crossing the river, yet only one seemed to not touch the water at all; pale and scarred, he landed on the grass and approached them with authority, his black hair sweeping out behind him, his light green eyes staring at the unconscious Vampire on the ground.

"What's happened to him?" an Enchanter asked from behind this Vampire; —it seemed no one wished to get too close.

"Unconscious," Nathanial answered tersely, moving to lift Xavier over his shoulder.

"Why? What's happened?" someone else asked.

Ignoring them, Nathanial pushed past the group of anxious Creatures and allowed his thoughts to travel to what it was he would now do. He had to uncover the book, but he could not do so, surely, with Xavier in the state he was in.

Eyeing the line of small cottages before the rushing river, he heard Rwnerog begin to answer the Creatures' questions. Gliding smoothly over the river, he landed on a small dirt path, a light Gnome running out from behind a batch of daffodils housed in a yard just before him. It eyed him warily and then ran with stubby legs over to another yard to Nathanial's left before disappearing behind a black rose garden.

Before he could decide what his next move would be, the scarred Vampire appeared at his side, sending the daffodils to bend away in the breeze created. "Take him into my home," he said in a commanding voice.

The Creatures that still lingered in conversation with the Dragons cast curious glances at Nathanial and the Vampire draped across his shoulder, and Nathanial knew he had no time to question this scarred Vampire—if he offered security, they would have to take it.

"Which one is yours?" he asked the Vampire, turning to watch him, taking note of the strange way his green eyes never pierced his face completely.

"This way," the Vampire said, stepping with swift, graceful steps towards the last cottage whose black door stood wide open. He moved for the door and swept inside, with little in the way of a glance back.

Nathanial stared at him as he moved, and when he'd reached his cottage and stepped inside, he set off after him, moving towards the small stone path that led up to the black door. He reached the doorway in a matter of seconds and stepped through it, jumping as the door closed with a quick slam behind him.

Adjusting Xavier over his shoulder, Nathanial looked around the small room, its bare stone walls dark and cold, but there was an obvious air of something more upon the walls, something Nathanial would call magic, but it could not be possible that this Vampire knew how to perform spells. And why would the Vampire need such magical protection?

Turning his thoughts from the strange Vampire, he eyed the three dark armchairs set around a small table in the middle of the room, the single fireplace set against the wall to the right of the door. There was a small staircase straight ahead that led to what must have been the second floor, but the more he stared, the more Nathanial realized the cottage did not look as though it possessed a second floor from the outside. More magic, perhaps?

Thinking this strange, he did not desire to remain for much longer than was necessary, but manners had to be observed, of course. Shifting Xavier over his shoulder once more, he eyed the Vampire that had moved to a shelf to his left and had not turned to him since he'd entered.

"My Lord," Nathanial said to the Vampire's back, "I am grateful you allowed us entrance into your home—"

"I did not offer you anything anyone here would not allow you, Vampire," the deep voice said.

His words shushed, he stared, but regained his tongue after a moment, and while shifting Xavier's dead weight against his shoulder for a third time, he said, "Of course...my Lord...but as I am sure you noticed, my friend here is seriously injured. Would you know of any...spells...to correct his misfortune?" Sure to make his words properly polite, for it was rude to suggest that a Vampire knew of such things. Magic was forbidden by all Dark Creatures that were not Enchanters or Elves, after all.

Yet the Vampire turned in a swirl of urgency all the same, his pale face deadly. It was in the flash of green eyes that Nathanial observed, now in the dark of the small room, the numerous scars upon the Vampire's countenance. A particular one cut across his left eyebrow and extended down across his nose and mouth, giving him a most vicious perpetual grimace.

The Vampire stared at him and Nathanial realized he could not know what this Vampire was thinking. How strange that was...

"You are observant," the Vampire said at last. "When did you realize my home was enchanted?"

"Only but a few moments ago, my Lord," he said. "It is a spell that gifts the dwelling of any home with the utmost of basic protection. Not a soul may enter your house unless you absolutely desire them to do so—but also I can detect a slight difference in this spell...it has been created in blood. A precaution, surely, to ensure that no harm can befall those who enter this house.

"But naturally, Vampires...cannot perform magic...."

The scarred Vampire said nothing to the words Nathanial had uttered, he raised a cut eyebrow, and his grimace intensified.

And then, much to Nathanial's surprise, he said, "There is a spell that will rouse your friend."

Nathanial's eyes widened.

"Yes," the scarred Vampire said, "I am versed in the Arts of Enchanting, though I, myself, have never cast a spell, but there is someone who can."

"Who?" It was not possible this Vampire knew an Enchanter. He looked as though he never left these dark stone walls if he could help it.

"A good friend," the scarred Vampire said. "Now please, take your seat, Vampire. I shall return shortly." And he swept forward causing Nathanial to step aside, further into the small room.

He watched as the Vampire moved to the black door and placed a scarred hand atop the doorknob that Nathanial realized was the golden head of a Dragon and turned. It emitted a faint hiss as the Vampire released it and stepped through the door back into the sun, the rush of voices outside drifting into the cottage as well. The Vampire did not turn as he closed the door, and Nathanial moved to settle Xavier within the armchair closest to him.

Once he was settled, he turned his gaze from the unconscious Vampire and stared around the small room much more closely. The Vampire knew of magic—*but how?*

Turning from Xavier, he moved to the shelf the Vampire had stood before just moments ago. There were books here, old, tattered, worn books. Perhaps, perhaps there would be some clue to the Vampire's knowledge of magic upon this shelf.

He ran a finger along the worn spines of books short and tall, at last reaching a book that seemed to shake as he lightly grazed it. He pulled it from its place on the shelf and eyed the old green cover. There were no words on its surface, but Nathanial was more than certain this book held great knowledge of magic all the same.

His fingers graced the edge of the cover, prepared to open it, when the doorknob hissed, and the door opened. Hastily placing the book back upon the shelf, he turned to eye the scarred Vampire entering the cottage, a woman following behind him, her black hair falling around a sharp, inquisitive face; she stared into the dark home with deep brown eyes.

She closed the door behind her and the knob emitted yet another faint hiss, her gaze moved to Xavier within the armchair and her eyes narrowed.

She whispered words to the scarred Vampire, words that Nathanial, for some strange reason, could not catch. With her words, the scarred Vampire nodded and stared at Xavier before bringing his gaze upon Nathanial, a gaze the woman shared as well.

He felt as though he were being heavily surveyed, yet before he could speak a word, the scarred Vampire said, "Why are you here, Vampire?"

"Why am I here?" he repeated, incredulous. "I was attacked by three Elite Creatures! I had to get Xavier to safety—"

"You misunderstand his question, Vampire," the woman said, and she stepped forward from behind Xavier's armchair, Nathanial noticing the deep red robes that swayed rhythmically with every step she took. "Why are you, a Vampire with a very rare affinity for magic, here, in this village?"

Was it so obvious he possessed magical skill? Thinking it incredibly strange that the Dragon, the Elite Creatures, and now this Enchanter had mentioned it, he wondered what the best course of action to take would be. They could not know the true reason he and Xavier needed to be in the village.

"We were ambushed," he began, "the Elite Creatures captured us, the Dragon brought us here—"

"If that is all you claim, Vampire," she said, resigned to his words, "so be it. But you must know that this Vampire," she pointed behind herself with a slender finger towards Xavier, "must be healed as soon as possible."

"I am aware," he said, knowing Xavier had to be awake to locate the book. But why would this Enchanter say such a thing? "Why do you believe he must be healed...?"

"My name," she said, "is Aurora Borealis. I am an Enchanter with the Modifying Magical Weapons Sect of Enchanting Sects in the Dark World. Xavier Delacroix's status in the World is one that is known by all Dark Creatures, Vampire. It would not do for the Vampire to be unconscious when there are Creatures out there who wish to harm him."

"Agreed," he said, thinking of the three Elite Creatures and if Worca had caught up to them. "But are you suggesting, Madame, that you are free to heal Xavier?" He could not help but glance curiously to the scarred Vampire behind her.

The Vampire did not share his gaze: he was staring at Xavier in his chair, as though if he looked away the Vampire would disappear.

"I am," Aurora said, turning from him and moving past Xavier's chair, stepping towards the fireplace, never glancing back. "And naturally, I would need your help. I believe he is lost to a madness he does not want to rise from." She turned along the fire to eye him, her eyes turning a deep black. "Are you prepared to undo this encumbering spell, Vampire?"

He stared at her. And when at last he could find his voice, he realized what she had said. "I am prepared to do anything I must to protect Xavier."

At this, both she and the scarred Vampire shared dark glances before she turned back to Nathanial, a small smile upon her lips.

Chapter Ten

THE WOMAN WHO
HOLDS NO BLOOD

Darkness swam before his eyes, the stark cold blowing all about him. He fell endlessly through the cold air, her voice filling his ears as though an echoing call:

"Nathanial Vivery!"

And as soon as he'd heard it, his falling slowed. He was floating... and then...

He landed atop the hard ground which was, he realized, dark water.

"Nathanial," Aurora's voice said frantically from somewhere and he looked up to see her walking towards him, her black eyes serious, "Nathanial, are you all right? Seems you had a harder entry...her energy is more disruptive to Vampires than Enchanters I'd imagine..."

And with her words, he could feel it all around him: the destructive dread of Eleanor Black's cruel energy. It swam through the air as though it threatened to become the air itself and if he had to breathe, Nathanial felt he would be easily subjected to it.

"I'm fine," he said turning back to the woman. "Xavier's mind—it's not as smooth an entrance as other Creatures' minds are."

"Indeed," she said, nodding curtly, her black hair bouncing along, "it is not." She turned from him to look around the endless space they remained in. "Now, we must venture to where Eleanor's pull is strongest..." And even as she spoke, a medium-sized ball of light appeared several feet from them and emitted a dense collection of what had to be Eleanor's energy: it was from this Nathanial felt it most.

Without a word to each other, they set off towards it, his black traveling cloak swaying behind him. But even as they stopped just before it, he began to feel as though Eleanor's dread was entering him, filling him with despair, great loss...

"Nathanial," Aurora Borealis said, staring at him, her voice echoing, "I know you don't need to breathe, but in my experience deep breaths do help when one is feeling off center."

He gave her a half-smile, hardly believing that a few cold breaths would calm him, when she reached out with a slender hand towards the ball of light. All at once, he found himself standing in a large hall, one that very much resembled the one in Carvaca's castle where the Council of Creatures meeting had been held.

They stood with their backs to the large hall doors, facing empty benches that were hovering serenely in the air before large arching windows that showed a snow-ridden forest beyond.

Before he could turn to the Enchanter at his side to ask what on Earth they should be doing, there, just before them, in the middle of the large hall, appeared Eleanor Black and Xavier Delacroix. But something was very wrong about the green-eyed Vampire.

Xavier wore a dark blouse, embroidered with dark red fabric along the cuffs and cravat, and his dark green eyes seemed to hold a greater hint of power than usual. He stared at them both with the coldest of gazes.

"Xavi—" Nathanial began. Aurora waved a hand through the cold air and he found his voice stuck hard in his throat. He stared at her in confusion. She grabbed the tail of his cloak and pulled him out of the line of sight of Xavier and Eleanor, and to his even greater bewilderment, they did not turn their gaze towards them, but continued to stare at the large hall doors as though expectant.

The hall doors opened and in stepped, looking downtrodden, ill-even, Christian Delacroix. Beside him a stoic-looking Vampire who held an icy gaze. He looked at nothing but Eleanor. The moment both Vampires stepped across the threshold of the doors, Eleanor moved forward, arms splayed as her long black robes swayed around her, giving her the air of a slender spider.

"Christian," she breathed, staring at the Vampire as though she desired nothing more than to embrace him, but he made to step from her when the Vampire at his side grabbed his arm, holding him steadily in place. "Oh dear, does one hate me now?" she asked the air, the trail of laughter in her words. "I have your family, Christian. I have your precious Alexandria! Your dear brother!" And with this she waved a long hand behind her to where Xavier stood, a smug smile upon his handsome face.

"Brother!" Christian cried with a snarl, his eyes a deep red. "How could you do this to everyone? To me?! *To Dracula?!*"

And Eleanor slapped him clear across his face, and he buckled, an aggrieved snarl leaving his lips.

"What does he mean?" Nathanial whispered to Aurora, aware the boulder in his throat had un-lodged itself some moments before.

"Shh," Aurora hissed. "We must find where her power is weakest and remove it at that precise moment. You remember the spell?"

"Aye," he whispered, saying nothing more: Eleanor had turned her back on Christian and moved towards Xavier, her eyes loving, her face softer than it had been but seconds before.

"My love," she whispered, and Xavier stared down at her, his own expression loving, "your brother does not appear to understand what sacrifice you have made for the Dark World."

"That is because my brother," Xavier said, staring upon Christian, "has always been a fool. Slow to act for his better gain—"

"You are the fool, brother!" Christian shouted, fighting to break free from his captor's grip. "You have forsaken Dracula! Left your mind! And you have given her control of it—"

"Watch your words!" Xavier roared and Nathanial felt his blood run cold. A strong wind blew around the large hall, threatening to blow them all from their places, but Aurora waved a quick hand and a dark blue wall was placed before Nathanial, protecting them.

"But brother—" Christian began, upon his knees now, for it seemed he had no strength to stand. Xavier released Eleanor from his hold and stepped towards him, dark green eyes crushing.

Christian did not reach the gaze as Xavier said, his voice incredibly deep, "You have always been the fool, little brother. You never understood what the Dark World was...and you hardly understand what it is now.

"Why do you fight me? Fight my Eleanor, the woman who brought such brilliant truths to us...the woman whose genius has been accepted by all...even your dear Miss Stone?"

At this, Christian gazed up towards Xavier, his red eyes wide with terrible rage. "She accepted none of this! You took her! She never wanted to be your prisoner!"

"But that, dear Christian," Xavier said with a cruel smile upon his face, "is where you are wrong. If only *you* could have defended her, protected her, *watched* over her, instead of letting your emotions get the better of you, all the more she would still be by your side..."

Christian's face fell to utter fear. "You have not...you did not turn her, you *could not* have turned her!"

And Xavier laughed, a deep harrowing laugh that Nathanial was sure if he were not protected, he would have felt as a chilling dread.

"Do you wish to see your sweet human so badly? Very well." And he clapped two strong hands together. Beside Eleanor appeared a Vampire Nathanial had seen several times in the course of his death, though he could not believe the stark difference that seemed to have taken hold of the Vampire all the same.

Darien Nicodemeus stood a charming six-foot-two, yet his jet-black hair was somehow longer, the trademark Elite Creature robes upon his slightly muscular frame, his black eyes somehow filled with malice as he held tight in a dark-skinned hand the arm of a terrified-looking woman.

Though beautiful she was, her features were marred with fear. She looked = worn, as though she could barely stand on her own two feet, the long red dress she wore tattered in several places and dirtied in few others. And she looked up towards Xavier, for he had turned to her the moment she'd arrived, the mark of fangs just there along her pale neck. She had been bitten.

"Alexandria!" Christian cried, staring upon her with utter desperation. "I am so sorry... I never meant... This should have never happened!" And no sooner had the words left his lips, did Xavier whirl to him, kicking him clear across the mouth with a dark boot, blood flying freely from his lips.

Christian sputtered and groaned on the floor. Xavier turned back to eye the two newcomers. "Darien, my old friend, I trust she has not been difficult in...keeping together..."

"Not at all," the cool voice responded. He pushed Alexandria towards Xavier, giving a curt smile to Eleanor at his side.

Alexandria flew into Xavier, who held her arms and gazed down at her with little care before snarling. She let out a brief cry of fear, and was thrown to Christian with little care.

"Alexandria!" the beaten Delacroix brother cried again and he grabbed her when she fell to her knees before him, clinging for dear life to his dirt-ridden cloak. She sobbed onto his shoulder, and he clasped at the back of her head, her long wavy dark brown hair riddled with what looked like dirt and blood.

"Look at how they grovel and cling to each other!" Xavier said, bringing all eyes to him with his thunderous voice. "They, the only two beings capable of it who have not joined us! And still they would resist, and why my Elite Creatures?" Darien and Eleanor eyed each other with knowing gazes. Xavier kept his green eyes on the shaking woman in Christian's arms. "It is fairly simple: She is born of Dracula's blood...her blood cannot be touched by us, and that foolish Vampire who cradles her as though she is his child is in love with her—he daren't leave her side."

"So what shall become of them, Xavier?" Darien asked.

Xavier continued to stare at her as though she was an insect he wished to step on. "She is close to death and as it is known, any... Vampire who is not yet so but remains in human form shall die a slow death until the time of their Vampire Age, when they must be turned to continue to live or they will cease to be.

"She must be given the blood of a Vampire and turned...and as the only true Vampire left in the Dark World is my foolish brother, it must be him to do it."

"But what will happen after she is a Vampire?" Darien asked.

Xavier turned to him and smiled. "She will be a testament to the other Dark Creatures that the last of Dracula's...pointless...blood resides within this concubine. The others shall do what they wish with her—"

"No!" Christian yelled, and even Alexandria stared at Xavier as though he were utterly mad.

"No? No?!" Xavier countered, stepping towards them, kneeling to reach their height. "You will come to understand, Christian, that the Dark World is not the same anymore—*nothing* is as it was. This human, you've been at her side for years, watching her slowly die, not willing yourself to see what was becoming of her, not willing yourself to turn her. Now you protest at the fate that has befallen you and your love?"

"I won't turn her for your ruthless means, Xavier! She will not be something to be passed along to your Creatures—" Christian began before Xavier's cold hand found its way to his jaw, ceasing his tongue.

Xavier moved ever closer to Christian, ignoring the woman who remained along the floor, staring at him in utter fear, stark anger, before whispering cruelly, "You have no choice. You are mine. Alexandria is mine. And the both of you worthless Creatures shall do what I say. You will turn this human into a Vampire whether you desire to or not!"

Before Christian could protest, Xavier removed his hand from his face and plunged it straight through Alexandria's chest, her pale face falling to sheer shock. Xavier appeared to have grabbed her heart and was squeezing it tight.

"No!" Christian and Nathanial screamed.

Nathanial felt Aurora's steadying hand upon his shoulder.

Ignoring her touch, he continued to watch Christian grab Xavier's arm with whatever faint vestige of strength he retained and pulled it from her chest, but not before Xavier laughed. "She's truly dying now, brother! Give her your blood...but first you would want to drink it, yes? You do look as though you could use the strength." He rose to his feet and stepped briskly away, blood pouring from the hole in her chest, spilling all along her red dress, falling onto the white floor.

Everyone watched as Christian turned his gaze back to Alexandria, and Nathanial thought he might cry, for it was so lost and distraught he looked, but instead he bent his head low and pressed his lips to Alexandria's wound, taking in her blood, her eyes fluttering closed at last.

Nathanial tore his gaze from Christian's feeding to eye the haughty glares of Xavier, Eleanor, and Darien and knew his blood to rise in temperature with anger. *Why the hell did the Vampire dream about this?*

He recalled the way the Vampire had looked back at *The Dragon's Cavern* upon awakening. Lost. Lost to deeper thought. And then he had mouthed a name Nathanial had thought was his mind playing tricks, but no, Xavier *had* thought of her, had believed with a strong conviction it was she who burned the café down right outside the inn.

He had just stepped forward when Aurora waved her hand through the cold air and the blue wall appeared to solidify, keeping him from moving any further. "No, Nathanial," she said, "the time is not yet."

"But he has taken her blood!" he said, stretching a hand to Christian, who rose from Alexandria as though he wished himself dead. "When is the time if not now?!"

"Our focus is not Christian Delacroix, but Xavier, Vampire," she said, waving a hand as to allow the wall to soften in its hold, and Nathanial felt as though he could step forward if he desired, "do not forget this."

Nathanial's golden eyes darkened in silent anger. Indeed, he knew very well that Xavier was their goal in this vision, but what the Vampire dreamed—seemed to pine for—it was madness! He eyed Xavier's haunted expression then and saw that all the Creatures now looked in fear upon Christian.

Turning his own eyes to where they all gazed, Nathanial let out a breathless gasp.

Christian Delacroix was glowing, glowing with a most familiar red light, and his eyes were no longer red with anger or desperation, but now red with sheer certainty, absolute knowledge.

"What becomes of him?" Eleanor whispered, moving forward to grasp Xavier's arm.

But Xavier did not respond. Christian bade him a small smile, one that held great mysteries, greater, perhaps than the ones Xavier had learned upon joining Eleanor. Christian lifted a small dagger that had remained around his waist, unseen by all, and dug it ravenously against his arm, cutting straight through the torn blouse with no care.

Darien stepped forward as well. "I don't...believe it..."

But what Darien did not believe, Nathanial could not know, for Christian had just pressed his bleeding arm to Alexandria's white lips, forcing her to drink.

If her eyes opened or not Nathanial could not know, for Aurora pushed him forward with a strong hand. "Now!"

And the blue wall disappeared as he moved towards Xavier, his golden eyes glowing furiously, the energy rising within his body at last. The Vampire turned to him once he was several feet away, his dark eyes widening in shock and he whispered, *"Nathanial?!* But you're dead!" before Nathanial placed a hand atop Xavier's chest, pushing the rushing white energy through his arm into the Vampire's heart before yelling, *"Divendividem!"* just as Aurora placed a hand upon a flustered Eleanor Black's shoulder, whispering, *"Claritorin!"*

Xavier exhaled deeply, as though all the breath within him had been forced out. His mouth opened wide as if he could not believe Nathanial stood before him.

White light filled the large hall, Aurora calling over Eleanor's shoulder. "He's no longer tied to her, Nathanial! Bring him back!"

And without another thought, Nathanial looked Xavier straight in his green eyes, the white light intensifying around them both, and whispered, *"Dilenvor."*

※

Christian pressed a white finger against the black curtain, the coach rumbling along the cobblestoned streets, his view of them a distasteful one: they now passed a street famous for its scoundrels and whores. Releasing the curtain and allowing it to fall across the window, he settled back against his heavily cushioned bench as darkness filled the coach.

And through the dark, her voice reached his ears, ever so careful. "What do you believe they wish to speak to you about, my Lord?"

"My brother," he said, sure to stare at her through the dark. She sat right across from him, her brown-green eyes never leaving his face. "He is wanted for the death of the constable. They wish for me to speak on his behalf."

"I see," she said, her gaze falling to the black lace gloves she wore upon her slender hands. He once again found his desire to reach forward and grasp them force its way to the center of his mind.

The coach came to a jarring halt along the road and he placed a hand atop the dark wooden panel around them to still himself from flying into her. "What the devil?" he breathed.

Alexandria let out a curious, "What's happened?"

The door to the coach was thrown open and against the glaring sun, Christian eyed the anxious countenance of Darien Nicodemeus.

"Lord Darien?"

"Christian," Darien said, other carriages passing in the busy street. "We must move, my home is in danger—"

"Danger? What do you mean?"

"Remove yourself from this damned vehicle, Delacroix, and I shall tell you more."

But he did not move. Urgent though the Vampire appeared, he knew he could not leave Alexandria unattended even for the slightest of moments. And was it not this very Vampire who desired to have Alexandria for himself those weeks before, breaking down Victor Vonderheide's door to do so?

Not sparing a glance to Alexandria, for the dark Vampire had not yet seen her, so steady was his gaze upon him, Christian said, "I shall not leave this coach, my Lord. Officers of Scotland Yard have sent it for me as way to venture to—"

"Yet you move a snail's pace when there is no time for it!" Darien said, a slight wind blowing past at his words, sending his long black hair to flutter in the breeze, his tan blouse rippling against his broad chest.

The breeze entered the carriage and as it was felt by Christian, the cold wind seemed to press itself against Alexandria, and she let out a startled gasp. At her utterance, Darien's black eyes narrowed, the bustling street continuing to curse their existence for being rudely, as some put it, in the way.

"You have another with you?" Darien asked, stepping forward to peer into the coach, his eyes gazing upon the confused woman therein. "A woman?" he remarked, turning his gaze back upon Christian.

"I shall explain—"

"Later, I'm sure," Darien interrupted with little care. He stepped back from the coach and Christian eyed Alexandria with the slightest hints of fear. If it was true that Darien desired Alexandria, would he not move to capture her as soon as possible? Why did he not do so? Was he truly too preoccupied with his supposed danger to realize the exact woman that remained mere feet from him? Had he even seen Alexandria before? Did he know what she resembled?

Christian realized he had to act. But what should he do?

"If you doubt my word, tune into the air, you will see I speak truth!" Darien said sharply, seeing the uncertainty upon Christian's face.

With little hesitation, he allowed his breath to leave him and focused his attention on the blood that surrounded them. He smelled the various scents, the blood of all in the air, and then he smelled it—dread-filled, thick in its wrongness, and close, indeed.

He moved from the carriage, turning to offer Alexandria his hand, and as he watched her step out onto the street and stare around in bewilderment, Darien said, "We must move—these Creatures have surrounded my home."

He began to move through the crowd of affronted people.

Christian took a quick stride to match the dark Vampire's as he had spoken, gesturing for Alexandria to follow close behind. As they passed the coach, Christian saw that the driver had disappeared. Figuring Darien had given him a few sharp words, sending him bolting down the busy street, Christian returned his gaze to the Vampire's back, wondering, dazedly, just what was going on at Damion's manor. If it had anything at all to do with what had transpired at his own. Lore, biting his brother's servant, Alexandria's belief that Lore had come for her.

He blinked in the crowd, realizing with a start that Darien's back had disappeared.

His black eyes narrowed as he perused the downtrodden crowd, vaguely aware the soft hand grazed his cloaked shoulder. Turning at the touch, he eyed the confused gaze of Alexandria Stone, her long dark brown hair falling partly out of its sophisticated hold atop her head as another slight breeze blew past.

"My Lord," she said, removing her hand from his shoulder, "do you think it is Lore?"

"I don't know," he whispered, mind lost on where it was Darien could now be. He could not have disappeared...it was broad daylight, after all, and he would have had to remove his ring. But was the Vampire even wearing a ring? Now that he thought on it, Christian realized he had not witnessed a ring on any of the dark Vampire's exposed fingers. But how strange that would be...

"We must move," he said at last, having felt the intense glares of all who passed them within the crowded street. Their abandoned coach remained in the center of the road, obscuring traffic. And it was with a quick movement that he grabbed her wrist, ignoring the thundering pulsing of her vein as his hand clasped it tight.

He pressed forward, muttering quick apologies as he brushed past miserable humans, Alexandria close on his heels. He knew he could not let her out of his sight, especially with the Vampires of Scotland Yard that wanted he and his brother's head.

He had made it but several steps when he could see, over the elaborate hats of wandering women, the tall dark manor that stood clear against the blue sky, before it the sea of tall green leaves of high trees swaying violently in the wild breeze that was increasing with the passing minutes.

"We are almost there, Alexandria," he said over his shoulder, not bothering to spare a glance towards, what he was sure, was a most bewildered expression.

He had not made it more than several feet from the first stretch of trees, Alexandria cursing and breathing heavily behind him, before he smelled it clearly: Fresh wind, thundering hearts, blood thick with anger, freshly ground dirt. Lycans were indeed approaching, and fast.

With Alexandria clutching at her side beside him, his gaze traveled to the many humans that continued to walk from home to shop, completely oblivious to the danger that awaited them. But what could he do to warn them? Could he be expected to take on Lycans with his bare hands once again?

Grimacing at the memory of such a foolish action, for he had let his cold instinct take over then, he wondered just what Darien was doing now...what had happened to Lillith Crane...

But before his thoughts could travel any further, he heard the loud roar ascend through the treetops to fill the morning air, causing several humans along the street to still in their ventures.

"Christian," Alexandria breathed beside him, and he eyed her, her gaze transfixed upon the shrouded woods before them, the thudding of heavy paws along the earth ground growing louder as the minutes passed.

He found it remarkable that he cursed himself then, for what could he do, indeed? And where on Earth was Darien? Was he not moving to stop the beasts from reaching the city?

Just as he wondered what more he could do, two large beasts thundered through the last stretch of trees and Christian felt his blood spike to a boiling point. The Lycans clawed at nearby trees in order to still themselves from tearing up ground any further. Their long silver claws left deep marks in the trees' bark. Christian felt Alexandria shake at his side, and then she was behind him, her sobs treading the silent air.

But Christian knew it would not remain silent for long. As he stared upon them in sheer disbelief, he was very aware numerous humans behind him were doing the very same, and it would be a matter of time before they came to their senses and panic ensued.

Dread swirled in the sky and he found it odd he didn't feel the need to throw himself towards the snarling dogs.

Panicked screams filled the street behind him at last, and he felt the surprisingly strong grip of Alexandria upon his arm, but he could not turn to eye her fear, for in the trees just beside the Lycans appeared Darien, sword raised in his hand, trained on the Creatures.

Christian wondered why he did not strike them. Before he could utter a word, the screams and cries of the humans and animals behind them faded as they ran off in the opposite direction.

"Attack, Delacroix!" he yelled.

And one let out a loud roar in the dark Vampire's direction.

Christian stared. "You must be joking, Darien!" He wondered just what kept the beasts in place, indeed, when another voice sounded from behind him, causing him to turn in alarm:

"What *in Tremor's name is going on here?!*"

Marching up the barren street, their badges gleaming in the morning sun, were several despondent-looking Vampires. The closest of which—a blonde, blue-eyed Vampire—brandished a broadsword with a darkly gloved hand. Before he could get very near, however, one of the Lycans let out a menacing growl, and several snarls left all Vampires present.

The blonde Vampire ceased in his steps, now able to eye the Lycans hidden in-between the trees, and his blue eyes widened in horror. "*Lycans?*" he whispered, aghast, the sword falling several inches within his hand.

At his word the other officers stopped where they stood, all eyeing the trees before them in sheer bewilderment. One, a black-haired, gray-eyed Vampire turned his gaze towards Christian. "Is it you, Christian Delacroix, who keeps this Lycan from stepping forward?"

"I—"

"Darien Nicodemeus!" the first Vampire to have spoken said in surprise having seen the dark Vampire at last. "What in the name of the *Phoenixes of the Nest* is going on here?!"

"These are not Lycans," Darien Nicodemeus's voice said from within the trees, and Christian turned to eye him, as he left them and stepped onto cobblestoned road. At his presence, the officers let out whispers of displeasure.

"What the hell are they, then?" the blonde-haired officer asked. "Not Lycans... They look like Lycans to me!"

"They are Eleanor Black's Creatures," Darien said, and Christian wondered if he was just imagining the way the Vampire's black eyes appeared to be glowing.

"Caleb!" one officer said, and Christian turned to eye the officers again. Alexandria let out a strangled sob at his side. "We must put this situation under wraps. The longer Xavier is allowed to roam free, the more things like this shall take place! You have not forgotten that that very Vampire," and he pointed to Christian's chest, "is wanted for his brother's crime on the death of our constable and several humans?"

"I have not forgotten, Benedict!" Caleb yelled. "Yes, yes, this has all gotten out of hand! I shall end it here and now! You, Christian Delacroix, are to come with me to the Vampire City in London and you have broken the code of secrecy, indeed! And—" But he did not finish, for just then, his blue eyes happened upon the terrified woman who clutched at Christian's arm.

"What?" Caleb whispered, and his eyes narrowed upon her. "What are *you*?"

Christian stepped in front of her, sure to shield their curious gazes; it would not do for them to realize, indeed, that a mere human was roaming about with a Vampire most famous for killing them. *How am I to explain my way out of this one?*

Before he could begin to formulate a plan at all, another voice sounded from down the street, a voice Christian had hoped he would never hear again.

"That," the voice of Devon Strumer sounded through the morning air then, "is a woman who holds no blood."

All Vampires turned to eye the newcomer who walked idly up the barren street, stepping carelessly over abandoned umbrellas and trampled hats, his dark eyes placed on Christian, a look of sheer triumph upon his pale face as he neared.

Oh, for the love of God, Christian thought, his cold heart sinking even further in his chest. The Vampire would surely change sides from an annoying investigator to yet another Vampire that wanted to see his blood along the streets of London.

Devon drew level with the other officers, a simpering sneer could be seen along his face, and he spoke again. "This is the woman I told all of you about last night. Mister Delacroix would not give up her truth, but this, I believe, proves that she was with him last night—indeed, has been with him most nights.

"Eleanor Black was here in London, my Lords. It was this woman she was looking for. The woman who holds no blood."

"*What?*" Caleb repeated. "Eleanor Black was here, here in London?"

Devon nodded, not bothering to speak further. He kept his gaze upon Christian and Alexandria as though he'd conquered them both.

"But what does he mean she holds no blood?" Azer said curiously, stepping forward.

"Pay attention, Azer," Devon said, annoyed that he had to repeat himself. "That woman...her blood cannot be accessed while she is awake...but asleep, her blood finds its way to all Vampires' noses. You recall the beautiful smell we had to endure for weeks now?" And as they all nodded, Devon continued, "It was her."

Devon stepped forward, his gaze on Alexandria. Christian took a few steps back, pushing her backwards along the street, ever closer to the Lycans.

"Christian, no!" she screamed. The Creatures letting out strange growls.

Realizing what he had done, Christian stilled and turned to eye them. They had taken a step out of the trees, causing the ground to tremble.

"Kill them!" Devon Strumer said. "Kill them here and now and let us end this—take these lying Vampires to their just judgment!"

Christian whirled to eye Devon, who stared towards the waiting beasts, the look in his dark eyes one of murderous intent.

But he had not made it but inches from the Lycans before another Vampire appeared within the air just behind Devon and pulled him back by the dark cloak, causing the large paw that had moved to swipe at the Vampire to press through air.

One Lycan let out a loud roar. Christian stared at the newcomer in bewilderment. He landed on the street just before him and released Devon Strumer from his hold.

The Vampire had barely spared a glance to any of the others before he said, "What are all of you waiting for?! Take down the beasts!"

The Vampires behind him roused at the Vampire's voice, and Christian watched them sweep past he and Alexandria, their swords high in their hands, their eyes dark with bloodlust—

They did not make it very far before the Lycans surged forward, ripping the Vampires apart with alarming ease. Christian stared in horror, the Vampires' blood spilling through the air.

Eleanor's Creatures, seeming to gain some bravado, sauntered forward into the sun's light, their gazes on him. And he could barely whisper his confusion before Darien appeared just before him, sword raised in protection.

"Will you fight, Delacroix, or will you continue to stand there?" Darien said.

He could not move. Even as the stench of the beasts reached him, Alexandria clinging tight to his arm, he was overcome with a strange sensation: He felt as though he was less than able to raise a sword the way Darien did now to these Creatures, their black eyes narrowed, their snarls filling the air. Why did they not move forward?

"Christian!" Darien yelled, the Lycan nearest him charging forward.

And as Alexandria screamed in his ear, he felt the rough hand on his shoulder and turned.

The strange new Vampire was badly scarred all across his face, his green eyes serious as they glared upon him. "We must go," he said before Christian could ask him what he meant.

And as the wind began to pick up around them, Alexandria hurling questions into his ear, he saw the strange gleam in the scarred Vampire's eyes, heard the snarl of the Lycan, the swish of Darien's sword, and all was lost to him.

Chapter Eleven

A RETURN

Christian Delacroix felt the strange change in the air before he saw them, and surely enough, just seconds later appeared two figures out of nowhere. They landed roughly upon the old floorboards just before the fireplace, the fire sending dancing light to bounce along their apparently unconscious frames, giving him the thought that they were to rise at any moment.

"Aleister!" he said, the heavily scarred Vampire moving towards the two figures without hesitation. "Aleister, what is going on? Who are they?!" And he stepped from the bookshelf he'd remained by and moved for the dark blue armchair where Alexandria sat just across from Xavier. She looked fearful but tired all the same, and he realized what a strain this must have been for her—seeing a servant bleeding to death along courtyard grass, seeing three more Lycans in broad daylight...

They had turned in broad daylight, he thought, Aleister slapping the pale cheek of the man along the floor, forcing him to open his eyes with uncouth words of encouragement:

"Get up, Nathanial! Get up. We've no time! Up. *Now!* You've had too much time in there. Far too much time!"

Christian and Alexandria watched as the red-haired Vampire Aleister had called Nathanial opened his eyes at last and Alexandria gasped: The Vampire's irises were gold.

Nathanial blinked at Aleister, the woman along the floor began to stir weakly, though for all the attention anyone gave her, she might as well have been the dust along the shelves. "Nathanial," Aleister said, the Vampire grasping his scarred hand, pulling himself up to stand, "what happened in there?"

"He had been taken under," the Vampire named Nathanial whispered in a low, ragged voice. "He was gone—far too gone—we had to wait for just the right time to undo her hold."

"Taken under?" Christian whispered, eyes drifting to the unconscious Vampire in his chair. *Was that what happened to Xavier?*

When they had arrived in the quaint little village, Christian knew that something was wrong, indeed: several Enchanters were still outside their destroyed homes, waving their hands through the air, sending colorful ripples of light to ascend from them. And then the heavily scarred Vampire had uttered what sounded like "Dragons" with an offhand glance to the mountains in the distance, and that was when Christian had seen the massive head and shoulders of a very large man standing behind the highest mountain—a Giant. Whatever had happened, he'd thought then, it must have been disastrous. But when they'd entered the scarred Vampire's small dark home, all Christian could get out of him was that his name was Aleister and that Xavier Delacroix had been taken there because the Vampire he'd been tasked with was in danger.

Christian had barely begun to ask who this Vampire was before he'd reached the bookshelf and had felt the change of blood in the air, rendering his next questions a distant thought. But this, Aleister had never mentioned that Xavier had been taken under! What on Earth was going on?

"What happened, Vivery?" Aleister asked the disturbed Vampire. He seemed unable to look anyone in the eye.

"When we arrived," Nathanial started, "Xavier was already deep in his mind—"

"His mind?" Christian interjected. "What do you m—"

"Let him speak!" Aleister snarled. "Go on, Vivery. What happened?"

"Eleanor," Nathanial continued, "she molded his thoughts, accessed his mind and coerced him. There in that dream, Xavier as one of those Creatures... He was worse than her."

"In what way? What do you mean, exactly?" the scarred Vampire asked.

Nathanial spared Aleister a weak glance and Christian realized how strange this Vampire was at last: despite his eyes being a mysterious gold, Christian also saw that they seemed to be glowing slightly. The Vampire did not appear to be upset or exuding his charm. Indeed, he seemed shaken, almost destroyed.

The woman had moved to the stairs while the Vampires shared words and now sank wearily down onto the third step, a hand gracing a bleeding cut on her arm, dressing the sleeve of her red robes in her blood. Christian felt his thirst (which had been high since the morning) increase and it was all he could do to continue to listen to Nathanial's words.

"The dread...Eleanor's...power. Once it was within Xavier, he was untouchable. Every word he spoke, every movement—it changed me. I could feel myself being filled with that strange power the more he exercised his force."

"But this was a dream. It can't come to pass," Aleister said, casting a horrified glance to the woman on the stairs.

She closed her eyes in resignation.

"Dream though it was, it took all we had to pull him from Eleanor's hold, Aleister," she said, the low fire's light sending the shadows of the railing to dance across her sharp face.

"So he dreams of Eleanor Black?" Aleister asked. "Why?"

Nathanial said, "He mentioned that he dreamed of her before, felt her presence nearby while we resided in an inn for a night. It took convincing to get him to release the thought. I see that he hasn't."

They were silent while these words filled their minds, and then Aleister asked, "What happened for him to drop his guard in the dream?"

"Christian Delacroix—his brother—" Nathanial began before his gaze found Christian's at last. His eyes then slid in incomprehension towards Alexandria in her chair, and then he looked back up upon Aleister in disbelief. "What—why are they here?!"

"There was a mess in London. Being the founder of Division Six, I naturally moved as I should—Lycans snarling amongst city streets is more than call for absolute correction," Aleister said. "When there, I happened upon Christian and this woman, and I moved to bring them here."

"This is no coincidence," the woman said from the stairs, bringing all eyes back to her.

"What do you mean, Aurora?" Aleister asked.

Only Alexandria's quick breathing could be heard throughout the small room. Then the woman named Aurora rose from her seat on the stairs and faced them, slender hand placed bracingly upon the dark banister. "I mean, Aleister," she began, "that Christian's presence in London, that woman's presence just when you felt called to take care of Lycans—it is no coincidence. It coincides masterfully with what we have seen: Christian Delacroix has a part in all of this as well."

"I what?" Christian asked.

"In Xavier's mind," Nathanial began, staring at the Vampire, "all Dark Creatures seemed to be a part of Eleanor's—Xavier's—

army. You were the only one. You and that human were the only ones that remained, for the most part, untouched."

His mind drew a fierce blank as the words swept through the room, and even as all eyes turned upon him in severe interest, he knew his senses to leave him completely. "I can't be. Xavier, he would never... You mean to tell me I faced him?"

"You did, Vampire," Aurora said from the stairs.

"And you did so with sheer determination," Nathanial added.

Christian stared at them both in utter disbelief. "Why would I do that?"

Aurora and Nathanial shared a glance, and their eyes happened upon Alexandria, who looked bewildered in her chair.

"What does she have to do with this, Vampire?" Christian asked. If she were in his mind—whatever it was this Vampire and Enchanter saw—perhaps Xavier knew her purpose...why she held such strange power.

"That woman, she seems to be very important in this war against Eleanor. In Xavier's mind, he mentioned that their power could not touch her, that her blood could not be touched by those Creatures," Nathanial said, staring at her. "He said that she bears the blood of Dracula—that she was close to her Age and would die if not given the blood of a pure Vampire. And as the only pure Vampire left in that world, Christian, Xavier forced you to turn her."

Christian cast a bemused glance towards Alexandria in her chair just as she glanced towards him in clear confusion, stark apprehension. *Power revealed in a strange red light*, Christian thought, searching her eyes for any sign of this power, indeed. *The power to fend off Lycans? The power of Dracula? Was this, then, what caused Darien Nicodemeus to fall into hysterics when he learned of who it was I remained with? Was this the truth of the mystery that is Alexandria Stone at last?*

"In the dream," Alexandria whispered, staring upon Nathanial, "I'm a...a *Vampire?*"

"It's safe to say that you are one now, Alexandria," Aurora said.

"But how," she choked, the words getting caught in her throat; it seemed all the breath had been taken from her lungs. "How can that be?"

Nathanial cleared his throat. "You must have been born from a Vampire—Dracula, to be specific. It is known that when a Vampire has a child, he or she must be turned before they reach their Age."

"Age?" she repeated. "I don't understand."

"A Vampire—if created at a young age—will continue to grow. It seems the curse of immortality placed upon our kind does not take effect until one is at their peak age. This, Alexandria, we call a Vampire's Age. A Vampire is never stronger then when he is at his Age," Nathanial continued. "It can be any age, but we have come to understand it has generally taken effect after one has reached their early twenties."

It seemed she understood. She blinked and said, "Oh. Oh, yes, yes, I am twenty-two this winter."

"Then we have no time to waste at all the process can speed up at any moment—there is no telling when—"

"But this," Aleister said from his chair, staring at the golden-eyed Vampire, "is not your concern."

"What do you mean?" Nathanial asked.

Aleister spared a serious glance to Aurora, who returned it. "Nathanial, your concern is for Xavier Delacroix and the book, not this woman and Christian."

Nathanial glared at him. "You would have me ignore what both Aurora and I have seen? That woman is Dracula's relation, his blood! Is it not my job as the King's Adviser t-to take this into account?"

"And what will you do once you have taken this fact into account as you have said?" the scarred Vampire countered, his green eyes narrowing in the light of the fire. "Will you watch over the woman as well? Will you tell Xavier, when he awakens, that this woman is Dracula's relation—that she must be cared for and bitten—when he must focus his attention on *The Immortal's Guide?* Do you think the Vampire able, Nathanial, to pay attention to a woman when his plate is already so full?

"Would you think it fair for him to deal with a human—for she is no Vampire yet—and what will happen when others see her cavorting around the Dark World with him? They will grow suspicious, and threats against him will increase—there are already enough Creatures searching for the book, it would not be fair for attention to be drawn to the woman so soon—"

"But attention has already fallen upon her," Christian said without thought, causing all eyes to move to him.

"What?" Aleister asked.

He stared down at her, her eyes alive with remembrance: the night before, the confusion, the fear, the uncertainty pooled through them, and he realized, for the second time, that he *had* saved her life. But why? Exactly *why* did the thought of that damned Devon Strumer discovering her existence send him running back to her? He had thought he'd moved to protect he and his brother's secret, that he had moved to protect the one thing Dracula had requested be kept safe...but was that the truth?

Pulling himself from her eyes, the thoughts they stirred, he looked up towards the heavily scarred Vampire and told them what had transpired last night, that a Vampire from Scotland Yard contacted him to explain that the other officers did not believe Xavier to be innocent in the murder of the constable. That the Vampire had desired to know what it was he and Xavier were hiding.

"He then told me," he went on, "that he witnessed Eleanor Black and the constable speaking in an alleyway just across from *The Dragon's Cavern*. Eleanor was the one who killed the constable, but before she did, she'd asked the constable about a woman."

Aurora and Nathanial gasped, while Aleister glared at Christian in silence.

"This woman," Christian went on, "did not appear to hold blood...and Mister Strumer seemed adamant to knowing just who she was—I assured him no such woman existed, but she had fallen asleep and her blood filled the air.

"I returned home and she soon awoke. I tried to keep her preoccupied while I scanned the room, the rest of the house, for any sign of the Vampire...and then I felt him. I moved as I could," he said, never looking to Alexandria, aware he could feel her gaze burning a hole into his face. "I bid her silence, cast off the only light that remained, and focused all my attention on distracting the damned Vampire from seeing her in the dark—naturally, Vampires are able to see their prey, but I assume, because her blood is lost to us when she is awake, her ability to be seen as our prey is taken as well. It was only a matter of demanding the sorry Vampire out of my home."

"Eleanor knows?" Nathanial asked in horror.

"If that Vampire can be believed," Christian said, wondering just how it had come to this. He had agreed to watch the human but only because his damned brother thought he couldn't—and was he not able? Was he not able to take care of the human? But, he thought darkly, that was just when he thought Alexandria a human, nothing more. Now that he thought on it, he saw that all the signs had been there. She had always been something more.

Aurora rose from her seat on the stairs and placed a hand on the railing. "This is not good, Aleister. If what Christian has said is true, then Eleanor Black... Were her men scouring Cedar Village for the book or for Alexandria Stone?"

"I do not know," Aleister said. He was still staring at Christian as though he couldn't understand where the Vampire ended or began.

"What?" Nathanial asked, his golden eyes wide. "What do you mean her men were 'scouring?' *They were here?*"

144

"Yes," Aleister said. "They were here two days before, tearing up homes and asking questions, as I hear it."

"And you just happened to let this little detail slip your mind?!" Nathanial shouted, indignation furrowing his brow.

"We could do nothing, Nathanial," Aleister said.

The snarl was vicious as it left his lips. "What do you mean you could do nothing?" Nathanial roared, causing Alexandria to jump and clutch tight the arms of her chair.

"Keep your voice down, Nathanial," Aurora said, but he rounded on her and shouted, "Why? So you can lie to me more? Pretend you know nothing when you know far more than you are letting on? I will not be lied to again! Who are you?" He turned to Aleister again. "And *you*?!"

"We don't have time for this, Vampire!" Aleister shouted, rising from his chair, and a strong wind blew through the small room, sending the fire to temporarily blow out. "You have been placed a great burden, this I understand, perhaps more than anyone else in this room! But that woman," and he pointed a sharp fingernail at Alexandria, "is not your charge! Leave her to Christian—the Vampire has proven himself capable of taking care of her! This is not your task! Your task is Xavier Delacroix!"

"But—"

"Enough!" His green eyes darkened. "Nathanial Vivery, you will stand down! Xavier Delacroix is your charge—your task—leave Christian and Alexandria to us!"

Nathanial glared at the scarred Vampire. He looked murderous.

Christian felt Alexandria shift in her chair, but he did not turn his gaze to her, he could not afford to, not now when the Vampire mere feet from them looked so ready to kill.

"Is this Dracula's word, Aleister, or yours?" Nathanial whispered through bared fangs after a time of silence.

"What?" Aleister blinked, and he seemed taken aback by Nathanial's words: his face fell from a look of stark impatience to utter bewilderment.

"Dracula," Nathanial repeated, and he took a step forward. The fire still burned behind him, throwing his front into shadow: he looked truly sinister. "Is your word, your command, for me to leave Christian Delacroix and this woman, this Alexandria Stone to you our late former king's orders?"

"Don't be ridiculous, Nathanial," Aurora began. She stood behind the chair Aleister had removed himself from only moments before, "Aleister has not had contact with Dracula for several centuries now—"

"So it must be you then," Nathanial countered viciously, turning his glare to the Enchanter. "You must have been told by Dracula to watch Xavier's brother closely."

Christian stared in confusion, Aleister and Aurora sharing dark glances. It was not long before Aleister said, "Dracula never mentioned Christian Delacroix to myself or Aurora, Nathanial. His place in any of this is just as much a shock to us as it is you."

"Lies!" Nathanial spat, his eyes turning a dark crimson. Alexandria tensed in her chair. Christian did not bother to gaze down at her, but took an instinctive step towards the Vampire, placing himself before her chair, Xavier's unconscious frame just before him. He watched the red-eyed Vampire's stare: something was gravely wrong with it.

"Christian Delacroix has a greater part in this—and it is all Dracula's plan, I know it!" Nathanial continued. "Do not try to steer me off course. You protect the Vampire and that woman with your words! What plan does Dracula have for the Vampire, for the woman who bears his blood?!"

"There is no plan!" Aleister said. "And if there is, Nathanial, we were never told it! Whatever you saw inside Xavier's mind—"

Nathanial's stared at Aurora lifted a finger to point towards her, the accusatory tone in his voice clear as it pushed Aleister's to silence: "You! You were the one. You stopped me when I was to prepare the spell for Xavier when Christian had taken the woman's blood! Why did you still me *at that precise moment*? Why did you wait until after he had taken her blood, why did you wait until the other Creatures realized they had lost? What did you not want me to see, Aurora Borealis?"

Christian cast a bewildered glance towards the Enchanter. She looked horrified. What was going on? Was he to understand that he, Christian, had *taken her blood* in this vision? Ignoring the great pangs of curiosity to the taste of her blood that he had only successfully dispelled several moments ago, he turned his greater attention towards the difficult conversation ensuing.

"You are mistaken, Vampire," Aurora answered him, her dark eyes wide with some kind of haunted truth. "There is no secret I keep from you. I only stopped you then because it was not time—Xavier had to be farthest from Eleanor's hold in order for you to pull him out, and he was in that moment—"

"But why?!" Nathanial roared, his chest rising and falling sharply, the breaths that did not need to leave him doing so in great heaves.

Christian felt his own blood begin to boil with alarming heat. What the devil? There was no manner of enemy about. What was going on?

Nathanial shouted, "Why was he farthest from the hold at that precise moment? What did Christian Delacroix know in that dream? What did he gain by drinking Alexandria Stone's blood?"

Christian felt his blood surge then, he felt as though a beast were somewhere, just lurking outside the stone walls...

But that was impossible, he'd smell it wouldn't he? And so would Nathanial and Aleister, indeed. But as he gazed upon the troubled

Vampire, he realized that Nathanial had not noticed any difference in the air. He looked far too gone with matters beyond his head.

His red eyes were glowing, his chest continuing to heave, his breaths growing deeper, colder...

"Nathanial, stand down!" Aleister said, stepping around the wooden table to stand before him. Christian barely noticed he surpassed the Vampire's height by at least three inches when Aleister placed a scarred hand upon Nathanial's shoulder. "You are not in your right mind—you are troubled, over-extended. Any stay in a Vampire's mind, especially one so lost, would drive any respectable Vampire to troublesome thoughts—"

It happened before Christian could properly see it: Nathanial had grabbed Aleister's wrist and had flipped him over on to his back; the Vampire landed roughly on the floor at Nathanial's feet. Alexandria sprang up at that precise moment, the alarm driving her more than the fear she must have felt, Christian deduced with a quick stare towards her apprehensive person.

Aurora waved her hands through the air, sending a burst of white light straight towards Nathanial. He wasted no time in moving from his place before the light could reach him. He appeared behind Aurora in the next second, a hand stretching forward to grip tight the back of her neck.

"Nathanial, no!" Aleister's deep voice sounded. And then Aleister was on his feet, a blur of black and blue, behind Nathanial, a hand upon his shoulder, wasting no time in pulling the Vampire with terrible force. He barreled back into the long bookshelf against the wall, books flew from their shelves and landed all over the floor of the small room. The shelves cracked in two, causing even more books to fall, landing atop Nathanial's head.

Christian heard a strangled sob leave the woman at his side and he turned to watch her, his blood still surging, still boiling: the overwhelming smell of Lycan stench filled his nose. Everyone watched as Nathanial Vivery slid books off his shoulders and, glaring at Aleister, rose slowly to his feet. He had made it but three steps when a great howling wind pressed against the stone walls surrounding them, and all froze where they stood.

"A storm?" Aurora whispered, sharing a reluctant glance with Aleister.

The wind continued, growing stronger as the seconds passed. Christian felt his blood spike higher with his need to kill, yes, it was impossible to ignore the blood rushing through his veins.

He caught the terrified stare of Alexandria upon him, as though for guidance, a desire to know just what was going on and what he would do to protect her if it were anything terrible.

All at once his blood ceased its flow through his veins. His desire to kill, to drink, vanished, and his mind instantly cleared. He realized how dark the thoughts that had swirled within his head had been. How maddeningly quick they had pressed together within his mind. How subtly they had intruded upon his common sense, pushing him to join in on the madness that filled the small cottage, pushing him to kill the woman at his side—

"Nathanial, stay where you are," Aleister said, returning his stare to the Vampire that had begun to resume his advancement upon him once the wind calmed. He pressed a scarred hand against the air, gesturing to the Vampire that he was not to be messed with. "You are not in your right mind—you are being controlled."

"Madness," Nathanial said with a snarl, cracking a shoulder, "my mind is my own. I'm very well aware of the secrets you and that Enchanter have been keeping from me."

"We keep no secrets from you, Vampire!" Aleister said. "Pay attention to the air!"

No sooner did the words leave his lips than the fire went out in its grate, the wind increased drastically, pushing against the cottage as though it threatened to tear the walls from the ground, the startling howl it made ascending into a frightening roar.

Christian had no time to react to Alexandria's arm wrapping itself around his, her body pressed tight against him as she shook. He had no time to react to her heart beating fast in her chest, a rhythm he could feel plain against his arm, the fabric of the shirt he wore a poor buffer against her touch.

He had no time to react to any of this because within the seconds of her movement, the walls did indeed tear themselves from the floor, sending the bookshelf to topple over at last, the unoccupied armchairs around the small table to fall forward. The fierce wind now blew against their skin. The walls up and lifted into the air, the fireplace no more, the ceiling descending upon their heads—

Aurora waved her slender hands despite the rush of wind that made it impossible to see anything at all. From her fingertips, there appeared a blur of large silver hands. They pressed against the weak ceiling, pushing it upward through the dark sky and away from their heads.

Alexandria screamed as the wind continued to blow all around them and Christian tore his gaze from the fading ceiling above to eye the dark village.

It seemed no other home had been blown apart. The brazen wind was centered on their cottage alone. Vaguely thinking it was magic conjured by some manner of Creature, he heard the gasp from Nathanial Vivery near an overturned armchair and stared.

The Vampire's glowing red gaze was focused on something far in the distance past he, Christian. Something beyond the rushing river. Something beyond the mountains of Cedar, it seemed. Steeling himself for whatever he might see, he let a cold breath escape his lungs, ignored the sobs of fright from the woman who clung to his now numb appendage, and stared into the swirling dark sky.

He did not know why it had not occurred to him. They had only arrived at Cedar Village in the early afternoon, not enough time had passed at all for it to be so miserably dark so soon. No, this dark was unnatural, just as this wind. And past the rushing river, Christian laid eyes on bouts of fire rising into the dark air at the top of the many mountains' heads. The Dragons were at war, it seemed, but with what?

He squinted against the unnatural dark. The large head of the Giant remained where it had been when he'd eyed it for the first time earlier. Why did it not move to aid the Dragons in their battle?

And then small black dots appeared in the sky, and he figured them dismantled stars, for only the strangest of objects would be hovering in the sky like that...

Oh.

His already pounding dead heart increased in its thrashing, as he realized, with a terrible jolt, that those stars were in fact—"Elite Creatures!" Nathanial roared.

Christian glanced at the maddened Vampire who ran the length of the old floorboards, right past Alexandria, and ascended into the air before he could grace the grass.

"What is he—?" Alexandria breathed before turning to Christian in alarm. "You can *fly?!*"

"Yes," he said. "And so can they." He eyed the blur of cloak that was Nathanial's, the Vampire ascending further, flying to greet the line of Elite Creatures that had seen him approach and encircled him.

"Christian," Aleister said, "you must take the woman and leave! Nathanial may not be able to hold them all off on his own."

"And go where?" he retorted. "Those officers must be waiting at my home—I cannot return to it!"

"Then you must go elsewhere!"

Aurora stepped up from her place near the stairs. She stared at Christian and said, "Aleister is right—Nathanial cannot last long—I imagine he needs blood and his magic is waning...not to mention he has been influenced by her Creatures with ease."

Christian stared at her for a moment, bright flashes of light brightening the air, temporarily bringing her into better light. "Did you say magic? That Vampire...he can do magic?" He eyed Nathanial, who was dodging swords and bolts of light that were leaving the Elite Creatures' fingertips.

"He is indeed a most adept Enchanter," Aurora said, bringing Christian's gaze back to her. "But in his state of mind... Nevertheless, we must get you and Alexandria out of Cedar Village—it isn't safe."

"As we are *aware*, Enchanter, but where can we *go*?" he said again. The sounds of battle were drawing nearer to their location. "I need blood and I am in no state transport, let alone take another along for the ride!"

Aleister stared down at the book-ridden floor. He ran a hand over his mouth, and his brow furrowed in concentration the more he stared at the scattered books.

The sounds of battle continued on.

"What is he—" Alexandria began to ask before Aleister swooped down on a green book.

Aleister lifted the book from the floor and stared at them, holding it open in his hands. The Vampire's green eyes were glowing, and his scarred hands were trembling...no...it was the book. *The book* the Vampire held was trembling vigorously as though it would take flight at any moment.

Christian wondered what he would do with it when. Aleister began to speak in a low, foreign tongue Christian was certain he had never heard before, alive or dead.

Aleister's words never rose above a whisper. The sound of doors all around them opened against the dark sky, the sound of battle continued on.

Christian whirled in the night to eye the many Enchanters that were leaving their own cottages, pressing past the destroyed one with conviction, their eyes black, their hands splayed before them, prepared to attack. As they lifted into the sky, a strange pulse filled his dead heart.

He watched Alexandria, her eyes were stuck on the line of Enchanters that had flown into the air, shooting bolts of lightning from their fingertips towards stray Elite Creatures.

No, this feeling...it couldn't be her, Christian thought, turning back to Aleister. The Vampire was still muttering in a foreign tongue, still staring at him. And when the pulse was felt again some odd moments later, Christian said, "Aleister, what are you—"

But he felt his heart tug hard in his chest, and his knees crashed hard against the old floorboards. *The pain*...the absolute pain. It was unbearable—but why?

Christian's head turned to Xavier, still in his chair; it was as though someone had forced him to stare there. Xavier—*Xavier*...the King of the Dark World. Xavier, the older brother—ruler of them all. His very duty was overwhelming, impossible, the burden would have killed any lesser Creature, any lesser Vampire...

And he felt it all: the pain Xavier had felt when he had seen their parents on the ground, the absolute love, the joy, the happiness when first in the Order, when first getting to know the Vampire named Eleanor Black, the honor and privilege of being trained by Dracula, the task of carrying the title Lord of Vampires...

Even through Alexandria's repeated questions and the sound of thunderous battle all around them, Christian was aware that the Vampire near him moved a hand to the grip of the sword at his side. Though very fast the movement had been, Christian had seen it clearly.

"No," he whispered, feeling the burden Xavier carried at all times, the pressure. If he rose from that chair, if he opened his eyes, he would feel it all again...

The hand that gripped the handle of the sword tightened around it and Christian stared at a face similar to his own, the face so sharpened, so edged with great duty, and it took him a moment to realize that the green eyes were staring coldly back upon him.

"Oh my God," Christian heard Alexandria whisper at his side, and if he could speak, he would have whispered the very same, for Xavier Delacroix was awake, and he was staring upon them all in darkened confusion.

Yes, Christian realized as he stared, unable to move from his place along the floor, something was different about the Vampire, of that he was absolutely certain.

Chapter Twelve
THE SWORD'S SECOND CALL

Wind howled through the small village. The many screams that filled the thick dark air were only overshadowed by the swirling rush of energy that filled a particular Vampire's ears. Even as the Creatures wrapped in thick dark cloaks dove and dodged blades and spells within the night sky, the ones that remained on the ground took the forms of beasts to rip through the flesh of the delicate Fae that were attempting to take refuge within their most ill-equipped homes.

As a group of Lycans leapt over the rushing river and moved ground straight for the unguarded cottage, the woman waved her hands and a solid stone wall appeared before them, causing them all to barrel into it, sending them to whine and howl with pain.

"Aleister!" the woman said, turning her gaze to a strange Vampire at her side, a Vampire who had dropped a green book to the floor just seconds before. "What were you attempting to do?"

"I meant," this Vampire said in a low voice, his stare glued to the floor where the book had fallen, "I meant to place Christian and the woman where they would be safest."

"Why didn't it work?" a new voice sounded, and Xavier Delacroix stared in the direction of this voice, his eyes widening upon Alexandria Stone. *Alive?*

The heavily scarred Vampire named Aleister stared at her. "It did."

Xavier squeezed the hilt of the sword at his waist. He looked upon the alarmed face of his younger brother, who still remained upon his knees before him. "Brother," he said aloud, his voice just barely able to rise above a delicate whisper. His voice was hoarse, as though he'd been screaming. Yes, there was that grand sense of righteousness again. *Not all had been lost.*

Christian blinked and Xavier knew instantly that something was gravely different about the Vampire. No, there was no hatred or indignation on that face, but instead a look of disbelief, of understanding? *But what,* Xavier wondered, *could the Vampire possibly understand?*

"Xavier," Christian breathed, and Xavier watched him attempt to rise to his feet, the movements slow, jarred with pain. "What happened? How are you fe...?" But the voice trailed just as it began and Xavier wondered why the Vampire did not try to attack him, why Alexandria was not a bloodied, bruised mess at his own hands. For he had not heard a word of Christian's questions: a strange buzzing filled his ears, making it difficult to hear anything that was not his own blood rushing wildly through his own veins.

Xavier did not notice the furtive, fleeing steps Christian took, nor did he see his brow crease, his black eyes shine with clear concern. No, all he could hear and feel was his mind, so utterly filled with a strange buzzing sound.

"Christian, what is wrong?" Aurora asked.

His brother turned to the Enchanter, bewilderment lining his face. "What did that book do? What spell did that Vampire place upon me?"

"Christian?" the human whispered tentatively next. Even through the immense buzzing, Xavier could hear that sweet voice. He stared at her. How was she still alive? Why was she not bitten? Dead?

Christian whirled to face Aleister. "What was that spell? My heart...the pain...what did you do to me? To my brother?"

Aleister stared at him. "That was a spell to get you and the woman to safety—to the safest place in the Dark World."

"And?" Christian asked, Xavier able to see how tense his brother was as the wind howled mercilessly around them. "Why didn't it work? Why did my brother wake up, instead? Why...why did I feel—"

"It did work," the Vampire said.

"No it didn't—"

"It did work," Aleister said, "you are already in the safest place you can possibly be."

Xavier's brow furrowed. Now this was interesting. *Why the urgency to remove Christian and the woman from...from... Where were they?*

He removed his hand from the handle of the Ascalon at last and flexed his fingers, staring around at more than just the strange Creatures he was surrounded by. A dark sky, sounds of brilliant battle. Yes, *there* was Nathanial, he saw as he gazed up at the sky so filled with all manner of Elite Creature. He recognized the Vampire's red hair as he swiped and blasted the Elite Creatures with bursts of light from his fingertips. Vampires were never known to do magic—it was beneath them, as Dracula had said many a time. *Dracula.* Hadn't the Great Vampire lied about a lot of things? Hadn't Eleanor Black shown he, Xavier, that magic—and many other things—were the birthright of all Creatures?

Xavier felt lost, drifting in between a world of miraculous power and this one of grand confusion. He continued to stare at the Elite Creature that Nathanial was focusing his attention on. An Elite

Creature that held a sword with such abandon, such fatigue. Indeed, he looked exhausted, his swings incredibly ill-formed, reckless. And as the Elite Creature thrust forward with the sword narrowly missing Nathanial's head, Xavier realized he had seen that sword before.

He knew that sword, but the name could not reach him, not when his mind was so heavy with fading direct rule, drifting absolute command, mindless grief...

Christian said, "We are safest...*here*? How can that be pos—"

An incredibly loud roar split the air in two and all Creatures, Elite and not, stopped mid-speech or mid-swing and stared around at the dark sky. Xavier wasted no time in rising to his feet with the earth-shattering roar. His head spun, causing the flashes of light and fire that filled the sky and ground to blur. The roar echoed on in his mind, sending a reverberating thudding sound to mar the next words spoken:

"What in the name of—" Christian whispered nearby.

Xavier blinked. The roar reverberated in his ears, a current of energy still rushing to and fro within his skull. And all at once, he remembered what he was. What he needed. *Blood!* Oh, what he wouldn't do for a grand gallon of the liquid.

"*Worca!*" the scarred Vampire cried, jarring Xavier, sending his mind to spin even more with the voice. He blinked at the scarred Vampire and saw that he was staring in awe up at the massive shadow that now passed across the cottage. The shadow exuded a grand burst of wind as it flew over their heads.

Xavier recovered first and watched the large red Dragon sweep from the cottage. It let out a particularly large gout of fire into the dark sky, flying straight towards the line of Elite Creatures, Enchanters, and the single Vampire that now flew in every which direction hoping to avoid the burst of flame.

The Dragon swirled in mid-air looked around at the hovering Creatures, its large red eyes appearing bright with anger. "Why does it still?" Xavier wondered aloud, his voice sounding strange to his ears. Amidst the buzzing, amidst the pounding of his head, he knew something was wrong. It was in his voice: something had been taken from him. He was not as he was before.

He was aware of eyes upon him as he spoke, but he did not tear his gaze from the large Dragon until Christian said, "Xavier, when did you awaken?"

"Just seconds ago," he responded, mind running as to why his brother wasn't furious with him. He thought of when that voice was not so genial, but angry, roaring.

"Are you well?" Christian asked, staring at him with concern.

"Fine," he said lowly, moving a hand to the hilt of the sword— only, his hand would not move—indeed, his whole arm was limp. He let out a snarl of disgust. *Broken*? When in the bloody hell did this happen? "Why is my arm broken?"

The scarred Vampire stepped forward. "Nathanial Vivery escaped with you on the backs of Dragons. Your arm must have been broken in the attempt."

He glared. "Dragons?"

"Yes," the Enchanter said, bringing Xavier's gaze to her. Her sharp brown eyes were placed intently upon him, although she looked wary of his nature all the same. "Nathanial said he escaped from Eleanor's Elite Creatures and that you had been knocked unconscious, lost to her. Do you not remember any of this, Xavier?"

He was not able to decipher her words, for it was all meaningless: the buzzing in his mind would not die. And he could not have been lost to sleep...all that he had been shown could not have been a mere dream! No, it was too real, far too real. Her touch, her voice, Christian's anger, Alexandria's blood, the feeling of absolute power that had canvassed him as he stood beside her, the knowledge, the absolute knowledge... It had to be real!

Another large burst of fire lit up the sky. The large Dragon spread its wings and said, "You Creatures enter the village we have been sworn to protect! You have killed my own! What you search for is not here! Leave Cedar Village, *at once!*"

And with its loud, haunting words, an Elite Creature—the one with the sword, Xavier saw—threw back his head and laughed, sending the large hood to fall back on to his shoulders to reveal short, black windswept hair. "Indeed? You profess to know what it is we are here for, *you scale-ridden beast!*" And he flexed the sword menacingly in his grip as the Dragon letting a stream of thick black smoke drift from its nostrils.

"Worca," the scarred Vampire whispered. *"Don't you dare...not now...don't—"*

Xavier stared at Aleister. What made the strange Vampire so worried?

"Your energy is unnatural," the Dragon continued, sending more black smoke to drift into the already dark air. "You are not normal Dark Creatures! As sickening as the Vampires are, you are—"

"You know nothing of what we are!" the Creature with the sword yelled, and all at once, a swarm of thick black cloaks surrounded the large Dragon.

A burst of wind blew books up from their place on the floor. Before Xavier could register what was happening, Aleister was in the air, heading straight towards the crowd of Elite Creatures that were slashing and attacking the large Dragon, making it scream with tremendous pain.

A silver blade was thrown through the air and an Elite Creature fell out of the sky. Another blade followed and hit yet another Elite Creature, and another, and another, until only eight Elite Creatures remained. It seemed none had realized they now took on a fully grown Dragon with lesser numbers.

The closer Aleister got to the Dragon, the more the Elite Creatures slashed and attacked it. Then the Elite Creature with the sword sent its blade straight into the underbelly of the Dragon.

"No!" Aleister cried. He pulled a beautifully crafted sword from a place around his waist and aimed it straight at the back of the Elite Creature who had struck the Dragon.

Nathanial appeared in that instant, and even from where Xavier stood, he could see the Vampire looked strained: his eyes were no longer golden, but a murky black, and there was something more—the Vampire looked changed. He held out a hand to still the oncoming Creature and began to shout in utter anger, but Xavier could not catch a word of it.

"What is Nathanial doing?" Christian asked. "Why does he keep Aleister from finishing that Creature?"

"Because he is not himself," Aurora said. She was wringing her hands, her sharp, inquisitive face dressed with concern and another unknown emotion. It was as if she were deathly worried, and not for Nathanial's wellbeing. "We must get Aleister and Nathanial—and you, Xavier—out of here. It isn't safe...the air here is too thick... Eleanor's energy...it corrupts..."

Xavier said, "Who exactly are you, Enchanter? What do you mean her energy corrupts? Is that what happened to Nathanial?" And as he spoke, he took several steps towards her, but she stepped away, almost stumbling backwards over the strewn books and wood that littered the old floor.

"I am Aurora Borealis," she said, eyeing him as though he were to strike her at any moment, "and Nathanial, when we went into your mind, to bring you out of Eleanor's hold—"

"You went into my mind?" he asked in bewilderment. The memories suddenly returned with blinding clarity: Christian upon his knees before him, Eleanor Black and Darien Nicodemeus at either side of him, the woman in Christian's arms, the hole in her chest sending her blood to fill the air, Christian's desperation sending him to feed from the woman. Xavier's mind spun with the image of Christian's smile as he cut into his wrist with knowing, the red light that filled the air blinding him—and then Nathanial was there... But Nathanial had died several years before. Xavier knew that well, after all it was he that had done it.

"We had to, Xavier," Aurora continued. "You were taken under by Eleanor's energy...you were gone, inside a future so thick with her hold—"

A bloodcurdling scream cut through the air.

Alexandria stared in horror at the dark sky, and as Christian turned to where her gaze was held. Xavier followed suit and his brow furrowed: Aleister's sword was pressed deep into Nathanial's midsection. His blood left him in a small river and spilled across the sword's blade.

"*Aleister!*" Christian yelled.

Xavier blinked, hardly believing the scarred Vampire could strike Nathanial Vivery so easily. But why did he do it? What had the Vampire told him to cause him to strike him? Then Xavier recalled how he had seen the truth of Nathanial, how it had driven *him* to madness. Was Aleister so wrong, after all?

He turned his stare towards Aurora as Nathanial began to fall from the sky, Aleister's blade now long removed from his body. "What is the meaning of this?" he asked. "Why does the Vampire attack Nathanial?"

"Xavier, we are protecting you and your brother—Nathanial cannot be allowed to act in his condition."

"His condition?" he asked.

Another voice filled the dark air: "Alex—*Alexandria!*" Christian yelled, and Xavier stared just as the sweet scent graced his nose.

There in his brother's arms lay the human woman, unconscious, the smell of her blood filling the air just as it had done previously, and before anyone could ask why it had happened, another body fell out of the sky and hit the rough ground with a shattering crash,

Dracula's sword resting just inches from an outstretched hand atop the cold grass.

"Alexandria wake up! Get up!" Christian continued to yell over her body.

In a moment of clarity, a brilliant burst of euphoria, Xavier eyed the woman, limp and lifeless in Christian's arms, and he eyed the sword several feet from where they remained within the cabin. A number of Lycans prowled and prodded the hard ground around the destroyed cottage, unable to enter it. He eyed the sword again just as he gripped the Ascalon at his waist and felt the surge of power rise up his arm.

Dracula's sword. *Yes, Dracula's sword.* He knew nothing in that moment, he knew nothing of Eleanor, of pain, of grief, of anger, of hatred, he knew nothing, he didn't even know if this was where he truly was or if were all in his head, all he knew was that he needed that sword, the power it held, the power used to forge it.

Without another thought, he leapt over the mountain of books that surrounded them. He darted past a confused Lycan, jumped across the rushing river, and ran for the body that lay several feet ahead, the sword there in the grass.

Then he was surrounded, many Lycan eyes glaring at him in a harsh circle. The remaining Elite Creatures that held Vampire forms appeared on the ground, continuing the circle where the Lycans could not.

Damn, Xavier thought, staring up at the underbelly of the Dragon that remained glaring down upon them. Even the scarred Vampire glared down beside the Dragon, disbelief filling his green eyes.

In the distance Xavier could hear Christian still uttering pleas to the woman to rise, and then a new voice sounded from behind him: "*N-no...no...I cannot, I can't be the o-one. I can't be the one...*"

He whirled in wonder as the Elite Creature on the ground continued to whisper, eyes still closed, sword still inches from his grip. *"Please...please...choose me...choose me...I can be—I am the one you need...I am...I am..."*

A red light surrounded the Elite Creature, and then the Creature began to rise from the cold grass. His arms and legs hanging limply at his sides, and he continually whispered pleas to something only he could see.

Xavier eyed the many Creatures around him. They all shared the same hesitant, bewildered expressions and none seemed to know what to do.

"Alexandria! Miss Stone!" Christian screamed.

Just over a Lycan's large head, Xavier could see the human woman had been covered by a red light as well and began to hover several inches from the ground just as the Elite Creature did.

"Xavier Delacroix!" a new voice issued from over the mountaintop and Xavier whirled to stare at the newcomer along with all the others in the large field. The Dragon in the air let out a stream of angry fire as it eyed the new Creature and Aleister flexed the sword in his grip.

Xavier looked to this stranger, unable to see what face remained beneath the large hood. He flew towards the circle, ignoring all other Creatures as he landed, his boots not making a sound upon the grass. His wind died, the overwhelmingly thick scent of lilac and blood jarring him where he stood.

Eleanor. He could not smell it before, no matter how close to her he came. All he was able to sense was her crushing power, the dread that filled the air wherever they roamed together. But now...the scent of lilac and blood was undeniably fresh. This Creature had just been near her—had just left her. A surge of jealousy filled him: this Creature had just seen her. Why wasn't he, Xavier, near her? Why wasn't he, Xavier, at her side?

As the Lycans broke the circle to allow the new arrival to enter it, Xavier was able to see the thin, snake-like grin the Creature wore beneath the hood and he tensed.

"Why the long face, Xavier?" Aciel said with a voice as thin as his smile. "You look as though you've...seen a ghost." The snake-like grin widened.

And once again memories returned, but they were not memories of Eleanor so close, Christian so angry, and Alexandria bruised and bloodied. They were of a night, one much like this, where this very Creature had led him to a cave and had told him that a new breed of Creature had been created by Eleanor's hand. Yes, the memories were of a time when Eleanor had changed into a Vampire just before him, had kissed him—cursed him.

Xavier gripped the sword before pulling it from its sheath and, mind mostly cleared, he allowed his vision to turn red. For nothing was making sense. He had been so close to her, so immensely wrapped up in her energy, her touch. But in this world, it seemed the only reality was that Dracula was dead.

Dracula, the Vampire who had lied to him. Dracula, the Vampire who had waited far too late to show him what he was meant to do. Dracula...the one who had kept the ultimate power to himself, power only Eleanor had mastered. Power Eleanor had once shown him—information that was now leaving his mind, making this world once again one of confusion. For what was true? What was real? Who could be trusted? And why, he wondered, did this Elite Creature leave the only Creature with the power to affect the entire Dark World to come to him when so many of their kind were already here?

He flexed the Ascalon in his grip and glared at Aciel, knowing he could not allow himself to get distracted, not when he was about to fight. But no matter how much he tried to focus on the newcomer, the wide unnerving grin stretching wide across that unsettling face, he realized all he could focus on was the thick, damning scent of lilac and blood.

✳

Aciel continued to grin even as the strange new blood filled the air. But he could not worry about that, not when Amentias remained hovering in the air, this strange red light surrounding him. It was curious. And what the Creature whispered in anxiety...he sounded as though he were begging someone, but on the same turn trying to show his worth.

Hm, he thought, *how strange. Thomas had acted the very same... glowing with a peculiar light...whispering strange pleas.*

His dark eyes fell upon the sword that lay in the grass, the red light bathing it in its pressing glow. Thomas could not handle its immense power and neither could Amentias, it seemed. Here was his chance to show the stupid Creatures that he, the first of the Queen's Elite Creatures, was the rightful one to carry the sword. Yes, he would show them all, her especially, and he would do it by injuring the very Vampire who would not submit to her will.

He hopped across Amentias's hovering body and snatched up the sword, tossing it lightly into the air, marveling at the sheer ease with which it landed right back into his grip. Such a beautiful sword... How was it that the simple piece of metal could cause such reactions within the lesser of Eleanor's Creatures?

Smiling to himself, he tightened his grip on the sword's fine leather and stared at the maddened Vampire before him.

"Aciel," Xavier Delacroix said, blinking hard as though he could not keep his focus, "why are you here?"

"Why am I here?" he repeated, waving the sword to and fro through the air. "You are incredibly daft. You, Xavier. When those three idiots returned just hours ago, it was not without Her Majesty's wrath. They are very dead. The Dragon," his gaze traveled upward to the large beast in the air above their heads, "unfortunately survived, but when she learned we had sent our own to this...village, she hurried back as soon as she could. She was no match for our own Dragons. Better than Tyrinian Dragons, Bagabills. They understand power, unlike these 'protectors' Tyrinians 'need' to be.

"But I digress, Xavier. Her Majesty did not want me to follow these...lessers, but she worried that Amentias would fall to the same unfortunate situation that our dear Thomas Montague did."

"What's happened to Thomas?" Xavier asked.

Aciel frowned. "It seems I've said too much. Sorry, Xavier, you'll get no more from me—all we need is for you to follow me."

The Ascalon fell in Xavier's hand. "Follow you?"

He nodded. "The Queen wants you, Xavier, as she always has, for reasons I will never fully understand. You must follow me if you want all of this mindless killing and chasing to end. I assure you that the book is not here. We perused this village two days ago. I don't understand why Dracula would ever think of hiding a book *here*." He sighed. "I grow bored. I was ordered not to provoke you and however...enticing this prospect is, I shall obey the Queen's command—she wants you," he eyed Xavier's limp arm with interest, "alive, more or less. And if we do battle here, I do not think it would be fair to you, being without an arm and all."

"Aciel—" Xavier began before a heavily scarred Vampire landed right at his side within the circle, his own sword gleaming in the night.

"Xavier, don't you dare listen to this Creature," the strange Vampire said, holding a badly scarred hand out to still him from going further.

"Ahh," Aciel breathed, eyeing this new Vampire. How piercing those green eyes were. "And who is this? A long lost uncle?"

"I hardly know him," Xavier began.

"But you should heed my word all the same!" the Vampire said. "Nothing can be gained by giving in to Eleanor Black's hold.

Nathanial was lost to her and started speaking madness—and you are not all clear of her yourself!"

"Who the bloody hell are you to speak so freely?" Xavier asked.

"I am Aleister...my King," the Vampire said, "and you mustn't go with this Creature, you must come with Aurora and I—"

"And why should I do that?"

"Please, Xavier. There is little time to explain."

"G-go with them...Xa-Xavier," a weak voice filled Aciel's ears next and he eyed, as did the others, the wounded frame of the red-haired Vampire on the ground mere feet from where the Lycans stood on the other side of the circle.

"Nathanial?" Xavier breathed, the Ascalon apparently forgotten in hand. It pointed towards the ground, just as limp as his arm. "Nathanial, what are you talking about?"

"You n-need to go with them—d-don't leave with that, that Cr-Creature," Nathanial breathed, the blood from his stomach glistening in the strange air of the night.

"Listen to the Vampire," Aleister said, turning his stare back to the flustered Xavier. "My blade brought him back to his senses. He was overtaken after he came out of your mind," Aleister began, turning his stare to Aciel, "thanks to *her* horrid energy!"

"Touching," Aciel whispered. "The weakened Creatures help each other through moments of crises. Though why you would fight Her Majesty's command... Does it truly affect you all so?" He amused himself with thoughts of the Vampires being subjected to her hold... their minds swirling with powers they were not able to comprehend.

He opened his mouth to comment on this when Amentias opened his eyes and fell to the ground abruptly, the red light gone from his body. "Amentias?" Aciel said, moving to the Creature as he sat up, his Vampire form gone, forehead damp with sweat, black eyes alive with preoccupation. Aciel half-wondered if the Creature knew where he was at all. This was only furthered when Amentias opened his mouth and spoke:

"Wh-where is s-she? Wh-where? *Where*?!" He rose to his feet, ignoring Aciel's concern, and began to look around the large field. It was not until Aciel slapped him across the face that he seemed to come around. "Aciel, did you see her? Where is she? Where is the woman?!"

"Woman?" he repeated. "What are you talking about? There's no woman here—"

But Amentias had seen something Aciel had not and moved past him, past a bewildered Xavier and Aleister, through the line of Lycans, and towards the rushing river. It did not take Aciel long to realize what it was he moved for.

Within the destroyed cottage remained a woman apparently asleep in another Vampire's arms, a Vampire that looked like Xavier.

"Amentias, wait! What are you doing?!" Aciel called, Dracula's sword tight in his grip. It was just his luck: He'd be the one held responsible if Amentias was returned to Eleanor stark raving mad, whining about a human just as Thomas had done.

Yet Amentias did not still in his venture. The Vampire so like Xavier rose to his feet and lifted the woman along with him, and an Enchanter Aciel had not noticed before waved her hands. A brilliant burst of green light filled the night sky for several minutes, and when it died, Aciel realized they had disappeared along with it. All that remained was Amentias, standing in the worn cottage, his frame one of utter exhaustion.

"Where did she take my brother?" Xavier asked the scarred Vampire.

"To safety," he responded. "But we cannot worry about that now."

Aciel saw that he was right: they could not worry about where it was the Enchanter had taken the human, for Amentias had turned to eye them within the circle then, his eyes alive with crazed determination.

What on Earth was happening to all those who held the sword? Aciel thought, his eyes moving to Ares. *It seemed harmless. Was it really so terrible? What about it changed them? Would it do the same to me if I hold it more?*

A scream of violent frustration left Amentias and Aciel looked up from his thoughts in alarm:

The Creature was headed straight for Xavier Delacroix.

※

He scanned the trees ahead of him, the moonlight peeking through the branches overhead, and his heart dropped. Or what had been left of it dropped, at least.

He had managed to flee this place, had managed to find some clothes, had managed to gather some human food, had managed— with great patience—to *think* on what it was he would do to the woman once he'd had her.

For she had appeared to him once more. And her power only seemed to have grown stronger in the month that had passed since he had been led to her.

But what a simple word that fled from her lips. What a simple command that was impossible to disobey. He had been lost to the Dark World for the few weeks that Eleanor Black made herself known, but now he realized he could no longer hide, could no longer make himself small when the Dark World called for a leader who could make order, for it seemed the Great Vampire had actually died. He remembered feeling a great sense of remorse when he'd first overheard this rumor, for he'd wanted to be the one to kill the Great Vampire, but it appeared his own son had done it, and with the Vampire's own sword no less!

He had been proud, right until he had learned that Thomas had joined Eleanor Black, had become one of those new Creatures. Then the very part of his heart that had not died when Thomas had walked away from him that those weeks before fell and he knew he could never replace it.

So he hid. And forgot what he was. But he never *truly* forgot. He never could. For it was in him every time he assumed the form of Lycan. It was in him every time he killed (although the victims had been few and far between, he admitted). And it was in him even now, as he eyed the young men that had come to this manor, apparently smelling his blood thick on the air.

There was pride in him once more. For they had come for him, surely. They had smelled his scent so thick in this place that they had come to find him. *He had been missed!*

And yet, he realized, although he stood a few feet away, none of them turned to eye him, none of them bothered to realize that he, their Great King, stood only but a few feet away. What was the matter with them? The flare in his heart had nothing to do with pride. Rage rushed through him. *They will learn, again*, he thought, bringing his hands together, beginning to clap.

Human heads turned to watch him, and when realization flickered across those faces, many mouths let out gasps of shock, disbelief, and fear. But still, he smiled.

"Men," he said, and for the first time in a long time, he spoke with authority, "what brings you to this Vampire's hovel?"

One brave enough to speak stepped forward, although he shook from head to toe: he was completely naked.

"I-is it r-really y-you?!"

Lore laughed and it filled the sky. "Is Dracula not truly dead?" he answered. "Of course, it is me. Don't tell me you all thought *me* dead, gone the way of my most celebrated adversary?" The flicker of anger and something like loneliness filled him at their expressions.

He waved his hands at them. "Don't think of it, men. Tell me, what brings you to Delacroix Manor?" He eyed the mansion in front of him through the trees.

Several stared around as though looking for the answer in the barks of trees nearest them. Others gazed at Lore, keeping him in their sights as though if they were to look away or blink too slowly, he'd disappear.

"Th-the smell, your Grace," one finally stammered.

Joy flared through him once more. "The smell—my smell, surely?"

They all looked uncomfortable at these words. "N-no," the first one to speak stammered, "it is the smell of a new one, one we are aware you've taken as your new heir."

"I haven't taken any new heir—" But his words were cut sharply. The man...his blood...his flesh... He did not understand. He had bitten many humans before but none of them had ever been considered his "heir" before. "What the devil do you mean?"

"The man you've bitten here, your Grace," one said, waving a hand towards the courtyard of the large mansion. "He is a young man...formidable, surely. With powerful...*extraordinary* blood. We waited here for him to realize his place and then—" But another gave him a sharp look that pushed him into silence.

Lore's own brown eyes narrowed darkly. And just like that, it all came falling into miserable place. "And then you would follow *him?* He would be your new King?" he shouted in disbelief.

The shame on their faces was enough to give him his answer. How foolish a mistake he made, but he could not be blamed, of course—he had not known the human man he had bitten would come to possess interesting blood...pure blood...Ancient blood.

No, he would not go that far as to assume the man had special blood, but indeed the blood that hung thick in the air around the manor was not his own.

He had to restore dominance or else he would lose his kingdom before it had a chance to grow once more. Clearing his throat, he said, "That man, whoever he is, was an accident. Have you seen him since the attack? Surely, he would have smelled your numerous scents lingering outside this place."

"We've seen no sign of him, your Grace," one said feebly.

"Then why do you wait for a king who does not show?" He allowed his smile to settle. He placed his hands upon his chest. "*I* am here. *I* am ready to lead you, my proud men, my glorious pack. I have made mistakes in the past, this I shall admit, and there are those out there who would mix our blood with that of the blood-drinkers, the nightwalkers! This is a disgrace! Are we not pure? Are we not strong? If you will follow Lore once more, Lycans, he will give you all the power you shall ever need. And together, Eleanor Black shall fall to our feet! So turn away from this boy who does not even know his power and look towards me, your vigilant and capable king!"

And just like that, as the men fell to their knees before him, Lore regained his kingdom—and vowed to keep it.

Chapter Thirteen

THE GIANT'S RETURN

Lucien Caddenhall continued to stare at the raucous scene before him. He had crossed the mountains of Cedar some moments before, had jumped across the slain Dragons that littered the top and bottom of the main mountain, but he had not moved from the snow and ice covered ground. What remained along the field before him made him hesitant to step forward: the corpses of slain Elite Creatures littered the field. But this simple fact did not seem to bother Xavier or the scarred Vampire: both remained focused on their respective opponents.

Long ago, Cedar Village had been set ablaze an Enchanter's misfired spell. Now those Fae and Enchanters that had not died in the fire fought, with admirable strength, the remaining Lycan and Vampire Elite Creatures that had left Xavier alone at the other Elite Creature's barking demand.

Though this Creature could not get far before the heavily scarred Vampire had interfered, leaving Xavier to fight the beleaguered and weaponless Elite, bewildered and very cross, it seemed.

"Give you who?!" Xavier shouted, the sword coming down again, narrowly missing the Creature's shoulder by inches.

"The woman," the Creature responded. And Lucien found it interesting that he did not change back into a Vampire, for he had seen enough to know that this Creature could do just that. "Give me the woman that was with your brother! Where did they go?"

"You think I have the slightest idea?" Xavier said, landing upon the cold grass after dodging the wild punch the Creature had thrown. The scarred Vampire landed behind him, his own sword gleaming with small traces of blood along the tip. It seemed he had cut his enemy: The Elite Creature landed upon the grass as well, the sword in his hand pointing to the scarred Vampire's chest though it shook. There was blood along his chest where the Vampire's sword struck.

"Xavier," the scarred Vampire said, keeping his sharp gaze on the Elite Creature before him, "we must get you to safety."

"I can handle a few Elite Creatures," Xavier shouted.

"I am not doubting your ability!" the scarred Vampire said. "We just cannot linger—"

Without warning, the snow-covered ground began to tremble.

"Aleister," a loud voice issued through the sky, causing all eyes to glance upward at the hovering Dragon that remained in the air, "Aleister, the Giant—"

Lucien looked up at the incredibly tall Creature that covered him and the Dragons' corpses in its massive shadow. He became one with this shadow, hidden.

He watched the Giant lift a massive dark bare foot into the air and step over the highest mountain in Cedar, its large black eyes glaring straight at the Dragon in the air.

A burst of fire lit up the sky as the Dragon flew towards it, flapping her large wings vigorously, spreading her flames to canvas the dark sky. The Giant lifted a large hand and swiped at the fire angrily.

"Let me go, you bloody—" Xavier's voice came, and Lucien stared as Aleister whispered unintelligible words with a strong arm around Xavier's midsection. He and the bloody Vampire were gone in a blink, a burst of green light flashing where they had been.

"What?" Aciel cried, the Dragon continuing to fly around the Giant's head, angering it further: it roared and shook more snow from the mountains, covering the Dragons' corpses. Lucien had to focus his attention on where the sword remained, allowing himself to move on the night air in order to avoid the avalanche of heavy snow. He landed beside the bewildered Elite Creature who stood in the field of his own brothers' corpses.

Lucien remained undetected as Aciel stepped right past him and knelt at Amentias's side, Dracula's sword all but forgotten in a hand. "Amentias! Amentias, *for goodness sake!* Get up! Get up this instant!"

But the Creature did not stir, even as the Dragon's wind blew their tattered cloaks and hair against their bodies. Lucien turned his gaze towards the skies: The Dragon let out another burst of fire onto the Giant's bare arm. It didn't leave a mark. The Giant lifted that very arm and brought it forward with a punch just where the Dragon had been but seconds before. The Dragon swerved gracefully, stabbing its silver talons into the Giant's shoulders, the Giant letting out a miserable cry that shook the air even more, sending more snow to canvas the mountains.

"Goddamn it all," Aciel said, and Lucien watched as he stepped forward, lifting the unconscious Elite Creature over a shoulder, the sword of Dracula along the grass.

"You must find out who has it, Lucien. And do so quickly."

With a pale hand, Lucien stretched forward, still unseen by Aciel, and bent to grace the handle—

The Dragon let another burst of fire fill the sky, the sword let out a thick pulse of energy, one that pressed Lucien back into the Giant's shadow along the ground.

His hand on fire, Lucien pressed it to his chest, the burning pain not ceasing in the least. Confusion gripping his senses, he watched the Elite Creature called Aciel grab the sword. He took one last look towards the Giant, the Dragon that battled fiercely still, and the bodies of the others that littered the cold ground before he closed his eyes, and disappeared from the field in a brazen gust of wind.

Chapter Fourteen

GOOD GRIEF

Xavier Delacroix felt his feet hit a rough surface and he fell to his knees. The Ascalon slipped out of his grip, clanging loudly against the hard stone road which he saw was a mixture of various cobblestone.

He could barely gather his thoughts, remove the sight of the exhausted Elite Creature from his mind's eye, when a familiar voice reached his ears:

"Xavier?"

He released cold breath with that voice and looked up from the hard ground to stare upon the burned street he had left a day before, black smoke thickening the air high above, trailing from the remnants of badly burned buildings. There, near the high black gates that resembled the bones of humans, stood Christian, his stare of bewilderment clear.

"Brother," Xavier managed to gasp amidst the fading dread that had so filled him but moments before. It *was* fading, but his mind...he could not release the thoughts of her, nor could he remove the smell of lilac and blood that had lingered on Amentias from his nose. It remained there, taunting him, just as the sound of her voice did when he could allow himself the thought of it.

A hand was on his shoulder, pulling him to his feet. He stared at the heavily scarred face of Aleister: The Vampire's green eyes were dressed with anger. Xavier almost felt it was directed at him. But why would that be?

"You are an insanely difficult Vampire to fight alongside, Xavier Delacroix," Aleister said.

"Difficult?" he repeated in bemusement, the tiniest seed of anger beginning to flare in his dead heart. Did this Vampire truly expect him to remain calm and ordered when faced with Eleanor's Creatures? "Diffi—who in the bloody hell are you?"

The rough hand tightened around his shoulder. "I'm the Vampire that saved your hide, Xavier. If it weren't for me, you'd be—"

Xavier pushed the Vampire's scarred hand off his shoulder with his free hand and glared at him, daring him to continue to speak his mind. When he did not finish the thought, Xavier snarled. "I'd be *what?*" he snapped, anger flaring in his chest with the Vampire's implications. "Permanently dead at the hands of Aciel?"

Aleister removed his hand and his expression darkened more. "No," he answered. "On the contrary, you'd be with Eleanor Black— lost in the throes of her power."

He blinked, the words unable to form on his tongue. He stared at the strange Vampire in front of him, the black smoke thickening the air. Why did this Vampire look at him as though he knew the exact place his mind traveled when left to its own devices? How did he know to appear just beside him when surrounded by Elite Creatures, keep him at bay, keep him from paying anymore heed to what it was Aciel said?

"Xavier!" Christian said again, this time closer to where he stood in the middle of the barren street, and he peered around Aleister's shoulder to see that his younger brother was indeed heading towards them, Alexandria Stone draped across his arms, unconscious, her blood filling the smoky air.

Aleister bade him one knowing glare before marching past him, most likely to tend to the wounded Nathanial. Ignoring the chill of extreme unease the Vampire's glare gave him, Xavier turned his attention to Christian. Aurora had appeared and was heading towards them as well.

"Xavier, are you okay? What happened?" Christian asked as he neared, and it was here Xavier was able to see the hopelessness that filled his brother's eyes.

"I'm fine, brother," he said, staring at Alexandria's unconscious countenance. Her blood radiated from her like a beacon, calling all Dark Creatures to its location. Hell, he could barely stand it from where he stood.

How on *Earth* could Christian hold her and show such brilliant restraint? He was never known for it, this Xavier could not help but remember: It had been a cold night when the Vampire had consumed the blood of several people during one of their self-proclaimed "Blood Balls," and had not even stopped to ponder the result of such a foolish action. He'd left Xavier with an excess of forty or more people to "take care of" once their panicked screams and thundering hearts filled Delacroix Manor's halls.

"The woman," Xavier said, sheathing the Ascalon, "what has happened to her?"

Christian's black eyes found Alexandria's face, his expression giving way to great pain. Whatever for? "She fell under," Christian responded at last, finally meeting Xavier's eyes, "when that Elite Creature holding the other sword..." His voice trailed with sudden question and he said instead, "What happened to that Creature, brother?"

"I do not know," he said, reliving with vividness how the sword had been just feet from his grip, how he had been surrounded, and then Amentias had begun to hover in the air, had begun to glow with a bright red light.

"Aleister," Aurora said, stepping past him and Christian, moving for the scarred Vampire behind them. Xavier turned to see just what it was she was prepared to say to him. Xavier saw that Aleister was kneeling beside Nathanial, hands stretched over Nathanial's gaping wound, a low white light reaching from his palms to the Vampire's torso. Xavier studied Aleister's face carefully for any sign of alarm or perhaps lapse of judgment. No, the Vampire looked perfectly capable, and he looked as though he'd done this a million times.

But, Xavier thought, *Vampires couldn't use magic.*

"Aleister, we must move," Aurora said. She remained standing and did not bother to assist the Vampire. She kept her concentrated gaze fixed on the home made of bones.

Aleister's head flew up, the white light dying, his hands falling to his sides. He stood, eyeing Aurora with the utmost seriousness. "Is it trouble?"

"It reeks of Eleanor's Creatures here."

"We waste time," Christian said, the woman letting out more and more coughs in his arms. "What is our next plan of action?"

The smell of dread, so thick and full in Xavier's nose, would not disperse. He blinked, the coughs filling his ears, drawing him out of his mind and onto the smoke-filled street where three Dark Creatures looked at him in alarm. Apparently they had seen his momentary lapse into his mind. But what they did not know could not hurt them, he decided.

He stared at the heavily-scarred Vampire, wondering just who *he* was. The longer he stared, the more it was he saw that this Vampire seemed to hold a feeling of familiarity for him, a feeling of great belonging, one he had not ever experienced with such a magnitude before.

"How much longer will it take to heal him, Aleister?" Christian asked.

Xavier knew his younger brother was fed up with the way things had turned out. Hell, the smell of such enticing blood was thick on all their noses and there wasn't a drop in sight—it was enough to drive any reasonable Vampire mad. Which was why Xavier wasn't surprised when Christian let out an aggravated growl as Aleister responded with, "Several more minutes."

"I can take her off your hands, Christian," Xavier said. "You gather your meal for the night."

The relief that dressed Christian's face then was palpable. He wasted no time in placing the human on the ground at their feet, giving Xavier a grateful nod. He disappeared with a thick burst of black smoke, sending Alexandria and Aurora to cough in his wake.

Xavier stared down at the woman as she quieted, her blood filling his nose, and he envied his brother.

The Vampire was free to do as he pleased, and in truth, he only watched over the human because he wished to impress his big brother—he truly did not *have* to endure such a miserable task. Xavier knew that it had had to have taken all of Christian's restraint—whatever he'd possessed of it—to remain standing there any longer. Be it far enough that he had to actually hold the woman in his arms...

To be so close, yet unable to touch. To take.

Yes, Xavier sighed as he tore his gaze from Alexandria and stared down the barren street filled with the ash of Vampires gone, he knew his brother's desires all too well.

※

The doors opened against the orange glare of torches high along the walls, and over the rocky threshold stepped a miserable-looking Aciel. Over his shoulder remained an unconscious Amentias, but it was the sword held tightly in his cold hand that caused Eleanor to rise from the stone throne.

"What happened?" she asked, anticipation rising in her chest with the hopes that Xavier had been there. But the doors closed with abruptness, giving her her answer: he had slipped through her fingers again. But how? She had been most certain that the news he was there was foolproof, so where was he?

Aciel did not respond. He dropped Amentias at her feet and eyed the Vampire that remained beside her throne. The scowl was apparent but Eleanor would not allow the Creature to be distracted, not when she needed to know what had transpired in Cedar Village.

Aciel retained his Vampire form but the glimmer of anger, of outrage, even, was tangible within his crimson eyes. He removed dark strands of hair from his face and returned his gaze to her before he said anything at all.

"I'm, I'm not sure what happened, exactly, Ele—my Queen." His words lingered on in her ears as though poison: her heart sank and the breath flew from her lungs in a rush of disappointment. But soon, anger found its place within her heart and she allowed herself to breathe slow, steady breaths, keeping at bay the rush of blood that threatened to boil.

Regaining her seat, she clutched the hard arms of the throne, begging the next words that left his lips to be those of the most positive, reasonable outcomes. She could accept that Xavier had been taken by another Creature, that that red-haired blood bank could have flown to Xavier's rescue and pulled him out of harm's way for a second time, but she could *not* accept that it had been Xavier, himself, to have winded her Creatures so. For if he was awake, truly awake, then he *should be here!*

"Find the truth, Aciel," she said, glaring him straight in his red eyes. He looked uncomfortable. *This did not bode well for him.*

"M-my Queen," he began, "when they arrived at the village, they were almost swept up in battle. They fought the Tyrinian Dragons at the mountains, but Amentias left the others behind and flew on."

It appeared that these last words were meant to be something of importance to her, but what it was she could not know. It sounded, she decided after a time of silence, as though he was trying to make Amentias out to be one that left his brethren behind in the thick of battle. *How tasteless.*

Eleanor Black lifted a hand to grasp at the many necklaces that fell along her collarbone and sighed in exasperation. "So you are telling me, Aciel, that Amentias was doing his job and went ahead to land in Cedar Village in order, I assume, to better see the state of what had transpired there?"

"I...yes, I suppose that was why. But," he seemed to regain his conviction, "he did not get very far before that Nathanial Vivery showed up and fought him with strange desperation. And then, my Queen, a Dragon appeared—"

"*What* Dragon, Aciel?"

"Th-the heavily scarred Vampire kept calling it 'Worca.'"

"Heavily scarred Vampire?" she repeated, frowning. "Who is that?"

Aciel's jaw hardened. He seemed to be searching his mind for the answer. "I am not sure—I assumed him to be Xavier's relative, for upon closer inspection of the two side by side, they did look simi—"

She rose to her feet, rushing him to silence. She did not dare breathe as his words thundered in her mind. Before she was fully aware of it, the stark cold had returned and she started to crave the blood of the nearest living human.

"*Side by side?*" she spat. "What do you mean?!"

She was hardly aware he had taken a slight step away from her along the dirt ground, or that Amentias had let out an involuntary shiver at their feet. All she knew was that it had been confirmed: Xavier had been awake and he had not come to her. *Why on Earth would that be?*

"Y-yes, Eleanor," he said, "Amentias had fallen in battle—and the Ares," he lifted the sword in his grip so that the long silver blade gleamed in the light of the torches along the walls, "began to glow. That was when Xavier Delacroix ran from a cottage he and few others were taking shelter in and moved for the sword. It remained beside Amentias, in the grass, my Queen, but Xavier was no more than a few feet from it before the others cornered him, and I needed to do something. If he held the sword...

"I revealed my location, my Queen and—"

"And?" How had Xavier awoken? What had he seen while encumbered?

"I grabbed the sword, but I did nothing with it. I swear! He l-looked madly disoriented, I knew he'd just woken up...he had no clue as to what was transpiring!"

She stared at him, reserving judgment even as the flare of bewilderment rose in her dead heart. "Go on."

Aciel lowered the sword and stared down at Amentias's unconscious body on the floor. "Amentias awoke, raving about a woman. I had not been aware a woman was there, but he darted for the cottage where the other Vampires remained, and the more I stared, there she was—"

"She?" Eleanor repeated, darker questions lining her mind. *It couldn't be...*

"Y-yes. A woman apparently just as unconscious as Amentias had been. Held in the arms of who I believe to be Xavier's younger brother, Christian—"

Her rage slithered through in a fantastic snarl, silencing Aciel's next words. How had they gotten a hold of the woman before her? It was she who had been told of the woman by Dracula. So *how* had the woman ended up in the hands of Christian Delacroix?

"What did she look like, Aciel?" she asked.

He said, "I-I'm afraid I didn't get a good look at the woman—Amentias had just woken up in a fit, like I said, and darted for them. But before he could reach them, my Queen, the *Enchanter* waved her hands and they all disappeared—"

"What?" she snapped. It was far more fantastic than she dared imagine. At this rate she much preferred it if Nathanial had grabbed an unconscious Xavier before either of her Creatures could do damage to the Vampire. "An Enchanter was there as well?"

"Apparently, my Queen," he said, seemingly scared of causing anymore outbursts.

Allowing her breaths to break the surface of her complete indignation at another plan gone to hell, Eleanor Black set about gathering her thoughts.

So he had awoken from his sleep, had he? And he seemed disoriented. That was a good sign. But why had he not traveled back with Aciel and Amentias?

She asked the nervous Vampire this and was surprised when he said, "Amentias swung for the Vampire in human form, my Queen, would not heed my word to stand down. I had the sword but he would not listen to reason.

"I had thought it strange enough that while he was out, he kept talking to the air, as though he were bargaining with someone no one else could see. My fears for him only grew, however, when, while he struck Xavier, he appeared physically exhausted and stuck in human form. He said himself that he could not transform into a Vampire no matter how much he tried."

She could not speak, could not gather thought, for how was it possible that it had happened again? And why wasn't Aciel subject to this reaction to the sword? Knowing she had to figure out just what was going on with her Creatures, she carefully asked, "And Aciel, with your exposure to the Ares, you did not find anything...strange to befall you?"

He looked as though he'd been struck with something hard: his face twisted into incredulity. "Befall *me*...my Queen?" He raised the sword. "No, no, I'm—I feel more than fine."

"Truly, Aciel? There are no...visions? No...strange...beings coming to you, demanding things?"

"Absolutely not, no, my Queen," he answered, tearing his gaze from the sword to eye her. "I daresay I am not as...weak-willed as the others." He stared down at Amentias still in human form, very much gone from their talks of wills and strangeness.

She eyed the unconscious Creature as well before pulling her gaze back to Aciel. Weak-will. Willpower. Did those with weaker wills, weaker minds, fall prey easier to the sword and its pull than others?

Aciel's red eyes flashed a murky black, the sword dropped from his hand, hitting the ground near Amentias's head, and Aciel fell to his knees.

"Aciel?" she whispered, staring into the Creature's distant eyes. It was the very same look she had seen upon the face of Thomas...

"M-my Queen," Aciel breathed.

"Aciel...what is happening?"

He said nothing for a long time, only the flickering of the torches' flames cast a sound against the hollow walls, and Eleanor was sure he would never speak again, until he said, *"Sh-she is terrifying..."*

Terrifying? She had not heard Thomas describe the woman as terrifying, indeed, he could barely speak, he had been so rattled... So what was this?

"Aciel, can you hear me?" she asked.

He made no response, even as Javier stepped forward from beside the throne and whispered into the still air, "M-miss...what's happened to him?"

Her eyes widened with the voice, and she whirled to face him. The young Vampire, Dracula's next prodigy, his innocent blue eyes alive with confusion, bemusement. Why, she had forgotten that he had remained just near her this whole time, privy to their entire conversation. How troublesome. She had not told the Vampire much of who she truly was, what her men were, she had wanted to know more about him first...a quest that had proven most fruitless, for he was a Vampire of few words.

"Javier," she said, "would you please take your leave of us for the moment? I will send for you when Aciel here is...feeling better." She attempted a comforting smile.

He cast one last wary glance towards Aciel before he stepped forward and grasped her hand. He moved for the two large stone doors behind them, their hold releasing as he reached the aloof Vampire.

Eleanor watched as Aciel grabbed the arm of Javier's black robes, causing the Vampire to still and stare at him in utter alarm. "What—" he whispered before Aciel turned his head towards him, though it appeared he could not see him at all: his eyes were still distant and black, long gone from the large stone hall they remained in.

"*Give her what she wants,*" Aciel whispered in a harsh voice, "*give her what she needs—you are the only one who can—who must do it!*" And he released Javier with a loud gasp as though harmed by the touch.

She could not utter a word before Aciel lurched forward, seemingly pushed down to the floor by a heavy hand, his head hitting the stone ground. He gasped for cold breath, his eyes remaining black and unseeing as his head remained pressed to the ground, and the paleness of his skin began to disappear.

I don't believe it, she thought with shock as he began to lose his death-filled glow. His gasping decreased, and as he slowly found the strength to lift his head from the ground, she saw that his eyes were their usual dark brown, though watered as if he were ready to cry.

"Aciel!" she cried. "What, why do you shed tears? What did you see?"

He looked defeated and his eyes could not meet hers as he said in a whisper, "I...I am not sure—wh-what I saw..."

"No—do not do this to me, Aciel," she said, taking a solid step towards him, "tell me, what did you see? What happened?"

His eyes found hers at last, the seething anger within them startling. "I do not know what happened, Eleanor. I truly... I do not know."

Frustration roared in her mind. She recalled the terrified, bewildered gaze of Thomas after he had seen what he had, and now, Aciel held the same hateful gaze. What was worse, she was not sure if it were directed at her, but it was clear the sword was the root of this all.

Straightening, she stretched a hand towards Javier. "Leave us, Vampire. I shall call for you when it is time for you to feed." But Javier did not move from his place at Aciel's side. His blue eyes were glued to Aciel's face, as though he couldn't believe the Creature kneeled there. "Javier!" she snapped, and he blinked, eyeing her, before turning from them all and sweeping for the stone doors at last.

Once they were closed Eleanor found herself just inches from Aciel, staring him dead in his dark eyes. "What games do you mean to play with me, Aciel?" she whispered, pressing a slender finger against his cheek. His breathing slowed at her touch, the shiver that left him at the coldness of her skin. Yes, this was what was needed. Control.

"I p-play, I play no games," he whispered, eyes closing. "Eleanor, you must believe me."

"I believe nothing until I see it for myself," she said. "You know this better than anyone, Aciel."

"But, my Queen—"

She removed her finger and his eyes flew open. "Yes." She smiled at the longing gaze he held upon her. "That is what I've missed. You think I haven't noticed it, Aciel—you think I haven't noticed your waning faith, duty in me, in what I am doing?"

"You place others before me—"

"I place those where they need to be."

"But, Eleanor—I...I was your first," he whispered, aghast, "yet you hand the sword off to the likes of lesser Creatures."

She stared at him, the anger seeming to settle within his eyes. Yes, he was returning to the present, returning to her, to his rightful place. "I hand the sword," she whispered, "to no one." And as he stared at her, she rose to her feet and waved a hand through the air.

The stone doors opened and two Elite Creatures entered the hall, their tattered black cloaks sweeping the dirt covered ground. They stepped forward, stopping just behind Amentias and Aciel.

"Take them to the cells," she said. "Give them nothing until I say otherwise."

"Yes, my Queen," both Creatures said together, before bending to gather the unconscious Elite Creature at their feet.

She felt Aciel's eyes narrow at her in earnest, but she did not look to him, even as he said, "Wait, Eleanor, what...what are you—"

"Him too," she said to the Elite Creature who had lifted Amentias over his shoulder eying the back of Aciel's head in question. And she watched as the other Creature lifted him to his feet.

"Eleanor," he shouted desperately, the Elite Creature beginning to pull him back towards the door. "Eleanor, please! You can't lock me in a cell! I'm your first!"

She stared at him, the stone doors opening and the Creature carrying Amentias disappeared into the darkness of the long hallway, while the one that pulled a bewildered Aciel stopped just before the opening and looked back at her, the sword at her feet.

"My Queen," he said over Aciel's shouts.

She stared at the silver blade at her feet and felt, for the first time, a strange energy emanate from it. Indeed, it seemed to pulse from the very blade itself, as though warning her to never touch it.

Eyes flashing with curiosity, anger, she returned her gaze to the Elite Creature that successfully held back a struggling Aciel and said, "Return for it when you have placed Amentias and Aciel in their new homes. Bring something to hold it with—this particular sword cannot be touched by bare hands."

"Aye, my Queen," the Creature said, dragging Aciel farther out of the hall and into the darkness of the hallway.

She kept her gaze on Aciel's and saw in them great question, the one that screamed loudest being the simple, *Why?*

And she knew she could not tell him, not when he had been subjected to the strangeness of Dracula's objects. She did not truly believe him to be free, no matter how much of her sway she exuded over him, over the others. She could not treat this situation lightly— she had lost three of her best men to a *blade!* What did it do to them to cause them to act so strangely, so...ruthlessly towards her?

Thomas had attacked her, and Aciel...he had moved for Javier. And Amentias...hadn't he moved to attack Xavier with no weapon, with no secure form?

What was happening to her Creatures?

The doors closed with a sharp slam, leaving her aware of her thoughts, the feelings of strangeness they had spurred. Yes, Aciel's frantic words still echoed against the walls, in her mind, and there was a seal of truth that had been broken there. He, like Amentias and Thomas, were no longer hers. She could feel it in her blood.

They had been taken...swept away by the "terrifying" presence of someone...someone else... this woman. What woman?

She felt it before she could stop it: the sword gave one jolting pulse, sending her stepping back against the stone dais with little balance. She stared at the weapon, confused by it. What magic, what

191

curse did it hold to do this? To harm her men, to send them from her, to pulse—why did it pulse?

A flash of red light filled her vision, the many screams of Aciel now fading as he was dragged further from her along the dark hallway, and she kept her gaze on the sword to see what more it would do.

Harmless it remained, laying there atop the dirt, a simple sword, the red gem embedded in the guard of the hilt shining dimly in the orange light that filled the room.

How was it possible that a bloody sword could do so much damage? As she thought of the Vampire who had once owned it, she remembered something Aciel had said when captured by the sword's visions:

"...*give her what she needs—you are the only one who can...*"

"The only one who can," she repeated aloud, thoughtful as to who this could be. Was it possible Dracula had set it so only a certain soul could hold the sword? Who was that soul? Could it, indeed, be Xavier?

She stared at the red gem again, a feeling of stronger conviction filling her. If it was...if it was Xavier...did the sword not have the potential to lead him to her? Was that why he was disoriented upon waking from his sleep?

Anticipation flared within her dead heart and her eyes flashed with excitement. The sword, the woman, the book—there was a connection there, yes, she was sure of it.

She disappeared from the large stone hall, only just missing the second pulse of energy that left the sword along with a blinding red light.

※

The knock on the door beckoned Victor's attention and he very much welcomed it: He'd been lost in the greater, deeper, darker parts of his mind, and was close to going for a walk in the sun sans ring.

"Do come in," he called without looking up the papers atop the black desk. Upon looking closer now, he realized they were Forms of Notice from two members of Division Six: a Whildon Strell and Octavius Reign. He sat up higher in his seat as the door opened. In walked the two Vampires that had seldom left his side since he'd been named Temporary King, their presence one he could not fail in despising. All they did when they saw him was impart horrible news about things he was no closer to handling. The Dark World was falling, and fast at that, and if Victor Vonderheide had anything to say about it, it had already hit rock bottom days, perhaps years ago. Everything else was neither here nor there.

Steeling himself for whatever news he would hear today, he did his best to focus on the papers before him, reading seriously for the first time that a Lycan had been present on Delacroix Manor property. Christian Delacroix had apparently saved a servant by the name of James Addison, but could not stop the Lycan from taking off a chunk of the man's leg. The Bite of New Life was to be administered but, it seemed, a call to Trollen Square for the Division Officers kept the procedure from taking place. Damion Nicodemeus appeared and it was this Vampire they had decided to place their trust in to see the situation through.

What a quandary, Victor thought, staring at the words scribbled so closely together atop the thin paper.

"Your Grace," the voice of Westley Rivers sounded over his head, bringing him from the paper to eye the dark-skinned Vampire.

The papers slid out of his hands. "What is it, Goldchair?" he asked the Vampire, Craven Winger stepping further into the room, closing the door behind him.

"Cedar Village, my Lord," Westley said.

"What about Cedar Village?" he asked, eyeing Craven's solemn face. A rush of anticipation braced him for whatever he may hear next.

Westley looked as though he did not desire to speak further, and it was Craven who said, "Cedar Village is destroyed, my king."

Victor stared. "Come again?"

"Cedar Village...it has been completely obliterated. The Enchanters and Fae who resided there are almost all dead, if not barely surviving in surrounding areas. All of the Dragons have been killed except for one—but she is barely holding on for all the good it's done her," Westley said. "And there's a Giant, Victor."

"A Giant?" Shock pooled through him. *What on Earth would a Giant be doing in such a remote place?*

"It's dead now, miraculously, but it seems it and the surviving Dragon were the last remaining Dark Creatures that remained alive enough to continue fighting," Westley continued.

"But why?" Victor breathed, not understanding it at all. "Why would they fight? What would put Cedar Village in such ruin?"

Both Vampires shared dark glances, and then Craven stepped forward, his expression somber. "It was Eleanor's Creatures, my Lord. When our men arrived on the scene, the peculiar energy her Creatures leave behind—it was everywhere. We also found the bodies of dead Lycans and few Vampires."

"Bodies?" Victor said. The word being the only thing he could cling to. "How can there be bodies?"

"It appears...when struck with magic as they must have been last night, your Grace, they do not resolve to ash—they die. The body, for whatever reason, remains."

"Last night? This happened last night? Why was I not told?"

"We ourselves have only just received word back from the soldiers we sent to check out the area, my Lord," Westley said. "When the Fae arrived here at the City...we thought it best to check out her story rather than rush to tell you—you've pressing matters to attend to, even without a Fae journeying to a Vampire's haven speaking of strange Creatures, Dragons..."

He glared. "Regardless of what it is I must attend to, Goldchair, news of this magnitude must be brought to my attention as it comes. Do I make myself clear?"

The Vampire bowed his dark head. "Perfectly, your Grace."

"Good," he said, eyeing both Vampires. "What would cause her Creatures to destroy the village like they did?"

"Well, my Lord," Craven Winger said carefully, "we have gathered that Xavier Delacroix must have been there. If Eleanor Black's Creatures were present, there is nothing else they would have desired more—"

"*The Immortal's Guide*," Victor said.

Westley shifted his footing. "You're saying her Creatures were there looking for that book?"

"It's the more logical choice, isn't it?" Victor said, moving to stand most near the door. The lit torch blazed brightly, casting its light against him, the desk, and the small number of surroundings most nearby. "We have no idea where Xavier is—"

"Last we knew, he was in London with that Vivery Vampire," Craven offered.

"Yes," Victor sighed. "That is the word we last received. But we have heard nothing of him since then."

"And now we have news of Cedar Village being burned to the ground," Westley said. "Forgive me for speaking out of turn, my Lord, but I don't think her Creatures would be burning down villages for a mere book. What if they burned down the book as well? It's far too reckless. The magnitude of ruin there—they must have been trying to coerce Xavier out of hiding—"

"Enough!" Victor snarled, his thoughts running to Xavier, if it were at all possible that he had remained there. "I will have none of this! Xavier Delacroix is gone! Missing! We do not know where he is and we can't possibly know unless he saunters forward himself. As he will not do that anytime soon, Mister Rivers, I think it is safe to say that her Creatures could not have possibly located him! And before *us* for that very matter!"

Silence fell over the room.

Westley said, "We sent our best soldiers to the task, Victor. But it is clear the Vampire does not want to be found."

"Regardless of what the bloody Vampire *wants*, it is your duty to locate him!" Victor shouted. "The Vampire left his bloody duty—his bloody post—and I'm the one... I'm the one that must look after all of this!" He waved a hand towards the three high arching windows that showed the rest of the Vampire City. "I can't do this, Westley, Craven," he whispered. "I can't bloody well do this! I am not the rightful king. The damned fire won't light no matter how many times I will it. Dracula shared none of his secrets with *me!* He told me *nothing*, nothing of what he *did!*

"The one Vampire who knows for sure is out there—out there fighting—doing something about the state of the Dark World, not just sitting behind a miserable desk! So don't you tell me, you damned puppets, that a village was burned to the ground because of him! I can't do any goddamned thing about it! I hold no honest power here!"

Westley stepped up to the desk and placed a dark-skinned hand atop it, fingers splayed as he met Victor's eyes. "We need to be seen doing something! Forgive us if we were left with no clear instruction on what it is we should do when faced with a threat the size of Eleanor Black's Creatures. But we are obeying Dracula's orders on the matter! At the time of his death, his most trusted Vampire was to be placed as king—*yes*, Victor, that is you. As far as I am concerned, that Vampire is you!"

Victor said, "But Xavier... Xavier was the one given the knowledge—given the bloody right to be *king!*" He waved a quick hand towards the unlit fireplace just before him. "The proof is in that damned grate! I will never—never for as long as I roam these halls—sit behind the desk of my creator and know what it is to see the fire spark to life! I'm a bloody placement piece. Don't you dare tell me otherwise, Winger." Victor snarled, for Craven had opened his mouth to speak, "I know what I am—what I've always been to that damned Vampire." He found his words to fall from his tongue. The truth, that he was in fact once a human man the great Dracula had all but shed his pity upon those many years before, could never, ever be uttered aloud: to do so would shatter the illusion of inner knowledge that he was *supposed* to have about the Vampire, having been his first turned.

An illusion that would all but fall with time, he thought, neither Chair saying another word.

He felt their questioning, shocked gazes upon him, but he did not turn to face them. To see in them what was mirrored in his own dead heart...he could not face it. Not now, when the truth was so fresh in his mind, so heavily squared within his chest.

The door opened then and in stepped a tall Vampire, glaring green eyes bright with unreadable coldness. He glanced from Vampire to Vampire, his long black hair sweeping out behind him, even though it was held high in a neat ponytail. Around his shoulders, he wore his familiar red traveling cloak, and Victor knew it was only fashioned in the best of fabrics for the King of Winfield.

Victor stepped behind his desk as Joseph Gail lifted a hand towards both Chairs, acknowledging their presence. They nodded curtly.

Westley said, "Your Graces...we shall take our leave. I am sure you have much to discuss. It is just my sincere hope, King Vonderheide, that you take my previous words into careful consideration."

Victor stared at the dark Vampire and almost laughed. *Such carefully spoken words.* He sighed, waving his response and bade them leave from his room. Westley and Craven nodded in subservience, and moved for the door as one, bowing low as they passed Joseph Gail.

It wasn't until the door closed that anyone said anything at all, and it was Mister Gail to do so: "I am sorry to intrude, as it seems I have done...your Grace."

"Think nothing of it, Mister Gail," Victor responded, low. *I am no king*.

Joseph Gail stepped forward. His stare intense, so much so Victor almost thought the Vampire to wish him harm. But why come all the way from Winfield, Middle Country, just to harm him? He'd done nothing, truly, in way of insult to the Vampire, he had never ridiculed him, never forced him away, so what then was *this* stare?

"I am here," Joseph's deep voice said, "to seek your...infinite wisdom on a matter most troubling, your Grace."

"Well, Mister Gail, I am all ears."

Gail turned to stare at Victor, a pale hand still placed atop the back of the chair, and his eyes widened with apparent question. "What, pray tell...do you feel having taken your predecessor's place?"

"Excuse me?" Victor said.

"I do not like repeating myself when the question has been spoken clearly, my Lord."

He stood straight and gave the Vampire a more serious stare, all lingering thought of Xavier Delacroix, Westley Rivers, and Dracula dissipating at once. "I felt like any other Vampire would feel, I imagine, Mister Gail. There's the sudden grief, the thrust of foreign responsibility now on your shoulders—"

"But the responsibility you must face...it is not all foreign, surely?"

"I beg your pardon?"

"You were Dracula's second in command...his right hand...and his left if I'm not mistaken...your Grace. I find it hard to believe that all of his responsibilities are not readily known to you. For why else would you be thrust, as you say, to the place of king?"

"I am no king. Xavier is the real king—"

"And yet...he is not here."

"Well...yes," Victor whispered. "He is not here. But he was given...a task by the former King...."

"A task, my Lord?"

"He is to locate a book. I'm sure you've heard of it by now. All have."

"*The Immortal's Guide*," Joseph said. "Yes, of course. But, you do not find this odd? Xavier Delacroix being given such a strange task when you were by Dracula's side for all these years? Surely it must have crossed your mind that Dracula meant for you to have that task."

"What?" he snapped.

Joseph Gail removed his hand from the chair and turned. "What are the odds, my Lord, that Xavier lied to you—lied to all of the Dark World—in saying that he had been chosen as king? I mean...it is not as though anyone present at the Council of Creatures Meeting actually knew what was said. Didn't most die? And Xavier...he could be off cavorting about the Dark World, laughing behind your back as he searches for his ticket into Dracula's mind." He turned from Victor as though wishing to examine the rest of the room. "But, of course, you being who you are, Victor Varick Vonderheide, you already *know* the inner workings of everyone's favorite Vampire."

The silence that lingered could not dispel Victor's anger. Xavier had taken his, Victor's, rightful place, had lied to him about what remained in that letter, had tricked him all into believing that he, Xavier, was the one Dracula had chosen as King.

But the stare Xavier Delacroix had bid him when he'd returned from the Meeting...there was something different about it, indeed. But could it not be that Victor had been imagining the change? The need to kneel then was not as overwhelming as it was when Dracula was still living... Was that not because that Vampire had been the one who had given he, Victor, immortality?

Not knowing what more to think, Victor said, "What I know of Dracula... Xavier Delacroix knows no more." He turned, and Victor was surprised to see a smile upon the Vampire's face.

Gail said, "But how can you be sure of that when the Vampire is out and about and you remain behind four walls?"

"I am just sure of it." Annoyance grew. "Why did you journey all the way to the Vampire City, Mister Gail? It's a journey no sane Vampire would make. You did not come all this way just to question me about our former king?"

"I came, Mister Vonderheide, to seek your counsel on a matter most troubling...a matter that directly involves you."

"I'm listening."

"Pardon me for saying so, but it would seem your position here is not to your liking. I have ears, Mister Vonderheide—I heard what you said to your man just before I so rudely entered. Is that how you truly feel? That you are not king?"

Regretting his words so loudly and rashly spoken, he closed his eyes. "I was speaking out of anger. The Chairs brought news that I did not favor—"

"You lie," Joseph said. "You just admitted it to me, Victor. It is in your stare, your stature—why, you've shed *tears* on the matter, haven't you?"

The air in the room seemed to crawl, and there was the sudden scent of derision so strong, Victor swore he could taste it on his tongue. It caused him to take a cautionary step away from the Vampire, and despite the desk that stood strong and resilient in-between them, Victor felt as though it would not be enough to stop the Vampire from doing serious harm to him if he so desired.

"Why are you here, Gail?" he whispered.

"I'm here, *Victor*," and the name resembled sharp knives slicing against each other, "for you."

"Wh-why me?" he asked, eyes widening, a single tear falling from an eye.

"You hold something interesting. And this thing you hold, Victor, is the exact thing we need."

He felt tears rise to his eyes, shame filling his chest, forcing him to cease breathing, for to continue do so would only drive him into further madness. He looked into the Vampire's green eyes, for he had a strong inkling that this sudden change in the air came from him. He was surprised to find the Vampire's eyes were a swirling black, and the smile had placed itself upon those lips.

"What is this thing I hold, that y-you could possibly want, Vampire?" Victor made himself ask. *How did the Vampire get in? How did I not sense him? Who is this Creature? And what does he want from me?*

Joseph Gail exhaled a cold breath and his eyes flashed a clear green once again. "Weren't you paying attention, Mister Vonderheide?" He extended a hand towards Victor as though showing him something he held on his own person. "Your sorrow, your indecision. You're standing in for a Vampire that, for all is known, could be mocking you at every turn. Why deal with that, Victor? It must be an extravagant weight on one's shoulders."

More tears fell, but he hardly raised a hand to wipe them from his face. The Vampire's words created even more questions, those he felt ashamed to admit.

"Someone," he said slowly after a time, thoughts of Westley's words forcing their way through his mind, "someone must be here when the Dark World is being tossed asunder by Eleanor Black's—"

"You shall not speak her name!"

Victor stared at him, the Vampire's wide eyes, bared fangs, and menacing scowl. He realized at last what this Creature actually was.

He stepped away from the desk and further away from Joseph

Gail, he found his tongue moving on its own: "You're *her* Creature? But how can you be?"

Joseph said nothing as he stared upon him, and it seemed to Victor that Joseph was bemused for a brief moment in time. But then his eyes resumed their unreadable glare and the Vampire straightened as though nothing had transpired at all.

"We see your indecision, your grief...your guilt, Victor," he said, his voice once more deep and controlled. "We see it and we welcome it." He stepped up to the desk, placed a hand atop the dark wood and said, "There is no place in this world for two kings."

And before Victor could think of a thing to say, the air in the room began to thicken until it was all he could feel, and Joseph Gail disappeared in a gust of wind that took the torchlight with it.

✳

Eleanor stared up at the massive manor atop the hill, the dark of the night beginning to give way to dim light. It was with a quick sigh that she started up the hill, moving to reach the large white gates of Montague Manor.

Once there, she pressed a hand to the white bars and they slid open. She maneuvered around the large fountain that split the path up to the large, beautifully crafted doors. Yes, Thomas Montague had done well for himself, whereas his father...well, that was another story entirely, but she needn't worry about him. She had his son. The Lycan Kingdom was as good as destroyed.

With this thought in mind, she climbed the steps and lifted a hand to slam the knocker against its post. One of the doors opened and there he stood, staring upon her blearily: it was clear he'd been crying. The stubble that had formed on his jaw was dark brown; he had not bothered to shave in days.

"Eleanor," he said, his voice cracked with obvious lack of use.

"Thomas," she said. He looked absolutely crushed. Was this the prolonged effect of the sword?

He blinked and seemed to realize they stood on his steps, and with the gentlemanly grace he had learned amongst the humans, he stepped aside and allowed her enter into his foyer. Here she held up her nose at his stench—apparently he had not bothered to bathe in days, either.

"Thomas," she said, again turning to face him within the large, darkly fashioned hall, "some strange things have been happening to the others."

He closed the door and resumed watching her with that misty-eyed, forlorn expression she had come to recognize as grief. Perhaps he mourned his wife, but what was the point of that? It had been *weeks* since she died. And he, Thomas, had her, Eleanor, did he not? So why did he cry for a Creature that no longer lived? But she knew the answer before she'd asked herself the question. He, like Aciel, and most likely Amentias, had all fallen prey to the damned sword and its strange charms.

"Strange things?" he asked in his low voice.

"Yes, strange," she breathed, allowing her Vampire form to dissipate at last. "I'd sent Aciel and Amentias to Cedar Village—"

"I know," he said, bitterness stretched throughout his words, "I was there."

She raised an eyebrow, demanding his silence, and his mouth formed a thin line. She continued, "And they returned to me... Amentias was out, but Aciel could still walk and talk. Apparently, Xavier was at the village, but there was someone else there that interests me even more as of the moment."

"Who?"

"Apparently they had been traveling with a human woman. Aciel could not tell me anymore, only that she had been in the arms of Christian Delacroix before an Enchanter took them both somewhere."

His puffy eyes widened. "What? That Vampire has her?"

"Yes," she said, searching his anxious gaze. He seemed incredibly troubled by this news, indeed. "I've decided, Thomas," she said, desiring to tear his mind from the thoughts of the woman, "to secure the sword away from any of my Creatures. At least until I am sure what it does to my men."

He said nothing, but continued to stare at her as though she were a ghost.

She clasped her hands together. "Thomas," she started, her voice low, penetrating, ever so careful, "what happened to you that night?"

"What night?"

"*Don't*," she whispered harshly, the seething anger flaring within her heart. No, no, she mustn't get upset with him. She must remain focused. *She* was in control here. "Don't pretend like you do not know what it is I am referring to. Tell me, what happened when you were on your knees, when you were saying...such odd things back at the cabin."

She could feel his resentment exude off him as strongly as she smelled his stench.

He did not answer.

"Thomas," she hissed. "What did you see?"

She thought for a moment that he would not speak, but then his mouth opened and he said, "I saw a woman. She spoke to me of such marvelous things. She promised me Mara if I could—" He gasped and tears began to fall from his eyes.

She recoiled. Tears. *Again*. What were her men becoming?

"If you could what, Thomas?" she breathed, ignoring his tears as best she could.

"If I could give the sword to the one who needs it," he said between gulps.

Her eyebrows rose. "The one who needs it?" she repeated. "The one who needs the sword? Do you think it meant you?"

"I-I don't know."

"But you have thought of this possibility?"

"Y-yes."

"I don't understand it," she said. "Amentias said the woman collapsed when the sword's gem began to glow—"

"It happened again?" he asked incredulously.

"Yes," she said, looking for any change in his dark brown eyes.

"Then it must be her!" he almost shouted. "If she is traveling with those Vampires...they must be waiting to turn *her* into a Vampire."

Eleanor stared at him. He appeared to be lost in deep thought, the tears fell no more, yet still stained his cheeks, and he seemed to have forgotten that she remained there—because of a human woman. "Thomas," she said, calling him out of his stupor, "Thomas, listen to me. You are saying Xavier and his cohorts are carrying her with them because they wish to turn her into a Vampire? Why would they do that?"

His eyes danced with thought. "That is Dracula's sword that we have, is it not?"

She appeared put off by his question in place of an answer, but said, "Yes," all the same.

"Then could she not be Dracula's relative?"

Her eyes narrowed. "What are you saying?"

"There must be a connection between her and the sword. If all of these Creatures are saying they cannot smell her when they are near her, then could her blood not be protected, guarded—something?"

"A possibility," she ruled. "A grand possibility. But if her blood was guarded by something," and she feigned her best skeptical expression, "what do you think that could be?"

Thomas paled, though he did not change form at all: he looked as though he'd seen a ghost. "The sword, Eleanor! The sword is what protects her blood. And whoever holds it..."

"Whoever holds it, what, Thomas?"

"Whoever holds it...falls privy to her presence," he whispered, tears filling his eyes.

"Her presence?" She needed more than this, indeed. She had to know for sure. "But...who is this woman?"

He wiped tears and gasped again, and when he stared back at her, his brown eyes were black. "She is Alexandria Stone, the same woman my father told me to find and kill before she could be used against the Lycan breed back when Dracula still sought her."

"Alexandria Stone. She was the one you saw when you held the sword?"

"Yes, Eleanor. It was her. She promised me my wife if I gave her the sword."

"Thomas, you know you cannot do that. It would benefit us all if you...acquired the woman yourself, do you not think?"

"Acquire her, myself?"

"Yes. If you were to locate Christian Delacroix, take the woman, and gather her for me, we could figure out just what her role is in all of this, once and for all."

He stared at her and she could not figure out what it was he thought, for his handsome face was dressed in a stark seriousness.

"Why were you searching for her that night?" he asked after a time.

"Ever since Dracula told me of her—told me to tell Xavier of her existence—I was curious. But," she said, turning her gaze from him as memories returned with swiftness, "other things were more important to me then. Now that they are sorted, I can continue my search.

"But it seems that she has been led straight to us. And we have Dracula's sword to thank for that. This is why I wish you to find her and bring her to me, Thomas. We can all find the closure we seek once this is done."

He said nothing for a time, and she almost thought he would not agree, it was so gone he looked, but soon he turned his gaze back upon her and said, "I will do it...my Queen."

She smiled. "I had no doubt that you would."

Chapter Fifteen

THE LYCAN

It was nearing morning when Christian returned with three bodies for them to feed from. Nathanial had risen from the ground after being healed by Aleister, and upon realizing where they were, looked around urgently, desiring to enter the high manor whose black gates Christian had arrived in front of the night before.

Nathanial would answer no one's questions as to why he desired to venture there. Aleister pulled him back by the collar and demanded he "get his head on straight." That they had to continue on, venturing for *The Immortal's Guide*. At this, Nathanial began again, questioning the Vampire's knowledge of what he and Xavier must journey for.

Aleister acted aloof, looking towards Aurora for help, but she would not give it. It was then that the scarred Vampire turned, venturing through the large, black piles of ash towards a place that was not London.

Resigned to the worst, it seemed, Nathanial took up pursuit of the Vampire, the rest following close behind. It was a long time before Alexandria awoke within Christian's arms, clawing at the black bodice around her abdomen.

Christian released her at once, and helped her, much against his better judgment, to loosen it. Once it released slightly, she breathed a sigh of relief and questioned just where they were headed.

The sun filled the sky and they'd long ago left the streets of the badly burned town, walking amongst high trees, following a single dirt path, a plume of dust filling the air ahead of them.

Xavier and Nathanial drew their swords and Aleister placed an involuntary hand to his chest, gripping something beneath his clothes, but Christian had little time to ask him what it was before Nathanial let out a shout:

"Lycans!"

And there they were, six fully-formed beasts along the horizon, their black beady eyes searching as though they couldn't wait to attack. But they didn't. *Why did they growl and paw at the ground as though bidden?*

"What the hell are they doing in daylight?" Christian heard Xavier yell into the air.

"*Oh damn,*" Aleister breathed, pushing Christian behind him, much to his bewilderment. He released his own sword from its sheath at his waist: "They're not Lycans! Xavier, do you hear me? They're *not Lycans!*"

"What?" Xavier asked, turning to eye him as a new figure appeared on the horizon behind the line of beasts.

Christian blinked, moving around Aleister's arm to see the new Creature that stood within the plume of smoke: He was tall, his black, tattered traveling cloak cutting an impressive shadow through the dust that filled the air. It was not until the dust cleared, however, that Christian was able to see the intense brown gaze the newcomer held, and even over the snarling growls of the Lycans that stood at least seven feet high while on all fours, Christian could hear Xavier's voice ring out as clear as day:

"*Thomas?*"

"Hello, Xavier," the man said, stepping in between two Lycans. They did not move an inch, but remained focused on the two Vampires before them. "I see that you have angered Eleanor again. She sent me to clean up the mess you seem to leave where ever it is you travel."

Nathanial lifted a hand towards the line of Lycans behind him.

"Who are you?" Thomas asked Nathanial with a sniff.

"I'm the Vampire that's ready to blast your Creatures back to the abyss they came from," Nathanial said, and a thick green light began to form within his palm, lighting Thomas's indifferent expression.

"Charming," Thomas whispered, turning back to Xavier, who Christian could see was tense: he held the sword tight in his grip, his shoulders a bit higher than normal, as though he were ready for a fight.

Christian remembered the piercing gaze Xavier had bid him the night before at Cedar Village and a swirl of dread flared within his dead heart.

It was the same dread he had felt when in Aleister's cottage, her Creatures heading towards them with rapt bloodlust...

His eyes widening, he realized what that dread truly was, but he had only looked towards Aleister for a second before the scarred Vampire whispered, "Yes, Christian—that is the feeling her Creatures give to those not of her likeness... Those are all her Creatures." He nodded in the direction of the Lycans.

He thought of the three Lycans in London. "And Xavier?" he whispered. He had felt as though he were in the presence of one of Eleanor's Creatures when he'd been surveyed by those dark eyes, indeed.

"He is surely on his way there—but he is not there yet," Aleister responded, "but being surrounded by her kind—her energy like this—it isn't healthy for him."

"What, what do we do?" Christian asked, Alexandria silent in her fear beside him.

"We get Xavier Delacroix as far away from that Creature as possible. Follow my lead."

Before Christian could ask what that lead would be, Aleister raised a scarred hand in the air as though wishing to draw attention to himself. Thomas's gaze traveled from Xavier to Aleister and when his bleary eyes found Christian next to him, he started forward.

"The woman!" he called.

Xavier and Nathanial moved, pushing Thomas back, their hands and swords pointed at his chest, keeping him from advancing while Aurora raised a hand as well. Christian could barely hear what Xavier said to him over Thomas's raucous shouting:

"The woman! Where is my Mara? Give me my Mara!"

What is he on about? Christian wondered.

Aleister let a frustrated snarl escape his lips. "He *knows*—he knows about Alexandria! Her Creatures saw her in Cedar Village—they bloody well saw her when she fell! I'm such a damned fool!"

"*What?*" Christian spat, Thomas continued screaming obscenities into the air, struggling rapidly against Nathanial and Xavier's hands. A burst of green light left Nathanial's hand as he pressed against the Elite Creature's chest, sending him flying back into the line of waiting Lycans. He fell atop two, making them fall over, a new plume of smoke rising into the air with their weight, obscuring all vision.

Through the air leapt an unharmed Lycan Creature, which landed right atop Xavier, sending him crashing to the dirt ground, the Ascalon flying from his grip, smashing a few feet from an outstretched arm.

The brilliant red light caught Christian's attention, and it was from Aleister's chest that it blared. The Vampire wore a necklace of some kind, for what else could be causing the brilliant red light?

A scarred hand flew up to cover the light, but the damage was done: The Lycan who had been atop Xavier, snarling and snapping at his face, looked up at the light, transfixed, and then Nathanial shot a burst of green light from his palm. It hit the Lycan square in its side and sent it tumbling with a loud whine against the dirt ground, away from Xavier.

Xavier had barely risen to his feet when three more Lycans lunged for them, and Nathanial and Aurora made quick work of waving their hands intricately through the air, causing a brilliant blue wall to appear. The Lycans barreled into the wall with terrible groans and two fell to the ground, unmoving, while one worked to recover: its strong legs trembled beneath its weight as it pulled itself up to stand.

"That shield won't hold for long—they didn't have enough time to prepare the spell," Aleister said, a scarred hand still clutching at the protrusion on his chest from which the red light still blared.

Wondering how on Earth the Vampire knew that, Christian opened his mouth to ask when movement ahead stole his attention.

The two remaining Lycans emerged from the cloud of smoke to join their brother at the blue wall, Thomas Montague on their tails, his face downright murderous. He glared directly at Alexandria.

Nathanial sent another blast of green light from his hands, blasting both Lycans back against the dirt ground in a flash. Xavier started forward with the Ascalon raised, preparing to swing for Thomas, when the Creature disappeared, re-appearing right before Aleister, a hand outstretched to grip at his throat. Aleister wasted no time in grabbing Thomas's wrist before he could get very far, and stared him straight in his eyes. They were a desperate black, the whites still tainted red from tears. "Why do you seek the woman?" Aleister asked coldly.

Thomas's black eyes shifted from the scarred Vampire to Alexandria, before finally settling back upon Aleister. "She holds the answers I seek to a long-asked question."

The scarred hand tightened around the Creature's wrist. "And what question is this?"

Thomas looked as though he wished to scream. Christian was taken aback when the Creature sighed, as though to still himself, and then said, calmly: "It doesn't pertain to you, Vampire. I just... I need her."

"Yes," Aleister said, never releasing his wrist, "but why?"

"You waste my time!" Thomas yelled, and Christian was almost shocked to see how sharp the Creature's teeth had become. They were lengthening, growing steadily, becoming far too much for his mouth, which elongated to accompany the size of his teeth. "You are incredibly foolish to do so."

"Back away from him!" Nathanial's voice issued over the loud growls that were leaving Thomas's large chest. And before anyone could move, a green burst of light hit the ground near Aleister's feet, causing him to release Thomas.

"What do you think you're doing?!" Aleister shouted to Nathanial.

"Saving your life!" Nathanial called back, Thomas ripping through his clothes, sending them to scatter in scraps against the ground. Christian stepped backwards in haste, pulling Alexandria with him, for the man had just transformed into a Lycan Creature— in no time at all.

What on Earth was going on?

"Christian!" Aleister snapped to him, causing him to stare into the glowing green eyes. "Get Alexandria to safety! Go! *Go now!*"

"But—"

Thomas started forward, a large claw swept for Aleister's head, but Aleister lifted a hand to still the large, hairy arm. As he struggled against the weight of it, Xavier appeared at Aleister's side in the next second.

Aleister released Thomas's wrist and allowed the Lycan to jump back, landing on all fours, sending puffs of dirt to blanket the air. Christian could see the focused glow of Nathanial's golden eyes behind the Lycan. "Get the woman to safety—I will take care of Xavier!"

He hesitated, indecision pulling at his mind—how miraculous it was that he was being told to leave—how utterly mad it was that he could not remain by his brother's side for longer than a moment. Did he truly have to remain by the insufferable woman's side?

Without warning, Thomas started forward again, kicking up earth underneath his massive paws. Christian realized with a jolt that it was her the beast's black beady eyes were trained on. A flare of panic seized his dead heart, and with it the dread amplified for a simple moment in time. Aleister said, "Locate me and transport to where I am. I will have taken these Vampires to safety once this is over." And the dread dissipated with the words.

Xavier moved to meet Thomas with a thunderous clash of sword against silver claws.

Christian found his voice. "How will I know where you are?"

Aleister released his own sword and prepared to charge forward with Xavier. He turned at Christian's voice and the sword lowered. "Trust me, Vampire," he said, the red at his chest glowing still, "Aurora will ensure you reach the right destination. Now get Alexandria to safety!"

Without another word, he was surrounded by a red light, and he could feel Alexandria squeeze his hand tight as it did, her alarm prevalent. They were both lifted into the air, her other hand quick to grab at his cloak as they were pressed towards each other. A gasp of surprise left her, the cold air engulfing them both and he looked over her head towards Aurora, who had a hand directed at them. She nodded and he understood. It was up to him now to lead them to safety. But how on Earth was he to do that?

He began to coast along the eternal cold, the darkness, until he felt his boots hit hard ground. He opened his eyes to stare at

Alexandria, her frightened expression glued on her face, her eyes closed tight.

✳

Xavier jumped back, Nathanial leaping over the Lycan's head to land just before it. He took but a breath before a blue light left his body, Thomas lifted into the air, writhing frantically to and fro. Nathanial flicked a finger.

The beast went barreling back towards the others that lay encumbered, the green flash of light they'd been hit with scattering over them like emerald strands of lightning. Thomas landed with a loud crash, but was on his feet, a loud angry roar leaving his long snout.

"Impressive, Nathanial!" Aleister said, moving to stand beside him, his own sword held upright. He stared towards the impatient Lycan that was padding the ground near its fallen brother's head.

Nathanial said nothing but eyed Xavier. "Now would be best to finish him off," he said, his golden eyes still glowing tremendously.

"Finish him off?" Xavier repeated, the surge of strange energy shooting through his gut and forming a vibrant target within his dead heart. The energy remained there, glowing excitedly, pushing his swollen mind to repeat the question, adding onto it only the words he could not form aloud: *"Why would I want to do that?"*

"Yes, Xavier!" Nathanial responded.

Thomas lunged forward again. He leapt through the air without hesitation and formed a dark shadow over Nathanial's person before the Vampire could realize what had happened.

He was on the ground, Thomas's front paws pushing Nathanial's back further into the dirt, and Xavier remained there, staring at the scene as though it took place far from him. For wasn't this, the Elite Creature atop a lowly Vampire, correct? Wasn't Aleister's futile attempts to remove the Lycan from atop Nathanial's person wrong? Why did the scarred Vampire slash the Lycan with myriad daggers fashioned from the bowels of his traveling cloak? And why did he, Xavier, find all of this so miserably *wrong*?

"Xavier!" Aleister said, Thomas snapping his teeth at the scarred Vampire, never leaving Nathanial. "Some help would be very much appreciated!"

He stared at the sword in his hand, unsure of why it remained there. *Help?* "Why would I help you, Aleister?"

The Vampire ceased his continued stabbing of the Lycan to stare at Xavier over the large, brown fur. "What?" he whispered, Nathanial summoning a large blue shield from nothingness, sending Thomas flying off him at last. "What do you mean?"

Xavier stared at the scarred Vampire as Nathanial rose to his feet, wiping the Lycan's saliva from his clothes with disgust. "Why would I...help you? Help any of you?" he repeated and the energy solidified in his dead heart. He let a cold breath leave his lungs, the feeling engulfing him in full:

The dread thickened from his heart and trailed outward, through his skin, blanketing him in its heavy hold, and all he knew was a remarkable, startling coldness.

"Xavier!" Aleister shouted, bringing him around to the present. He blinked at the scarred Vampire and stared, Aleister moving towards him. "Xavier, what in the bloody hell is wrong with you?"

But the Vampire's green eyes narrowed, and then Nathanial's voice filled Xavier's ears: "Aleister! A little help, here?!"

Aleister turned to eye Nathanial, who held the Lycan off with another large blue shield of light. The Creature continued to charge towards it: cracks were beginning to appear in the shield's body and Nathanial's hands, held aloft, looked strained. Even Aurora was struggling against it.

A slight chuckle left him before he could help it, and it was this sound that caused Aleister to turn back to him in horror. "What, Vampire?" Xavier asked him, feeling the unadulterated power surge through him. *All of this was meaningless.*

"Nathanial!" Aleister shouted instead, "leave the bloody Lycan! We're taking Xavier out of here! Now!"

"What? Why on Earth would we do that?!" Nathanial shouted back.

Xavier was not prepared for what the scarred Vampire would do—or say—next: Aleister lifted him over a shoulder, and said, "Because the Vampire is not fit to find the book—he's not fit to rule the Dark World—he can't do *a bloody thing* while he's under her hand!"

Nathanial's shield disappeared with his surprise; the Lycan did not charge, it remained standing on all fours, staring towards Aleister as though shocked to hear what he'd said as well.

Xavier growled at the way he was being handled—and spoken about, for that matter—by the scarred lump of a Creature. But he could hardly pay attention to the bemused expression that graced Nathanial's face before Aleister shouted, "Follow me, Nathanial!" and swept them into complete darkness before Xavier could do a thing to stop it.

Chapter Sixteen

SEPARATED

Cold air whirled about them and Christian tore his gaze from the woman who still clutched at his cloak and held tight his hand to eye the many thin trees around them. Woods. Brilliant. But there was no sign of the heavily scarred Vampire in sight.

Where had they gone?

He turned back to Alexandria and placed his free hand on her shoulder. She opened her eyes with his touch and released his hand, pressing both hands together to warm them.

"Are you—" he began to say, sure the woman was disturbed by what she had witnessed.

"P-please—please," she whispered through chattering teeth. He was aware just how cold it must have been for her: he could see her breath on the morning air. And she pressed a hand to her midsection as though she were about to release whatever contents of her stomach remained from breakfast days before. She inhaled great gulps of air. And all at once he realized she was possibly having a fit of panic.

Her brown hair lay disheveled down her back. The wind swept it up in its hold, and a grand shiver engulfed her. Without thought, he undid the clasp of his own cloak and removed it from his shoulders, extending it to her. She turned from a blank stare at a tree at his movement to watch the cloak in hand, and he half-wondered if she would take it. She gave him a wary smile and placed the thick cloak about her shoulders; her shivers died at once.

"Wh-where are we...m-my Lord?" she asked after a time.

My Lord. It was a title he was beginning to severely question the importance of, all the more when it left her lips. They were no longer in society, was the need to be addressed as such still so damned important?

"Christian," he said to her, watching her surprised expression, "please, call me by my name—Christian."

She looked as though she desired to ask why she was allowed to do so, but instead, she said, "Christian," and the name left her lips with far too great an ease. "Do you know where we are?"

"I've no honest idea, Miss Stone," he said, staring around at the innumerable trees. "Aleister and my brother don't seem to be anywhere nearby—I cannot smell their blood—"

How she tensed at the word. He could not help but still his tongue when he'd uttered it. She looked as though she was going to be sick.

"Does it bother you...the word?" *And by extension*, he finished in his mind, *what I am?*

She did not answer. She drew the large hood up over her head, hiding the rest of her long locks from view, and she stared at the dirt ground, the dried leaves that remained at her feet. It was several minutes before she said, "It does bother me, honestly—all of this bloody bothers me. Why I'm here, with you. Why those...those beasts are there at every turn! Why no one can tell me what's going on. Why I'm supposedly some Vampire's...*relation!* It makes no bloody sense—and I-I..." She placed a hand atop her midriff, inhaling deeply. "I need to know why I'm in this mess at all!"

Her voice had risen to a shrill scream, and Christian was aware several birds had ascended into the air from their places atop trees. He stared at her, lost for words, for what could he truly say? He knew she was scared, knew she was gravely out of her element, for he was as well—and this made nothing better with talks of her supposedly holding Dracula's blood within her veins.

Her stare was one of anger and determination. And he realized she wanted answers—from him. Her breaths came in quick and shallow; he realized that she was waiting for him to speak—had been waiting since she'd stopped.

Damn.

"Alexandria," he began, the name lingering on the morning air as though it did not belong amongst trees, but instead somewhere much safer, much more enclosed.

"Christian," she breathed. The tears in her eyes had begun to fill and more tears fell as she stared at him.

He was aware that a drink of blood would ease the uncomfortable edge he felt with her stare. "I've already told you—I know not of why you must remain with me."

"But you jumped at the chance all the same!"

The shock of her words pooled through him, and it was a moment before he could form the words. "I *only* did so to quell my brother's incessant talks of my inferiority!" he snapped and she jumped as though he'd slammed a door square in her face. Her brown-green eyes were wide.

Several moments passed, and she opened her mouth and then closed it, opened it again and a sound much like an inadequate whimper left her lips. "So—I am n-nothing more than...than a bloody *job?* On top of not knowing why you must look after me, you only jumped at the chance to help me because your...that V-Vampire thought you couldn't? What are you, some, some *child?*"

"I am no child, human!"

"Oh, I would not have thought so," she said, sending his blood to boil despite the ring, "if it were not for the fact that only children react so wondrously juvenile when faced with such a choice! You bargain my life over a show of bravado!"

He moved before he realized he'd done it: The wind pressed against him, sending his hair to fly behind him as he stepped against the air towards her. He squeezed the ring on his finger, taking one cold breath as the metal clamps released themselves from his skin. When he had reached her, the ring was safe in the breast pocket of his shirt, and he allowed his eyes to turn a brilliant red.

He was aware the startled gasp left her lips, aware how her breasts heaved with every tremulous breath she took, but it hardly mattered. She had spoken to him as if she understood why he did what he did! How dare she! But as he watched her breathe, he found himself remembering with a great pang of nostalgia, the time *he could* breathe—needed to do so, but as soon as the notion had come, it had gone, and he stared down at her, aware his stare rattled her far more than his sudden movement had. As it should.

"You speak," he whispered, "as though you know me, human. Do you profess," and he lifted a finger to her soft cheek, aware he wanted to taste her elusive blood, whatever she truly was, unable to feel the warmth that must have remained there, "to know why I do what I must?"

Her lips trembled and she did not speak.

"An answer, human," he snarled, showing her his fangs, "is the polite custom when asked a simple question."

Several tears left her eyes and he knew a fleeting pang of remorse to fill his dead heart, but that died when she said at last: "J-just as you so rightly answered mine?"

What the devil? Was she truly *questioning him*—to speak so freely when he exuded his charm—a charm no bloody human had ever, in all his years as a Vampire, been able to ignore? She *was* terrified, shaking vigorously, yes, she was, but *why on Earth* was she able to speak words of her own mind and not of his?

"You profess to know me!" he snarled. "You profess to know who I am—you *dare* speak so freely to me when I can rip your tender heart," and he pressed a hand to her chest where her heart beat thunderously within its cage, "from its home and make you my meal?"

He felt her tense at his brazen touch, but he did not remove his hand. How easy it would be to claw through her chest, through her ribs, and show her—show her at last what he was truly capable of. But he did not move, did not dig his nails into her skin, he remained watching her eyes as though they had called his gaze.

Minutes passed, or hours, he did not know, all he knew was that her heart continued to beat madly, its rhythm the only thing driving him to remember where he was, indeed. In the middle of a wood, and what if more Dark Creatures—or worse—were nearby? How could he allow himself to get caught up in a meaningless quarrel with the woman?

"I profess," she said at last, her voice shaking, her stare somehow softening; he half-thought she had accepted her fate at his hands before she continued with, "to know nothing, truly, of you, Christian Delacroix. But I know you have not hurt me thus far, and I know you truly know nothing of why I-I must be h-here. You have always been there when danger loomed, and despite those...things that have come after me...you have remained...by my side.

"This is why I believe—no," and she shook her head, sending brown tendrils of hair to partly cover an eye. He had to keep himself from lifting a hand to tuck it behind an ear. "This is why I know you won't—or perhaps you truly can't—harm me in anyway." A spark of hope at her words shined in her eyes then, and he released his hand from her chest.

He felt nothing. Nothing. No vestige of anger remained, no indignation tore at his dead heart, threatening to engulf him with its madness, no. He was perfectly...perfectly numb. And he found he could not form a proper thought, for the woman—she was absolutely right, and he knew it somewhere deep in the remnants of his soul.

He turned from her to better gather his thoughts, for he found her stare most distracting: the hopeful gaze, the fearful stare, the anticipation for his next word or action, he could not bear it.

What an insufferable woman, he thought, finding a sight that was not her. *First she sparks an astonishment within me that I have seldom witnessed except from other Vampires—and now she speaks as though she knows. But how can she?*

And before he could spare another thought for his current predicament, her voice sounded through the air, "Christian." He turned to eye her and saw her face was filled with fear. But it was not a fear for him, she stared at him as though she desired his assistance.

"What is it?" he asked her.

She turned her gaze to a place to her left and he followed it, stiffening, for there stood a man, his cautious eyes placed upon them both.

Christian smelled the thick scent of blood and dirt, and he realized he had been training his senses on recalling the smell of Alexandria's blood this whole time.

"Get behind me, Alexandria," he said stepping towards her, keeping his eyes upon the Lycan in human form, aware he could do nothing but take a hard hit in order to buy her time to run.

She obeyed, stepping behind him, and he felt the slight touch of her hand upon his arm. He found his thoughts running to how her skin had felt beneath his hand. Shaking it away, he focused on the strange man said, "What do you want?"

The man ran a dirty hand through his sandy brown hair, and his face changed from cautious to content. "Well, Vampire, funny you

Chapter Seventeen

A MEETING OF MINDS

Christian dodged the Lycan's paw as Alexandria let out a terrible scream. He turned his head to eye her pressed up against a tree, fear full in her eyes, and he vaguely wondered if that fear was for his safety or her own.

"Pay attention to your opponent, Vampire!" the Lycan said, deep snarls escaping his throat. It lunged for him again, and Christian pressed a hand against the Lycan's snout to keep it at bay, feeling the thick saliva drip down his arms.

"Alexandria! Run!" he screamed at her, surprised when she shouted back, "And go where?"

It let out a terrible roar and pushed on his hands, sending him barreling back against a tree, which he smacked into with tremendous force.

"Christian!" he heard Alexandria scream in panic through the low continuous buzzing that pierced his ears now, and why were there *two* Lycans stomping towards him on tall hind legs?

"St-stay back, Miss Stone," he called to her weakly, waving a hand in the general direction of frantic breathing. He tasted the blood in his mouth and felt it escape down his chin, the grimace finding his face, for everything hurt.

"Christian—but you're hurt!"

"I said *stay back*, Miss Stone!" he repeated with ferocity, although the sight of two Lycans continued to swim before his eyes; he pulled himself off the tree at last, his knees trembling with the pain that pulsed along his back. Flexing both shoulders, he stifled a scream, for the pain was great, but nothing was broken this time and he was silently grateful for the fact. He'd rather suffer through the pain than taste Unicorn Blood again.

The Lycan let out a haunting laugh and Christian blinked against the shroud of larger shadow that was descending upon him. He stared up into the four black beady eyes, and inhaled the terrible breath the Lycan exhaled, its large chest rising and falling beneath its lowered head.

"D-don't hurt him!" Alexandria screamed, and Christian wished she would cease her screaming, for not only did it send his mind to ring even more with pain, but she was drawing more attention to herself.

All the Lycan did was laugh. "Well, it seems you've got the human talking since last we met, Christian."

What? he thought, his mind further pounding with every shuddering breath he dared take. He must have heard the beast wrong—for he had never seen this Lycan before. He blinked at its shaking frame, both Lycans finally merging, and the pulsing in his mind began to steadily wane. "What?" he said aloud, trying his best to ignore the pain.

"*What?*" it repeated incredulously. "You don't remember me, Vampire?"

"Remember—" And all at once it returned to him: the towering beast amidst a red light filled night. How could it be? How could he have found us? And so soon? He tensed when the Lycan snarled appreciatively at him.

"Ah yes, you do remember me," Lore said. "Funny how fate has pulled us together."

"Alexandria, get out of here!" Christian shouted. The bloody Lycan King, and here he was just standing, trying to get the woman to leave with shouts—he'd have to do more to get her to budge. He'd have to...

"No, no, no, Christian," Lore snarled. "I've got you exactly where I want you—and since your little friends aren't here to save your arse this time, I can finish you in one sweep before I work on that piece of flesh—"

"You're not touching her!" he shouted before he could stop himself. *What the hell am I saying?*

"Aren't I now?" Lore growled. "Well, seeing as how I was the one who found her first—"

"*I said don't touch her!*" he screamed before the words could find reason within his mind. The pain dispersed in a sweep of cold air as he turned to look at her, her brown-green eyes filled with tears. And there he saw it. Her fear...for him.

He was thrown back against the tree again, Lore pressing his claw deeper into his chest; his ribs cracked beneath the pressure, eliciting a scream.

The stench of old blood and dirt filled his nose next, Lore's long snout appearing mere inches from his eyes as he said, "You hold no power, Christian. Nowhere near your miserable brother. So do not tell me what to do to your little follower. She holds more power than you do in your finger. And that power...I can't let it remain in this world—*my* world."

Before Christian could utter a word over the thick trail of blood that left his mouth, another Lycan appeared behind Lore and tore up ground to reach Alexandria Stone.

Christian barely had time to collect himself before he was on the ground. Lore had released him, having heard the newcomer arrive as well. Stars forming in bleary eyes, Christian watched in horror as the Lycan stopped just before a shaking Alexandria and pawed at the ground hungrily, but it did not do anything more.

"Thomas?" Lore said, eyeing the new Lycan, and Christian saw the surprise that seemed to grace the new Lycan's face: it ceased all movement, and stared back at Lore as though it had seen a ghost.

Christian turned his weak gaze to Alexandria, the fear wide in her eyes, the tears falling faster. He coughed, his entire body trembling with pain, and he felt the shards of broken rib move around in his chest, the blood continuing to pool within his mouth.

How can I protect her? he wondered, the scene before him beginning to darken. *How can I bloody well protect her? How can I do* any *of this?*

"*Alex—andria...please...run,*" he forced himself to whisper. He could barely keep her and the Lycan within his sights.

The new Lycan growled at him, but Lore stepped in front of Christian and began to shrink. He blinked several times upon the ankles of the Lycan, the fur disappearing, the well-toned legs of a human man replacing the large paws that had just been there, before the man stepped forward hesitantly.

The man reached the new Lycan he had called Thomas and stretched out a strong hand, as if to stroke the Lycan's fur. It took a quick step sideways as though it would be harmed by the touch.

"My son, it's me, your fa—" Lore began.

Thomas snarled and even Christian felt the ground tremble with the sound, and it was then that he wondered just where the other Lycans were. He knew neither of these Creatures would be roaming the Dark World alone.

"Why are you here you goddamned tyrant?" Thomas asked, and Alexandria let out another wail of terror.

Christian felt his dead heart pulse with the sound of her fear, but the pain would not cease. He dug a hand into the hard dirt and felt his nails fill with it. *Alexandria...get away....*

The heaviness of the pain descended over his eyelids, the darkness growing thicker; he could barely keep them open, he could barely see the scene before him, but he heard the loud voice of Lore respond:

"I followed a hunch and it led me straight to her."

"Why on Earth would you be looking for—"

"Why would *you*?"

He heard the snarl escape long rows of sharp teeth, but he could not open his eyes, could not begin to focus on the sounds around him, his mind swimming with vagueness, darkness...

"Wh-why do you w-want me?" he heard Alexandria whisper amidst the low growls.

And just before all was lost to him, he heard both voices respond together as loud rustles left the trees around them: "Why wouldn't we?"

✳

"And how is the situation in Quiddle?" Eleanor asked.

The large fire that blazed high in the center of the stone room sparked with greater life, and he shifted his footing. "The situation is moving along...er...wonderfully, my Queen," he said, beads of sweat forming along his brow. "The Vampires that reside there know nothing of the ones we have sent to infiltrate their city."

"So when Xavier and his little gang show up there..."

"They will be monitored constantly and the link will be sent to you from one of our own—Trent, I believe his name was, my Queen."

"I see," she whispered, thoughts full with the image of Xavier entering Quiddle, only to lead her straight to the damned book. They had their orders, of course, her men and women that were stationed there—they were not to allow Xavier to get the book no matter what, hold him off for as long as possible until she could venture there and claim him at last...

"Take your leave," she told him, and he bowed himself out of the door with a look of great relief.

Javier took the other Vampire's place, blue eyes narrowed in question.

She rose from her seat as the door closed behind him and beckoned him forward with a slender hand. "Javier, my child," she said, watching him step towards her, the large fire illuminating his handsome face, the tattered robes he wore, "what troubles you?"

"Is it true?" he asked once he reached her. "Is it true you're heading off Xavier—going to all the places that he is for a book Dracula created?"

She stiffened at the questions so abruptly asked, though it was not long before she recovered and smiled, a hand placed reassuringly atop one of his own. "I see...you're incredibly intelligent, Javier. Dracula did well in teaching you... But it seems," and she rose from her seat and stared down at him, "you are ready to learn more."

"More, my Lady?" He stared at her hand as she ran a gentle thumb over the back of his, and a cold breath escaped him at her touch.

"Yes," she whispered. "More. What I truly am...what your former mentor, Dracula, could never tell you." She let the cold air of the dark dungeon engulf her, her blood chilling, her gaze taking on a red hue. He gasped and removed his hand from hers.

"How are you able to—"

"The question, Javier, is how am I not."

Chapter Eighteen

WINGDALE

Alexandria had kicked off her shoes some minutes ago and pounded the hard ground as the snarls resounded all around her. *I'm going to die. I'm going to die. I'm going to bloody well die—*

And there they were, two more Lycans in human form appeared before her through the many trees, their eyes all black, and she inhaled the windy morning air as her heart thundered vibrantly in her chest.

Before she could decide which way to move, she felt a swarm of heat at her back and she turned, several more Lycans appearing, the one that had pinned Christian to a tree still in human form. She averted her eyes at once: he was completely naked.

"First one to claim her, my son," Lore roared, and how incredible that voice was, "gets to do with her as they please."

And the Lycan at his side growled low. "Fine," he said before he charged forward, ripping up earth as he moved, "but I will claim her first!" And how strange it was that Alexandria saw time still, how strange that the maddening Vampire was not here to step in front of the beast, no matter how foolish it was—

231

A loud sound filled her ears and she lifted two hands to cover them, for the sound would not cease; it was like a horrible, screeching wail.

The Lycan that ripped up ground to reach her stilled and all other beasts that surrounded them seemed frozen as well.

She watched in alarm, the Lycan let out a brazen cry and began to whine as though every spot upon its body was being prodded with daggers.

"Thomas!" Lore cried.

Thomas was doubled over, knees upon the ground, hands to ears as well. But even as she watched him, she realized she could still hear the sound.

She blinked, realizing that all of them had ceased, and this was her only chance.

She turned towards the two men that had appeared and saw that they were on their knees as well, ears covered by their hands, faces twisted into grimaces; it seemed the sound was causing them incredible pain.

That was when she saw it, the large shape that passed overhead and blanketed the ground in greater shadow. Without thought, she looked up into the sky and squinted past the many trees' leaves, a massive bird zoomed overhead, its long blue tail the last thing she saw before a large dark blue feather appeared right before her eyes. Her surprise propelling her now, she released her hands from her ears and reached out a hand to grasp it when it burst into flame. She inhaled the warm air as the fire dispersed and blew into her face, her fear disappearing completely.

The loud screech filled her ears, and she looked up to see the large shadow flying steadily away from her.

All Alexandria knew was that she needed to follow it, for she had a strong feeling that if that sound ceased when she was still here, the beasts would recover and move to rip her apart.

Shaking hands clasped at her skirts and she lifted them, moving past the two stunned men, their hands still stuck tight to their ears, and she did not look back as she ran through the many trees, never ceasing even as a painful stitch resounded in her side.

Tears fled her eyes as she ran, and they slid into her ears, but she did not wipe them. She pressed forward, keeping her eyes upon the large shadow that flew forward, almost guiding her out of the woods, but that was preposterous.

So why am I following it?

What do you mean why are you following it? It's the only thing that's putting distance between you and those monsters back there!

But what about Lord Delacroix?

What the devil about him?

He tried to keep me safe—he truly did attempt to save me—

And what did that get him? Crushed by a damned Lycan—again!

But I should still go back to save him....

I should keep moving!

But he's saved my life—I can't let him die!

Technically, he's already dead, Alexi....

Goddamn it all!

Run—come back when you're safe!

Come back? With who?

Help, of course!

Where on Earth *am I going to find help?*

Before she knew it, the trees had cleared and there was a stone road that led to a quaint town, odd shops and brick houses squished together on either side of the hard sidewalks. Several tall men with large pointed ears walked the streets, while several normal-looking humans clad in long dark robes walked among them. Some held long golden staffs.

Alexandria let a sigh of immense relief escape her and she pressed forward on bare feet, the soles of them sore and hurting. She was sure she was bleeding, but she did not stop to look: there was no telling what those beasts were doing—if they had recovered and followed suit...

She hobbled over the ground and her feet soon found the smooth surface of stone as she reached where a sidewalk began. Tall lampposts stood several feet before the first building and, as she neared it, a large wooden sign just above the dark wooden doors could be clearly seen:

Terch and Terry's Furnishings: All of your magically-enchanted furniture Enchanted or De-Enchanted here, for less!

Magically-Enchanted Furniture? she thought in slight amusement as she passed the wooden doors and stepped gingerly past the brick building, thinking wholly of a couch bewitched to dance in mid-air.

The stitch at her side labored with her small chuckle, and she clutched it, passing a lively cafe whose patrons seemed to talk to each other with muffled hisses.

Turning from their curious gazes, she stepped across the hard sidewalk, eyeing the rest of the small town. It seemed the entirety of the place was just one long street straight through.

Her stomach let out an incredibly noisy grumble, and she remembered with an abrupt start that she was absolutely famished.

Food, food, I need food, she thought, passing another brick building whose sign read:

Randvell and Rita's Dragon-Taming Books and Equipment

She wasted no time in pulling open the wooden door, prepared to beg the next person (or whatever) she saw for a plate of food and some water, but the dank air of the dark store held her mouth shut. A few feet from the door remained a stand holding something that looked very much like hanging eyeballs, but she could not be sure in the dark: there were absolutely no windows near the doors and only the faint glow of a candle atop a desk pushed against a cluttered wall gave any relief from the gloom at all.

Inhaling as much air as she could possibly muster, Alexandria stepped carefully towards the desk and the light of the candle. She was able to see now the many portraits that hung along the wall. And she almost thought that no one remained in the strange shop, but the more she stared against the dark, the more she was able to make out the sanctimonious glares of two incredibly pale people who stood facing each other, their heads facing the front of the painting. Their long brown hair did nothing to soften the piercing glare of their eyes: the man's was a startling blue, the woman's a pressing brown.

As her stomach rumbled again, she vaguely wondered if they were Vampires, for their intense gazes were something she had been subject to many a time thanks to the horrifying Christian Delacroix. *Christian!*

She almost slapped herself. She had forgotten that the Vampire remained in the woods—and what was she doing? Looking about with vague curiosity in shops and cafes. Yes, she needed to find help, needed to find food—*bloody hell was she hungry!*—but food could wait. She couldn't allow the damned Vampire to die...again...for her sake. After all he *had* moved to protect her. And no matter *how* miserable he was...he *had* stuck to his word that he would not, could not harm her.

She pressed a shaking hand to her head as a terrible pressure began to fill it. Being frightened at every turn on an empty stomach did nothing to help her body, this she knew perfectly well, and it was then that she cursed herself for refusing the food sent up to her while in Delacroix Manor. What she would not give for a plate of freshly prepared potatoes and steak...

The flood of regret filled her then as she realized just how safe she had been within that mansion...at least she was able to remain within walls, free of the madness of a world she had never known. And she agreed then that it was one thing to hear that beasts and... Creatures wanted her but to actually face it time and time again... She wished she had believed Christian Delacroix when he had told her that Lore was going to return for her. She had hoped, wildly, that it was some maddening dream, that she would awaken in her own room after a particularly long slumber.

The sound of movement somewhere deeper in the shop beckoned her attention, and she stared through the gloom to eye a collection of long swords held up on a horizontal rack. It hung from the low dark ceiling. As her eyes found the rest of the ceiling, she realized there was what seemed to be a Dragon's blue wing hanging from five thick ropes above her head. She wondered how indeed one tamed one of the large, terrifying creatures.

"May I help you?" a smooth voice sounded through the gloom, causing her to jump and step away from the desk at once.

God that voice. If her head wasn't hurting, she would have been sure it would have warmed her heart on a better day: it was rich with command, but now in the dim light of the strange shop, his eyes gleaming from darkness, she felt much more on edge, much more alone.

"I-I...I'm sorry, I shouldn't be here... I shouldn't—"

He took a step along the ground and into the light of the candle. His eyes were not a piercing blue like the portrait displayed but a deep familiar red...

Oh no, she thought, casting a quick glance to the door. How far away it seemed now. *Damn it, Vampires. Always Vampires!*

He didn't say a word as he took another step forward, but she heard it clearly and turned to eye him. A white hand moved through the gloom for a silver blade and she watched in horror as he removed a sword from the rack and flicked it through the air, catching the black handle in his open hand.

She stared in horror at the long blade, it appeared to gleam in the dark as he tightened his grip around the leather handle, and she noticed his red eyes flashed with hunger. He could smell her blood— but how?

She took a miniscule step away from the Vampire and felt the slippery liquid that trailed along the dark cold floor at the bottom of her foot.

Of course.

Ultimate fear filled her: Christian was not here, and here was a Vampire with a blade that could smell her blood and did not seem to want to ignore her existence.

There was nothing for it—she knew she wasn't going to die in the hands of a Vampire that wanted her blood. She turned as fast as her slippery feet and aching head would allow for the darkly painted door and reached out a hand for it only to hear the voice behind her bark with command, "Rita!"

And there she was in a swirl of suffocating wind that did nothing to make breathing in the small shop any more bearable, the woman from the portrait, only her piercing eyes were not brown but instead a similar red as the Vampire that must have been Randvell.

A door opening to the right of her caused her to clutch at her heart, for it felt as though it was going to find itself out of her skin. Both Vampires turned at the sound to eye who had entered and Alexandria felt her mind pulse with pain even more.

A woman clad in long dark purple robes moved past a shelf of large books that seemed to hover several inches from the shelf itself. She stepped into the faint light of the candle. Alexandria watched as her blue eyes found the Vampires, and then her, and then she said, "Come with me, human."

"But Wenefore, a human!" Randvell said in disbelief as several loud roars filled the air outside the door.

"Enough, Randvell," Wenefore said calmly, extending a hand for Alexandria to grasp. "We have protocols for dealing with any trespassers—they have been activated. I will get the woman here some food, she looks like she hasn't eaten in months."

"Th-thank you," Alexandria whispered, knowing the woman was an Enchanter at first hazy glance: she had kind, yet stern eyes about her. The same Aurora held. And she carefully placed a shaking hand in hers and let out a soft sigh at the exact warmth that filled her at the touch, and she vaguely wondered if the woman had done that for her.

Not turning to eye either Vampire, Wenefore led her to the door just behind the shelf of hovering books. As she left the light of the candle, Alexandria realized that both Vampires had retreated back into greater shadows, though their piercing gazes still held on her. She felt them burning holes into her hair.

The dark door closed behind her. She had to blink at the marvelous brightness that filled her eyes, for the entire room was lit with various lights: torches around the four high walls, several candles placed precariously upon tottering towers of thick books, there was even a miniature sun against the ceiling leaving no shadow in any corner.

The Enchanter moved to a back wall and waved her hands over a small stove. The kettle, which had sat dormant atop a cold burner, sprang to life and began to whistle as though it had been burning for ages.

"Tea, dear?" Wenefore asked, without looking over her shoulder. She had waved a hand over a pot and it began to bubble over with a creamy-looking froth. "I hope you don't mind oatmeal."

"N-no, not, not at all," she whispered. The smell of the oatmeal and herbal leaves filled her nose. A silent scream of relief filled her lungs as she moved weakly for a small table to the right of the stove and wooden counter and sat down in a hard chair without a second thought.

A bowl of steaming oatmeal was placed right before her, the large mug of tea just beside it. Tears almost left her eyes as she picked up a spoon and dug in, only stopping to let out a wail of brief pain: her tongue burned as a result of her impatience.

As she ate, she was very well aware that the Enchanter was watching her, and it was not until she saw the bottom of her bowl that she started on the cup of tea, which had cooled a bit now. Alexandria looked up at last to see the blue eyes of the Enchanter staring at her over a green book.

"Thank you. Thank you so very much for the meal," she said.

"You needed it," she responded, closing the book as the roars of Lycans thundered through the stone walls of the shop. And as she looked up at the main white doors with this roar, Wenefore said, "Would you like to see them again?"

"What?" she breathed, thinking for a foolish moment that she meant see the Lycans as they ran through the streets.

Wenefore smiled. "The Vampires. Forgive me, but as it seems you are free of them now...one cannot help but wonder why you would want to go back."

"I...I'm not free of them," she said, "no matter where I go, I will always run into them."

"No, human," she said, "not just any Vampires. The Delacroixes. You want to go back to them—it is all over your face. Now that you have eaten, you want to save him."

Alexandria stared at this woman closely now, wondering how on Earth she could read minds, for surely she could not have only known that with just twenty minutes of being near her.

She looked at her empty mug and traced the line of the handle with a finger. "He's been there for me...I can't just leave him in the woods—he's dying."

"But he is a Vampire, Miss..."

"Stone. Alexandria Stone."

"He is a Vampire, Miss Stone. You cannot expect him to keep his word."

"Yet, he has. When Lore found us he, he jumped up and, and *moved* to defend me."

"But why would he do this? Why would he, a Vampire most known for his...recklessness, move to defend you?"

"Because I... I'm Dracula's granddaughter—"

"Dracula's granddaughter? What? Do you really believe that you are his blood relation?"

"I...I don't know," Alexandria said, rising slowly to stand. "But it remains that I must go back for him—help him—I can't...survive this world...all of this alone."

Wenefore said nothing to these words but appeared to be in careful thought, for her blue eyes narrowed upon Alexandria intensely.

As shouts and cries of panic filled the street beyond the walls, Alexandria realized that this woman was not being kind regarding her desire to go back to Christian and save him. This Enchanter seemed to have a grand dislike for Vampires, indeed.

The door opened, sending the afternoon sun to beam in past the outline of a man with short black hair, his own purple robes swaying around his boots. "Wenefore, what is the meaning of this?"

Alexandria stared.

The man said, "Lycans! Tearing up the streets and you're doing nothing about it!" And Alexandria saw his brown eyes finally turn to her in further bewilderment. "And who are you?"

"I'm—"

"A human that got her paths crossed with the Lycans," Wenefore said.

Alexandria stared at her and she stared back, her eyes shining with silent command to not repeat her words to anyone else.

"A human, hmm?" the man repeated, his breathing slowing as he stared more closely at her. And she felt it was strange how the man was surveying her, as though he wanted to know what made her tick.

Wenefore stepped right in front of her, directing the man's eyes to her, instead. "Who is out there fighting, Carnvoy?"

"Hm? Oh, er...the Elves and others, of course," he said, and over Wenefore's shoulder, Alexandria could see his eyes move back to the Enchanter. "I imagine the Vampires are...dying to join the fray, but well...yes."

"Have they succeeded in holding the Lycans back? What is the state of the town?"

"You should just, just come see, Wenefore..." And he stepped away, moving towards the still open door, and as he disappeared through it, Wenefore stepped in his wake, Alexandria moving uncertainly with her as well.

When she reached the door, Alexandria blinked in the heat of the sun and stared down the street to where several large beasts lay in the center of the stone road, several tall-eared men and women stood around them, their long golden staffs gleaming in the sunlight. "What's happened to them?"

"The Elves seem to have finally succeeded in casting the Spell of Burden upon them," Carnvoy said, his brown eyes narrowed in the light as he stared upon the beasts as well. "They were trying to rally enough magical power to do it when I arrived back in town."

"Ah," Wenefore said with a sniff. "Well...the beasts seem to be... burdened enough... Shall we get on with sending the human on her way?"

"On my—" Alexandria breathed. "You must come with me! I need to save Christian."

"Christian?" Carnvoy said, looking around at her. "Who's this Christian, Wenefore?"

"A Vampire," Wenefore said without looking to Alexandria, and Alexandria could not help but feel the woman was profusely bored with the situation and did not desire to help at all.

"A Vampire?" he repeated, his demeanor darkening, and then his eyes appeared to spark with realization as he looked from Wenefore to Alexandria and back. "This isn't Christian *Delacroix*, is it?"

Wenefore nodded.

He looked towards Alexandria. "Christian did this, didn't he?" he said with conviction. "That damned Vampire—*of course!* And you human, you're with him, aren't you?"

"I-I," she stammered, not understanding at all what would cause the man to react so violently when it came to Christian. "He needs help, Enchanter p-please, you can't send me back in that...world a-alone!"

"But we can!" Carnvoy yelled, causing several Elven heads to turn in their direction. He stared towards Wenefore as though looking for reassurance to his claim: it seemed he had it, she gave him a look of silent reinforcement. He said, "We can and we will! Get out—out of Wingdale! Get out now! Go back to your Vampire and save him with your damned *blood* yourself!"

She stared in disbelief. *Why did everyone refuse to help him?*

"I don't understand—you can help him, you can!" she almost screamed, and she was aware a few Lycans rustled against the ground at her voice. "Why won't you move to assist him?"

"Because, human," Carnvoy said with clenched teeth, "we're damned Vampire Specialists!"

"Vampire Special—"

And from a pocket on his robes, he pulled out what looked like a sign one would pin to their chest to denote their position within a store. She stared at it carefully and saw that it read:

Vampire Specialist: Carnvoy Regale / Hunter

"Hunter," she read aloud, wondering what on Earth that meant. As she stared at it, she realized just why one would be called a specialist of Vampires at all. The slight step away she took matched the hesitant breath that escaped her lips as she stared upon the both of them in renewed wonder. "You...kill Vampires?"

"We do more than kill them," Wenefore said, bringing Alexandria's eyes to her. "We help other Creatures who are having particular trouble with the bloodsucking monsters."

"A-are you serious?" she breathed, not understanding it. Why would Aurora be so keen on helping Aleister as she did?

"You look surprised, Miss Stone," Wenefore said. "Why, you look as though you have never known the truth of we Enchanters, that we are not particularly fond of the Creatures... Always forced to do their dirty work...we are their damned slaves. Which is why I would beseech you to still in your quest to help the Vampire.

"I don't know what tricks he pulled over you, or what lies he whispered into your ear at night, but the truth of Christian Delacroix is not as pleasant as you may believe. He is a monster, Miss Stone," she whispered, "a monster that would not hesitate to rip you apart if he were driven to it—no matter *whose* blood you may believe yourself to harbor."

And that was when she felt it, the cold hand of Christian upon her chest, and she could almost see the look of hunger that lined his face as he'd gazed upon her. The fear, the complete fear, she remembered it, the utter fear that filled her at that touch, that look. She had known that he had seen it in her, she had known that it filled him with what he craved, second only to blood...

But he had done nothing, and that was when she had felt her fear retreat, for there was his resignation, a mere flash, but she had seen it, and that was when she had known beyond a shadow of a doubt that he would not, indeed, rip her heart out.

She blinked, the present a startling revelation of sun and scalding looks, and she knew just what she had to do.

To hell with damned Enchanters that desired nothing more than to tell her of a Vampire that they had not seen, had not seen as she had, so how could they know?

And mind just how she was to save the Vampire, herself, she turned from both Enchanters without a word and stepped along the stone ground, very aware her cut had almost healed: less and less blood trailed from her foot as she walked.

✳

Christian inhaled a shallow breath, the heat of the sun piercing his hand, and he grimaced. The pain of his heart and the warmth of the sun could not be ignored now, and ignore it he had by trying to fall sleep. But now he was awake, aware, and he could not feign sleep, not when his mind—so full with thoughts of Alexandria Stone and where she'd run off to, if the Lycans had reached her at all—berated his skull with his pain.

Damn, he thought weakly as the smell of burning flesh reached his nose, and he used the last bit of strength he retained to remove his hand from the light of the sun. How foolish he had been to remove his ring just to scare the woman into her place. If he still had it on... nothing would be different would it? He would have moved towards Lore and what? Gotten his back cracked again, his arm torn off by the beast's teeth?

I can do nothing, truly. I was a fool to think I could—a fool to think I could protect her. She's probably dead.

And he froze as he heard the crunch of dried leaves, felt the faint footsteps move rapidly towards him. He forced himself to look up from the hard ground at last, the familiar sight of dirtied ankles and horribly bruised feet coming into blurry view.

He blinked profusely. *It couldn't be, not her—she's dead. She should be dead.*

The smell of her blood filled his nose, an involuntary snarl leaving his lungs as he watched her step uncertainly over leaves, twigs, dirt. *She's looking for me,* he barely registered, *but why—why would she come back?* Surely she has help? But even as he lay there, tracking her movements with his eyes, he knew that no one else had traveled back with her: there was no other smell to fill his nose but her own. But why? If she had survived the Lycans, how had she done it? Had they chased her in circles? What on Earth propelled her to come back?

He cleared his throat, aware the smell of her blood was driving him mad, sending his own blood to boil with the desire to taste, sending his brain to pound painfully against his skull. *Damn, damn, damn. I need that blood,* he thought coldly, barely questioning why he was able to smell it while she was up and about and not asleep or unconscious.

She had neared him now, but still looked lost. He opened his mouth to call for her, but he was surprised to find his voice had been taken from him—he was far too weak to speak.

It stung him, this loss, why, he had never been this weak before, in this much maddening pain. And the light of the sun that would pierce him every time a breeze caused the leaves to sway did nothing to make his situation any better. He snarled again in further anger. How ridiculous that he be this way! Weak, unable to press forward and defend the human against a damned beast!

Why in Dracula's name did I not get the damned training I desired? But even as he thought this, he let a cold smile tear his pain-filled face in two. He had been brooding that night, impaling himself repeatedly upon the daggers of ridicule. He thought himself unworthy of training at the hands of the mighty Master of Weaponry. How funny it was that he had stumbled upon her and Lore, and had moved to attack the beast regardless.

I am a bloody fool, letting my urges get the better of me, he thought with resignation, the sound of Alexandria's hesitant footsteps nearing ever closer.

Her feet stopped just beside a thin tree and he had to force himself to roll over onto his back in order to see her face, for a startled gasp had filled his ears the moment she'd ceased walking.

"Christian," he heard her whisper as she stepped hesitantly towards him, and he stared at her carefully, the pain still spreading throughout his body.

Her dark brown hair was windswept, even more so than before, but her cheeks were rosy with...wind? No, it was something else... healthiness that he had not seen upon her since they had first met. She had eaten. But what? And where did she do so?

She seemed to be reading his mind for she knelt at his side and kept her gaze from his eyes. "There is a town a few yards from here...I...it's a fantastic story as to h-how it happened..." A tear left an eye, but she hastily lifted a hand to wipe it away.

Without thought, he forced himself to lift his hand to her own and she turned to eye him, wonder filling her brilliant eyes. *Tell me... more,* he thought with great concentration, wondering indeed if the words would reach her.

Her eyes widened with alarm and he knew the thought had hit its target. He smiled, and was surprised when she returned a hesitant one before saying, "Christian...what—what can I do, to-to..." And she sighed, gesturing to the rest of his body.

If you could not find help in that town, he told her, *then do not worry about it, Miss Stone. We will...find a way.*

"You don't truly believe that, do you?" she asked, and her stare was knowing.

He let a small chuckle escape his lips, but he grimaced as the action sent a piercing shot of pain through his chest. And before he could stop it, blood left his lips and he rolled on his side, away from her, and coughed his blood to the ground.

Two hands were placed upon his dirtied sleeve but he did not turn to eye her as more blood left him. *I need blood. I need Unicorn Blood*, he thought.

"*Unicorns?*" she asked. "Christian, are you okay? Please—"

He rolled to her in great alarm, for he had not realized all of his thoughts would find her mind. Why, he had not directed those last two to her at all...how was the connection able to remain open?

I'm fine, Miss Stone—fine. Please, do not think on it. It was just a thought...in the moment... I'm afraid I'll have a few of those without the proper blood in my system... There are things I cannot control... when I am like this, he thought, directing these words to her, rolling onto his other side. He propped himself up on an elbow, grimacing. He caught the scent of her blood much more clearly here. A snarl escaping him with the closeness of it.

She gasped and jumped, moving away from him, and his gaze turned red.

Don't, don't be alarmed, please.

"Christian, you—"

I won't hurt you, I swear. It is just...your blood... You have been cut somewhere? And he searched her person for any sign of injury to her being.

A hand involuntary moved to a foot as she sat on the ground and she stared back at him. He knew she wouldn't say a word, for she couldn't—most humans didn't when they saw his true face.

Your foot? he wondered. She removed her hand before long, a faint trace of blood smeared across her palm. *You cut your foot?*

"Yes," she whispered, her stare never leaving his eyes.

And he smelled it—the horrid scent of Lycan blood as it rushed to his nose and caused him to growl.

"Christian? What?" she whispered in alarm, and Lore stepped through the trees, a winning smile plastered upon his handsome face as he sauntered right up to Alexandria and pulled her up to stand by the hair.

Her cry of fright resounded in his ears but he could do nothing as Lore breathed hungrily into her neck.

"*What* dear Vampire? Did you think me truly gone? I am not as foolhardy as my inane son and his cohorts!" He pressed a hand to the front of Alexandria's neck, stroking softly the vein that pulsed with her fear, and Christian realized with a terrible jolt of anger that he was mocking him. "I have her, have her all to myself and no one—not even *you*, Christian Delacroix—can stop me."

Aurora Borealis appeared behind Lore and placed a hand atop his head, whispering words that Christian could not catch. He could only watch as Lore let out a horrible scream and release Alexandria as though burned. She fell to her knees just before him, but he was only able to let his eyes flash upon her briefly before Lore went up in vibrant green flames, his eyes bulging in their sockets. Then, in a puff of golden smoke, he was gone, his screams lingering on in the air, filling the afternoon sky.

Alexandria was breathing rapidly, clutching at her throat as tears left her eyes in droves. Aurora stepped to her, a hand upon her shoulder reassuringly.

Christian stared at the woman's hand before turning his gaze to her black eyes and found that she was already staring at him.

Christian, she said in his mind, and he thought that she did not want to alarm Alexandria further, *we must reunite with Aleister and Xavier.*

How? he forced himself to respond—his brain was still reeling with the scent of Lycan.

Magic, of course. She lifted a free hand into the air, looked down at him and said, "Take her hand, Christian." He turned his gaze to Alexandria, her eyes wide with tears, and he realized then that he wanted nothing more than to rip Lore's fingers from his hands for touching her. She did not deserve this—any of this. She deserved a life, a normal one. This is why he hoped, feeling his dead heart slow all the more, that she wasn't truly Dracula's granddaughter.

No one deserves a life like this, he thought, more blood sliding past his lips, *especially not a soul as pure as hers.*

Chapter Nineteen

JOURNEY TO QUIDDLE

Aleister stared at the Vampire at his feet. They had traveled to a couple of Elves known for their healing abilities with releasing binds, but it did not seem to have worked. Nathanial was waving his hands across Xavier, who had long since stopped struggling and glared up at them in anger.

"Enough, Nathanial," Aleister said, and turning to eye him, Nathanial noticed the Vampire was looking somewhere past him. "We've guests."

"Guests?" he repeated in bewilderment, following the scarred Vampire's gaze through the many trees. There, walking steadily towards them, was Aurora Borealis, her expression stern, carrying a glowing man easily over a shoulder. Beside her walked, with something of a limp, a dirtied, windswept Alexandria Stone.

"Aurora?" Nathanial called through the trees.

Even Xavier sat up along the ground to stare in beleaguered silence.

Aleister stepped past Nathanial and moved for her, waving a

hand to dispel whatever spell she'd placed upon the body on her shoulder, which Nathanial soon realized was Christian.

"What's happened to him?" he asked as Alexandria gave him a weak smile. Aurora lowered Christian to the ground with Aleister's help. Once the Vampire was safely atop the grass at Xavier's feet, Aurora kneeled at his side and began waving her hands across his body.

"What are you doing?" Alexandria asked Aurora.

"She's rousing Christian," Aleister answered.

Aurora nodded. "Yes, he fell under somewhere between the waking world and the spirit one—he must be roused so he can feed."

Nathanial stared at the back of the Enchanter's head in confusion. "And how do you plan to rouse him?" he asked, his gaze shifting to Alexandria, who returned the gaze with uncertainty.

"Simple," Aurora answered, removing her hands from over Christian, working to pull back a sleeve of her red robes, "with my blood."

"What?" Alexandria shrieked before Nathanial had the chance to. He watched Aurora extend a hand to Aleister for one of the many daggers he held, to which he obliged, releasing a dagger from the leather strap around his waist, handing it to her without a word.

She took it, pressing the blade to the inside of her arm, moving it across her wrist easily, and Nathanial watched with red eyes as the blood began to leave the cut. Aleister turned away from her blood as though it harmed him to smell it, and Xavier stared at the woman's arm with apparent desire: his red eyes would not leave the crimson drops.

Nathanial stared at Aurora with a hardened jaw as she moved her arm to Christian's lips and forced him to drink. His eyes would not open, but before long, a hand found its way to her arm and he began to shown signs of consciousness. His eyes opened at last and how red they were, and his hunger, Nathanial could see it clearly; the Vampire fed as though it would be his last.

After several birds flew from the trees, Christian released her arm, letting a long cold breath escape his lungs.

As Aurora nursed her still-bleeding wound, Aleister turned back to face them all, his expression pained. He cleared his throat and said so all would hear him, "We must move."

"Yes," Xavier whispered, and even his face held great traces of longing, "we must." He moved to stand although one arm was still wrapped carefully around his midsection, the other extended to push himself upward as steadily as possible. Aleister was at his side before he could fully arrive to his feet, a scarred hand upon Xavier's shoulder. "Easy, Vampire," he said sternly, "you must be feeling off-center."

Xavier stared at him. "I just had water thrown on my face and was taken...wherever the hell we are—of course I'm off-center," he snapped, brushing the Vampire's hand off his shoulder. "And I don't need you constantly on my back."

Aleister had opened his mouth to respond when low rumbles shook the grassy ground. "What on Earth is that?"

Nathanial tensed as the rumbling grew greater with the passing seconds, and Aleister said to Aurora, "The Whispering Winds Spell of Location placed me here—where *is* here?"

"The outskirts of Wingdale," Aurora responded.

"I see," Aleister said. "We've no time, we've no blood—we must run. Now."

"Why?" Christian asked and Nathanial stared at him, able to see his worry.

"Because, Christian," Aleister said, pointing a sharp finger through the trees where the rumbling was beginning to form something akin to an earthquake, "Eleanor's Creatures are coming."

Alexandria eyed him next. "Where can we go?"

Nathanial said, "Quiddle."

※

"We see your indecision, your grief...your guilt...and we welcome it."

How cruel that voice, how taunting, how it never seemed to leave him, especially when he was left to his thoughts. And no longer did he find himself blaming Dracula for his predicament, but instead, he found the words of Joseph Gail to linger on incessantly, pulling the thoughts of Xavier to the forefront of his mind every so often.

"You're standing in for a Vampire that could be mocking you at every turn..."

He had no clear idea where Xavier was. He only knew the Vampire was moving freely about the Dark World. But Victor gained some comfort in the thoughts that Eleanor Black's Creatures surrounded him at every turn.

"M'Lord," a concerned voice said then, bringing him out of his thoughts.

He looked up and blinked, realizing indeed that he was in the First Meeting Chamber within Dracu—*his* mansion, and round the long table were the prestigious men and women of the various Vampire cities and towns within the Dark World. And they were all scared.

He cleared his throat, dispelling thoughts of Xavier. "Sorry, was a bit distracted."

"I'll say," a jovial Vampire said, bouncing along in his seat, his dark curly hair shaking. He peered over thin glasses to stare at Victor. "You haven't said a word and we've been in procession for over thirty minutes!"

"What ails you, your Grace?" another Vampire said, her blonde hair vibrant in the many candles' light.

"Ails me?" Victor asked, rising to sit up higher in the large, tall-backed seat. *Uncomfortable*, he thought. "Nothing...truly, my mind is rapt on thoughts of Cedar Village...how terrible that attack was."

Whispers of assent drifted around the table and Victor was almost surprised that the candles were not extinguished in the wake of the wind they created.

"Truly horrible," a dark-skinned Vampire said from next to a Vampire Victor recognized as the King of Rore. "But we wonder, your Grace, how that was allowed to happen?"

All waited in silence for what he would say: it made him all the more uncomfortable, those pressing gazes, those silent questions that filled the shimmering eyes.

Folding his hands together atop the dark wood, he found the words at last, "It was not allowed, Mister Grove, it was something we had no way of knowing would happen at all. When I received word, it had already happened, and at that time there was no way we could rectify the situation."

"But, surely Your Grace," the blonde-haired Vampire said, and Victor realized it was none other than Catalina Zey, Countess of Lane, her brilliant brown eyes questioning, "you know the whereabouts of Xavier Delacroix."

And when he stared at her, the Vampire at her side said, "Forgive us, your Grace, but...we all assumed the reason Cedar Village was destroyed was because Xavier Delacroix was there."

Marvelous, he thought darkly, wondering what else was public news. He eyed the searching gazes of all the Vampires that surrounded the table and forced out a meaningless breath before he said, "As I said, we knew not what happened in Cedar Village, and if it were because of Xavier Delacroix or not, there is no clear way to say."

"But Victor—er, your Grace," a gorgeous Vampire with dark red hair by the name of Odette Chrisanti said next, "we were under the impression that you knew where Xavier Delacroix was—what he was doing. Was that not why you agreed to take the place as Temporary King...waiting until he returned?"

Unbelievable! "I agreed, Odette," he said, fighting hard to keep the venom out of his voice, "because the Dark World needed a leader, and Xavier Delacroix is not it. We know not where he is—though we *are* tracking him—he continues to slip our reach."

"So you are saying," a stuffy Vampire Victor had come to loathe as the Duke of Trenn, said next, "that you have no idea where our king is? Just how in the world do you profess to run the Dark World in his stead?"

He glared at this Vampire, unable to keep the anger out of his voice as he snarled. "I have never professed to run anything! The Chairs and I are hard at work trying to locate the damned Vampire. Would you, Fitan Trenn, like to go out into the Dark World in this state to try to locate one Vampire that apparently doesn't want his place?"

He looked affronted, but Victor did not care. Even as the whispers of bewilderment flittered through the dim air, Victor found his thoughts to return to the insufferable Vampire and what, if anything, the Vampire was truly doing in the Dark World. *It was not dealing with the troubled voices of the other royalty, that was for sure*, he thought miserably.

The dark doors opened and in stepped a Vampire that seemed to fill the entire room with his pressing green eyes, an aura of great command. And Victor inhaled sharply, the sudden dash of fear propelling him to his feet.

Joseph Gail paid him no mind. He stepped deeper into the large hall, and Victor saw that he still wore the same clothes that he'd been wearing the day before. The Creature had never left. So why show his face again?

"Gail," several Vampires said, all rising to their feet much like Victor had done, though he expected they knew not of his true reason for leaving his seat.

"My friends, my family," Joseph said, waving a pale hand through the air in greeting.

"Why, why are you here?" Victor forced himself to ask, unable to keep his gaze off the unsettling Vampire, his previous words filling his mind once more: *"I'm here Victor...for you."*

And those green eyes found him at last, and Victor understood that he had come to check up on him, to keep him from spilling the truth to the others. The cruel voice drifted to his mind as though it belonged there:

"They doubt you...your position...they still cling to the Vampire that has lied to you...what kind of king has no true command?"

Chapter Twenty

THE MEDALLION

They'd journeyed to Merpeople's waters and night fell about them, Aleister moving to secure passage across the water. They'd watched in horror as he had been denied and slipped beneath the surface as though pulled by hands unseen. It had not been long, however, for Xavier Delacroix to pull himself from battle with Thomas Montague and join them at the water's bank, completely oblivious to all that had just transpired, arm healed, Dracula's voice filling his mind. He'd stepped forward, and as they all watched, submerged, just as the heads of many Merpeople did.

✳

Xavier spun in the water, eyes narrowed as he searched through darkness for any sight of the scarred Vampire. Only the moon above gave him any light, and he was aware that disturbances in the water were the causes of the Merpeople swimming about him...but what they would do, if anything, he could not know, and he would not wait to find out.

He moved, propelling himself through the water, though he knew it to be fruitless, for nothing remained before his eyes but more darkness, more water.

Then she appeared, and he was forced to still, for it could not be possible...

"Eleanor," he said, water filling his lungs the longer he stared.

She said nothing, her long dark hair just floated around her effortlessly, her skin pale, breasts bared, but her legs—Xavier saw at last that she did not have any: black scales shimmered atop a long, powerful tail, two strong fins flitting through the water, and he realized that a Mermaid had shown herself to him. It was not bloody Eleanor...

Anger fueling him at his momentary lapse of sense, he stared at her, wondering just what she was doing, wondering just where Aleister was, if they had him...

An odd sound filled his ears next and she turned from him, her tail swishing through the black water. He was almost amazed at how fast she swam. He was aware his traveling cloak was heavy, weighing him down.

With quick hands, he shrugged out of the cloak and pressed on behind the tail. She never stopped, never ceased, never once looked back to see if he followed, indeed, he was hardly sure that the Mermaid was leading him to Aleister at all.

He was just about to make his own trail through the water when the sword at his waist began to buzz with a calling energy and he removed it from its sheath. At once, a brilliant red light filled the dark water and he stared at the sword in alarm. It glowed red just as it had done when he'd pointed the sword to Aleister's chest back in Scylla...

Could it be?

He pressed on, the Mermaid falling away from in front of him. The red light blared, but he ignored her, the sword was his guide. As the red light intensified, the more he pressed on. He knew he was getting close...

The sword had begun to tremble in his hand when another red light a few yards ahead of him blared through the dark water.

There. And he swam faster, the sword buzzing violently in his grip the more he neared the second source of red light. It was not long before he saw the outline of the Vampire: Aleister's head was down, his eyes closed, his arms in front of him, hanging limp in the water. It was as though he'd drowned, but that couldn't be. *Vampires don't need to breathe.*

Xavier reached him and sheathed the sword, even though it had not ceased vibrating. The large red medallion found its way out of Aleister's shirt and hovered just before him in the water, shaking angrily as well.

"I don't believe it," Xavier said, and he lifted a hand to touch the glowing red gem. As soon as he had done so, a thunderous voice filled his mind, as though the person who held it was right beside him:

"Protect the Dragon."

✳

Christian narrowed his eyes: something flew out of the water, a brilliant red light filling the air for a moment, and then it was gone. "Did anyone else see that?" he asked as Aurora and Alexandria nodded.

"It's them," Aurora said, and he saw her eyes were wet with tears.

She and Alexandria shared grateful glances, but then Alexandria said, "Are we going to have to swim through—"

"Oh, no, of course not," Aurora said.

Christian saw she looked happy: gone was the stern gaze she normally held, replacing it was a soft look of relief.

"But you said," Alexandria began, and Christian could not help but see how pleasantly the moonlight graced her face, "that we had to—that Mermaids..."

"Things have changed, my dear," Aurora said. "Now, stand back, all of you." And she spread her arms wide to push them all back against the grass.

Christian looked skeptically towards Nathanial, who mirrored the glance, and Aurora waved her arms through the night. From them, a purple light fled, moving in a narrow line across the lake.

Christian watched in amazement as the grass from all sides of the lake lifted up from the ground, mounds of earth coming with it, and flew over the lake to form a narrow bridge that ended where Xavier and Aleister rested in a wet heap on the other side.

"Wow," Alexandria breathed in astonishment, and Nathanial smiled in appreciation.

"Lovely Spell of Alteration, Madame."

Aurora gave a false bow, and when she rose, the smile was still upon her lips. "We can only cross it one behind the other. Miss Stone...if you would."

"I...okay," Alexandria whispered, moving barefoot to step on the grass bridge.

She moved carefully, and when she was in the very middle of the large lake, several dark heads resurfaced from the water. She gasped at these appearances and Christian thought she was prepared to fall. He took a step along the ground in preparation, but she soon recovered, her tattered skirts swishing around her ankles. She stepped across the bridge and reached Xavier and Aleister, the former of whom was on his feet, careful hand upon her shoulder as if to comfort her.

"I'm next," Christian said, and he kept his eyes upon Xavier and Alexandria, wondering what on Earth they could be discussing, for it was so animatedly they spoke. He stepped across the narrow ground and reached them.

"...I wasn't in my right mind, I do apologize for scaring you if ever I did, Miss Stone," Xavier was saying to her, and Christian could not help but envy how even dripping wet the Vampire retained his charm. He was partway to wishing the Vampire was still lost when Alexandria turned to him and said, "Christian, your brother was just telling me that he was...trapped in Eleanor Black's...energy, but Aleister saved him."

"Continuously," Christian muttered. "How would the Vampire know where we were to go, anyway?" he continued, wishing for a distraction from Xavier's genial nature.

A harsh cough filled the air, forcing their gazes downward. Aleister was slowly rising to sit atop the grass, his coughs never ceasing, and the red medallion around his neck seemed to shine.

"What is that?" Christian asked, and Aleister looked up at him briefly before catching his gaze: he lifted a scarred hand and stuffed the medallion back into his shirt.

"It's nothing...family heirloom," he rasped, more coughs leaving him as Xavier extended a hand for him to take.

He seemed to be hesitant to take Xavier's hand, Christian thought, but soon relented, allowing the Vampire to pull him to his feet. Once he was standing, Xavier said, "I must apologize for my actions, Aleister. I was not in the right—"

"Mind?" Aleister said, staring hard at Xavier. "It's fine...what matters is that you are in the right mindset *now*."

"But it does not explain," Nathanial said, stepping from the bridge, Aurora close behind, "how you knew that we were to travel to Quiddle."

"Ah," Aleister sighed, wiping his wet brow with his wet sleeve, and Christian could not imagine away his terse gaze upon Aurora who would not reach it. "I...a simple guess," he breathed, returning his eyes to Nathanial.

"Hardly a guess," Nathanial said. "Now that we are moderately safe, I'd say the mystery that is Aleister must be solved. How did you know we needed to travel to Quiddle?"

"I knew...because—"

"Because you are closer to Dracula than you were letting on," Nathanial interrupted, and Xavier narrowed his eyes upon him.

"Nathanial—"

"No, Xavier, he has helped you, that I can thank him for, but he knows far too much than he is letting on. My contact in Lane was told from Dracula, himself, where he would leave the book if ever it came to hiding it. This Vampire...he *has* had a special interest in you ever since he saw you in Cedar Village. What more do you hide, Aleister?"

Aleister looked as though he were going to be sick. "I knew Dracula, Nathanial. I knew him, yes I did, but I left him, I left the Vampire City. Dracula was going to kill me if I didn't...didn't do... what he wanted me to. I did it...my hands were tied...but I left him forever after that."

"Except you didn't," Nathanial said, and Christian eyed him.

"How do you mean?" Aleister said and Christian almost thought he looked scared.

"That medallion," Nathanial said, nodding towards Aleister's chest, "only those close to Dracula held one. Evert the Ancient Elder has one, and it is from him that I receive my orders. An Enchanter in Lane, whom I have studied with closely, has one. You only get that medallion if you were someone Dracula trusted, absolutely. No offense, Xavier."

Aleister looked lost. Christian thought he'd never seen the Vampire so off-kilter. "I...Vivery—"

Many yards ahead of them came a deafening sound; it reminded Christian of a massive earthquake, and as they all stared ahead, the blast of dread hit them all in one complete sweep.

"What in the bloody hell was that?" Alexandria screamed.

Xavier tensed and Christian half-wondered if his wish had come true. There was no doubt that this was Eleanor's energy, the swarming dread could not be mistaken.

"It's her men," Xavier whispered to the air. His eyes scanned the dark horizon.

"But that's where Quiddle is," Nathanial said, looking troubled.

"And is that not," Xavier began, turning to eye them, and not a trace of strangeness in his gaze could be detected, "where we must go?"

Chapter Twenty-One

LANE

Damion Nicodemeus lifted a hand to stroke the Creature's gray skin, his eyes soft, for extracting the blood of a Unicorn was a task that had to be taken seriously. His dark fingers ran nimbly through the Unicorn's black hair and it let out a comforting neigh at his touch.

"Yes, girl," he whispered, "yes, relax."

He continued stroking her hair with one hand while with his other he moved for the small blade atop the ground. With his next cold breath, the blade was in his hand. He knew he had to make quick work of it, there was no telling when a Centaur would come bounding out of the woods—or worse.

He moved, pulling the dagger against the underbelly of the Unicorn, its frantic neighing reaching his ears.

"Shh shh shh, my sweet," he whispered reassuringly as the blood spilled into the three empty jars he had placed beneath it some minutes before.

As it drained of life, its black eyes rolling into the back of its head, Damion became aware of rustling in the trees around him. He stood, ignoring the Creature as it swayed without his hand to steady it any longer before plopping to the ground, knocking over the half-filled jars, spilling the blue blood along the ground.

"Shit," he hissed, staring at the bleeding Unicorn, the blood from the jars getting crushed underneath the Unicorn's dead weight. *There goes the damned Vampire's healing.* "Who's out there?" he called to the dark trees before him, eyeing them closely for any sign of Creature.

"Master Damion," the voice called, and he felt his dead heart surge with anticipation.

"Lucien?" Damion whispered, stepping from the horrible smelling blood towards the Vampire that appeared through the trees, a thick hood atop his head. "What more did we learn?"

"Eleanor Black's men, Master, have the sword—" he began before Damion let a vicious snarl of frustration leave his lips, ushering Lucien into silence.

"And you did not take it from them?" Damion asked next, brown eyes alive with murderous intent. The Vampire's next words had better be good.

"I could not, my Lord," he whispered apologetically, his stare placed upon his boots. "I reached out for it, but I could not touch it."

"What the devil do you mean you could not touch it, Lucien?"

"I reached out for it while one of her men was distracted, my Lord—I was not seen, of course. It appears to have some curse around its body, I was not able to touch it at all."

"How curious. I presume you followed her men—you did not just rest on your laurels..."

"No, Master. I did follow them, they arrived several yards from a place that seemed to venture underground. It had a gate, my Lord, and a stone staircase...but I could not follow them in there."

"And why not? This place sounds familiar...it was not the Vampire City was it?"

"No—it was someplace else. The mouth of a dark cave, my Lord, that headed down into terrible darkness. Even with my...abilities, I could not step foot in there. That is the last I saw of the sword, my Lord."

Interesting, Damion thought as he stared at the pale Vampire, blond hair swaying slightly in a passing breeze. "So this must be where Eleanor...resides. Tell me, Lucien, could you lead me to this place if ever I asked you to?" His mind set on how he could accomplish this impossible task.

Lucien's eyes seemed to shine with question. "Yes, of course, my Lord. But...your blood...you do not need it for that Vampire anymore, Master Damion?"

Damion let a smile tear at his lips, for he knew he would get nothing out of Dragor Descant—the Vampire never talked. It was a waste to keep him there any longer. He'd have to kill him. He stared at Lucien and said, "No, no, I don't think I have any need for Dragor anymore. He has served his purpose."

✳

Her eyes widened as the voice called to her through the narrow tunnel: "Eleanor! My Queen!"

She whirled and stared at the Vampire whose lips were curled into a smile of confidence, the radiance one she would only acknowledge in one other Vampire...

"*Joseph?*" she said, thoughts of the Vampire he was ordered to manipulate springing to her mind. "You've returned so soon?"

His brilliant green eyes flashed in the light of a nearby torch along the wall, and she saw he looked uncertain. "Was I not to return once seeds of doubt had been planted within Victor's mind, my Queen?"

"You were. I assume this task has been successfully completed then?"

"He is noticeably stirred—and you were correct, my Queen. He sheds tears as easily as the clouds hide the light of the moon. It took nothing more than simple words of betrayal...the idea that Xavier knows more than he does to get the Vampire's mind further frayed. He truly does not want his seat as Temporary King. It is miraculous how the Vampires fall without their creator to steadily hold their hands."

The smile rose to her lips, for in this she knew the Creature spoke perfect truth. "And a pity that is, my dear Mister Gail." She said relishing the thought of Victor Vonderheide lost. "The Vampires are at a loss, truly, defenseless... And with Xavier falling to the trap of those stationed in Quiddle...they are no threat. We may move for the Vampire City sooner than expected."

A harrowing scream sounded from farther down the hall, and she watched Joseph's eyes widen in question before she smiled and reached for his hand. "Thank you, Joseph, for your work. You may return to Wingfield—we shall be using it for...headquarters if anything were to go wrong and this...cave...fails me. Though it shouldn't."

He smiled his appreciation and bowed low, turning on a heel to disappear into darkness.

A worn-looking Creature came barreling down the tunnel, his expression fearful when he neared her. A hand pressed tight against a rib, he said, "A thousand apologies, my Queen, but Quiddle—Xavier never entered it! He marched right past the stone marker for the mountains that hide Lane..." He took great breaths, his human form shaking.

She could not find the words to speak, for how horrible was this? Why would the Vampire not enter Quiddle? Why would he not enter the place he had to go in order to acquire the book? If he'd sensed the Creatures within the city, what then? Why would he run? Would he not stay and fight? What was the cause of this sudden excursion?

How I hate it when things don't go to plan.

She cleared her throat and dismissed the man who had given her this information a curt nod, for she knew what she had to do next. If the Vampire was already moving for Lane—had possibly reached it by now—then there was little she could do, for if he found the book and traveled through it...why, acquiring him would be something of a task, wouldn't it?

No, he was a lost cause, at least for the moment...which was why Eleanor prided herself on her endless supply of plans and countermeasures. If one were to rule the Dark World, did one not need to account for any contingency? And if Victor Vonderheide was as lost and distraught as Joseph Gail let on, then would that not be the best course of immediate action to take?

After all, Xavier could have already claimed the book, could already be trapped within its ruthless, damaging pages...

She shuddered at the thought of what she'd seen whilst in there, whilst seeking fervently the truth. And she'd gotten it, hadn't she? Yes, she'd faced what Dracula had hidden and she didn't much like it at all. So that was why she fought this truth and made her own, and successfully survived the damned book once and for all.

And she was done with it. Done with it, but the knowledge remained.

"Thank you for telling me this, Trent," she said to the man, whose breathing had finally slowed; he now stared at her with apprehensive admiration.

He nodded at once. "Not at all, my Queen."

"Have the remaining Elite move for the Vampire City in London. We have a sufficient number of Creatures, a few Giants and Dragons have not hurt our cause. To delay this any longer is foolish and tiresome. I grow weary of waiting for my dear Xavier to make the next move—we shall make it for him."

"M-my Queen..." Trent whispered in utter astonishment.

She knew what her words meant. But she knew, also, that nothing else could be done—if he *did* acquire the bloody book in Lane and faced it all, survived, he would be much harder to touch, let alone bend to her will. It would have to be Victor.

"What, what of Aciel, Amentias, your Highness?" an Elite near the door asked.

She stared at him and was not surprised when he removed his gaze. "They are of no consequence to me. They have been poisoned and there is no telling when they will return to their minds. Trent, call for the others, spread the word—I want bodies moving for the Vampire City within the next three hours. Any less, and I shall be most cross. You have my permission to kill a few Vampires—but save the rest—the better to build our forces. Show those pathetic Creatures what true power resembles. But leave Victor for me, I shall need time alone with him. Do I make myself clear?"

"I...yes, my Queen," Trent said. "Shall we utilize the Bagabills for this? The Regarocks?"

"Hmm. Only just obtained and already looking for uses to our cause. I appreciate your mind, dear Trent. Yes, I don't see why not. Let us put our newfound friends to good use. Round up the Regarocks, I shall handle the Bagabills myself."

"At once, my Queen. And...the humans?"

"What of them?"

"They will surely be murdered if we lead the Giants and Dragons straight to the Vampire City—there is no other way to get to it but to go through London, my Queen."

"I am aware, but my concern is not for the humans. Our cause has grown. We have gained a considerable amount and even more shall join us once we have taken over the Vampire City. We are sowing the seeds of our very foundation."

"Yes, my Queen."

"Now tend to the Regarocks—the sooner the Giants are out of the way; the sooner it is we can move. Dragons are much...easier to persuade."

And she did not blink as he turned on a heel and disappeared into darkness.

Xavier, she thought, *ever the confident, hands-on soldier...* As she stepped down the hall, the thought of Xavier brimming with knowledge and purpose sent a strong chill up her spine. For even if it weren't the knowledge of what *she'd* gained for her sacrifice, it was a knowledge that could build the world anew or tear it asunder all the same.

And both had to be done for true order to be restored.

✳

Xavier Delacroix heard their whispers, their words, but he paid no mind to any of it for long, for the voice of Dracula sounded clear now, rendering all other thought and action obsolete. For the Elves' magic had done their job, his arm had finally healed, and he was no longer tied to Eleanor...at least, not lost in his mind. Nothing else rang true but Dracula's voice of command, of hope, of direction.

For that was what he needed now—what he'd needed the moment Eleanor had returned from the grave speaking of Ancients, power, and secrets. But if there was one question he was plagued with, despite the encouraging words of his former mentor, it was "Why wait so long to let this be known?"

If Dracula knew he was to die like Evert the Ancient Elder had let on, then why would Dracula keep all of his secrets until the very last moment? *Why would he not just spill everything to me so I'd be better...*

No, he could not make himself finish that lie, for he was not sure that he'd be better equipped to deal with any of this had Dracula told him. But, perhaps, Dracula would have taken him on his journeys, perhaps, even, Dracula would have been a helping hand.

Instead, he was stuck with Vampires and an Enchanter that seemed to know much more than they were all letting on. Dracula's... touch had been painfully branded on each of them, one could not miss it. It was a touch Xavier was all but familiar with: after having being bestowed the title of "Dracula's Favorite," one would have to get used to the enclosed environment of fame that came with it.

And Nathanial, why, the curious Vampire held grand traces of it. If not famous by namesake, then famous by Dracula's eyes. After all, Nathanial Vivery was a Vampire that had been with Dracula, in close quarters, seeing things perhaps no other Creature got to see. And his magic...Xavier could barely recall why the thought of the Vampire performing magic was not a complete surprise...but he suspected it had to do something with her, so he turned his attention to the most mysterious of the bunch, Aleister.

The scarred Vampire was hiding a load of burdens. The way the Vampire continuously saved him, kept him in line, didn't even give him a chance to fail...the Vampire was personally invested, this much Xavier had worked out...but why—and in *who* was he truly invested?

True, his cottage, Aurora's cottage had been turned to ash by the battle in Cedar Village, but they did not *need* to travel with them. Being a Member of Division Six surely afforded Aleister another place to remain. Somewhere that did not entail following he, Xavier, around like a lost animal. And why did Aurora stick around? Surely she had a Guild or some such where she could recharge herself? If so, why did she not move for it? Why would either of them stick around like they had?

It could just be because you've taken the place of the Vampire that's held something important for them.

Ah, it could. Or it could be that they wish to see the self-assured Xavier Delacroix in action with no overhead authority figure to stop them.

The words trailed from Xavier's his mind as a new sound filled them. Over the biting snow, the howl of wind, there appeared a band of voices from somewhere over the mountains' snow-drenched tops.

He thought of who it could be—there was no lingering scent of strange dread nor of Lycans. So these newcomers had to be Vampires, but why allow Vampires to leave the high gates of Lane at a time like this?

"Shh!" Xavier hissed to the three bickering Creatures behind him. "Someone is coming over the mountain!"

They fell into silence, stepping closer towards him. The severity of his words had hit them rightly: they all appeared cautious.

Xavier kept a steadying hand on the Ascalon, preparing himself to use it, when a figure appeared at the top of the lowest mountain, a royal blue traveling cloak thick with white fur at the collar and cuffs around the stranger's body. "Xavier Delacroix? Is that you?" the figure called down.

"Don't answer," Aleister said, but Xavier recognized that voice—it was none other than Reginald Zey, the King of Lane. Why would he leave his beloved city?

Xavier stepped forward, releasing the Ascalon as the Vampire left the top of the mountain and jumped carefully down the mountainside, landing smoothly just before him, sliding a little with the movement of the snow. A white gloved hand was extended, however, and the smile was wide as he stared at Xavier with something of joy.

"My boy!" the Vampire said. Xavier finally took his hand and shook it, the other gloved hand moving to cover Xavier's warmly. "We've been waiting! Why, I was just about to go to the Vampire City myself to gather Catalina, and I had hoped to run into you along the way!"

"I'm...sorry?" Xavier said

"Xavier—we don't have time for this," Aleister said. "You need to get to Lane and get that book—"

It was the first time the Vampire's blue eyes found Aleister, and here, even through the fur of the blue hood, Xavier saw those eyes were cold. It was as though the Vampire truly despised Aleister, but how did the Vampire even know him?

"Aleister," Reginald said, the pep had drained from his voice. "I didn't know you were with our king."

"And I did not know you ever left your City," he responded.

"Aurora," the King of Lane said, ignoring Aleister's words. "But this must be Christian Delacroix! And—" His voice died abruptly as his eyes found Alexandria.

Several figures appeared atop the mountains and King Reginald nodded as though he knew they were there, but he had not turned to look. His sharp gaze moved instead from Creature to human and back with something of great reverence.

"We shall talk more inside the gates," Reginald said, the snow continuing to press against their cloaks and hair and his stare moved to Xavier. A sliver of sadness in the Vampire's gaze. "This way."

And they moved over the lowest mountain, Xavier only turning once atop it to eye his brother and see how he'd decided to help the woman up the freezing, loose snow, with nothing to protect her feet. Christian held her across his arms as he climbed up the slope behind Aleister, the Enchanter bringing in the very rear. The smile was brief as it graced his lips, but it was there. For he never imagined, in all his years as a Vampire, that his bloody *brother* would be hauling a woman in his arms to protect her from things like snow.

A younger Christian, he knew, would have let the sorry woman fend for herself. But was it because Miss Stone was no normal human that Christian moved so to assist her? Or had they...bonded in their time together?

He let the laugh escape him with that fleeting thought as he turned and saw the large walls of solid ice that protected the crystal blue City of Lane. He stared, marveling at the tip of the largest building in

Lane, which could be seen just beyond the high walls. The last time he had been here, it was a gathering party for the royal family and he'd been tasked to accompany Dracula. That was when he'd met the lovely Liliana Zey and, for all the time he had been there, enjoyed her company ravenously.

"Xavier? Something wrong?" the rough voice of Aleister called.

Spinning around, he found the curious and worried gazes staring up at him from the side of the mountain and he moved, stepping in Reginald's footsteps over the snow, down the jagged rock beneath.

When they had all safely reached the other side, the Vampires that had appeared atop the mountain stood in a line just before the tall walls of ice, their fur-lined gazes placed on Xavier. The King of Lane spread two gloved hands wide through the air, and Xavier blinked: There was no snow at all here, nor was there the harsh wind, it seemed it had all but disappeared. But as he turned to the high blue walls before him, he saw that there was a light sprinkle of snow over the city alone. He remembered when Dracula had told him, *"The snow of Lane is a protector—a buffer, actually. None but the purest of Creatures may enter, none but the most royal of blood may pass through the ice gate. It is The Impenetrable City."*

"Men!" Reginald Zey said with impressive command, and all seven of the Vampire soldiers stiffened, but Xavier saw no protrusion of sword along waist against their cloaks. They each held arrows in white quivers along their backs, and a large white bow tight in a white-gloved hand. *When did the soldiers of Lane switch to archery from their coveted golden staffs?*

"We have very important guests here, today! Our beloved king, his brother, Madame Aurora Borealis, and Lord Aleist—"

"*Your Majesty!*" Aleister interjected before the Vampire could finish his speech, and Reginald looked around as though annoyed: his hands dropped from the air and his stare found Aleister's. "I have been here before—is this truly necessary?"

"It is," Reginald said, but his stare found more than just Aleister now. He looked from Aurora to Alexandria and back, "But...for the sake of the women who find themselves here, perhaps we can skip introductions." He turned away from a relieved Aleister, who would not lift his gaze from the ground, and addressed his men with a lower tone:

"We have important guests. Open the gates and let them in, they need not pass through our Introduction Committee—give them whatever they desire, deny them nothing. I shall be heading to the Vampire City for Catalina and shall return as soon as possible. *Live long the City of Lane!*"

"*Live long the City of Lane!*" they chanted in reverent unison. And even as Reginald turned and faced them once more, Xavier's questions died in his throat. He watched the Vampire climb expertly up the lowest mountain before disappearing behind it without a glance back.

A loud noise drew Xavier's gaze from the mountaintop to the high gates before him, and he watched as the others took several steps away, for the seven soldiers were pushing the gates open with nothing but their hands. Their eyes flashed red as the snow along the ground moved slowly against the thick ice. Xavier realized they were cutting a fresh path: no one had left Lane in a long time. So why did dear Reginald continuously mention Catalina? And how had he found his way through the gates if they had not been opened until now?

"Xavier," Nathanial called, "coming?"

He saw that they had all stepped together to venture into the bustling blue city, and it was with a slight nod that he followed in their wake, pressing a hand to the Ascalon, only just realizing that it had been steadily pulsing at his side the moment Aurora's medallion had glowed.

Chapter Twenty-Two

THE IMMORTAL'S GUIDE

"*T*his is where he's been taken?" Peroeneus Doe asked the old Elf at his side.

"Aye," Arminius said. "And all we must do is gather him. I'm afraid he will not be well enough to stand, however."

The Vampire at his side let out a slow sigh. "And the Caddenhalls... they will just let us take him?"

A long-fingered hand clutched at the red medallion along his chest. "They are not here; the house is empty. We will find no complications in this venture."

Peroeneus Doe stared at the tall white manor, its old black gates around it as though they didn't belong on the ground they stood on, and he felt the medallion along his neck pulse. "He is right. Only Dragor remains, but what does the Vampire know of any of this?"

He saw the thin smile rise on the Elf's lips as the old cane was pressed into the grassy ground. "He knows enough," he wheezed, hobbling towards the black gates, Nicholai moving with him. Peroeneus felt the briefest hints of hesitation before he stepped forward as well, following in their wake.

It was all strange, he thought, keeping his eyes upon the silver hair of Nicholai Noble. *The Vampire...what had he done for Dracula? And Arminius...how miraculous was it that the old Elf was a part of this hair-brained scheme? What had* he *done for the Great Vampire?* They drew nearer to the black gates, Arminius pushing it open with a white hand. *Did imparting that damned spell really cause me to be tied to all of this?*

Arminius moved up the small steps to the door. He waved a hand and it swung open. Peroeneus watched him step around a finely polished wooden table, disappearing into a larger room, the Vampire following suit.

He stayed at the threshold of the door, however, as the smell of blood and horrible death found his nose. Stifling an upheaval of his dinner, he pressed the sleeve of his dark purple robes to his nose and pressed forth for the room the Elf and Vampire had disappeared into.

There was comfortable-looking furniture here, brown thick curtains lining the quaint windows. But that smell... He saw the door that remained open in the back of the room and stepped for it, the smell thickening through the sleeve of his robes. *Bloody hell,* he thought as he neared it, *is the Vampire even alive?*

"Help me get him up, Nicholai," he heard the hissing voice of Arminius command from somewhere down the stairs. As he stepped slowly, nose still covered, he saw the dimly illuminated frame of a disheveled, unmoving heap of bloody cloak along the floor. Nicholai Noble and Arminius were on either side of it, and as Peroeneus stepped down the rest of the stairs and removed his sleeve from his nose at last, he saw the battered, bruised face of Dragor Descant in the light of a nearby torch.

Nicholai had grabbed the Vampire's worn boots and had lifted them off the ground, while Arminius waved a free hand, sending Dragor's bloody head to rise as well. Peroeneus stared at them, not understanding how a Vampire could cause such terrible damage to one of their own, when the medallion underneath his robes, which had never stopped its steady pulsing, gave one lurching throb and then ceased. Arminius's, Nicholai's and Dragor's medallions let out a brief haze of red light as well before it disappeared.

"Good," Arminius wheezed, turning for the stairs, hand aloft, "we can go." But he and Nicholai had not made it but two steps before an alarmed voice rang out through the house: "The door's wide open! Someone has been here!"

"Who on Earth is that?" Peroeneus whispered, staring at an annoyed Arminius. *"I thought you said we would have no complications!"*

He said nothing.

The basement opened wide and down the steps came none other than Damion Nicodemeus, a Vampire Peroeneus knew by name and horrible reputation. He was surprised at the exact anger and coldness that seemed to fill the Vampire's eyes as he stared around at them in disbelief.

"What brings you...curious Creatures here?" And his brown eyes moved to the still-hovering Dragor in between Arminius and Nicholai; the slightest quiver of an eye gave away his displeasure.

Arminius clutched tight his white cane and nodded, bringing Damion's gaze to him. "The truth...of what is to come, what has *already* come, brings us here, Vampire," he said, his voice leaving him in a low hiss.

"Master...what troubles you?" another voice sounded from the top of the stairs.

"Nothing, Lucien. Remain where you are," Damion called back, never tearing his gaze from Arminius. "I can handle a few... misguided souls."

Nicholai let out a sound, something like a snort, and Damion stared at him. "Something funny, Vampire?"

"Hardly," he responded with a small smile, readjusting Dragor's boots in his hands. "It is just...you say you can handle us...when you've been the one handled all along."

Damion's eyes narrowed, and he dug his nails into the wood. "Excuse me?"

"Enough, Nicholai," Arminius said. "We have places to be—we cannot dawdle any longer."

Damion stepped down the rest of the stairs, placing himself just before the Elf, barring them from the stairs. "I'm afraid," he said, "I am interested in what it was you are doing here and...claim to know of me...what it is I do...what it is I know."

"You know nothing, Vampire," Nicholai said, to which Arminius gave him a scathing glare.

"What don't I know?" Damion asked. "Why are you here, gathering Dragor at that?"

"It does not concern you, Damion Nicodemeus," Arminius said, and as Peroeneus stared at them in confusion, the dark Vampire smiled.

"Is that your word on the matter, Elf?" he countered. "Or are you trying to hide what more is going on here? For you say this does not concern me, yet here you are, in my bloody basement, handling my damned Vampire. I'd say I was much more involved in whatever's going on than any of you are letting on."

Peroeneus watched as Arminius let out an impatient sniff, the Vampire now glaring angrily towards Damion as though he were the reason they were there at all.

"You think because you kept a Vampire in your basement that you know anything at all?" Nicholai said.

Damion stared in his direction. "I daresay I know that this Vampire knows of Dracula's power—and that his power is held in that damned sword he carries. But no matter, I know who truly has the sword, and I will acquire it for myself. If you want the damned

Vampire," he stepped aside, "take him. I'm sure you won't get any more use out of him than I."

Arminius did not hesitate in gesturing with his head towards the stairs, before moving, the head of Dragor hovering just out of reach of the steps as he was pulled along by absent strings, Nicholai's hands still holding aloft the Vampire's boots as he stepped behind them.

And Peroneous stepped to the stairs, moving carefully past Damion as he climbed them, leaving the stench of death and blood far behind him as he moved for the dining room, its finely polished wooden table shining in the candlelight as he stepped for the open door.

He swept through it, not stopping as he reached the black gates, pushing them open against the night. He watched as the Elf and Vampire set the bruised Vampire down upon the ground carefully. Once he reached them, the Elf nodded and said, "Reveal your medallion, Enchanter."

Wondering just what more they would do, he lifted the necklace from his robes and let it rest against his chest, plain for all to see. Once the Vampire and Elf had done the same, they began to glow once more, this time a much brighter light than before, and even through Dragor's bloody robes the red light could be seen.

A slight hum filled Peroneous's ears.

Arminius spread a hand over Dragor's body then, bringing all eyes to him, and the red light from the Elf's medallion pressed itself against the long arm, moving down it. It shot down into Dragor's limp body. Peroeneus watched as the Vampire became filled with the light, his entire body glowing with it, until a voice, jarring and deep, sounded from somewhere around him:

"Protect the Dragon!"

He staggered backwards, not understanding where the voice had come from. The Vampire on the ground opened his eyes and rose to sit up. His rough face was battered, an eye partially swollen. He blinked before he rose to his feet within the red light, and then, much to Peroeneus's surprise, turned to Arminius and said, his voice rough from lack of use:

"So...it is time then?"

※

Tall buildings made of a gleaming white stone captured his attention, and he stepped with the others along the main street. Light snow fell here, never resting upon the ground: it remained dry and untouched, and Christian almost thought a bit of magic had brightened his every step here, for it so illuminated the ground. He could see Alexandria's reflection with every step they took.

"And here we have the Enchanter's Guild, Lane Section, naturally," a Vampire introduced as Vincent upon their entrance said now, a pale hand pointed towards the tall building whose wide white double doors were thrown open. "There you shall find food for humans...other Enchanters," he said, and his gray eyes found Aurora and Alexandria.

"Excellent," Nathanial said, nodding towards the Vampire before disappearing inside without another word.

Aurora eyed Alexandria before extending a hand. "I'm sure you are famished—I am the same."

Christian watched as Alexandria hesitated before taking the woman's hand, the slightest glance in his direction one of (at least it seemed to him) gratitude. "You have my thanks," she said, and he was very aware the words seemed as though they'd been spoken in foreign tongue, for he had never heard them directed at him before. They climbed the steps and disappeared within the doorway, and Christian stared after it in bewilderment.

Aurora reappeared in the building's doorway. "Sorry. Alexandria would like to speak with you, Christian. And Aleister—Nathanial, and his mentor, wish for a word as well."

Christian met the scarred Vampire's green gaze and it was with one last apologetic stare towards Xavier that he moved from the sidewalk and stepped towards the Enchanter who had begun to retreat back into the large building. As Aleister stepped within it as well, Christian was aware the Vampire clad in a thick white traveling cloak named Vincent said to Xavier, "Will there be...anything else, my Grace?"

He barely heard the Vampire respond with, "Yes, take me to Zey Manor," before he was too far away to hear anything more.

✳

He stepped with the Vampire through the streets, the crowd thick. Xavier kept a hand on the Ascalon as he walked.

Vincent stopped and Xavier barreled into him. "Wh—" he began, when he saw her, the Queen of Lane. She was walking towards them, her long white dress spilling along the smooth ground behind her. He watched in awe as the older Vampire drew closer, her high cheekbones, beautiful face proud. The high hold her blonde hair took atop her head strengthened this visage.

"My Queen," Vincent whispered, never rising to his feet as the woman reached them at last; she paid him no mind, but stretched a small hand for Xavier to take.

He obliged, clasping it, remembering Dracula's quick reminder to show the proper etiquette when surrounded by others of higher blood. It was her stern smile that made him release her hand and give her the lowest of bows. "Your Highness," he said.

"Xavier Delacroix," she said. Her voice was as light as her appearance, but the sliver of pride had not fled her tongue as she removed her hand from his and waved it gently, bidding him to stand. "I trust your journey here was without incident?"

"No, Ma'am," he responded. "I was met with a few...incidents, but nothing that could not be corrected."

"When Dracula ventured here some weeks ago," she began, much to his surprise, "I was worried for him. He could barely speak— only kept harping on about 'Vampires that were in over their head,' and of course, he desired only that you see the mysterious book he kept hidden beneath this...old-looking leather wrap—"

"Sorry," Xavier said dimly, not able to get past the words "Dracula ventured here." He said, "But Dracula *did* come here? He spoke to you? To the King? *The book is here?*"

She did not gaze at him as she spread the folds of her dress so that she could climb up the steep steps that led to the large black doors that allowed one to enter Zey Manor. They were wide open against the snow-filled air, and when Xavier followed her towards them, the Vampire named Vincent bowed from their presence, Liliana stepping in their wake, looking bemused as Xavier glanced towards her.

"Mother," she started as they entered the large hall, and Xavier stared at the black walls here, the tall white fountain in the center of the large room spouting water with flecks of ice within it. "Mother, what's this about Dracula? When was he here?"

"This does not concern you, Liliana," the older Vampire said, waving a hand through the air. As Xavier turned to eye them again, the Queen had gestured for another Vampire who had remained in the shadows: his black clothes and traveling cloak doing nothing to reveal him until he stepped forward into the light of the torch and sparkling water.

"My Queen," he said expectantly as he drew closer to them, his black eyes never moving from the Queen's face as he gave a curt bow.

"Take Liliana to her room, and do not let her leave it."

Xavier stared at the Vampire in confusion as Liliana let out a gasp and said, "Mother? What's going on?"

She did not stare at her as the Vampire in black grabbed the Princess by the arm and led her through a doorway to the left through a grand sitting room. Xavier could see the white furniture that remained within.

What on Earth...

"Now, Xavier——" she said as though nothing had happened, moving past the large fountain to a black door, "I've no time to properly explain, but you will get your answers in due time." And she waved a hand across the doorway, a brief light flashing from a finger, the light traveling down what appeared to be stairs into what looked like a cellar.

His eyes found the finger from where the light had come and his brow furrowed as further question filled his mind. "Where...did you get that ring, my Queen?" he asked as the small red gem flashed with color in the presence of his question. He thought it resembled a brilliant shade of blood.

Another hand was waved through the air and his gaze was drawn to her cold brown eyes. "Please...return safely, my King. We——I—— could not bear it if we lost you as well." And before he could say another word, she had turned on a heel and had stepped back through the main doors of Zey Manor, leaving him alone.

He stood there for a moment, wondering what had just happened. Why did the Queen of Lane wear a ring resembling the necklaces that Aleister, Aurora, and Evert the Ancient Elder wore? Was it possible at all that she and the others were...a part of some guild that were to, to help him along with his quests?

Xavier thought of Aleister who had never left his side once he'd awoken, he remembered the abled Aurora who had seen to it that Christian and the woman were always safe, the mysterious Nathanial who could do magic, who was at Dracula's side for many years....

What did they all have in common? Was it Dracula? It had to be, surely, for they all had known him in some way—that much they had revealed. And the Queen of Lane? The king? What more did they know? Why, they almost seemed like they'd been expecting him—but how would they know he were to travel here in his quest for the book?

And how had Aleister known where they were to go next?

And the book...

He turned his gaze to the dark stairs before him, only now barely illuminated by the small red ball of light that had fled the queen's finger. The light was hovering there...waiting for him.

The Ascalon pulsed at his side, and as he placed a hand upon the leather-wrapped handle, a remarkable fear swept over him.

Despite all he had been told of the book, despite Dracula's words that still rang through his mind with terrible prominence, *"Xavier, you must become greater than you are. Please listen to me—you need to be all you must for this world. With the power I have given you, you alone can do it—must do it,"* he could not deny that uncertainty filled him now as he stood on the threshold of grand change. For this book...this guide...was it not supposed to be treacherous, filled with terrible truths?

Realizing now how far away Dracula's voice sounded (for could it not just be more lies?), he took a cold breath and stepped over the threshold of the doorway, down the stairs, further into the red light, at once seeing how large the cellar was. It seemed to span several miles in either direction, and when he found the red light, he stepped towards it, aware the Ascalon was pulsing rapidly at his waist.

There it was. The small red book lay plain against the dark wood of the desk, and there was nothing but the red light to further illuminate the book's simple red cover, the golden words etched into the skin:

The Immortal's Guide.

He reached out for the book, aware the dark corners of the large room held no one, nothing—only he remained. But it was jarring to realize it now when he had to...travel through this most mysterious book and uncover the secrets within...

His hand hesitated over the red cover, for he found his thoughts traveling to Eleanor Black, and just what'd she'd possibly gone through to get this book...to journey through it...to end up so changed...

Knowing, somewhere deep down, that he could end up the very same, he let Dracula's words resound through his mind again, letting his hand grasp the red cover, the material smooth against his skin. He realized with a jolt that it was Dragon skin before the book flew open and an aged page stared back at him. The page turned on its own and more red ink showed itself. The Ascalon let out a searing heat that he could feel against his thigh, and as he cried in pain, his vision blurred, the red light disappearing into abrupt darkness, and the coldness of nothing greeted him.

Chapter Twenty-Three

REVELATIONS

Christian had found Alexandria sitting in a lavish room, several Enchanters placed around their respective tables here. He had stepped up to her, curiosity lining his mind for whatever she desired to speak on. Neither Aurora nor Aleister were here and he'd found that strange. Before her was a plate of food she'd already begun to eat: a generous slice of roast chicken was all but cut in half, the other bit in her stomach, he'd guessed, and when he sat across from her, she'd pushed her plate away from her and said, "I was led to London by a Count Dracul."

"What?" he'd said.

"As I understood it from his letters, he was a most respected... man of power. I believe I...knew...that he was a strange man, when I arrived at the hotel he designated I stay once I'd reached London."

Christian stared at her in alarm, wondering where this was coming from at all. "Miss Stone..."

"At the...hotel...he...sent...a man—well it must have been a Vampire, now that I look back on it—and this man...was...scary, if

287

I'm honest. He said I was to journey with him the next day for Count Dracul's...place of residence."

Christian remained silent as the exact meaning of these words hit him with the horrible truth. "...Dracula led you to London and sent a Vampire to...gather you to be brought to him? But...why? Who was this Vampire that came to you, Miss Stone?"

She stared at him, and he found it miraculous that her eyes were not filled with water. She looked odd: it was as though she had accepted what had become of her life and knew that it would never be the same again. "I know not who he was, Christian. But I know his name. It was Nicholai Noble—I won't forget it because it was so... fantastic. He had a thick accent, Russian, perhaps, and he stayed with me the whole night I was there."

"The whole night?" Christian's thoughts ran to matters of indecency, the sight of her fully naked against white sheets, cheeks flushed with the heat of her desire...

"Yes, he said it was to...keep watch over me—that I was an important...acquirement of the Count. But," and she'd hesitated here, "when I awoke...I was in Lord Nicodemeus's home."

He'd sat back in his seat, realizing what night it was that she'd been talking about, and he'd said, "This...Noble person, why did he let you just...leave the hotel? How did you get into those woods?"

"I hardly know, myself, but I did...somehow. I expect it was something at that Vampire's home that drew me there." And it was as though she'd thought what had crossed his mind the moment the words had left her lips—that he, Christian Delacroix was the reason she had been drawn to the Vampire's manor. That he was the reason Lore had gotten his claws on her.

Now he stood in the large hallway as Alexandria Stone finished her meal, his thoughts still wrapped around what she'd said. It was incredible. How Dracula had led the woman there—how he had had another Vampire—whoever was that?—look after the woman for the night. Ignoring the thoughts, he had not been able to stifle when just before her, he turned his attention to what had drawn her to Damion's Manor at all. Was it truly him? Had that just been...wishful thinking? What did he have that would draw a woman with such interesting power to him? What did he have at all?

He moved for the place he had seen Aleister enter. Perhaps the scarred Vampire would be able to air the muddled mess that was his mind.

He walked down the long hallway, the blue of the walls shining with a coating resembling ice, and he passed several Enchanters that were carrying piles of scrolls in their arms, talking jubilantly about someone named Equis.

The tall golden doors stood before him and he raised a hand to knock against them when the low voices beyond it caught his attention. He lowered his hand, for the conversation seemed most heated:

"...You were bloody well there and you couldn't tell me?" came Nathanial's angry voice.

"Now, now, Nathanial," another voice Christian did not recognize said, "that isn't the way to handle this."

"How would you have me handle this, Master? The damned Vampire stood beside me—Xavier—and he would have us just believe it was happy coincidence that we journey to Cedar Village, that he has no choice but to get swept up along for the ride?"

"The damned Vampire led you to me, Nathanial," the deep voice of Aleister snarled. "I know he did. He just wouldn't allow me my peace my mind. Yes, I did oversee the Enchanter-Vampire project with Victor Vonderheide, yes, I monitored your progress for all the years you grew until your Age was reached, but I left when what he wanted me to do was done—I couldn't stay there another minute with the knowledge weighing me down—"

"But you live with it even now, Aleister!" Nathanial screamed, and something heavy hit the floor.

There was a long silence next, and Christian could hear another's terse breathing, yes, the smell of fear was great in this other being that was not a Vampire. But what had happened?

"Nathanial," the unfamiliar voice said after a time, "screaming will do nothing. What is done is done. We must put our focus on helping Xavier once he leaves the book."

No word was spoken for a long moment.

And then:

"Very well, Master," and it was Nathanial that said so, "but let me make it plainly clear—this Vampire is a coward, a bloody farce, using magic to block our memories, to push himself into the shadows of obscurity so that when this damned day came he could continue to hide from his past.

"Of all the years I've worked alongside Dracula, never once did I besmirch my title, my name at his side, no matter what he'd made me do—and my hands are not clean, Vampire—but at least I did what I did with the sense to own up to it."

What the bloody hell are they on about?

Christian listened closely.

Nathanial said, "They are as good as thrown into this world because of you. How long will you hide behind your bloody spell, keeping their memories locked tight within their minds?"

"As long," the low voice of Aleister said, "as I can."

There was a snarl of disgust, and then further silence, and Christian pressed a hand on the gold of the door, pushing it open to reveal a grand room filled with piles of paper and books against the high silver walls. There in the center of the room stood Aleister, a look of surprise replacing his previous grimace.

The Enchanter beside the scarred Vampire gave Christian a glance of knowing before bowing low to both of them, his long black hair spilling over his shoulders. He swept around the wooden circle of a table they'd stood in front of, and moved to the back of the room, his red robes swaying around his boots.

When he'd disappeared behind another set of golden doors, Aleister opened his mouth, but it appeared he was lost for words: he closed it after a short while, his green eyes dark with a mixture of embarrassment and humiliation.

Nathanial moved from the room as Christian narrowed his eyes. A strange pulse filled the air and they stared at the ceiling from whence it appeared to have come.

Aleister smiled, and how strange it was. "He's in."

✳

Whispers filled Xavier's ears as he lay there, not knowing whether it was safe to stand, for he was very aware his leg had been burned—he could not remember the last time he had been able to feel physical pain at all.

"Damn," he groaned as he opened his eyes, a blinding white light keeping him from seeing anything. He lifted a hand to rub his wounded leg and cringed as he touched the raw flesh. "What?" he breathed as he squinted and focused on his leg.

He saw the dirt ground that his leg rested upon, but his eyes widened as the bare burnt skin glistened in the strange light. All down his leg, in the shape of the Ascalon's blade was a brilliant burn that still pained him...

The Ascalon—it was gone!

Turning from his singed pant leg, he searched his waist for any sign of the leather sheath, the sword it would hold... No, it was gone. Not a trace of it along the dark ground anywhere.

"Should we help him up?" a light voice said from somewhere nearby.

"Well," a deeper voice said, "he is awake. It wouldn't be fair to just leave him in his mind, would it, Flora?"

"Yes," Flora said, "we must broaden the man's horizons."

Who on Earth? Xavier thought, forcing himself to look around against the light. He could see the tall shadows of thick trees all around him, and the more he squinted, the more he was able to see.

He was in woods of some sort, and the bright light he'd seen had been the sun. It was shining in the crystal blue sky, not a cloud in sight through the trees' thick branches and leaves.

"Who's out there?" Xavier called, raising a hand against the light.

"Flora...I'm a Fae," the light voice said, and as he turned his attention towards it, the tall, beautiful woman stepped out from behind a thick dark tree, her blue eyes large within her small face, her long blonde hair covering her breasts. He looked away from her, as she was completely naked.

"And I," the deeper voice said, "am Bartabus. Enchanter, naturally." The man stood tall beside the same tree the Fae stepped from, his eyes a dark brown, and it seemed a permanent scowl was etched upon his face: a large scar from a corner of his mouth trailed downward to his jaw. He wore long black robes that swept across the dirt ground around his feet.

"Why are you here?" Xavier asked, carefully rising to stand, aware he could not stand on his wounded leg—it hurt far too much to rest on it properly. "How did you get into the book?"

They bade each other a glance before Flora said, "We're dead, of course. Only those who have died can enter this place—but more on that later, you've things to learn." She held out a hand for him to take.

He stared at her hand, not entirely sure that he desired to take it, but did he not have things to learn, things to figure out, indeed?

Stepping forward, he took her hand and was surprised that it was warm—warmth he could feel. Why, the last time he could feel anything was when he was alive...

He stared at his hand more now and saw the color that remained against it, the blood that filled his fingers, the back of his hand. Yes, he hadn't realized it when he'd first opened his eyes, but his blood was warm!

He looked up towards the Fae. She smiled and said, "You couldn't expect yourself to remain dead, could you, to learn what you must?"

The Enchanter said, "Now Flora, don't tell him everything all at once. Let us go—we've a journey ahead of us." He stepped from them, moving through the trees, the Fae following suit, pulling him along with little regard for his wound. He limped forward, marveling at the feel of her skin.

They passed through tree trunks and bare dirt ground, the sun ever overhead, the green leaves keeping most of it from reaching them. Xavier wondered if ever they were to see...well, anything at all when the Enchanter stepped past a tree, into a large clearing and the Fae did the same.

His eyes scanned the grass that appeared once the trees ceased. He looked out upon a large field, the sun's light illuminating it, making it shine with unguarded beauty. It was a beauty he seldom had the chance, or thought, to appreciate. But he did so now.

There was little here but the field...and a wonderfully large Dragon, its black scales shimmering in the light, its large black eyes staring at them with vague interest.

"Why...is a Dragon here?" he asked the Fae who would not release his hand.

"Were you not just thinking of Dammath, your subordinate's Dragon?" Bartabus said, his own brown eyes never leaving the Dragon's frame.

It spread its large wings and rose from the ground. Xavier admitted that he had been thinking of the green and black Dragon for the slightest of seconds.

"Yes, well, this is the result of your thoughts. You thought of a Dragon—so a Dragon shall appear."

"But this is not Damion's Dragon," Xavier said, staring at the black Creature that tossed its head side to side with apparent impatience.

"That is neither here nor there, Xavier," Flora said, and she released his hand at last. "He wants you to travel with it. Your...desire to know what's going on, and yes, know where Dracula is, is part of the reason this Dragon has appeared. He is your vehicle—you must use him."

"I...are you not coming?" Xavier asked her, feeling the absence of her hand within his, the sudden cold that had replaced the warmth she'd provided.

She and Bartabus exchanged pleasant glances.

"We...cannot go where you must. You wanted someone to appear to tell you what must be done, Xavier. That is who we are—that is all we are," Bartabus said.

"So...all of this...is because I wanted it to be?"

"Yes...and no. I cannot say you wanted Dracula to die, but it has happened—as have our deaths. No, this is not a place of acquiring what you want—it is a place of gathering what you must. You will have more help than the others," Flora said.

"The others?" Xavier whispered, feeling the sun press against his skin.

"Those that could not...do," Bartabus said, and for the first time a hint of grimness left his voice. "But you can, Xavier, you must. Now—the Dragon."

"Yes, yes, off you go," Flora added.

He stared at them before he stepped towards the large Creature. He lingered on the ball of a foot before he sprung forward, knowing he had to move—had to get to Dracula...

The Dragon obliged, bending his head low to the ground so that Xavier could hop up on its neck. Once he'd done so, he had but a second to stare at the Fae and Enchanter before the Dragon lifted itself into the air with an incredible burst of power and circled the clearing once, before pressing for a large building many yards from where they remained.

"Is that where Dracula is?" he shouted into the Dragon's ear, feeling the burst of cold that came with every sweep of wing at their sides. A shiver to arose from within him and he marveled at the feel of it.

"No," the deep voice roared back, "but that is where someone else remains that can take you to him."

"Why can he not just show up? If I think about him enough, wouldn't he—"

"You are a very strange human to think that if you wish for something enough it will just spill into your hands," the Dragon countered.

"But Flora—the Enchanter—they just said—" he began, feeling confused now.

"They only said that this is a place of getting what you absolutely need, not that if you desire it, it will come," the Dragon said.

"But I need Dracula," he shouted as the Dragon dove then and landed on the grassy ground just in front of the incredibly large manor that stood far too tall for Xavier's liking. He could not see where the manor ended: it was hidden in clouds.

He slid off the Creature's back, letting out a cry of pain as he, once again, landed on the wounded leg. "For bloody—" he began to cry before the Dragon pushed him with his long muzzle towards the large black doors.

They opened against the sun and Xavier almost lost his breath (how incredible that he needed to breathe!), for the woman that remained there looked exactly like Eleanor Black.

Her long black hair was unbound in tight, neat curls around her face, but there was a rosiness beneath her cheeks, a subtle glow of wizened years deep in her brown eyes. And as she stared at him, he grew weak in the knees.

"So you're the one he's chosen?" she asked him, the voice not Eleanor's not all. It was smoother, kinder, and more pleasant as it left her lips and drifted to his ears.

"Who are you?" he breathed, working fast to reclaim his breath. How fleeting it was against those eyes.

"Come inside," she said, turning from him and moving further into the darkness of the manor, the long black dress she wore fitting her slender body perfectly. Xavier bade the Dragon one glance of question before he followed after the woman, limping painfully up the stairs and through the doors.

Chapter Twenty-Four

REUNITED

"You are ever the attractive man, aren't you?" she said, moving to take a seat in one chair, gesturing a hand towards the other for Xavier to sit. As he stepped towards her, she continued speaking: "I see now, why Eleanor took such an interest in you. You hold the tenacity of one used to power...but now..." and her brown eyes lingered on his damaged leg, "you are more man than ever, aren't you?"

"You know of Eleanor, do you?" Xavier asked.

"I know of her," she said, crossing her long legs beneath her long dress, "though I had...something of a time *getting* to know her."

"And why's that?"

"Dracula, of course. When she ventured to his city, he had just killed Julius Dewery—I knew his mother, lovely woman—the poor Vampire only wanted to branch out and...learn how to be better as a Vampire. When he came upon Dracula, fear overtook reason or sense and Dracula put an end to him. I have seen how Dracula gets when he feels threatened."

He stared at her, not understanding. "Dracula killed a Vampire born from an Ancient?"

She nodded.

"But—what does this have to do with Eleanor?"

She sighed. "Everything. Like I said, when Dracula killed Julius, Eleanor and I had just arrived, hoping for a safe place for her to... understand her talents... When he saw me, Xavier, he lost it...again. Killed me...locked my body in his bloody dungeon. But my Eleanor he decided to keep alive."

"You're Eleanor? You're...her mother?"

"The one and only," she said, sinking back in her chair. "My name is Sindell, Xavier, and I was not physically present for the more important...aspects of my daughter's life. Such as the trainings and the feedings. Dracula took care of all of that. Of course, whilst here I was able to regain all I had missed before the book was created, and I saw how curious my daughter had become.

"She desired more from her mentor...once she got the slightest inkling that he was keeping from her the truth of her origins—I was never able to tell her, being dead and all—and that occurred...yes, it was the day the Nicodemeus brothers showed their faces in the City as the Invaders.

"*Eleanor*...took an interest in the younger brother, Darien, and it was he she convinced Dracula to let join the Order. Of course, Darien's past here is what captivated her, the branding of other Vampires... the power that came with it. She...convinced him to learn more of Dracula's secrets for her and together, for a while, they conspired... pulling together the pieces of information they had gathered.

"Darien, naturally, thought their ventures insightful. He had no intention of learning Dracula's greatest secrets to use for his personal gain. It is why, I believe, when he learned the truth, he could not face it and barely survived this book.

"And when he was out, Eleanor saw his difference and was intrigued by it, but he would not speak of what he knew. She was made all the more incensed when Dracula took Darien out of the Order and kept him closer than ever and put, in his place, the Vampire's brother—"

"I was but a few years into the Order when this happened," Xavier interjected in astonishment.

She stared at him, a finger placed idly underneath her chin. "Were you? Yes, you had to have been—Damion was named your subordinate and then...Lillith Crane was pushed into the prestigious place as well..."

Xavier shifted in his seat, prepared to hear more on Lillith, but she said nothing else. Lost on thought of her story, he cleared his throat when he realized she had said that Darien Nicodemeus had been close to Eleanor Black. The Vampire's words to him whilst in his living room then returned as easily as he drew breath:

"*I do admit she was acting weird ever since Damion was inducted, but perhaps she was just... You know how woman are. Fine one minute, angry the next. There is no figuring them out.*"

Xavier said, "When Damion was inducted...that was when she'd entered the book—learned the secret."

She nodded as though pleased he had figured it out on his own. "Yes, my darling daughter traversed this book, but, because she was not ready, because she had not yet been chosen by Dracula—who'd had a number of Vampires to use—she fell to a most abrupt turmoil.

"Why, the moment the pages sucked her in, she was gravely lost—she did not have the ease of guidance that you had, Xavier— that Fae and Enchanter. This world was not as pleasant, either. She stumbled, nearly died several times—permanently—and had gotten lost so much, I fought with myself and Dracula to see her to safety."

Xavier's hands trembled slightly with that name, the thought of seeing him again. "He keeps you here?"

And at this, her face lost its calm pleasantry. She now looked grim and even sad. "Those who have died by his hand...find our place within the book's pages. We cannot rest, Xavier. We are forever commanded to harm or guide those that fall into this guide. We've even had to do it when Dracula himself first traversed these pages."

"And who did he have to guide him?"

She was silent for a long moment, as though the answer was hard to whisper. "The Phoenixes."

"I'm sorry?"

"The Phoenixes of the Nest were Dracula's guide...but I can say no more on that, Xavier. I am only here to speak on Eleanor so that you may better understand how it is she has come to be so warped in her quest for power."

"How...how did the Vampire seek the counsel of the Phoenixes?" he whispered in awe, knowing full well that no one had ever seen them before, that they were removed from the Dark World.

She sat up higher in her chair and he saw she looked most uncomfortable. "I really shouldn't, Xavier, I have already overstepped my bounds—"

"That you have, my dear Sindell," a familiar voice sounded then, and even against Xavier's human ears, he felt the chill run down his spine.

Slowly tearing his gaze from the beautiful, otherworldly woman, he turned in his chair and eyed the single door that had been opened. He stared at the man who stood there. And all at once, the grief hit him as he recalled the sight of the very Vampire's body dissolving to ash right before his very eyes...

He slowly stood. "Drac—" and the name stuck hard in his throat as he was privy to something he had not known in many years: tears.

He smiled slowly and took a careful step into the large room, and his brown eyes moved from the woman in the chair back to Xavier. "You've done it, my boy," the voice said again, and how he knew the exact unsettling air to linger in his vibrant heart with those words. *Was that how all Vampires sounded to humans?*

"I really didn't think you would make it so soon," Sindell said from her chair.

"And miss Xavier as a human man?" Dracula countered, a hand moving to the sword at his waist.

Xavier hastily wiped the tears from his eyes as he stared at the Vampire, the sword he carried, and he was aware then that he was just a human, this man a Vampire, the very first—why on Earth would this Vampire be here for him when he was so utterly wounded? So useless?

"Dracula," he whispered, bringing the brown eyes back to him, "wh-why put me through all of this? Why allow me to suffer?"

An eyebrow rose in question as Sindell stood from her chair. No one paid her any mind, however, as Dracula took yet another step towards him. "Is that what you think I've done? Allowed you to suffer? I was under the impression, Xavier, that I had allowed you to find your own way—I thought it would have helped you appreciate what it is I've had to deal with all these years, indeed, what has propelled you forward thus far?"

"Y-you! You, you goddamn... How can you stand there a-and tell me you've allowed me to find *my* way? *You were gone!* Eleanor— she was everywhere I dared turn! I was lost for years in a vision that seemed every bit as real as the breath I dare breathe now and you— *Dracula!*" he cried in exasperation. "I have n-nothing, but...but lies, deception, *secrets* that are all meant to be revealed here, now! *In this damned book!*"

"And they are!" Dracula snarled, causing him to step away, the fear alarming. He could all but feel the ascending terror as Dracula's eyes flashed to an aggrieved red and a pale hand moved to the hilt of the Ares at his waist. "You want to be told everything—all at once—

in one fell swoop! But if any of us were to do that in your state, you'd cripple over with the weight of it all! Or go insane!

"This place," Dracula said angrily, gesturing a hand to the high walls, "is your mind. Everything you think, exists here. The only reason it is not completely in ruin, Xavier, is because of me. I am the glue that keeps your world together—Darien did not hold fast to my words like you, nor did Eleanor. It is for this reason that I chose you to take my place. I knew, no matter what, you'd listen to me. And you have. Your unwavering faith to me, believe it or not, is what has kept you going thus far.

"Darien only made it to the very end before his mind made acknowledgement of me—that is the only reason he was able to escape—survive. Eleanor..." A dark gaze moved to Sindell, who returned it just as knowingly. "Eleanor never called for me. Her mind never desired me. When she ventured through this book, she had decided that I was never to be trusted again. She did not need me. She never did. Not like you."

He could not speak with the pressure of his heart pounding in his eardrums, his throat. The anger, the terrible anger the Vampire exuded...it was palpable, and he desired nothing more than to be away from the Vampire, but he knew he couldn't, knew the Vampire's words held a semblance of truth, for he had ventured this far only to know what Dracula had never told him whilst he lived...

"But Dracula, you've bloody well used me—"

"Oh, don't try that, Xavier!" Dracula spat. "Of course I've used you! I've used every bloody Creature I could get my hands on! What makes you think you're any different?!" And he withdrew the sword, pointing the blade at Xavier's chest. "If you knew what I must undergo for the bloody *sake* of the world—*damn it all, Xavier!*" He snarled, lowering the sword, and stepped towards the door. "We don't have time for this. Come on! I won't get anywhere with you here...we can't linger."

Xavier stared after the Vampire, not able to get over the fact that he'd drawn a sword on him. An intense fear kept him glued to his place beside Sindell, and as he cast a quick glance to her, he saw that she looked miserable once more.

Dracula stopped just before the door, the sword still in his hand. "Are you not coming, Xavier? We can't linger. They know you are here and I won't let them get their hands on you before you understand more from me."

"I...wh-who's c-coming for me?" he barely managed to stammer.

Sindell cast them both a fearful look before bowing low to Dracula, stepping backwards into darkness: Xavier was aware the building around them had begun to fade into the recesses of nothingness. He figured the scenery was about to change.

Dracula's red eyes looked despondent as he glared straight at Xavier. "Keep your bloody wits about you, Xavier Delacroix. This is not the time to lose me—you don't want to face them alone."

"But how can I trust you?"

"You must!" he screamed. "Now trust me and *let us go!*"

"Dracula!"

"The bloody *Phoenixes* are headed here, Xavier. Here for *you,* and I promised them once you reached the book, you'd understand, but you don't, and we can't waste any more time! If they see you are not ready, they will kill you where you stand! And you must be a Vampire when they lay eyes upon you, do you understand?"

He truly didn't, not a word of it, but the ferocity in the Vampire's eyes could not be willed away.

What have I gotten myself into? Xavier thought as he stepped gingerly on his bad leg, not at all surprised it still pained him.

✳

He limped, the Vampire several steps ahead of him against the fading light of the sky, its misty gray air foreboding. Xavier knew it fruitless to ask the impatient Vampire anything, indeed, for he would receive nothing until the Vampire felt like sharing.

The long white hair flew wildly in the wind that had only just begun to pick up, and Xavier clutched a hand to his ribs as they began to pain him with his fast movement—he knew he could not keep up with the Creature for long, hell, he was barely keeping him in his sights now.

For every step Dracula took, Xavier had to blink several times to retrain his eyes on the Vampire: his steps, his movements, they were all much too hard to keep track of, especially against the wild wind.

"Correct your thoughts, Xavier," the deep voice commanded.

Dracula had not turned, he kept storming his way over the barren land, the hills all but gone now, and there was not a Creature in sight.

"What?" Xavier called, trying his best to pace his breathing. Every inhale brought a sharp pain to jab his lungs.

The Vampire stopped and turned, his eyes narrowed with dark intention that made Xavier still where he stood at once. "You're making the world worse—stop thinking of things that don't pertain to you and focus. Focus on me."

"How am I meant to do that?" The wind lifted the hair from his shoulders. "I'm all but left in the dark again, aren't I?"

"Not for much longer at all," Dracula responded. "Now let us go. You will get all you need when we reach my place of rest."

"Your place of rest?" He limped once more after the Vampire. "You need a place of rest?"

"It is a place unchanged by the shifting landscapes of those that traverse this book—my haven, if you will."

They walked over the dry land, Xavier's eyes scanning the gray sky as he wondered what this haven looked like. No sooner had he thought this, did a broken castle appear atop the dirt ground several yards ahead of them.

He stopped and stared at it, marveling at how high it seemed against the gray, cloudless sky. "Is that it?" he called to the Vampire, and as the wind died, Dracula turned to him, the smallest inkling of a smile upon his lips.

"Thanks to you it is," he said. "Can you make it to the door, Xavier?"

He turned his gaze to the burn that still resided on his leg. It hurt something terrible and showed no sign of dissipating. "I've...come this far."

"That you have," he said, and Xavier thought he heard a sliver of pride in that voice. Dracula turned from him before he could figure out anything more and stepped briskly across the ground that was beginning to sprout small green blades of grass.

They walked in silence towards the building which held no doors: a large hole waited just in front of them, and as they drew ever closer to it, Xavier could see the dark outlines of an almost empty room within it.

Dracula pressed forward for it and waved a hand, many torches' light springing to life as he did so. As Xavier entered the room at last, he was able to see the large sitting room that remained, littered with large gray stone bricks and the accompanying rubble.

"No, not here," Dracula said, moving for another room right across from them, a tall black door opening against the dancing light.

Stifling his wonder for just where he was being taken in this run down castle, he stepped for the door, Dracula holding it open as he reached it. He turned from him and moved further down a long hallway whose stone ceiling was falling as they stepped through it. Xavier's every step was made more difficult with the mass of stone that littered the black floor.

They soon reached another tall black door but not before they passed a dirty, cracked mirror, Xavier stopping where he stood as he saw his muddled reflection for the first time in many, many years:

He stared at his green eyes, surprised at the pain, the exhaustion, and loss that filled them. His skin was pale against the lack of light here, his hair reached the beginning of his shoulders, unkempt, frayed with the wind. He touched a hand to his face, feeling the stifled warmth that remained beneath his skin. Life. Pain. *Bloody breathing.* To be human...*why am I human?*

Dracula opened the door and disappeared behind it, leaving Xavier to struggle with opening it. Inside, he found himself in a large wide room, a set of stairs to the very right of him, stairs the white-haired Vampire was now climbing, his long black traveling cloak swaying at his back.

Xavier followed after him, stepping carefully up the large steps, his thoughts traveling to why the sword had burned him, why it was now gone...

Dracula opened the door at the top of the stairs and slid through, never turning as he strode the length of the room towards a large red chair. He sank comfortably into it and Xavier watched as his brown eyes narrowed upon him, a large hole in the wall revealing the thick gray sky as it swirled above their heads, a slight breeze blowing through it every so often, sending the red torn curtains that remained against the high arched windows to rise from their places, the large bed in the corner to ruffle its deep red sheets.

"Step forward, Xavier," Dracula said.

He obeyed, moving forward, knowing, indeed, that he did not want to get any closer to the Vampire than he had to. He knew a Vampire's bloodlust and only imagined what the bloodlust was of the first Vampire to have been born.

"Kneel," Dracula commanded next.

A hint of confusion touched him, but kneel he did after a short time, ignoring the pain that still filled the side of his leg. "What will you tell me?"

"Only," he interjected, "what it is you need to know. Now, let's begin with your words back in that woman's home. You think I allowed you to suffer, do you, Xavier?"

"I knew nothing of what you desired for me to do—how you expected me to find this book—"

"You had Nathanial Vivery, he had his Enchanter feeding information into his ear, you had Aleister...Aurora. Hell, as I understand it, you also had Alexandria," Dracula said, the disappointment clear in his eyes. "What was it about Nathanial that made you so uneasy?"

He recalled the utter calm the Vampire had exuded while the high flames burned Scylla to the ground, the vague words Eleanor had bequeathed explaining the Vampire's special power.... "He can do magic, how can a Vampire..."

Dracula settled back in his chair. "My project to ensure I had an edge over the Lycan race even while I was on task to keep the Artifacts safe. Victor and several other Vampires I...trusted were sent to oversee the young Vampires I had chosen for this special task. All of them from royal blood, all of them...different in some way from your average Vampire.

"Aleister was his Vampire mentor...yes, he worked...ever so diligently to ensure Nathanial made it."

"Aleister was Nathanial's mentor?" he repeated in wonder, thinking of the scarred Vampire's knowledge of...well, everything. "Is that why he had one of those medallions, because he'd helped you with your little project?"

Dracula bade him a look of disdain. "Hardly was that project 'little,' Xavier. It helped me breach a wall that I had previously been wary to touch: That Vampires, and not just myself, could perform magic. Keep their book of Equis nearby and still take in their blood.

Of course, for a Vampire of Nathanial's talents...the Fyre of the Phoenixes had to be...acquired from their ashes for his magic to be replenished every now and again."

"I thought Vampires were not able to do magic, Dracula. You, yourself, had told me this."

"I lied."

"Lied about everything, then, did you?"

"Only the things that mattered."

Xavier burned with unguarded hatred then. The Vampire *had* lied, had done so profusely at that! And here he was just asking to be trusted?

The sky outside the windows and the giant hole began to churn and thicken with black clouds and Dracula sat up higher in his seat. "I had to lie," he said, "again, do you think it smart of me to tell you, a Vampire quick to jump at my call, that Phoenixes were a part of anything I was undergoing? You would have sought them out without my word—gotten yourself killed."

"I am not Eleanor!" he said, knowing full well that there was a time that he would have taken that news in stride, not stepped out of his bounds. "I would have listened to you, *yes*, I would have been surprised by that news, but only because you'd told me that the Phoenixes had nothing to do with our world! What would you have me do when the one I trusted absolutely began to contradict himself with his words? I only started to question your bloody rule when I thought Eleanor dead and you would tell me nothing of her!"

"That is neither here nor there," Dracula said dismissively then, waving a hand, "what matters is that you know now—I have been in contact with the Phoenixes for the majority of my...undesired life. And it was...a task getting them to listen to me, an unwanted creation, an abomination.

"But they soon heard my pleas to be released from my...pain. To be released from my curse of existence. At this point...I had bitten a few humans—okay, several hundred—and they, themselves, got creative, learned that giving their blood could make more of us. But these early creations died out. They died with their stark desire for blood consuming them. I only survived because I taught myself restraint, I...wanted...nothing more than to be human like my father, something as close to normal as that if I could help it.

"The Phoenixes said they would help me when they saw I was truly sincere. So they created a goblet—a cup that if drunken from, by, me, would end the tyranny that is our existence. Lycans would fall to the same fate, surely, being from Ancient blood as well."

Xavier stared, his hatred waning. "What would that mean? The ending of our existence?"

Dracula gestured towards him. "You and all other Vampires, Lycans, would be what you are now, Xavier: human."

"Eleanor...once she learned this—the truth of what I was doing—she decided that she couldn't allow it. She, someone that never had the opportunity of being human, could not fathom a life that was... simple. She always wanted power...always wanted...more. I'm sure her mother's told you this."

Xavier could only nod.

"Darien, when he knew this, it frightened him. But he, like Eleanor, took the same form you take now. Yes, they were both human when they entered the book—and this is because I wanted those that dared traverse it to understand that their limits are only created from their minds. If we, as Vampires, could only change our ways of thinking about the humans, we could be one step closer to achieving...peace, within ourselves and within our world.

"For it was only when I was born that the Dark World fell into disarray, Xavier. The Dragons never cared a lick for the state of the Giants, the Merpeople's waters were free to swim, the Elves' magic was the only kind that existed, not allowing there to be discord, not allowing the Elves to desire to show their worth, thereby tacking on underhanded means to achieve their state of respect.

"Once humans were born, a select few given the power of magic from an Ancient named Equis Equinox, who had learned magic from the Elves, they were pushed to the forefront of the Creatures' minds. They were bestowed the title of Enchanters, and by the time I'd sought one out for this spell of immortality, they were a household name among those that desired their talents.

"I can only assume," Dracula said with a slow sigh, "that I only furthered that legend, forcing one to push their limits and give me the power to live forever. But of course, no one lives forever, Xavier. I knew I had bought myself more time to locate the Goblet. By the time the Phoenixes had finished creating it, I had had no time go back and procure it. A trip to the Nest takes years at best and that is at a blinding pace, stopping for *Anima* along the way."

Xavier remembered the refreshing blood that had boosted his spirits and his strength once he'd reached the Council of Creatures with Dracula those weeks before. "You knew we were not truly immortal? So how could you allow us to think we were—that we could not die?"

"The necklaces and rings I had Spelled in order to make the others walk in the sun, they were not permanent either. And I knew that prolonged exposure to the trinkets would result in...immunity from their desired uses. After a time, they would no longer work. To see if I could use them in the long run to further my goal, I procured a drop of the Head Phoenix's blood to be added to Victor's ring. It was the only way I could ensure that if I never handled the Goblet or drank from it, then at least my first victim could live his life as a human, enjoy his life as one."

"So you meant for Victor to take your place?" Xavier asked, understanding that it would have made a lot more sense if this was true.

Dracula bade him a dark stare. "I meant for Victor to be as free of me as he possibly could. I never wanted to turn him—never did I want to give him a life by my side, forever indebted to me. I tried to spare him the best I could of my exploits. I only think it made him hate me more."

Xavier said nothing to this assessment.

"But even if I wanted to use him, I couldn't," Dracula continued. "The one that drunk from the Goblet had to be approved by the Head Phoenix—and that is you Xavier. When Evert told me what would happen at the Council of Creatures, I knew there was a very real chance that you would abandon my cause and join her. I had to keep you from that as best as I could. Right after you were introduced to me and met with the others, I moved to tell the Phoenixes that I had found my replacement, and that, given any possible determent to that end, you would have to be guarded endlessly.

"That is why, upon my death, the medallions given to certain Creatures who had aided me throughout the years, were activated. Beacons, they were called by the Phoenixes, to ensure that all that wore one, could locate each other and help you where I could not. For this book will burn once you are free of it, Xavier, and though by that time you would know all you need to seek out the Artifacts for your own, I could not rule out, again, any determents. Eleanor's energy being once such thing.

"When you went under after the sword connected to one who held the medallion, Xavier, I was there, trying to reach you, but you were swept up in Eleanor's hold. That was when the first three Creatures who recognized the medallion's call could keep you from her—"

"Wait a minute," Xavier said, "I vaguely recall an Elf in that dream—"

"It was Arminus, alongside him Peroeneus Doe, and Nicholai Noble...and far from them, but still present, was Aleister... I believe he felt the pull first but chose to ignore it."

"That was why the Vampire would not leave me alone?" he asked. "He was one of yours?"

A dismal expression found Dracula's face then and he stood from his seat and moved to the large hole where the sky had brightened considerably now, the wind all but calm. "Aleister...would not leave you alone, as you say, because...he is your father and the one that turned you."

Xavier rose to his feet. "Come again?" he whispered as the sky began to fold under low clouds again and a quick fog began to settle over the land.

"Aleister Delacroix, your father, found by Victor, turned by Victor, brought to me with the news that he bore two sons, the mother of them a bloody Ancient Creature. He was a goldmine to me, Xavier, not one but *two* sons that I could use to take my place, and if one of them died or some other horrible matter...I had another of Ancient blood. All that was needed," he eyed Xavier, "was for the both of you to be turned and brought to me."

Xavier could not speak, his mind swimming with blinding pain now, flashes, thoughts of the man who had smiled upon him when he was but a boy, vague glimpses of the Vampire that had turned them... It was as though a veil was being pulled off his head, the clearer picture much harder to bear.

He recalled the way the Vampire had stuck to his side in Cedar Village, how he had moved to see him freed from thoughts of her...

He turned from Dracula and threw up the blood that remained in his stomach. It left him in painful, quick spurts.

"Of course it didn't turn out like that—only you, Xavier, were brought to me, only you were trained and groomed to take my place," Dracula's cold voice went on. "Your brother...well, I meant to bring him into the fold when I'd sent you both to Eleanor to learn of Alexandria—but as I understand it, he discovered the woman first— and I truly did make it easy for all of you.

"What *has* Christian been doing with the woman, Xavier?"

He lunged at him before he knew he had done it, tackling him to the ground, his weak, tired hands wrapped around the Vampire's throat. Dracula's head remained off the side of the building, out in the air. His white hair flew in the brazen wind, and it took all of Xavier's remaining strength to scream his anger:

"How *could* you make him turn us?! And why didn't you tell me he was still alive? *Why didn't you tell me you made him turn us?*"

"How could I have done so?" Dracula whispered in surprise. "When I learned he'd tasked Aurora Borealis to perform the Calling of Void upon you and your brother, I knew nothing I could have said would have registered."

"The Calling of... But you removed it once when Eleanor placed it upon me!"

"Only just barely—some of it still lingered. You were still under her command until...well, I don't know what happened, do I?"

Xavier squeezed Dracula's throat tighter, his hands growing numb the more he did so. "*Aleister* took me to some Elves—made me drink some water that cleared my mind. Returned me to you—you damned—"

"Ah!" Dracula gasped. "The Gabbling Elves—of course! Their waters can remove any Enchantment, any spell of binding, with the simplest of sips!"

"Enough games! Tell me more about my father! Why didn't you intervene and at least try? Not once did you even hint that he was still alive! That you knew him at all!"

"More important things were going on, Xavier! I had this damned book to protect, the Goblet to locate, and the Lycans to keep from killing the humans or more of our kind!"

"You filthy liar! How do you expect me to believe anything you say?!"

"You have no bloody choice but to believe me!" Dracula

snarled, the fangs spurring fear within Xavier, causing him to release the Vampire and stagger away.

"Perhaps Victor," he said, voice gone from screaming over the harsh winds, "was right—perhaps you are a murdering, mad Vampire."

Dracula rose to his feet and readjusting the front collar of his traveling cloak. "Is that what he thinks of me? Damn, I guess I must abandon all my plans because one Vampire is at odds with what I must be."

Xavier said nothing for a while. Did the Vampire truly believe his words? Had he truly ventured to the Phoenixes, sought out their counsel, had a goblet created to save the Vampires and Lycans from their ways?

"These Phoenixes...you say you are working under them?" Xavier asked.

"What of them?" Dracula's brown eyes narrowed in question.

"Well, if you what you say is true," he whispered, focusing his thoughts on the Phoenixes he had never seen before, "then I can bring them here, let them tell me the truth for myself."

"Xavier, don't you dare!" he shouted, but it was far too late:

The sky outside the large hole had begun to brighten, so much so, Xavier could barely see the clouds, all of the sky was one massive bright golden light. Then three massive birds appeared through the gold, their large wings flapping serenely as they flew straight for the castle. He could barely continue to stare upon them for long before Dracula was before him, and the Ares was released from its sheath, the blade brought through his stomach before he could know it had happened.

A sound of surprise left him and Xavier sunk to the floor, Dracula's hand upon his shoulder, guiding him down, before the Vampire slit his own wrist against the blade and brought his blood to Xavier's lips, Xavier barely able to taste it before Dracula's voice whispered very close by:

"Believe me or don't, you must get the Goblet and drink from it—and Alexandria—you must let her die, Xavier! Let her die and turn her, her blood will keep away any Lycan that attempts to keep you from your goal."

The flapping of large wings could not be ignored now.

And before he could open his eyes, just as the taste of the Vampire's blood found itself upon his tongue, nothingness reached him, the touch of the Vampire's cold hand the very last thing he could feel.

Chapter Twenty-Five

LONDON

When Xavier opened his eyes, an impossible weight covered him, keeping him against the floor, but the high flames atop the dark desk drew his attention and he stood, no pain greeting his leg, nothing, indeed, but the cold of death. He stared at the book as it burned, the Vampire's last words to him reaching him through some way of memory. *"You must get the Goblet and drink from it..."*

To make us all human, Dracula?

There was a bang and then hurried footsteps moved down the stairs, and he turned to eye who it was. The Queen of Lane. Blinking at her as the light of the fire died atop the desk at last, he saw she looked panicked.

She did not leave the bottommost step. Her eyes traversed the burned desk, his bemused stare, and then she let a cold breath escape her as she said, "Thank goodness you're back! We just received word! The Vampire City is being attacked by Eleanor's Creatures! Xavier, my daughter and husband are there!"

He ran a hand to his side, surprised to find the Ascalon greeting his movement with stern coldness and, he looked down at his leg, he saw his pant leg was not burned away at all, but was brand new, as though it had never been damaged...

"I," he said, glad to find the command, the purpose return to his voice, "will move for the City at once, Madame, you have my word."

He stepped forward, brushing past her on the stairs, leaving her trailing after him. They reached the landing and he saw through the open main doors leading out to Lane the pandemonium that was ensuing.

Vampires, their white cloaks flying out behind them, ran and flew every which way across the city, and Xavier soon discovered why.

Two large white Dragons and one massive tan Giant were hovering and standing just before the mountains. The Dragons shot fire from their mouths. The Giant welded a large stone club in his mighty grip, waving it through the air.

The more Xavier stared, the more he realized that the Dragons' fire was aimed at Vampires that flew towards them in an attempt to thwart them, but their still-on-fire bodies fell out of the sky. The Giant was swinging his club to hit more Vampires that dared fly towards it, and Xavier winced as these bodies fell out of the sky as well.

"Oh no," the Queen whispered, aghast.

"I must get to my brother—the human I arrived here with," Xavier said, not attempting to think that Christian or the human had been injured in anyway.

"O-of course," she stammered, tearing her eyes from the sight of her Vampires falling and burning to their permanent deaths as she waved for him to venture back to the others. "Be safe, Xavier. Please."

✳

Christian felt the building shake once more and placed a hand on Alexandria's shoulder to steady her slight trembling. "What can we do?" he asked the Vampire that had been pacing the ground in earnest for the past half hour.

"I don't bloody well know, do I?" Nathanial answered, the frustration clear in his eyes. "We can't leave Xavier in that book—we don't even know if he's out!"

"Enough, please!" Aleister snarled and Christian saw how rattled he looked. "We will—we must wait to hear from Xavier. When he gets out of the book—we will deal with the intruders."

"But they're bloody Dragons and a Giant!" Nathanial said. "How—even with all of our magic, we can't fend off a damned Giant!"

"There must be a way," Aleister said, rising from his seat around the wooden table.

An Enchanter with large eyes appeared in the open doorway. "My Lords! Xavier Delacroix is heading this way!"

"*What?*" Christian shouted just as Aleister, Nathanial, and Alexandria did the same in utter bewilderment.

They all offered each other skeptical glances before moving from the room, stepping down the long hall towards the high front doors where Christian now saw, through the burst of Dragon fire in the sky, his brother, running through the crowd of terrified Vampires and Enchanters. His eyes were wide with his fear, but as he drew near, flying up the steps to the buildings, he said, "We must get back to the Vampire City! Eleanor Black is there!"

Nathanial reached his side. "Eleanor Black? Why?"

"She seeks to destroy it," Xavier said, and Christian noticed the different gleam in his eye.

"But how will we get there?" Alexandria asked.

The Enchanter that had been at Nathanial's side whilst they cornered Aleister appeared in the doorway in the next moment and said, "I believe I can be of assistance."

✳

Eleanor stepped to the door as the screams and shouts filled the floors below her, and she shrugged some hair off her shoulders as she lifted a hand to bring it to strike against the hard black wood of the door.

"I don't need to say 'come in,' do I?" a tired voice sounded from beyond it.

She let the smile grace her lips as she pushed down on the silver handle and blinked in the light of the torch most near the door, her stare around the room quick until she found the Creature she sought.

Victor Vonderheide sat around the long table pushed near the first window beside the desk, his frame slumped and sullen. He looked as though he'd been lost in thought or possibly shedding tears.

She stepped into the room, pulling the door closed behind herself as she moved, a hand at her throat, rubbing idly the small chain that held her many necklaces together atop her chest.

"You must know why I'm here, Victor," Eleanor started, striding past the fireplace, eyeing the books along their shelves just beside it, remembering the time she had been forced to read them all.

The Vampire did not stir from his chair. "You want me to join you."

"Yes," she said, passing the bookshelf, moving for the green curtains placed against the stone wall. "I could use a Vampire with such...need on my side."

"Need," Victor repeated in surprise. "What need of mine could you possibly want for your...aims, whatever they are?"

She eyed him. "Victor...Xavier...is out of my reach and he's out of yours. What better way to...figure out just what he truly knows than to look for it together?"

"Look for it?" He turned to eye her at last. His eyes watered, but were not swimming with tears...yet.

"Yes," she answered, "I have...a growing number of resources at my disposal and you have desire...the grief that propels you from Dracula...all of his lies."

He stood with those words, and Eleanor could not help but see his fear. "I desire—what do you know of what I desire?"

"Because you have been left behind, but you needn't remain here where his secrets hide, forever torturing you. Why look," and she waved a hand to the windows that showed the Vampire City being torn asunder by Creatures in tattered cloaks, "your seven armies are no match for what I have created—see, they are being blown apart by the magic I have allowed my creations."

She watched his face as he turned to eye the destruction that filled the streets: he looked defeated.

"Dracula denied your kind magic," Eleanor said, placing a careful hand on his shoulder; she saw it as a good sign that he did not brush it away. "He denied your kind freedom, the freedom to be as powerful as you could be...to possess the blood of a Vampire and a Lycan and regain the humanity that you once held...without letting it destroy you as it does now."

He looked up at her, his violet eyes wide with his bewilderment. "How did you know I—"

"Dear, Victor," Eleanor said, "one left to his own devices after their creator has died...I can't imagine it's any good, the lack of direction, proper guidance..."

"I don't need to say anything to you," he said defiantly, regaining himself.

"You hardly need to, Victor. Your manner, your actions, speak louder than any of your words have thus far. You know why I am here...you know what I want. Why did you not move to defend your city when the alarms sounded? Why have you allowed me into your office without so much as a sword to defend yourself?"

When he did not respond, she went on: "It's because you wanted me to get here, Victor. You wanted me to arrive at your side, to speak the words you have been thinking since Dracula died. You want," and she stared him deep in his eyes, "answers. And you know I can give them to you."

"I daren't take your words at face value."

"But you needn't," she said, allowing her energy to thicken within the room, within the Vampire's chest. "Can't you see...I have been showing you the truth of what I am since I stepped into the room."

"What do you mean?"

She allowed herself a simple breath as she stepped from him and pressed a hand to the green curtain against the wall, her eyes darkening as she knew what she was prepared to do...but she had no choice, did she?

"What are you doing, Eleanor?" he asked her, but she did not respond as she pressed a hand to the bare wall and whispered the name of the woman's corpse that remained behind it.

Much to his surprise, it opened to reveal a narrow passageway large enough for anyone to enter through. "Here, I can show you what that Vampire has kept from you," she said before turning back to face the dark stone staircase that remained just before her.

Eleanor stepped forward and descended the many steps, hearing the footsteps of Victor behind her as she moved. When she reached the floor, she snapped her fingers just as Darien had told her to, and laid her eyes on the withered corpses of a black-haired woman, a man, and the freshest corpse there: Armand Dragon, the Silverchair.

They sat against the wall, and even as the torches cast a dancing light over their bones, Eleanor felt a shadow of the Vampire's panic as she remained there. All his secrets, to keep them safe...the sword against his back propelling his hasty actions.

"What are those?" Victor's bemused voice sounded from the stairs.

"Those," she said, regaining herself, for it would not do to get lost on thoughts of the Great Vampire when she was trying to take the Vampire's very first victim for her own, "are the corpses of my mother, Sindell Black, Julius Dewery, and Armand Dragon, Dracula's...victims in his quest to keep the truth his alone."

"I—" he began, his gaze never leaving the bodies along the floor. "I knew he had reacted strangely towards Julius and his mother, your own...but I never thought—he killed them? Even Armand? Why would he do this?"

"To keep his secrets safe. *The Immortal's Guide*, the truth of being a Vampire...all of these things threatened life as we know it."

"But what," he breathed, turning his gaze to her, "what is the truth?"

She smiled and then stepped towards him. "Now that, Victor, is a wonderful question."

※

They appeared in London in a haze of red, black, and green energy, and once the swirling colors died, Xavier snarled.

The buildings were all but demolished, broken, and dark flecks remained on the ground, dark pools of red around them as they filled the street.

Whimpers left Alexandria's throat as she stared around at the destruction, the death, and Xavier smelled the lilac and blood, so thick, so complete. *She had already reached the City.*

He said, "Christian, get to the manor—take the woman there, see her to safety."

"Xavier—" Christian began, tearing his gaze from the ruined street to eye his brother.

"Enough," he said shortly, spreading his hands to what remained around them. "I must get to the City—if Eleanor is there, I *will not* put you or the woman in harm's way. Do as I say!"

He was relieved when the Vampire did not put up an ounce of protest but gave a grim nod, the understanding deep in his black eyes. He grabbed Alexandria's hand and turned from them, running up the dark street. They had not made it far before Aurora said, "I shall go with them. They can use all the protection they can get," and followed in their wake, the scent of death and blood reaching Xavier's nose as she ran.

Aleister said, "You ventured through the book, Xavier?"

"Yes," he said, tearing his gaze from where Christian ran, "but I learned less than I had hoped."

The scarred Vampire looked as though he desired to inquire further, when new sounds filled the air.

They all turned towards it.

Twenty Elite Creatures were running towards them, and before they had a chance to defend themselves, a thick dread filled the air around them, and Xavier closed his eyes, for it hurt far too much to keep them open.

When the dread dispersed, he opened his eyes. He stared at the black gates leading into the Vampire City.

"On you get, Vampires," an Elite said from his back.

He heard Aleister snarl near him but he did not turn, thinking only that he was glad he told Christian to venture home when he did. He stepped forward, much to the protests of Nathanial and Aleister. He kept his gaze on the darkness where he knew the stairs would be, ignoring the snickering tongues of the Elites at his back, for Eleanor had control of the Vampire City, had destroyed all of London, had killed countless humans, and he had wallowed in his mind, trapped in thoughts of her, a future not at all present...

He stopped just before the stairs, letting his mind empty. Even as Aleister and Nathanial whispered their urgent pleas for guidance, he held onto the quiet, seeing Dracula's brown eyes flash in red. He saw Eleanor's ever-changing eyes. And he wondered, truly, what he had been kept from in *The Immortal's Guide*.

Chapter Twenty-Six

VICTOR'S CHOICE

They stepped for the doors, and to Xavier's dismay, the words that had been so carefully crafted into them were now torn, ripped through with what looked like a Lycan's claws. He halted here, an Elite pushing him forward the only thing that allowed his feet movement.

Two Elites pushed open the doors.

The eerie silence that issued throughout the city struck him as strange, and he almost spared a glance to Aleister when an Elite said, "Now, now. Onward, Vampire."

And so they moved, stepping on the short path of the building. They stepped inside, seeing no one near their desks, the large entrance hall deserted, nothing but sheets of paper, quills, and ink lining the floor.

"This, is not what I expected," Aleister said, snarling at an Elite that had nudged past him.

"Indeed," Xavier whispered, a twisting feeling of fear full in his gut. He squeezed tight the Ascalon as the Creature moved for the doors to the city and opened them, resolute darkness greeting them all.

Dracula's light had been extinguished.

Trying his best to stifle the boiling dread, he stepped forward, mind blank.

He only stopped when he felt the rough lump of the ground beneath his feet. *The dead*, he thought, a snarl leaving him in frustration as he pressed on despite the Elites' excitement at their backs: They were beginning to chat amongst themselves.

Xavier saw the small dancing flames several yards ahead of them. He pressed on faster despite the fear, wondering what had become of Victor, when he finally saw up close the river of torches, held aloft by what looked to be despondent Vampires. The Elite Creatures, Xavier saw, were on the steps leading to Dracula's mansion, several holding their torches aloft, shining their flames on the two Creatures in between them.

"No," he whispered, eyeing the unreadable expression of Victor over the heads of the Vampires that remained along the street. *What? Why was Victor standing beside her?*

"You are here, still alive," Eleanor said, making sure to catch everyone's attention with her words, "because you will bear witness to the most...celebrated addition to my ever-growing Kingdom!" She waved a hand majestically towards the Vampire at her side. "Victor Varick Vonderheide!"

The silence that stretched on throughout the barren, dark City was tangible.

"Victor, you can't do this!" Xavier shouted before he could stop himself, and all heads turned to him along the street.

He watched as Eleanor narrowed her eyes, attempting to see who had spoken.

He stepped forward, knowing Nathanial and Aleister did the same for their footsteps matched his as they moved into the light of the torches. Victor's face fell to utter horror and Eleanor looked genuinely surprised.

"What is the meaning of this, Victor?" Xavier yelled to the Vampire.

"Xavier—why are you here?" Victor called, looking lost.

The Elites took their places in front of him and Eleanor stepped forward as well, further shielding the Vampire from Xavier's sight, but he had made it to the bottom of the stairs when Eleanor said, "So you went through the book, Xavier?"

"I did," he said shortly, the Ascalon rising slightly in his hand.

"And?" she breathed.

"And the truth...to be human, is admirable," he said, forcing his thoughts to turn from Dracula's last words. "What you are, however, is not. How could you kill all those humans? What do you expect those that remain to feed on?"

"That is just it—they will have nothing to feed on, and I will visit all their hovels and take them down—just as I have done your beloved City, Xavier!"

He took a step up the stairs, eyes moving to her with her words, all Elites stepping forward.

At his sides, Nathanial tensed and Aleister released his sword from its sheath. "Careful, Vampires," Eleanor said, having seen their movements, "you would not want to do anything risky."

"We won't, if only you will release Victor."

At this, she let out a hard laugh, her head thrown back revealing her many necklaces as they dipped into her breasts beneath her open cloak. "Release him?! Why, he has agreed to join me, Xavier! It seems you've reached here far too late to save him, if that was what you intended to do."

"He wouldn't join you if it were the last thing he'd do—"

"You don't seem to understand what it was like once you left... gone on your little adventures, Xavier," Victor's bitter voice sounded from behind the Elites and as he pressed forward to stand beside Eleanor atop the stairs, Xavier saw the Vampire's face was one of coldness, it was the same as when he, Xavier, had returned to tell them that he had been named king.

"Hardly an adventure, what I've had to endure, Victor," he said, staring the Vampire dead in his eyes, "and Dracula—"

"Don't tell me about that bloody Vampire," he said, and the crowd of Vampires behind Xavier shifted their footing with, it seemed, surprise at Victor's words. "I know you and that sorry sod of a Vampire had your secrets—kept them close. Well I know them now, Xavier, and I am all the more disgusted at what my creator was."

"What do you mean you 'know them now,' Victor?" he asked, eyes shifting from Eleanor to Victor and back.

Victor let a dark expression grace his face. "I mean I know what Dracula did—what he did it for—all of this so he can keep our world down—us, his own, down. And you would still follow his lead, Xavier. It's pathetic."

"Whatever's she told you, you can't believe it—"

"And I am just to believe you, hm? Just bow down once more to the untouchable Xavier Delacroix! No, Xavier, I can't adhere to you or Dracula's *ridiculous* rules anymore. I've made my choice. Eleanor knows what she's doing, and unlike you, running across the world to gather Dracula's lies, she was here, with me, showing me her support...where the true power remained."

"Victor—" Xavier began when Aleister raised a hand to silence him.

And as he stepped forward, Victor's violet eyes widened in shock. "*You?!*"

"Sorry to intrude," Aleister said, "but it seems you owe the Vampire a great bit more than just a dismissal, Victor. We here have all faced Dracula's...deception in one form or another, but for the bigger picture you are only aiding a side that is surely destroying our world."

"I don't bloody well care about the 'bigger bloody picture' or anything like that, Aleister!" Victor shouted, glaring at the Vampire. "Dracula turned me to torture me and he has! And even with his death the torture lives! Why must I suffer while he gets his peace, while you, Xavier, you, Aleister, get to know all you know under him?"

"That is not how it is and you know it, Victor," Aleister said, still stepping up the stairs, and Xavier saw the sword twitch in the Vampire's scarred hands, "we have shared a great deal of suffering to acquire these secrets. Now, stop this foolishness and let us explain the truth."

He had made it but three steps below the Vampire before several Elites moved forward, their swords brandished out of thin air. One swung for Aleister, barely missing him as he jumped back, out of the way, landing on a much lower step, closer to Xavier.

"Take care of them," Eleanor could be heard saying to the others.

With quick steps, Xavier moved up the stairs, dodging the blows of the Elites, keeping his sights trained on the beautiful woman as she gripped the arm of a dismal Victor.

He had just made it to the landing of the steps, his sword raised high, when she turned to him, her red eyes bright, her words jarring him where he stood: "Perhaps next time, my sweet." And she disappeared in a burst of strange energy.

An Elite moved for him, sword outstretched as he aimed for Xavier's midsection, but sensing the blow, he stepped aside, flipping the sword in his hand to send it upward, straight through the Elite's heart, up through his head.

He pulled out the sword as a burst of green lightning left Nathanial's fingertips, reaching for three Elite Creatures that were attempting to bring down Aleister with their swords, all of them falling over as the green lightning hit them.

The Vampires that remained on the streets finally moved to action, dropping their torches and moving for the remaining Elites, but as Eleanor's Creatures saw them, they disappeared in a swirl of dark energy, leaving them all alone.

He sheathed the sword, not able to speak as he stared around at the angry, bewildered Vampires that stared at Nathanial or Aleister, or kept their gazes to the floor: they seemed scared to look Xavier in the face.

"My King," Nathanial said, moving to him, and as he did, Xavier saw the three Elite Creatures that remained motionless along the floor, their eyes wide with their fear, "what would you have us do with them? Shall we finish them or let them live? Figure out what they know of Eleanor?"

Xavier caught Aleister's cold glare as the Vampire stood just beside the three captured Creatures. Was what Dracula said true? He had stamped it down whilst focusing on the Vampire City, but now...

"What do you think, Aleister?" Xavier asked him.

He glanced down at them briefly before returning his gaze to Xavier. "If you would, my king, I'd like to have my Division...get from them what we can. You needn't get your hands dirty. You've enough to contend with as is." And he motioned with his head towards the mass of startled Vampire that would not stare him in the eye.

An eyebrow rose. "I would like that, Aleister," he said before he moved for the group of Vampires, all of whom looked up in alarm as he neared them. He knew not where to begin, but only that he needed to be their peace of mind. "I am sure these past few days have been... trying, but I am here now. What Dracula was attempting to undo was years of death, needless destruction, and mindless war. We have a long road ahead of us, and all of you are free to leave me forever if you please, but those that stay, they will have my eternal thanks as we move to rebuild our city...our world."

And he saw in the flickering green light of Nathanial's spell, the looks of bemusement on their faces. "I would ask that those of you who have family in other Vampire Cities to send them letters—"

"And just how are we to do this?" a sniveling voice said. And as the crowd parted, a bloodied, damaged Civil Certance emerged, his eyes thick with disbelief as he glared up at Xavier.

"There is a group of Dark Creatures," he said, turning to eye Aleister, who stared at him in confusion, "that shall be coming to my aid soon. Once we make sure the city is absolutely safe, we can call upon them."

"What group is this?" another Vampire asked.

"It is not important," Aleister interjected, stepping towards them, stopping just beside Xavier. He looked at him. "We must talk."

And as the Vampire led him through the ruined doors of the tall mansion that was now his, Xavier thought on Christian, wondering if the Vampire knew at all, perhaps, that their father still lived.

Inside Dracula's office, Xavier stared at Aleister as though he couldn't believe the Vampire existed—and he couldn't. He daren't believe the Vampire was his father. It must have been Dracula's lies, surely. Yet he didn't dare take a seat behind the dark desk that remained against the wall, but remained standing as the scarred Vampire took a seat at the long table just before the high windows.

They said nothing to each other for a time, the fire in the fireplace dancing brightly, and it was not until Xavier's thoughts turned to Dracula for a third time that Aleister said, "He told you, didn't he?"

"He told me...many things."

There was silence, and then: "You have grown beautifully."

"It was not without consequence."

He inclined his head forward as if to say "Ah well," and said aloud, "Whatever consequence that entails...if it means you have kept you and your brother alive, I won't take it as a bad one."

His eyes darkened with these words, as they reminded him wholly of what Dracula caused in his desire for a better world. Aleister must have seen this, for he said, "I never wanted this life for you, Xavier."

He stared at the green eyes, not desiring to see the truth that remained within them. "Damn," he whispered, feeling it full in his heart. *My father.*

Aleister pulled out another chair just beside himself and motioned for Xavier to sit, having seen the realization on the Vampire's face.

Once he did so, he said, "I knew it was wrong. As a man—a human—to know yourself involved with a woman that is anything but, you prepare yourself for the risks of getting thrown into her world. But when I met Dracula, I knew then that I had been severely in over my head.

"It was why I begged Aurora to cast the spell—I could not do it myself. I could not bear what I'd done to you, to Christian."

A strange comfort settled over Xavier with the words, and the more he watched the scarred Vampire, the more he saw their resemblance, just beneath the scars. "Your scars. How did you get them? Did Dracula—"

"Oh no," Aleister said, heading him off, "this was the work of a few rogue Enchanters many years ago when I was on a mission with my Division. They made it so we would forever bear the scars of our battles."

"How poetic."

"I thought so as well."

Another silence fell over the large room and it was not until Aleister opened his mouth to speak again that Xavier said, "Do you truly think I can do this?"

"Do what? Take Dracula's place? Remain King of the entire Dark World when it is close to ruin?"

A fresh feeling of despair encircled him, but then Aleister said, "Of course you can. He may have left you his spoils, Xavier, but you have me, Nathanial, Christian, Aurora, the Order, and those Vampires that remain out there if ever you feel overwhelmed—if you cannot do this," and he waved a hand, "I can't think of a Vampire who could."

He blinked in the firelight, astonished. He knew the Vampire was right, he was not alone, had never truly been, he had just been looking for guidance in all the wrong places.

The door opened and in Nathanial stepped, his golden eyes wide with panic.

"What is it, Nathanial?" Aleister asked.

"Sorry to intrude, but I have found a Vampire in a hallway, barely alive. He said his name was Westley Rivers."

"Westley?" Xavier repeated, rising from his chair.

Nathanial nodded, not waiting for them to follow him. He turned from the doorway and swept down the hall, Xavier's gaze finding Aleister's.

"Aleister—"

"Tend to your matters, my son," Aleister said, rising from his chair, "I imagine we will have all the time in the world to talk now."

He hesitated ever the slightest, not entirely sure that were true, but Nathanial's voice rung out for him down the hall, and he decided that he would have to trust the Vampire at his word, for as he stepped from him and moved for the door, he knew he would have to learn to trust himself as well. It was the only way he would truly lead anyone, indeed. Dracula, at the very least, had shown him that.

About the Author

Besides being addicted to vampires, blood, and a good, steaming cup of tea, S.C. Parris attends University in New York City, and is the author of "A Night of Frivolity," a horror short story, published by Burning Willow Press. She is the author of *The Dark World* series published by Permuted Press, and enjoys thinking up new dark historical fantasies to put to page next. She lives on Long Island, New York with her family and can be found writing ridiculous articles for CLASH Media.

BOOK

IS COMING

PERMUTED
PRESS

PERMUTED PRESS
needs **you** to help

SPREAD INFECTION

14

Peter Clines

Padlocked doors.
Strange light fixtures. Mutant cockroaches.

There are some odd things about Nate's new apartment. Every room in this old brownstone has a mystery. Mysteries that stretch back over a hundred years. Some of them are in plain sight. Some are behind locked doors. And all together these mysteries could mean the end of Nate and his friends.

Or the end of everything...

PERMUTED PRESS

THE JOURNAL SERIES
by Deborah D. Moore

After a major crisis rocks the nation, all supply lines are shut down. In the remote Upper Peninsula of Michigan, the small town of Moose Creek and its residents are devastated when they lose power in the middle of a brutal winter, and must struggle alone with one calamity after another.

The Journal series takes the reader head first into the fury that only Mother Nature can dish out.

PERMUTED
PRESS